HOW
THE
MISTAKES
WERE
MADE

HOW THE MISTAKES WERE MADE

TYLER McMAHON

St. Martin's Griffin
New York

HOW THE MISTAKES WERE MADE. Copyright © 2011 by Tyler McMahon. All rights reserved. Printed in the United States of America. For information, address St. Martin's Press, 175 Fifth Avenue, New York, N.Y. 10010.

www.stmartins.com

Book design by Rich Arnold

ISBN 978-1-250-00091-0 (hardcover)
ISBN 978-0-312-65854-0 (trade paperback)

First Edition: October 2011

10 9 8 7 6 5 4 3 2 1

FOR DABNEY. FOREVER.

ONE

ONE

I don't mind the hate. It doesn't bother me anymore. There was a time when I was adored by the same brain-dead sheep who despise me now. I don't miss that. Behind every dead rock god, there's always some uppity female scapegoat. Why shouldn't it be me? The public eye sees only love or hate. Fans aren't capable of anything in between. So let them hate me; I can handle that. The part I can't abide is having my own history ripped right out from under me, my life rewritten by magazines. It's true that I've made mistakes. But it's also true that I made the Mistakes.

All the quickie-biographers and poseur journalists say I stumbled across those two boys in some basement in the mountains some-where, already playing amazing music—that my eyes turned to dollar signs and all that was left to do was shove them into a recording studio and a stadium. That's not how it happened.

The first time I heard Sean and Nathan play, there was an elk heart bouncing on the floor. The beer-soaked attic of a venue would've never met fire codes in any state besides Montana. The first of the two local bands on the undercard called themselves Venison in Unison, and ran everything through distortion pedals, even the drums and vocals, resulting in a slush of chords and screams that was little more than a soundtrack for the mosh pit. Their lead singer sang draped in a fleshy vest fashioned from a deer's rib cage. Meat was their thing. At the height of the set, they tossed the elk heart into the pit, where the kids kicked it around like a half-deflated soccer ball. Everyone thought this was awesome.

It was August 1990. Fires raged through the surrounding forests. Walking around town earlier in the day, my eyes stung. The air in the valley was dense and gray, the sun a dim glow through the smoke.

After the first band, I went to the bar. The place served only Pabst Blue Ribbon and Jägermeister, both from a tap. I ordered one of each. Above the stage, a skylight had been painted over. Little streaks of smoky night sky came in through scratches in the black paint. As I walked back to my table, one kid pointed at me and whispered to his friend.

There were times when I liked to see these small-town punk enclaves. It used to make me proud, like my teenage years weren't all a waste. But this particular night, it put me into a foul mood. I sat by myself and smoked, picking my feet up whenever the heart bounced too close. The rest of the Cooler Heads—the band I was on tour with—ate dinner somewhere downtown. They were a hipper-than-thou bunch of college kids from Seattle who sang poppy odes to their own record collections. I'd excused myself to come straight to the venue. Even so many years later, I still followed some of Anthony's rules, like never missing the opening act.

There was nothing remarkable about Sean and Nathan when they climbed onstage. Wearing faded T-shirts and threadbare jeans, they carried instrument cases and a grocery bag full of cords and pedals.

Nathan lowered the microphone stand, then set about plugging in gear. Sean held a hand up to shield his eyes from the overhead lights.

The singer from the previous band sat down behind the drum set, also of the previous band. On the floor, the elk heart lay still. They tuned up and nobody paid much mind.

Nathan laid a list of songs down on the floor of the stage, then whispered last-minute comments into the ears of his bandmates. He wore his blond hair in a sort of disheveled bowl cut, not unlike one of the Beatles. Back then, his face was clean-shaven. I remember thinking that he had good posture. To start off their set, he strummed the bass line with a pick. The drummer dropped in after a bar but was terribly off-rhythm. Nathan turned and nodded his head along with the downbeat until the guy got it.

Their sound cracked open once Sean came in. His tone was nothing special—a cheap Stratocaster knockoff, a half-open Cry Baby, some kind of fuzzbox—but he had this pins-and-needles style that was impossible to ignore. It made my skin crawl. Kids in the crowd shivered during certain lines. The taller of the two, Sean slumped his shoulders and stared down at his strings. That bush of dark hair already covered part of his pale face. Half the time, his back was turned toward the crowd.

Their final tune—something like an Irish drinking song sped up—brought out the best in them. Nathan did a call-and-response thing, and the boys from the first band shouted along. Behind the microphone, his face clenched tight, eyes retreated farther into his skull. He might have been singing to a million people, for how serious he took it.

Sean, on the other hand, didn't seem to know or care that he was onstage. While his sidelong lines wove in and out of the melody, he looked curious—more than anything else—like he was surprised at the sounds coming from the speakers.

They didn't sound great that night. The mix was bad; the drummer was off. Nathan's microphone was too quiet to hear the words. Still, they had something that a lot of bands didn't. There was drama in their music, a critical tension between order and chaos. Much later,

I would understand that Nathan tried his hardest to hold the songs together, while Sean did everything he could to pull them apart.

The rest of the Cooler Heads showed up as Nathan and Sean finished. Jack, our front man, was red faced and smiley from booze. The other two girls, Claire and Kristina, giggled at something he'd said. I didn't look forward to our set.

As their bassist, my job was easy: Stand there playing simple lines and looking aloof. Jack twirled around in his ridiculous dances. I watched him perform, the way he raised his eyebrows up and pointed into the crowd. It struck me that night as phony to the point of terrifying.

Something came over me as we started our final song. I found a pick in my pocket and turned up the gain on my amp. Instead of plucking, I strummed the bass as Nathan had an hour earlier, playing it double time. Claire didn't miss a beat on the drums. Kristina caught up a couple bars later. Jack glared at me. I leaned forward and hid my face in my hair. Eventually, he sang without enthusiasm.

I drank more Jägermeisters while waiting for the van to load. By the time the boys approached me, I felt well buzzed.

"Are you Laura, from SCC?" Nathan did the talking while Sean stood silent by his side.

In the middle of lighting a cigarette, I nodded my head to confirm what he already knew.

"We"—he pointed back and forth between himself and Sean with his thumb—"we're huge fans."

"You guys sounded good tonight." Smoke came out my mouth along with the words. "If you ditch that drummer and get serious, you two could be onto something."

"You think?" Nathan said.

"Wouldn't say it if I didn't."

He let out a breathless half laugh.

"But ditch that drummer," I said.

Nathan and Sean exchanged glances and smiled, communicating in that nonverbal language of theirs that I'd become familiar with over time, but never quite fluent in. I took another drag from my cigarette and looked around the room, wondering where my band members were off to. Half our gear still lay on one side of the stage. The singer from the venison band, Sean and Nathan's drummer, picked the elk heart up off the floor.

"I remember the first time I heard your records," Nathan said.

"I think that guy's going to take the heart home with him," I said.

"Back then, did you know what a great band SCC was, how important you all would become?" Nathan asked.

"I used to believe that what we were doing was important. Sometimes I still do. Most times I think that band could've been a hobo pissing in the woods for all anybody cares, in the bigger picture."

The vocalist/drummer walked by and pushed the elk heart into Nathan's chest. Nathan put his hands around it, still looking at me. It was as big as a grapefruit, colored in the dull whites and deep reds of raw meat. Dust and hair from the floor clung to every side. The severed tubes at the top looked like they must be part of some machine, not possibly an animal.

Nathan caught me staring. "Do you want to hold it?" He extended it out toward me.

I took the heart from him with both hands. It was cold. The grit from the floor felt oddly more alive than the actual flesh. I held it rightside up with one hand and lifted it to my eye level.

"I never held a heart in the palm of my hand before," I said.

Nathan nudged Sean and the two of them smiled, pleased by my reaction.

"Does he talk?" I looked at Sean. He slouched farther forward, as if trying to make himself a few inches shorter. A couple brown curls crept down his forehead.

"Once, I went camping with my family." Sean's eyes darted around as he spoke. "My grandfather brought one of those along. He cut it into strips and cooked it like kebabs over the fire. It's good."

"Would you sign this?" Nathan held out an old SCC seven-inch and a felt-tip marker.

I took them from him. The cover of the record was a black-and-white drawing I'd done a long time ago. It showed a small figure crouching in the corner of an empty room, his head cast down in his hands as though crying. The threatening shadow of another figure stretched along one of the walls. SECOND CLASS CITIZENS read the blocky script. There was a chance that I'd glued that sleeve together and put the record in myself.

"If you guys ever come to Seattle, or if you get serious and want to go full-time, give me a call. I could help you out." I wrote my phone number on the white space of the wall in the drawing, but didn't sign my name.

PHILADELPHIA: AUGUST 1984

This is how you make mistakes. This is how you hurt people that you care about. It's not hard to confuse love and hate. There are good reasons to fear adoration, to suspect anyone who would put you up on a pedestal, be it a screaming fan or a selfless lover. It's not sick. It could happen to you. Here's how it works.

For the first couple hours, try to call your parents from the hospital. No answer. After that, give up. The long night passes there at the side of the bed, the air going in and out of Anthony's lungs via a plastic hose, machines beeping and ticking, late-night traffic outside. Every so often, a pair of headlights sweeps through the room and circles the ceiling. The hospital staff performs tests—pricking him with pins like a voodoo doll, hitting his bones with a rubber mallet. They speak in a lingo you don't understand. In the end, there's nothing they can do.

The band stops by in the morning. Hank hands you a wad of bills, everything you made last night. Stare at the currency as if it's from a foreign country. Billy asks if you want a ride home. You think he must be joking.

"No violence." Hank shakes his head back and forth as he looks down at Anthony. "I told him that shit would never work."

That's when you see just how bad this part will be.

"It's kind of ironic, right?" Hank flips the curtain of hair out of his eyes. "I mean, that is irony, isn't it? I'm not trying to be a dick or anything. But I think that's, like, the definition of the word."

Billy punches him in the shoulder.

"Would you two please leave?" You've been waiting all night for something that is not coming. From now on, and for the first time, you'll have to cope with this world all by yourself.

Neither boy looks back as they walk away.

Out of habit, you turn to the body in the bed, the one who always knew what to say or do when you were at a loss. You are eighteen years old, and have never been without your big brother. Watch those two boys disappear down the hall of the hospital. Memorize the image of their backs and heads getting smaller. Machines tick and beep along with your brother's mechanized breath in a sort of unbearable music. Promise yourself that you will not forget this. You will not forget those boys, or the fans, and where they all are while their hero lies motionless in a hospital bed, with tubes down his throat and pins in his toes.

TWO

As months went by in the city, I forgot all about those two Montana kids. My days were spent fetching lattes and muffins for the newly rich employees of Boeing or Microsoft, hoping one might drop a bill into the jar by the counter.

It's a popular misconception that early nineties Seattle was a town full of unshaven lumberjacks in flannel and torn jeans, swilling beer and starting rock bands on every corner. In fact, it was one of the most yuppie cities in America. My workplace swarmed with young white professionals in Eddie Bauer and Nordstrom clothes, washing down their Prozac with shots of espresso. Like D.C. in the eighties, the music scene here was an underground.

I rented a studio apartment above a nightclub in Belltown. It was a shithole, but big enough to hold all my instruments—even my drum kit and performance amps. After the club opened its doors downstairs, I could be as loud as I wanted and nobody cared.

The Cooler Heads rehearsed in a storage locker near Pioneer Square. We'd screwed in a power adapter to the light socket, ran an extension cord to the floor, and plugged in a series of power strips for our amplifiers. Every so often, a breaker would blow and we'd call it a night. At the start of winter, we brought in a kerosene heater. I played bass in fingerless gloves on colder nights. With the temperature changes, our instruments constantly went out of tune.

Claire, the drummer, had a massive crush on Jack. He took a sort of cruel pleasure in leading her on and pushing her away. I seemed to be the only one who saw this with any clarity.

Tonight, she'd brought in another old portrait in a brown paper bag. She handed it off to Jack, her head bowed a bit, making an offer on the altar of infatuation.

They'd decorated the practice space by hanging framed portraits from thrift stores and estate sales. School pictures, family photos, posed shots from weddings and graduations—yellowing strangers smiled hard in outdated clothes. The girls brought new ones to every practice. Somehow, the whole thing was endlessly amusing to the three of them.

Jack pulled the picture—a fair-skinned teenage boy with freckles and a crew cut—out of the paper bag. "I don't know." His faux-childish voice had so come to annoy me. "I don't think I like this one. It's too . . . obvious, you know." He handed the picture back to Claire.

Claire's smile deflated. "I guess it is a little obvious."

To me, it looked exactly like all the other stupid pictures they'd hung up. "Let's do our songs already," I said. "It's fucking freezing."

We went through our set list once, without stopping, then took a break. My bandmates looked on nervously as I smoked a cigarette too close to the kerosene heater. Kristina, our guitarist, volunteered to run for doughnuts and coffee.

"Hey, guys," Claire announced once it was just the three of us. "I've been working on a song. I could, like, play it if you want."

Claire sat on an amplifier and tuned up the acoustic guitar. She crossed her legs and strummed a few chords. It sounded like a ballad— something I've always been a sucker for. The slowed-down tempo and the minor chords were a welcome change from the bright bouncy shit that was our standard fare. Claire sang and I was shocked at the beauty of her voice. She didn't have perfect pitch, but there was a dark and haunting quality. I was so taken by the sound that I barely noticed the lyrics until she got to the chorus. It went:

something, something . . . still remember my name
when you walk away from the mix-tape hall of fame.

It was a little cheesy, but a good fit for this cheesy band.

Claire's tone cracked as she went through the second verse. There was an awkward moment of silence once she finished.

"Claire," I said. "You've got a beautiful voice."

Her face turned red. She mumbled a thanks.

"This reminds me of that old joke," Jack said. "What was the last thing that the drummer said before getting kicked out of the rock band?"

I knew that joke, but I didn't think that even he was rude enough to mention it.

"Hey, guys, I've been writing some songs!" Jack laughed and clapped his hands together.

Claire looked down into the sound hole of the guitar.

"I mean, it was nice. Don't get me wrong," Jack condescended. "It's just . . . the song takes itself a little too seriously, if you ask me."

Claire nodded. Her throat constricted as if actually swallowing his criticism.

"It . . . tries too hard to be a rock song, you know?" Jack squinted at her.

"Give me a break," I said. "She just sang in a voice that's ten times better than you could ever sing in. Where do you get this shit? 'Takes itself too seriously'? 'Too obvious'? Take this seriously: You're an asshole!"

Jack held his hands up in the air as if to say, *What did I do?*

"And you." I turned to Claire. "You let him get away with it. Put your foot down. What do you need his blessing for?"

"Laura, it's okay," Claire said. "He's right. The song isn't a good fit for us."

"Nothing will fit if you act like a goddamn doormat!"

She turned back to the sound hole.

"I didn't realize that you felt this way about my singing, Laura," Jack said sarcastically. "Thanks for sharing."

"Don't ask how I feel about you as a human being." I lit another cigarette.

"Hey, guys!" Kristina walked in with a white box and a tray of paper cups. "They just came out of the oven!"

"These fucking portraits." I picked up the picture that Claire had brought from off an amplifier. "It's bullshit. You hide behind this corny naïve façade and pretend it's some edgy-ass ironic art thing. But really it's a cop-out." I waved the portrait at Jack. "It's easier than taking shit seriously. It's safer."

Without my intending, the bottom piece of the frame came loose from the rest, and the whole works fell to the floor. Claire flinched at the sound of the shattering glass.

"Here we go," Jack said, "another elegy for the hardcore scene. Guess what, Laura. It's not 1982 anymore."

"Maybe not"—I let out a lungful of smoke in Jack's direction—"but the world's no less fucked up. And there's more to it than mix tapes and thrift store treasures."

Claire wiped at the edges of her eyes.

"What are you trying to say?" Jack asked.

I hadn't planned this, but it seemed the only way to win the argument. "I quit." I turned to Claire. "If you were smart, you'd do the same."

I walked all the way home with my bass. The stiff leather of a new pair of low-cut combat boots pinched at my heels. Suddenly, I wasn't even a musician. I was a restaurant employee, before and after enlightenment.

The stairs to my apartment shook under my feet with the trumped-up low-end tones of the club below. It was a hip-hop track; the lyrics boasted of cars and guns. The crowd—the same white professionals that I served all day long—sang along. They cheered for the man in the corner playing records and pushing faders. This is what passed for a live performance in America in 1990.

I closed the door and went through my record collection until I found my favorite SCC seven-inch, "The Ballad of John Hinckley Jr." The record hissed and crackled on the turntable. I mixed myself a vodka and Coca-Cola—a drink Hank used to call a Cold War. We'd sneak these on tour when Anthony wasn't looking. I gulped down the first one and poured a second.

It was a live recording, and poorly done. The screams from the crowd come first. There's a few odd beats on the snare drum, some random notes as Hank tunes up. Then my brother's voice: "This is a song about a lunatic, a deranged killer, a murderous madman. . . ." The crowd shouts a few words, eager to jump around. Anthony was a genius at teasing them along, breaking into song only when they couldn't wait a millisecond longer.

"And this is a song about the man who tried to bring him to justice!" *Boom*. A slight move of the head, some unspoken signal from my brother, then Hank, Billy, and I playing as fast as our fingers allowed. The crowd went nuts. The recording maxes out a little. Hank's amp feeds back.

> *Today, Mr. President*
> *we are all deranged*
> *If this is called sanity*
> *then I must not be sane*

The tune was good for stirring up controversy. But it was deep, when you thought about it—a hard look at how we decide what normal and abnormal is. I gulped the rest of my cocktail and bobbed my head up and down in the easy chair. It wasn't until the track faded out that I heard the phone ring. Before answering, I turned down the stereo and finished my drink. Most likely, it would be an earful from Jack or a teary plea from Claire. Nobody else called me.

"Hello."

"Is Laura Loss there?"

"This is Laura."

"Laura from SCC?"

"Who the fuck am I speaking to?"

"Sorry. My name's Nathan. I met you in Missoula a couple months ago. Sean and I have been talking about what you said."

"How did you get this number?" I had no idea who this person was on the line.

"The album cover."

"What?"

"You wrote your phone number down on the record. You told us to call when we got serious. You don't remember?"

"Oh, wait. You're the guys who handed me the heart."

"Right! That's us." He let out a relieved sigh. "So what do you say?"

"Say about what?" The conversation still didn't make much sense.

"Can you put us up in Seattle, help us get started?"

"Hold up. I'm not running a boardinghouse here."

I looked around my apartment. At the far end, by the radiator and window, was all my music equipment—my drum set, a couple amps, my good bass, an acoustic guitar in need of repair. On this side was my bed, a too-short Salvation Army sofa and easy chair, a Formica table covered in takeout wrappers and makeshift ashtrays, clothes strewn all about. The tiny kitchen was crammed between the bathroom and the front door. Beside the telephone, my drink trembled with bass notes from the floor below.

"Sorry," went the voice on the phone. "I thought . . . We thought you were going to help us, once we got serious."

"Did I say that?"

"Basically."

What was wrong with me? I had no problem stomping over the feelings of the Cooler Heads, arguably my best friends in this city. But here were two perfect strangers, and I couldn't quite swallow the thought of letting them down. I remembered all the floors that I'd slept on, all those fledgling bands that had stayed at our house in D.C. over the years.

"Fuck it," I said at last. My speech slurred a bit from the two strong drinks. "You can stay here if you need to."

"Thank you so much!" Air rushed out of the guy like a popped tire.

"You got a pen?" I asked. "Let me give you the address."

The thanks kept coming, so I said good-bye and hung up. The bass speakers thumped away below. Lights from the traffic shone in. What had gotten into me? Most of those poseurs in that rat-hole bar in Montana made me sick. What was different about these two?

Fuck it. They'd probably never show up anyways.

WASHINGTON, D.C.: DECEMBER 1980

If there's one thing that everyone needs to know about growing up in the D.C. metropolitan area during the early 1980s, it is this: You are all 100 percent certain that you will die in a nuclear holocaust. Your parents believe it. Your teachers believe it. Your older brothers and sisters explain mutually assured destruction before they tell you about sex. Full-blown war with the Soviet Union is inevitable, and your city will be the first to go. Whenever your family car passes the Capitol or the Pentagon—which it does several times a week—you see them as giant bull's-eyes for warheads, a red button somewhere on the other side of the world under a sad old man's trembling finger. You believe in an imminent Russian attack at the same time that you believe in Santa Claus.

This is a totally abstract fear. You have no real idea what a nuclear bomb looks like. Somebody tells you that they're about the size of a suitcase, and you figure that they must look like suitcases as well. For a while, you burst into tears if left alone with a piece of luggage of any kind. Later, you're told that the real nukes, the ones that will destroy your city and end your lives, are as big as a house. Picture a brownstone from your neighborhood suspended by wires underneath an airplane.

All holidays are haunted by the threat. Rumors circulate that the Soviets plan to attack on Christmas morning, when America least expects it. With every New Year's countdown, some older kid always asks out loud if this will be the last year in history.

This is important. Punk rock had everything to do with the Cold War. When your brother sings, *"They took the future without a please or thank you,"* he isn't being coy. He's being honest. Look at what government has done for you. They built a perfect machine for destroying life on the planet, then put some Hollywood-cowboy-action-hero at the helm. That plus cops and taxes. The mass hallucination of the twentieth century is this: that all these national governments, which each year kill or threaten way more humans than they protect, and take a big chunk of your income to do so, are for some reason a great idea, an inevitable force of fucking nature.

Punk rock is your first peek behind this ridiculous curtain.

THREE

On my way to work, I pondered not being in a band. After first moving to Seattle, I went without any music projects for a couple months—the longest time since I was a teenager. It was a strange feeling, like an amputee might have for a missing limb. But I was older now. Jamming in basements and storage lockers was cool when you're a kid but pathetic in adulthood. There might not be a next band for me. Food service was my only other skill set. I stared down the barrel of life behind a coffee counter.

"Laura!" the owner of the Daily Grind called as I walked in. "Laura, I need you!" Maxine was a giant lesbian who'd played basketball for a European league in her youth. She fell in love with Italian espresso and brought back the equipment and recipes.

We went to her office before I could take off my coat.

"I've got to figure this out." Maxine ran her hands through her short red hair, until her index fingers settled into a pattern of tight circles along her temples.

One of the regular girls had quit. "I'll hire somebody as soon as I can, but I don't have anyone who's trained as a barista." Maxine was a perfectionist when it came to espresso. "I need to know if you can work some overtime."

"Sure," I said.

"I'm serious. You've got your band and all, but this—"

"It's fine," I cut her off. "I quit the band last night." She was the first person I'd told.

"Oh." Maxine took a moment to guess what the appropriate response might be. She settled for, "I see."

"Put me down whenever you need to. I could use the money."

"Okay." She jotted something on her calendar.

"Also, Christmas and Thanksgiving. I'd like to get those shifts if I could."

Maxine looked up. "I'm going to close on Thanksgiving and Christmas this year. But I can put you on for Christmas Eve."

"That's cool."

"Is everything okay, Laura?" She seemed to suffer from a misguided mothering instinct.

"Just fine."

"All right. Could you get out there and take the machine?"

This was a good thing. I did need the money, and it was something to keep me occupied during the holiday season that I loathed. Making espresso was my favorite part of the job. I wouldn't have to interact with the customers except to call out their drinks.

I stood at that Italian machine, pulling levers and popping milk bubbles. I packed my shots hard and slammed steam pitchers. The customers flinched and shivered with my bangs and whirs. It was like playing abrasive music, only this instrument was bigger and easier to hide behind than my bass. The hours flew by. I directed my own private orchestra of clanging steel and whistling steam. Before I knew it, break time arrived. I put on my coat and took a handful of day-old scones and a double espresso outside.

Even in the cold, I took breaks at our outdoor tables. I could smoke there, and the autumn air felt nice after the hot counter. I was pleased with the winter coat I'd found at the army surplus store: black, mid-length, with elbow patches and a waxy surface that kept out the rain—perhaps it was designed for snipers.

Boeing Bob sat with his cappuccino and the paper. He called me over to join him. The trench coat was wrapped tight all the way up to his neck, his gray hair and beard draping down over the collar. Bob had been an engineer for Boeing back in the day but was laid off when the commercial aviation industry had its slump in the seventies. He decided he didn't care to work anymore and took to the streets. Every so often, he came here and bought coffee with the change he gathered panhandling. A self-described news junkie, he'd sit reading every single paper we had.

"Any good news in there?" I sat down and munched through my scones.

"Germany is now reunified."

"Is that so?" I asked through a mouthful of crumbs.

Bob folded the paper around and showed it to me. "Yes, indeed. Looks like Gorbachev will get the next Nobel Peace Prize."

"Just wait. They'll find somebody more menacing to replace him."

Bob smiled through his whiskers, the sides of his eyes breaking up into clusters of wrinkled skin. "Why are you such a cynic, Laura?"

I shrugged then wrapped both hands around the coffee cup to warm them. "I quit my band last night."

"You'll find something else."

"I don't know. It feels final this time."

"That, too, might be good." Bob sipped his coffee. "There's value in giving up something that you love."

"Value in being a quitter?" I took my cigarettes from the pocket of my sniper coat and lit up.

"I'm not talking about quitting," he said. "I'm talking about sacrifice."

"Like killing a goat or something?"

"Sacrifice is an ancient concept, a part of every major religion. The idea is, if you give up something you desire, you throw the cycles and organs of the world out of whack for a second. What you'll end up with is something different, something unexpected."

"Yeah, well"—I took a long drag from my cigarette—"I could use that."

Bob smiled and reopened his paper.

I let Bob's words sink in. The harsh sounds of the traffic and the soft exhales of cigarette smoke were all we had to share for a second.

"I got to get back inside."

Bob slurped down the rest of his drink. "Don't work too hard."

Around three, Maxine came out of her office with the new schedule. I'd be working ten-hour shifts. She thanked me again. I clocked out and walked home through a light rain. Bob was right. I didn't have it so bad. I had my coffee and my cigarettes, my records and my drawings. What had being in a band ever brought me, other than trouble?

On the way up the trembling staircase to my apartment, my head filled with the familiar scent of unwashed males—an odor I knew well from years of traveling in vans and sleeping on floors.

There, in front of my door, sound asleep and fresh off the Greyhound, were those two kids from Montana that I'd been foolish enough to encourage.

"Wake up." I kicked the boy who was closest to me and jingled my keys. "You're here."

He cracked his eyelids, then looked around. A few feet away, his buddy slept soundly. I opened the door and walked in, hung up my coat, and fixed myself a Cold War while the two of them got their things together.

A minute later, the tall one came in, his eyes barely open, and lay down on the floor over by the radiator. He curled up in a fetal position on the hardwood and fell back asleep a second later, in his belt and shoes and everything. The shorter blond one carried in all their things and made a pile in one corner by my instruments. He pulled a sleeping bag out of their duffel and spread it out over the body of his friend.

"He's a deep sleeper." The awake boy smiled at me. "Thanks for this, seriously."

"What are your names again?" I sat down in the recliner with my cocktail.

"I'm Nathan; he's Sean." He wore one of those quilted flannel jackets, with a pattern of red and black squares.

"Are you guys brothers or something?" Nathan stood before me and stuck his hands deep into the pockets of his jeans.

"Just friends. Known each other since kindergarten."

I started to remember them. Nathan was the talker, the one who stood up straight and approached me in the bar. Sean was the shy one with the insane guitar skills.

"You want a drink?" I held my glass toward him.

"No thanks." He gave me a funny look.

"What? You're underage?"

"No. We're both twenty-one. It's just, I thought you were straight edge."

I laughed so hard, I almost blew Coke-and-vodka all over both of us. Nathan smiled along, as if he'd meant it as a joke.

"That was a long time ago. And I was one of the straight edgers sneaking drinks and smokes when the others weren't looking."

He tried not to act surprised.

"Sit down, at least. You're making me nervous." Him standing in front of me in my big chair, it felt like a trial or something.

Nathan took a seat on the corner of the couch. "Do you play all these instruments?" He pointed to my gear.

I shrugged. "I'm sort of mediocre at all, master of none."

"I learned to play bass listening to your—"

"Look, Nathan." I stopped him. "SCC was a long time ago, and I got more bad memories of those days than I do good ones."

He stared at me for a second. The radiator across the room came alive with a clang.

"Right," he said at last. "Thanks for letting us stay here."

"You said that already. Find some floor wherever you're comfortable. This"—I patted the arm of the sofa where he sat—"is too damn short to sleep on." I drained the last of my glass. "You can plug in those headphones if you want to listen to records or something."

"That's okay. I'm tired."

I stood up. "Listen, I'll be working a lot over the next few weeks." I took off my work slacks and hung them on the closet door. Draped across one of the kitchen chairs, I found the surgical pants that I slept in. "Tomorrow, I'll leave early and be gone all day."

"Right." Nathan turned his head. His cheeks reddened at the sight of me in my underwear.

It'd been a while since I shared a room with only boys. I went into the bathroom to finish changing and brush my teeth. When I came back out, he was already curled up in a sleeping bag on the floor. He'd at least managed to get his shoes off.

"Good night," I heard Nathan say as I killed the light.

"Sleep tight."

———

In the morning, little water droplets clung motionless to the outside of the window. I heard the sounds of light snoring, and then something else, something even softer. It was music.

I opened my eyes and looked around. Nathan's body lay by my drum set, snoring away inside his sleeping bag.

The music in my ears was bizarre; it slowed down and sped up, but still made sense. Like a game of peekaboo with a baby, it tempted with a few whispers, then let loose half a measure later. And the tone was unlike anything I'd ever heard. This was not one of my records. I sat up in bed and saw that the stereo was off.

The music came from the bathroom. It was the other boy, Sean, the quiet one. He played an electric guitar that wasn't plugged in, but the sound of the unamplified strings reverberated off all the tiles and the bathtub.

I rubbed my eyes and got out of bed. Tiptoeing across the room, I noticed something even more remarkable about this guitar piece: He played in time with the snores coming from his friend. That was what kept it together. I think it was even in the same *key* as the snores.

Right outside the bathroom door, a plank of the hardwood creaked underneath my feet. Sean stopped short. He turned around, shocked to see me standing there. "Sorry," he said in a whisper. "I like the echo." He used his eyes to indicate the tile walls. His mop of bushy hair was bigger than it had been back in August.

"I need to get ready for work," I said.

"Right." He stood up off the toilet seat. Taller and leaner than Nathan, his limbs were long and gangly, his shoulders slumped forward.

"That was nice," I said as our bodies crossed in the narrow doorway. "I liked it."

He offered an awkward smile. The angles of his face were all quite severe—sharp nose and chin, high cheeks. For the first time, I noticed the faint scar on his upper lip from cleft-palate surgery.

In the shower, I remembered that my work clothes were out in the main room. Great: based on what I'd seen so far, these two would probably memorize the sight of me in a towel and call it up later for jerking off. I wiped the moisture from the mirror and had a look at my body. It wasn't bad, all things considered. My hair still had the shiny blackness that other punks always believed to be a dye job. A few wrinkles formed around the sides of my eyes, but I'd been lucky in the skin department, considering how much I smoked. My stomach was as flat as when I was a teenager. The bones of my hips still poked out a little at the top of my waist. I pressed my index finger into the fleshy part of my ass and was satisfied with the firmness. Hell, why shouldn't these two guys take notice?

MINNEAPOLIS: MARCH 1982

On either side of the drum kit, you and Hank widen your stances, as if something might try to knock you over. A basketball hoop hangs above. It's late. In hats and gloves, anxious kids file into this gymnasium. They're sick of waiting.

Your brother crouches in a tight ball in front of Billy's bass drum. Wearing cutoff jeans and a pair of black boots, Anthony looks like he's trying to fold himself up into the smallest possible space. His head is between his knees. His arms hug his shins. The microphone dangles from one hand.

It sounds overdramatic. But you know that it's necessity, part of his process. This room full of kids, they will expect him to perform—full-throttle, every-synapse-firing perform—for the next several hours. There is no backstage (or stage at all). He needs a second or two to gather himself. Doesn't he deserve that much?

The crowd keeps a safe distance. Wonder how long that'll last. You've recently cut Anthony's hair, a soft and even buzz with the one-guard. He's already sweating. His upper body—dirty, moist, hairless—

looks like a piece of meat dressed and marinated, ready for roasting. See the face muscles tense around his ears.

Anthony's head turns toward Hank. Hank looks at you and Billy, and mouths the numbers: *one, two, three* . . .

Hit the first note of the set. You are all together. The crowd jumps backwards with the noise. Anthony explodes into the air as if suspended on wires. Everyone sings along with him. Like an angry dog inside a fenced yard, he runs back and forth across the space that has been arbitrarily determined as the "stage."

After the first verse, Anthony sprints straight toward Billy, as if he's about to throw himself into the drum set—something you've seen him do before, but never so early in the show. Instead, he takes a running step off the bass drum and jumps upward. By his fingertips, Anthony manages to grab the net of the basketball hoop and hangs there by it. Everyone—the crowd, the band, yourself—watches with disbelief as your brother puts the mic cord in his mouth and climbs up the basketball goal. Within seconds, Anthony has hooked his legs into the metal rim. He sings the rest of the song upside down, in midair.

Later, he will show you the scars on his legs where the hooks for the net dug into his shins and drew blood. But for now, you only wonder how he will top this, with hours of playing left to do. Hank looks up and laughs as he brings in the second verse.

As far as you've ever been from home, and all these strangers scream for you. This is it, you think to yourself; this is where you belong.

FOUR

"You did what?" I threw my coat down on the kitchen table along with the paper bag and figured I must've heard Nathan wrong.

"I got us a gig."

"You don't even have a band yet. I thought you were going to find jobs, maybe an apartment. First things first."

Sean sat on my amplifier and tuned his guitar.

"It just happened. Things came together."

"How?"

"Walking around, talking to people."

"Where's it supposed to be?" I turned over the paper bag and dumped day-old muffins and cookies all over the table. Both of them hurried over.

"It's a place called the Wreck Room. Have you heard of it?"

"Oh, Christ." I pulled the vodka from the freezer and a can of Coke from the fridge.

"You know the place?" Nathan asked.

"Take that hellhole where I met you in Montana, multiply it by a pile of shit, add a ton of garbage, and you have the Wreck Room."

"We saw it." Nathan shrugged. "It's a big space. The sound system is solid."

"Here's the thing. The Wreck Room is all ages. It's a place where high school kids hang out. There's no bar, which means no drinking, which means no money. They sell sodas and snacks. On the night of a show, the whole place smells like hot dogs." I collapsed into the recliner with my drink.

"A lot of our listeners might be underage." Nathan unwrapped the cellophane off a second cookie.

"What kind of hot dogs?" Sean asked.

"What listeners?" I took a long pull from my Cold War. "When is this show, anyway?"

"One week from today," Nathan said with pride.

"A week from today? Thursday night?"

"That's right." He grinned and took another bite.

"You dumb-ass, they set you up." I rested my forehead in my free hand.

"What do you mean?" Nathan spoke through a full mouth.

"A week from today is Thanksgiving!"

The boys stopped chewing and stared at me.

"Everybody'll be with their families, full of that chemical in turkey that makes you tired. The college kids will be out of town. High school kids won't even be allowed out."

After a few seconds of silence, Nathan said, "We'll come up with something."

"I don't care if anybody shows up." Sean wiped his mouth on his shirtsleeve and strapped his guitar back on. "It'll be fun."

"You guys don't even have a band," I reminded them.

"We've got the songs," Nathan said. "All they need is some words. I'll make flyers. We'll get people to show up."

"Why don't you play drums for us, Laura?" Sean said it like a brilliant idea.

"You're not pulling me into this mess." I sucked down the last of my cocktail.

"What mess? This is our music." Nathan spoke in earnest. "We're serious about this."

I walked over to the kitchen to refill my drink. "Look, it's good that you have ambition and stuff. I'm happy for you." The rest of the Coke can didn't make it halfway up my glass. "But this is a bloody road you're starting down. At least find a decent day job that pays the bills . . . do music as a hobby." I put in more vodka than the last time. "Look at me. I'm still scrubbing the crust out of coffee mugs. You don't want that, do you?"

"Laura," Nathan said. "If I made one song that was as powerful as an SCC song, I wouldn't care if I spent the rest of my life shoveling shit."

"Psshhh." I rolled my eyes. "Careful what you wish for."

"Our sound is good, Laura." It was the boldest statement I'd heard Sean make.

"Oh, really? Your sound is good? Well, hold everything! I didn't realize that your sound was good!" I slammed my drink down and picked up the telephone. "Hello! Is this MTV? I've got two kids here from some Podunk town in Montana with a good sound. . . . A million bucks? Sure. Would you like to write a check, or send over some shopping carts full of cash?" I slammed the receiver back down in its cradle so hard that the bell inside gave a dull ring.

Both boys hung their heads. What happened? Did they get close enough to me that I needed to crush their feelings?

"Look, I'm sorry." I picked up my new drink and finished it in two long gulps. "Fuck it. Let's see how good your sound is." I sat at the drums and unlaced my shoes.

"What, right now?" Nathan said.

"SCC used to do forty shows a month when we were on tour. You don't get to wait until you're in the mood. You have to be in the mood all the time." I threw my Docs to the side of the kit.

Sean didn't flinch. He plugged in his guitar and fiddled with a couple of knobs on the amp. Nathan opened up his instrument case. I got the feel for the pedal—it had been months since I'd played drums. They turned on their amps and plugged in. Sean strummed chords and Nathan played a scale.

"That blue one, from before," Sean said.

Nathan started us off with a kind of heavy metal bass line. I liked it. The beat was easy enough to pick up. I did a slower tempo thing with a lot of kick in between the notes. Then it was all Sean. His line sounded like a cross between a lullaby and an air raid. Even then, in my cynical mood, I couldn't deny that the three of us had musical chemistry. Sean stopped playing and ran his hand across his throat.

"Hold up," he mumbled at Nathan. "You're a little bit red. Here." He twisted one of the tuning pegs on Nathan's bass. "Let's do that greenish one from before."

"Right." Nathan strummed his bass. It was in tune now.

"What are you guys talking about?"

They both turned to me, like they'd forgotten I was there.

"A little red? His bass was flat," I said. "What do you mean by a green song?"

"Nothing." Sean blushed and looked to his feet. "It's nothing."

I might have let it go if not for his reaction. "What the fuck is going on here? Don't jerk me around."

Sean played a fast run up and down the neck of his guitar. His hands shook. It was like a child covering his ears and screaming.

"She's going to find out soon enough!" Nathan shouted over the staccato notes.

Sean stopped and Nathan whispered something into his ear.

"Okay," Nathan said to me. "If I tell you about the color thing, will you play drums for us on Thanksgiving?"

"What?" It was my first taste of Nathan's salesmanship. "Fuck that. I'm not even a real drummer."

"All right, then," Nathan said. "We keep our secret."

Sean let out a stream of frustrated harmonics. Nathan looked on, stone-faced. They were serious.

"Fine." I looked to the ceiling and bounced up and down on the drum stool. Ever since these two boys came into my life, they'd consistently made me act against my better judgment. "I will sit in with you guys at your waste-of-time Thanksgiving show at the Wreck Room. Then you find your own drummer, you find your own apartment, and you find yourselves jobs. Just save me a ticket when you sell out RFK Stadium with your 'good sound,' okay?"

"Okay." Nathan smiled. "Here it goes."

Sean turned the volume switch down on his guitar and sat on the amp. He strummed the chords to some classic rock song, sped up like he was trying to remember it.

"Sean has this thing," Nathan said. "He can see sounds. Notes and chords have their own colors. Songs and riffs have different shades and hues. The colors get deeper and lighter, depending on how the music is."

There was a pause. Even Sean stopped his quiet playing.

"You're shitting me."

Sean strummed a minor chord and bent it with the whammy bar.

Nathan shook his head no.

"Okay," I said. "That's cool. Let's jam."

Nathan smiled. Sean stood and turned the volume back up on his guitar.

"So," Nathan said. "This one has a weird intro with these vamps." He played me the notes and I came up with a little drum crash to do along with it. Sean filled in the spaces with one of his goose-bumply lines. The song was like a time bomb. Sean counted down the seconds, and the big vamps with all of us were the explosion. Nathan shouted out lyrics, but we couldn't hear him over the music. Once we were done, he wrote some words in a notebook on the kitchen table.

They had several more riffs to jam on. Watching Sean play, with that vacant stare in his eyes and the invisible music swirling about the room, I had some sense of how gifted he was. But this evening, I didn't spend much time pondering it. Mostly, I enjoyed beating on my drums and bobbing my head along to the music we made, on a night that was more fun for me than any night in years.

Ladies and gentlemen of the press, fans of all ages: Let the record show that there was no money, no fame, no advantage to be taken when I first sat down on a drum stool behind those two. They had to twist my arm.

I woke up early the next morning, hours before I needed to. The boys snored away inside their sleeping bags while I showered and dressed. My ears rang a bit from all the noise last night, but I felt myself twitching with a kind of electricity. I doodled in a sketchbook that hadn't been opened for weeks.

A groaning sound came from the floor. Nathan stretched his arms out of his bag. He turned to me with half-opened eyes and said, "Morning."

"Good morning." My legs crossed in the kitchen chair, I bounced one foot up and down.

"We sounded good last night, huh?" Nathan stood. His disheveled blond hair stuck out at odder angles than usual. Several days' worth of stubble clung to his face.

I stared up from my sketchbook and tried to look serious. I couldn't help it. My smile was as giddy as his. "Yeah, we sounded good."

Nathan nodded, now satisfied.

I turned back down to the page and bounced my foot even harder. "We've got a lot of work to do." For one thing, I needed to hone my chops. Drums were never my forte.

"True. I got to write lyrics to all those songs."

"And find a way to get people to come to this thing."

"Nice turkey." He looked down at my doodles. Without thinking, I'd been drawing little cartoons of plump roasted turkeys on platters, over and over.

"Thanks." I closed the cover on the sketchbook and stood up. "We need some way we can spin this, turn the Thanksgiving thing to our advantage."

"You must know people in the music scene here," Nathan said.

I laughed out loud. "I've got more enemies in this scene than I have friends." But underneath my dismissal, I knew that I would indeed have to make some calls.

"I'll think of something," Nathan said.

"And write those lyrics." I picked up the full ashtray off the table and slammed it into the trash can.

"We can jam tonight, right? Once you get home?"

The thought of playing music again filled me with pleasure. "Yeah," I said. "We have to." I washed my hands and put on my coat.

"Hey, Laura," Nathan said before I walked out the door. "Sean's color thing, let's keep that between us, okay? He's real sensitive about it."

"Right," I said. "See you tonight."

The rain was bad on the way to work. The dampness soaked through my sniper coat and finally put out the small fire of nervous energy that had been lit inside me last night.

It was a busy morning at the café and Maxine was stressed out. People stopped in to escape the weather. Umbrellas and jackets hung over all the chairs and tables.

Everybody wanted hot drinks. I got sloppy—spilled milk, screwed up orders, threw full cups into the garbage. The late night and early morning caught up with me. A new girl, Liz, the one Maxine had just hired, worked the register.

The rain ended around noon, but the sky stayed gray. The place slowed down and had almost no lunch-hour business. Maxine sent me on my break early. I went outside with a coffee and day-olds.

"Look who's here." Boeing Bob let go of one end of the paper and motioned me over with his hand.

"What's going on in the world?" I noticed that his clothes were damp, but was too shy to ask where he went in the rain.

"It's mostly more on this Kuwait invasion mess, the UN sanctions, and whatnot." He folded the newspaper and put it to one side. "How are you, Laura?"

"I'm good, actually." The chair's metal grid was wet against my butt. "I've got a show planned, to play music."

"Yeah?" Bob slurped his cappuccino. "You see: You can take the girl out of the band, but—"

"Don't go overboard." I cut him off mid-cliché. "It's a temporary thing. These two guys need someone to sit in on the drums. It's a favor." I finished off my muffin and worked the cellophane into a tight ball inside my fist.

"Look at you: mentoring a new generation of punk rockers."

"Yeah." I brought my coffee cup up to my mouth and blew. "Me, a fucking role model—that's a good one."

He reopened his paper. I brushed the crumbs from my hands and lit a cigarette.

"Bob, can I ask you something?" I tried not to sound silly. "Have you ever heard of somebody who was able to see music?"

"After a few hits of acid, you mean?" Bob laughed.

"No: all the time, no drugs. Like different notes and chords have their own colors and stuff."

"You mean synesthesia?" Bob asked.

"What?"

"It's a neurological phenomenon," he said.

"Like, a brain disease?"

"I believe it's more of a condition than a disease."

"So it's real? It's not an urban legend or something?" I washed a drag of cigarette down with hot coffee.

"The word itself means 'sense fusion.' It involves confusing two or more of the senses together. Have you ever read Nabokov?"

"The author?" I recognized the name from my father's bookshelf.

"He was a famous synesthete. For him, words had different textures, or feels to them. One might be rough and woody; another might be like polished metal, or an old rag, a piece of fruit, or a cloud."

"But it could happen with music, too?"

"Sure. I think Leonard Bernstein had something like that."

Had Sean been born into different circumstances, he might've been a celebrated virtuoso playing concert halls full of tuxedo-clad dignitaries. Instead, he grew up listening to the records me and my brother made when we were kids.

"Why? Does that happen to you?" Bob asked.

"Me? God no. I can barely tune a guitar." I looked at my watch. "Excuse me, Bob. I have to make a call before my break ends." I ground my half-smoked cigarette into the sidewalk and balled it up with the cellophane from my muffin.

There was a phone in the office that we were allowed to use for local calls if Maxine wasn't on it. I hadn't talked to Mark in a long time, but if anybody could rally the indie rock in-crowd to an unformed band's unknown first show in Seattle, it was him. Mark was the front man for Thieves as Thick, the alpha males in this city's underground rock scene and now the flagship band for the most revered of the local independent labels, Gawk Rawd. Years ago, we'd briefly been in a retro surf rock band together. We'd also dated—which was even more short-lived and an even dumber idea.

"Laura, what are you up to?" Mark sounded like he'd just woken up.

"I want you to come to a show I'm playing next week. And bring people."

"The Cooler Heads?" he said the name of my old band with indignation. "No thanks."

"I quit Cooler Heads. I'm working with these two young guys from Montana."

"Great." More sarcasm.

"Listen, Mark. One of them has this thing. He can see the music. He's like the Rain Man of electric guitar. You got to check it out."

"That's interesting. Where's it at?"

"The Wreck Room, the night of Thanksgiving."

"A dry gig?" A groan came through the receiver. "Laura, I couldn't get my friends to go to that place even if you'd put SCC back together."

"Well, that's the thing. . . ." I plucked nervously at the small hairs along the edges of my eyebrows. "We're going to play a bunch of the old SCC stuff."

"For real?"

From the other room, I heard Maxine call my name.

"Yeah. This kid can play Hank under the table. The other one has a voice that's the spitting image of Anthony's." In actuality, I'd never had a proper listen to Nathan's voice. But it was a moot point: my brother could never sing. "This is a one-time thing I've got with these kids. Thursday is the last chance to hear SCC with original members." I felt ridiculous. "So tell whatever wannabe punk rock girl you're dating that you've got the inside line on the last real show of a great band. Bring your buddies so you can brag to them about how you pulled the first lady of hardcore."

"I'll see what I can do."

"Laura?" Maxine's voice came from the next room.

"I got to go," I told Mark. "Bring a flask or something, and friends. You won't regret it." I dropped the receiver down in its cradle as Maxine rounded the corner into the office.

"There you are." She sounded out of breath. "It's been great, the way you've stepped up lately. I want to create a new position—assistant manager. You'd be in charge whenever I'm not around. I can pay you more, maybe put you on salary, now that you're not leaving to play music."

"That's cool." This job was the last thing on my mind today. "Can I think about it?"

"Sure," Maxine said. "How much time do you need?"

"I don't know, a week?" I had no idea what was appropriate.

"Okay." Maxine was disappointed that I didn't accept her offer here and now. "After Thanksgiving, then."

"That's cool," I said again.

We were slow all afternoon. My mind raced in two different directions. As for the show: I needed to come up with a way to get bodies into that venue next week, and now, I had to teach the boys at least a few SCC songs.

Also, I considered Maxine's offer. I'd always sworn never to take a management position in food service. I'd seen too many perfectly good waiters lose their minds over clean spoons, empty grease traps, and the temperature inside the fridge. But I could use the money. And it would be nice to boss other people around for once.

As my brain spun, my hands scrubbed circles into the portafilters. Liz, the new girl, still worked the counter.

"So, Laura." She tried to start a conversation. "You've been here for a while, right?"

"Too long." I blew a puff of steam into a rag and wiped the caked dairy foam from off the steam wand.

"Any plans for the holidays?"

"Working." I paused in my scrubbing and looked at the machine. It was pristine. Why was I still cleaning it? If I was considering becoming a manager, I should make some effort at having a rapport with my co-workers. "Actually, I'm playing a show on Thanksgiving Day."

"Oh, yeah. What kind of show?"

"Punk rock . . . loud, hard."

"That sounds cool."

I considered inviting her, but figured she was too preppy for this sort of thing. We chatted for my last few hours on the clock. I never got around to asking why she worked here. It was obvious, at least to me, that she came from money.

I said good-bye to Liz as I clocked out, and took a double espresso with me for the way home. It would be a late night. We had a lot of material to work on before the gig. This morning, I couldn't wait for practice. Now, all I wanted was a nap.

A few blocks into my walk—still in the commercial district—I did a double take on a piece of paper taped to a light post. It was one of my doodles from this morning—of the plump cooked turkey. But this one had a circle around it and a slash through it, like the no-smoking symbol. Above the picture, in big black letters, read the words TURKEY KILLS, ROCK HEALS.

I walked over to the flyer. Below the no-turkey logo were more words:

Stop the Violence!
Turkey Freedom Concert
This Thursday at the Wreck Room

It was followed by the time and the address. All I could think when I finished reading it was: Nathan. I wanted to be pissed off that he'd gone into my sketchbook without permission. But mostly, I was impressed. I walked to Belltown with a buzz a bit stronger than I normally got from an evening coffee.

WASHINGTON, D.C.: SEPTEMBER 1981

With a box of Xeroxed copies, a bucket of paste, and a couple of paint-brushes, you and Anthony take to the streets of D.C. There is little speaking. Your brother is visibly annoyed that Hank and Billy begged off this job. You don't mind the work. It's fun to get your hands dirty, to see something that you've made hanging all over the city. But your feet and back ache after a few hours, and you can't help thinking that Anthony is leading you into neighborhoods where you're more likely to get hassled.

Find yourself posting flyers all over Georgetown's posh shopping district. Speed up. Gain a block or so on your brother. The stack of papers under your arm, sticky brush in your hand—lose yourself in the rhythm of flapping paper and setting paste. Don't even hear the car as it pulls up.

"Freak!" comes the first shout.

Turn and see a European sedan slow along the curb. A group of blown-dry college students rolls down their windows. One of them holds a bill out the window.

"Hey, here's a dollar." His shirt has a tiny alligator on the breast. "Buy yourself a bottle of shampoo!"

His friends laugh hard.

Grip the paintbrush a bit tighter in your hand, as though it were a weapon. Work up a wad of saliva inside your mouth. You can handle this.

Hear the breaking sound before you see him. Anthony kicks the grille of the car and manages to shatter a headlight. The pastel-clad college kids are shocked. For once, you think, those heavy steel-toed boots are good for something.

Your brother isn't big, but he cuts an imposing figure—the leather jacket with its spikes atop the shoulders, the blood vessels trembling along his bare scalp.

"Get out!" he screams at them, his arms held up in the air. "You wanted a fight, didn't you? Get out and fight!"

The rubber squeals as the car pulls away from the curb. "Fucking freak!" shouts the kid in the passenger seat.

Your brother always seems to win his battles through fearlessness, by calling someone else's bluff. He spits on the trunk as the car pulls away and stares them down as they go.

"That's good enough for today," Anthony says once the car has gone. "Let's go home."

FIVE

The set list became a problem. Sean remembered the songs by their color: "that blurry gray one" or "that bright yellow one." I could call them up with a brief description; my shorthand was more like "the fast one in C" or "that metally one without a chorus." Nathan did his best to name them based on the unfinished lyrics.

This was our lives for the next few days: me working late, the boys putting up flyers, all of us practicing at night. Nathan and Sean found jobs wrapping Christmas presents in a department store, but that didn't start until after Thanksgiving.

I brought home all the day-old baked goods at the end of the night, and the boys always ate heartily. Other than that, I wasn't sure what they were eating. They'd brought an enormous bag of jerky with them—deer or elk, probably killed by one of their fathers or uncles. Macaroni-and-cheese boxes turned up in the trash can, sometimes ra-men noodles wrappers. The two of them didn't have a taste for junk food, not like SCC did. Nathan and Sean, at least when I first met them, would've chosen a glass of milk over Coca-Cola.

None of this was any of my business. I wasn't their mother, much less a model of good health and clean living. But for some reason, on my walk home after work on Sunday, I found myself picking up a dozen eggs, a loaf of bread, and a block of cheese.

I had Monday off, so we stayed up late jamming and slept in. It was my first free day since their arrival, and I made us a big breakfast. Nathan and Sean ate like starving dogs—layering pieces of white bread with scrambled eggs and ketchup and sucking it all in with a few bites. I liked this: sleeping late, having food in the fridge, feeling busy and tired enough during the workweek to enjoy doing nothing come my weekend. Perhaps the manager job was the right decision. I'd given the past ten years of my life to music. When was it enough?

After breakfast, I took them for a walk around the city. The day was cold and overcast. We went past the Pike Place Market and felt the wind blow hard. Sean pulled up the fake sheepskin collar on his denim coat. Nathan carried around another stack of flyers and taped them up on every wall and telephone pole we passed.

I dragged them to the Seattle Art Museum, where I often spent days off. There was an Edward Hopper exhibition that I wanted to see. They followed me in and looked at the paintings with polite feigned interest. I loved Hopper's compositions, the way he painted loneliness into the hearts of urban dwellers as if it had its own color. My favorite was called *Morning Sun,* which showed a woman seated on a bed, staring out the window of what looks like a hotel. There's a blue sky above the city that spreads out below her like a long day with nothing to do.

"Wow." Nathan was at my side all of a sudden, staring at the picture. "That's so sad."

"It is sad." I was surprised that he noticed the woman's subtle melancholy. We stood there side by side for a few minutes, soaking it up.

Sean found us and walked over, frowning. "Is there someplace to sit down? My feet are killing me."

"Let's get out of here," I said. "I want more caffeine."

Liz stood behind the counter at the Daily Grind. Her breasts managed to look perky even underneath the starchy uniform shirt. I could find no blemishes on her ivory skin. Her wavy black hair was pulled into a ponytail, and under the café lights, it shone like a vinyl record.

"Hey, Laura." She smiled at the three of us. "Coffee?"

"Please. Do you guys want anything?" I turned to the boys. Sean looked up at the speakers, which played some of our mellow café fare. Nathan's eyes were fixed on Liz.

"We'll have what Laura's having." He kept staring as she filled the order.

Liz put our drinks on the counter. I grabbed a handful of sugar packets.

"Thanks. By the way, I'm Nathan . . . from Laura's band." He reached across the counter.

When their hands touched each other in a shake, I felt something fall within my chest, an organ dropping several inches lower.

"Hi. Liz." She offered him a smile and turned to make sure that no customers approached the register. "So you guys are playing in the Thanksgiving concert?"

"We'll be outside." I stuck one paper cup in Sean's hand and pulled him toward the door.

We sat down at a metal table.

"Whoa," Sean said as he took a sip. "It's bitter."

"Here." I handed him three sugar packets. He dumped them all in at once.

"What's Nathan doing?" he asked.

"Striking out." I put a cigarette in my mouth.

"Huh?"

"He's chatting up the chick who got us our coffee, but it won't work.

She's a rich girl, from Mercer Island. I don't even know why she's working here." I cupped my hand around my lighter.

Sean nodded. He tucked his hair back behind an ear. As he went for another sip, I got a good view of his harelip scar.

I took a drag off my cigarette and stared through the storefront window. Nathan leaned on the counter with his elbows. Liz cocked her head back with laughter. Why was it taking her so long to brush him off?

"Could you work here, Sean?"

"I don't think they'd hire me. I have no experience in this kind of thing."

"No. I mean hypothetically. Like if you were me, would you hate it?"

"Of course not," he said. "It'd beat working at the mill."

"What mill?"

"The pulp mill, back home. That's where our dads work. It's dark and stuffy there, no windows. I don't like it: standing around, washing machines down with hoses, helping them turn the forests into cardboard boxes."

"Is that where you two have been working since high school?"

"Part of the year. It pays good. During the winter and spring we've had a bunch of odd jobs: shoveling snow, washing dishes, changing tires. Could I have one of those?" Sean pointed at my cigarettes.

"Be my guest." I pushed the pack toward him and handed over my lighter. I'd never thought to offer one to either of them.

"Thanks." He knew how to light up all right.

"Inside there, just now," I said. "Could you see the music coming out of the speakers?"

"Sort of," he said.

"Does it take over your eyes? Does it, like, blind you?"

"The colors are there in the room, or on the street, wherever." He took a long drag and considered the tobacco and the question all at once. "They might be shapes or blurs. Most of the time they line up, like long clouds—appearing then fading away with the sound. I can see through the colors if I try hard. It's like"—he held up his cigarette at eye level—"like smoke."

"What about other noise? Sounds that aren't music?"

"It's funny." He ran his hand through his hair and scratched at his scalp. "When I was a kid, I used to see things when a dog barked, when a dish dropped into a sink, or an engine revved. Now, it's almost always during music. If somebody has a nice-sounding voice, I might see colors when they speak."

"Does it ever get distracting?" I was fascinated. "Do you ever wish it would go away?"

He looked from side to side, as if afraid that somebody might listen. "For most of my life, I didn't even know I was different. I thought everybody saw shit like that. It wasn't until junior high that I figured it out. Once we were teenagers and started playing music with other kids, I got sick of people treating me as a sideshow freak, like I could make their band better. For most of high school, I didn't jam with anybody besides Nathan." He shrugged, then took another drag. "To be honest, I don't understand how people play instruments or listen to music without the colors. That seems weird to me. It might be cool to see what that's like."

I laughed. "You're not missing much."

"Still, it makes you wonder how things sound to someone else's ears, what it is that they see."

"Hey!" Nathan burst through the door with his paper cup in hand.

"Give it up, Nathan," I said to him. "You're not her type."

"Is that so?" He wore a self-satisfied smirk. "At least I got her to drive us to our gig."

"What?"

"All our instruments and everything. She's got a station wagon."

Sean took a slow drag on his cigarette.

"You're kidding me. She must eat Thanksgiving dinner with her family." Why did this bother me so much?

Nathan shrugged. "Maybe she's going through a rebellious phase. You guys are smoking? Can I have one?"

I took out another for myself, then handed him the pack. "Listen, Nathan. You can't come into my workplace and bum rides from my staff. It's not professional."

"What staff? Don't you two have the same job? It's just a coffee shop."

"I'm serious about this. Don't fuck with my workplace."

"We need a ride." He sparked the lighter. "You got a better idea?"

That stumped me. We stopped talking for a second and focused on the smoking.

"Hey, guys." Liz walked out and dropped a paper bag on our table. Nobody took the day-olds home last night, if you all want them."

"Thanks," Nathan said.

She waved at us, then went back inside. I spent a little too long watching the eye contact between her and Nathan, feeling my face redden. This was embarrassing—taking scraps and begging rides from a girl so much younger than me, a girl who's supposed to be my employee soon.

"Let's go home." I picked up the bag from off the table and walked. "It's gonna fucking rain."

WASHINGTON, D.C.: NOVEMBER 1981

No extended family shows up for the holidays anymore. It's just the four of you, with nothing to talk about. Anthony is experimenting with vegetarianism, and piles his plate high with mashed potatoes and cranberry sauce. It's a bit of a contradiction: He still wears his first leather jacket, with its spikes and studs, the SCC logo and a sort of manifesto written on the back in Wite-Out. Chains jangle at its shoulders as he scoops green bean casserole. Your father glares. His tolerance of Anthony's music, dress, and lifestyle has always been a sort of theoretical tolerance, based more on principles that he's read about in books than on actual emotions.

Despise this part of the year. Both parents are off for the winter break. For three boring weeks, they take you to a cabin in West Virginia inherited by your father's side. There, they busy themselves with academic work while you sit around and do nothing. What's worse: Anthony, now nineteen, didn't go last year and surely won't this time either. The quiet is what gets you the most—the dull hum of central heating, a few clacks on the typewriter from the word or two that your parents type per hour, the hurried and then slowed-down flipping of yellowed pages. It's what you imagine prison to be like.

"So," your father finally speaks up over pie. "We're going to the mountains earlier than usual this year. Your mother has some important work to do, and we've got to give her all the time that she needs." Even at this age, you already recognize the way he condescends to your mother when it comes to her career. Though they're both professors, he speaks of her work like it's a diversion. "You'll need to have your things—" He's talking to you.

"She's not going," Anthony says. "Laura's in the band now. We've got a tour."

Your father looks back and forth, not sure whom to respond to. "No," he says at last, lifting his eyebrows to punctuate. "Absolutely not."

"Yes, Dad." Anthony is calm. "She's in my band. I need her."

"She's coming with us, Anthony!" your father yells. He's grown lopsided and hunchbacked by his passion for English literature. Watching him turn confrontational is two parts scary and one part pathetic.

"Dad, calm down. Laura's gone to the mountains every winter for the last eight years. Can we agree that she's learned all that she can from this experience? The band is important. This is a good opportunity for her."

"I want to do it, Dad." You know you have to speak. "I'm going to do it."

"You're a child!" He stands up and swings his arms around. "I'm your father. You will do what I tell you, and that's how it works. That's how normal families are!"

Look at your mother. Why doesn't she say something? Wonder if she hasn't kept her career subservient to his, purposely never published as much, neglected to apply for promotions.

"Dad, with all due respect"—Anthony's calm is unfazed—"I don't think we should appeal to what's considered 'normal.' Look where that's gotten us."

Your father picks up the half-full pie dish and hurls it across the room. The glass bounces off the wall, leaves a hole in the Sheetrock, then thuds onto the wood floor.

"Don't you patronize me!" he screams at Anthony.

Your mother buries her face in her hands. The wallpapering of this room was a recent and time-consuming project for her. The pie-shaped hole shows rough-cut lumber and pink fiberglass insulation beneath.

"You two are academics." Anthony's voice has the slightest quiver. "How did you get so conservative? This band, this movement—we're rewriting those dusty old books of yours. You think Emerson did what his parents told him? You think Picasso worried about being 'normal'?"

Your father's face curls in disbelief. He looks down at his two soft hands, surprised at what they just did. As you and Anthony head out the door, your father finally goes over to comfort his wife.

The two of you walk in circles through the cold park across the street. Little puffs of steam show with each of your breaths.

"I'm sorry," Anthony says at last. "I thought they'd take that better."

"I don't mean to upset them," you say, "but I want to go with you."

Anthony looks around at the leafless trees, the brown grass. "I guess it shouldn't be easy, you know. If it's important, then it won't ever be easy."

Turn back and look at your block—your own home in the center of a row of well-kept houses. Inside each of them, their inhabitants are dressed in their holiday sweaters, eating with the dishes and forks that come out two or three times a year.

It's true that you don't want to upset your parents, that you mean them no harm. But it's also true that ending up like them, in lives like theirs—ruled by wallpaper and good china—is the only fate you can think of worse than a nuclear strike.

SIX

On Thanksgiving Day, I shelled out for a bucket of chicken with mashed potatoes and biscuits. This was probably the first holiday Nathan or Sean had spent away from their families.

The boys ate fast and without words, until the table was a mess of empty Styrofoam tubs and chicken bones with even the cartilage sucked off the ends. A siren whizzed by outside on what was otherwise a quiet evening in the city. I made myself a Cold War, while the boys drank plain Coke.

"So," I said. "What do we do now? Talk about what we're thankful for?"

"You're supposed to do that before you eat," Nathan said.

"Sorry," I said. "I didn't think of it in time."

"Fuck it." Sean spoke up. "We'll do it now."

I'd only meant it as a joke.

"I'm thankful for Laura, that she let us crash here and agreed to play drums with us." Sean was sincere. I was touched.

"To Laura." Nathan raised his plastic cup. Sean did the same.

"Cheers!" We all brought them together.

A knock sounded from the door. Nathan ran to get it. Sean cleared up the bones and trash. It was Liz, right on time. She wore a pair of torn jeans and—much to my surprise—an old SCC T-shirt.

"Hi, Laura," she said. "I love your place."

I barely swallowed a laugh. My apartment was hard to see under the beat-up instrument cases, dirty laundry, greasy fast-food wrappers, and overflowing ashtrays. It smelled like a mix of sweaty feet, cigarette smoke, and fried chicken. "Thanks," I said.

Between our drums and guitars, the amplifiers, and four people, we needed every inch of Liz's station wagon. The boys used their sleeping bags to cushion the cymbals and snare.

The owner of the Wreck Room was known as Fat Paul—a chunky balding guy who played in a cover band and bought this place to live out some frustrated rock-and-roll fantasy. He let us in through the back door. Liz went to find a parking spot.

My enthusiasm faded once we took our equipment out onstage. The place was empty.

"Fuck!" I said.

"It's still early." Nathan looked around the room.

By the time we had the drums set up and the guitars tuned, Liz was back. A few young kids in SCC T-shirts and leather jackets wandered in. The Wreck Room had high ceilings and a big stage, though the floor space itself was small. With the windowless walls and the dim houselights, it felt like the inside of a cardboard box. At the snack bar, a wheel of limp hot dogs turned under the orange glow of a heat lamp.

"I can't believe I got talked into this."

"There's still time," Nathan said.

"Fucking empty room on Thanksgiving." I should've known better.

Nathan frowned at me. Sean retuned with his guitar, hair in his eyes, head hung forward. Fat Paul called for sound check. I reluctantly banged out the rhythm from "My Sharona" while they mixed the levels. At least we'd get this over with early and I wouldn't be too tired for work tomorrow.

A couple more kids came in during sound check.

"Hey," Paul's voice echoed through the monitors. "What are you guys called, anyways?"

Both Sean and I turned to Nathan, but he shrugged.

I grabbed the microphone suspended above my tom-toms. "We're the Mistakes," I said, and I meant it.

Nathan glared at me hard. I met his gaze. He wore a red T-shirt with a faded white number eight from a recreational soccer league.

Paul spoke over the PA system now, in his cheesy announcer voice. "Ladies and gentlemen, coming to you live from Seattle's own Wreck Room, please give it up for . . . the Mistakes!"

Nathan continued to stare me down, still upset about the band name that he'd one day fight me tooth and nail for.

Sean, of course, couldn't care less. Wearing a threadbare flannel shirt not quite long enough for his arms, he started us into the song that until then I'd known only as "the time bomb one." With his guitar, Sean ticked down the seconds for two, three, four bars . . . longer than we'd ever let it go in practice.

Finally, Nathan hit the vamp as hard as he could, those three notes each sounding as if he'd broken a string off his bass. And I was right there with him, each beat a different tom plus snare, a grace note on the kick drum in between.

Two of those vamps we did instrumentally; then Nathan came on the microphone. It was the first time I'd ever heard his voice:

> some wadded-up bills and a knife in his pocket
> a bottle at his crotch and a car like a rocket
> going NO-WHERE-FAST!

The three syllables of the refrain hit on the three notes of the vamp with a tuneful, howling scream. In between, there was only Sean's ticking guitar riff and Nathan in the microphone.

His jacket and his hair and his pretty little cousin
Jesus on the dash and the devil in the engine
going NO-WHERE-FAST!

It was beautiful. Nathan had one of the greatest rock-and-roll voices I'd ever heard. By the time we reached the chorus, I decided to take a page from Sean's book and enjoy this, the raw pleasure of playing good music, loud and hard. I let my hair hang down before my eyes and got lost in a song I'd had a small part in creating.

When we returned to the verse, I found myself desperate to know what happened to this redneck incestuous drunk driver that Nathan had invented, this character that was both the hero and the villain of his own story. I opened my eyes and whipped the hair away from my face.

Everything was different now. There were people. A bunch of kids had shown up—perhaps they'd all been outside smoking. But the more shocking sight was Sean, all of a sudden performing. He was on his knees in front of the crowd, playing his licks as they reached up and touched his guitar. When we got to the vamp, he somehow exploded to his feet and jumped up in time with the three strikes of the *no-where-fast*.

I saw the door open in the back. There was Mark, still wearing black jeans and that too-small Bob Dylan overcoat. As always, his stubble was at the same sexy middle length; as always, there was a girl on his arm. She was thin and Asian with pouty lips and a dyed-red bob, tattoos all over her shoulders. The rest of Thieves as Thick followed them in. The whole of their party looked shocked at what they saw: kids jumping up and down, shouting the lyrics to a song being played for the first time ever. I didn't quite understand it myself.

The tune came to its end. Everyone screamed and whistled. Sweaty, panting, the three of us onstage looked at one another, awestruck.

Nathan played the bass line to "The Only Good Cop," an early SCC classic. We'd practiced that one a few times. Nathan put his own spin on the singing. In his hands, the song sounded less like a rant, more like a tortured confession.

The crowd went crazy over the SCC tune. I noticed Mark and his friends in the back, mouthing the lyrics. They passed a silver flask back and forth, out of sight from Fat Paul in the sound booth.

People continued to fill in. The front of the stage grew crammed with kids. Even Mark's überhip crew and preppy Liz came forward.

We played every song we'd practiced and took no break. Finally, an exhausted Nathan spoke through the microphone in a hoarse voice, "Thanks a lot for coming. We are——" He looked at me. "We are the Mistakes."

The crowd hollered, and the three of us ran offstage. Sean and Nathan still had their instruments strapped over their shoulders. In the dressing room, underneath the no-smoking sign, I lit a cigarette and we passed it back and forth.

Over the PA came Fat Paul, "Ladies and gentlemen, let's see if we can get them back out for one more song."

We took turns peeking at the audience. They held up lighters and stomped their feet. The front row banged their hands on the stage.

"What do we do?" Nathan looked over the spent set list, which had meaning only to him.

Sean played a silent riff along with the stomps and chants of "Encore!" coming from the crowd, as if we could write a new song on the spot.

Nathan let his piece of paper fall to the floor and looked up at me.

I said, "John Hinckley Jr."

Sean stopped playing. Nathan plucked a few notes on his bass, trying to remember the tune.

"No"—I put the nearly finished cigarette in my mouth—"in E." I took his finger into my hand and guided it over the frets: an inverted version of the bass line that I used to play live forty times a month, in another life. Nathan's fingers were warm inside my own. I repeated the verse a couple times, humming the tune. After a few seconds, he looked up from the fretboard at me and gave a little nod, as if to say, *You can let go of my hand now.* Sean chimed right in once Nathan played the line on his own. I drummed my palms on my thighs.

"All right," said Nathan. "Let's hope that satisfies them."

Once we were back onstage, the crowd screamed. Nathan did his best to shush them. I saw Mark, looking drunk now, all the way down front, shouting with the high school kids. He'd left his girl in the back.

Finally, the crowd settled enough so that Nathan could speak. We hadn't discussed how to start it off. His voice came through the speakers, "This next song is about a madman, a deranged killer, a murderous lunatic. And this next song is about the man who tried to bring him to justice."

Nathan looked back at us. He raised the head of his bass like an axe, and when he dropped it, the three of us hit the first note.

His feet together, Sean bounced up and down. Nathan closed his eyes and sang the lyrics that everybody said would lose their relevance after a couple years. How I wished my brother could've seen this: a room full of disenfranchised high school kids in 1990 being moved by this tune, even if they had no idea who John Hinckley Jr. was. It didn't matter. The world was still mad enough to call mass murderers heroes and to call geniuses lunatics. I looked down and saw little bursts of clear liquid jumping each time I hit my snare drum. I was weeping over a fast and angry three-chord punk rock song. I whipped my head around to be sure that hair covered my face.

We got toward the end of the song. Mouthing something that I couldn't understand, Nathan looked back at the two of us. Finally, he took a hand away from his bass and held up one finger. I read his lips at last. *One more,* he was saying. *One more time through.*

We hit the last note, and Nathan again raised his bass and took us back to the start. We played louder and harder this time. Nathan resang the first verse. Sean played with his back to the stage, heels hanging over. Once we made it again to the chorus, boom, he fell straight backwards. I almost jumped up to try and grab him. The audience caught him, of course, and carried him around atop their hands for a while. I worried that his cable might come unplugged.

Sean managed to get back onstage before the end of the song, and never missed a note. The instrument cord was wrapped around his waist a couple of times, so he spun in circles until he was untied. We came to the finish and blew it up with an extra loud crash. The boys looked like they'd been beaten—covered in sweat and breathing hard. Nathan nearly lost his voice.

"Happy Thanksgiving everybody!" he wheezed into the microphone. "I'm thankful for rock and roll!"

Everyone shouted and we stumbled off the stage, exhausted and trembling. The three of us sat down side by side on the floor of the backstage room, our heads against the wall. Nathan fetched a bottle of water from off the table and passed it around. We continued to sit there and suck air. Somehow, without deciding to, the three of us were holding hands—me in the middle, the boys on either side.

Fat Paul came in a minute later, carrying cash and gushing about our performance. "You guys killed out there! When can you play again?"

Suddenly embarrassed, the three of us dropped hands. Nathan stood up. I followed.

We went back out to break down our equipment. The houselights were up, and most of the kids had gone. The boys took a load to the alley. Liz went to get the car. I stayed and packed up the drums.

"You guys rocked." Mark stood at the foot of the stage.

"Hey, Mark." I checked to see if Fat Paul was looking. "Anything left in your flask?"

He handed it up and I took a discreet swig. *Whiskey,* I thought.

"Listen, we're going over to my place for some after-hours fun. You guys should come." His girl reattached herself to his side. "Hey," he said to her. "Laura, this is Scarlett. Scarlett . . . Laura."

"Hello." I handed the flask back to him.

Scarlett smiled, said hey back, and gave me a once-over from my feet up to my face.

"I'll talk to the guys," I said. "See if they're up for it."

"You should come," Mark said. I could tell Scarlett was pulling him toward the door. "We need to talk. You guys have to play with us, and soon." They left. The rest of their people followed them out.

Sean and Nathan came back onstage and loaded their arms with equipment.

"You guys up for a party?" I asked.

CLEVELAND: JUNE 1983

Once again, the skinhead is here. He comes to all your shows now. His uniform: orange and black flight jacket, full-length combat boots, tight straight jeans, head always shaved down to the nub. The edges of dark tattoos poke out around his neckline. His eyes are close together and buried deep within his head, protected by that carapace of knobby flesh that seems to cover all his body like armor. His mouth is always in a crooked state between smile and frown. In the back, he stands beside a trash can and grinds a fist into his palm. There are rumors that he punched out the singer of another band. He is everything that your brother and you will go on to hate about hardcore.

Try not to stare, but miss a note and get a reprimanding look from Hank. Anthony leans over the crowd. You want to tell him not to jump tonight, not with that skinhead lurking about. *Stay here, together, where it's safe*. A ringing in your ears drowns out the noise from the amps.

The skin marches forward through the crowd, pushing the kids who get in the way and then scowling at them, begging for a confrontation. Your brother is on Hank's side of the stage, his head turned away from you, only his toes still touching the wooden platform, suspended above the sea of hands and heads as if on a cable.

The skinhead makes it all the way up to the front. With your hands, test the weight of your instrument, wonder if you could unstrap it, hit him across the face, and have time to run away out the back. He walks up to the foot of the stage, within kicking distance. You take a step back. The skinhead blows a wad of white spit as fast and straight as a bullet, which hits Anthony around the kidneys. Your brother takes no notice.

A million hands reach up from the crowd toward Anthony now. He drops himself into them. From behind, a thin slam-dancer bumps into the big skinhead. In a blur of black clothes and pale flesh, the skinhead turns and punches somebody in the face. A body falls to the ground. Your brother is lost in the crowd, but taken in the opposite direction, as the kids all move away from the scuffle.

The skinhead kicks the body on the ground once, then marches back off toward the back.

What will become of him, this object of your fear? Will he wind up in Northern Idaho somewhere, in one of those colonies too stupid to oppress other races economically and so left to do it with violence, as if it were a sport? Perhaps he will still listen to your music, in his pickup on his way to work, pounding nails for more per hour than SCC ever made. In ten years or so, he will likely be nostalgic for hard-core punk, this thing that he helped ruin.

SEVEN

"There they are!" Mark shouted as the four of us entered. "The men and women of the hour." The Velvet Underground played on the stereo. Beer cans lined up along every piece of furniture. Mark's whole band was there plus members of other bands and their girlfriends. The Lower Queen Anne house was as I remembered it. Something in the lighting made the whole place look different shades of brown and yellow.

Tony, the drummer from Thieves as Thick, held up a half-full twelve-pack of PBR and said, "Beer?"

I reached in and took out a can; Sean did the same. Nathan took out beers for both himself and for Liz, who was now attached to his side.

"I've got something for you guys." Mark stood up and motioned for us to follow him into the kitchen. The linoleum was still dirty. The pile of dishes in the sink looked as if it hadn't moved since the last time I was here.

Mark opened a silverware drawer and took out a plastic Baggie full of white pills.

"We all took ours, like, ten minutes ago." He opened the bag and held it toward us. The other three looked at me.

"MDA?" I asked.

"Mellow Drug of America." Mark smiled.

I reached in, took out a pill, and washed it down with a sip of my beer. That was all Sean needed; he was next. Nathan followed. Liz hesitated and looked over to me. I shrugged. She went ahead.

"Thank you," Nathan said, though he could've just taken birth control, for all he knew.

"He's the guy you need to talk to." I spoke to Mark and pointed to Nathan. "About booking gigs." I almost said: *I'm not part of the band.* But the words didn't quite make it out of my mouth.

"Right on." Mark turned to Nathan. The two of them shook hands. "Let's talk," Mark said. "I want you guys to play with us." Nathan and Liz followed him into the other room.

"Laura," Sean asked, now that it was the two of us in the kitchen, "what did I just take?"

I choked back a laugh. "MDA," I said. "They call it the 'hug drug.' In half an hour, everybody will start smiling and telling you how great you are and how great life is and shit."

He looked back at me, incredulous.

"Once it kicks in, it'll seem like a good idea." Nowadays, all you have to say is that it was an early form of ecstasy.

Sean peered into the living room. Nathan and Mark were deep in conversation, each of them with a girl at his side. Liz and Scarlett appeared to get along. Scarlett pulled her shirtsleeve farther up her shoulder and showed off a tattoo. They all sat on the floor, at the foot of the old couch where Mark and I used to make out.

"C'mon," I said to Sean. "Let's go smoke."

We crossed the living room without looking over at the rest of the party. Lou Reed's voice swelled—*"I'm . . . waiting for my man"*—until we closed the front door behind us. Sean sat on the brick banister of the front porch. I lit up and then handed the pack and lighter to him.

"Playing with Thieves as Thick would be good for you guys," I said to Sean. "They've got a following, and their label might hear you."

Sean got himself lit and exhaled smoke from the side of his mouth.

"You guys kicked ass tonight," I said.

"You kicked ass, too."

I looked back through the window into the living room. On the floor by the couch, Nathan and Liz connected at the lips. This didn't seem awkward to any of the other partygoers. I stared at them. A small black emotion, a mix of hatred and envy, took shape and buzzed around my face like a gnat.

"Will you keep playing with us?" Sean asked.

"I can't. They offered me a promotion at work." I kept staring at Liz, no longer kissing but resting her face against Nathan's. "I'm getting a little old for this kind of thing, you know."

Tony burst out the door with another partly full twelve-pack. Droning notes came from the stereo as the front door opened and closed. "More beer anybody?" He wore the shorts, combat boots, and long underwear combination that was—for some reason—gaining popularity in this town.

I finished my first can and dropped the spent cigarette into it, then took another from Tony's box. Sean did the same.

"Fuck." Tony fumbled with the buttons on his jacket. "It's tough being single at these MDA parties."

I looked inside and saw that several other couples were now in liplocks. Sean and I made muffled sounds of understanding.

"So this is the guy, huh?" Tony put his hand on Sean's shoulder and shook him a little.

"What do you mean?" Sean asked. I wondered the same thing.

"The guy who can fucking see the music!"

All the color drained from Sean's face.

"What did you call him?" Tony turned to me. "The Rain Man of electric guitar?"

Sean's nearly full beer hit the ground with a thud. A fizzy puddle spread across the concrete patio. He was down the stairs and heading up the street before I got my cigarette stomped out.

"What?" Tony called from behind. "What did I say?"

Sean didn't run so much as walk swift and fast, his hands tucked deep into the pockets of his denim coat.

"Sean!" I gained on him. "I'm sorry, okay. It just slipped out. I was desperate to get people to come to this show."

"You think I'm a fucking freak, like everybody else does." He stopped suddenly and turned around.

"That's not true." We were face-to-face now. "It was to draw people." I put my arms out at my sides.

He turned around and kept walking.

"Sean!" I followed behind him. "Where are you going?"

"Right here!" He stopped walking and then grabbed the handle on the nearest car, which I only then recognized as Liz's station wagon. Because the street in front of Mark's was so full, we'd parked two blocks away. Sean opened the door to the backseat, which was inexplicably unlocked with all our gear inside.

"I'll wait in the car until you guys are done partying."

I hadn't expected his answer to make so much sense. In the absence of any sound explanation, I acted on my first impulse, which was to kiss him on the mouth.

Sean trembled a little at first, but calmed down a second or two into it. I reached my hand up to his hair and pulled his head a little closer to mine. His two hands froze out at his sides for a moment, then wrapped around me. I pushed him down into the backseat and managed to get the door closed behind us.

I could've guessed that it was his first time. He lay back across the bench seat of the station wagon. On hands and knees, I held myself above him. Nakedness sprouted at each of our waists and then blossomed in both directions until all our clothes formed a pile on the floor of the station wagon. Strings and drumheads resonated with every motion.

Just like that, I was once again inside a dark automobile, helping an awkward boy figure out sex. The MDA kicked in, and this felt like the most natural course in the world, despite years of disparity in our ages, much more than that in our mileage.

Clothes completely off now, I crawled downward along him. His hands slid up my sides. He shuddered as I wrapped my lips around his dick, his body tense and taut as a guitar string. He came within seconds, his hands clenching lopsided fists inside my hair. I sat up straight for a moment and caught my breath.

I lay down with my back against him, wrapped up in his frayed sleeping bag and slender limbs, his breath heavy upon my cheek. Above us hung the station wagon's dome light, which I kept mistaking for the moon. It seemed the only fixed point in the universe, and that the two of us, the whole of the car, were orbiting around it somehow.

His boyhood curiosity about a woman's body never abated. Sean's hands—which only hours ago drove a crowd of people crazy and which would go on to awe others on all continents—for a few minutes, they were nobody else's but mine. Years from now, teenage boys in their bedrooms will spend hours attempting to unravel the miracles that these two hands performed. But for a moment, there was something that I could teach them.

I guided his fingers across my body the way that I'd guided his best friend's across that bass fretboard before our encore. Even without speaking, it wasn't hard to show Sean where the note was that he needed to play. It took him another second to understand that this wasn't a fast verse-chorus-verse number. This was more like a ballad. It had a beginning, middle, and end—several movements that built upon one another and then finally culminated into a moment of transcendence.

I wondered what color Sean saw then. In which key did I climax? Was it something dim and blurry, or did he see a deep and brilliant hue? I closed my eyes. We curled up even further into the seat of the borrowed station wagon and gave no thought to what might happen next.

SOMEWHERE IN TEXAS: AUGUST 1982

"Would you just relax," Hank says. "Try not to make noise."

All you can think of is your brother, asleep along with Billy on the other side of some amplifiers, here in the van. Your body trembles nervous underneath Hank's hands as he wrestles with your clothes. You've heard that it will hurt and have a low threshold for pain. But more frightening is the possibility that your brother could wake up and see you.

"No," you whisper at last, and beat the underside of your fist against Hank's chest. There's a terrifying moment as his weight shifts to his knees. Is he about to let you up, or get a better grip and pin you to the floor? In L.A. not long ago, you saw what you think was a man forcing himself on a girl. You know it happens.

But it doesn't come to that. Hank sits up, holds his hands in the air with fingers splayed.

"Not here," you whisper to him, then open the rear door of the van and walk out into the night.

The moon is at the far side of the sky and lights up the fence posts along the road. You'd hoped to reach Austin and stay with friends, but

Texas turned out to be even bigger than anticipated. So you pulled off the interstate, moved some equipment around, and crashed in the van.

Don't recall ever seeing a piece of land so long and flat and empty. The point where the road disappears at the horizon looks like the curvature of the whole earth. In the middle of I-10, you squat on the yellow lines and piss all over the blacktop because you can.

Stand up and start back toward the van. Pluck at the tiny hairs along the sides of your eyebrows. Hank meets you halfway with the filthy woolen blanket you both lay on a moment ago. Though you're not cold, he wraps it around your shoulders and hugs you to him. Now that you're outside and farther from Anthony, don't mind his advances so much. Hank guides you over to what is essentially a ditch at the side of the road, and lays you down atop the blanket. With his wadded-up jacket, he makes a pillow for you and then goes about lowering your jeans and underwear. Close your eyes. Dig your fingernails into the dry earth on either side.

Once it's over, Hank lays down beside you, lifts his hips in the air, and raises his pants.

"Don't tell Anthony," you say to him.

"Why?" He works with the buckle on his belt. "Does he have a rule against sex, too? Just because he's never done it doesn't mean that nobody else can." Hank turns onto his side and falls asleep in seconds.

Think about that last sentence for a few minutes. Hear footsteps from the ground above. Don't be afraid. It appears at last, poking its head past the rim of the ditch. Even having never seen one before, you know it to be a coyote—wilder than a dog, not so scary as a wolf. It looks you right in the eye and cocks its head a little, as if trying to remember your face from somewhere. Then it turns and runs off.

Sit up and watch the animal disappear through the wire fence and then into the taller grass on the far side of the road. In one pocket of the jacket that Hank made into your pillow, you find his cigarettes. You can't help but look back to the van as you light one up, now seated on the rim of the ditch, your first and only lover asleep at your feet. Middle America stretches out before you, infinite in every direction but down. The landscape lightens as the sun breaks at the horizon. Soon, long shadows stretch themselves out from off the fence posts.

Smoke your stolen cigarette right down to the filter, looking back toward the van every so often, checking your pocket for gum so you can cover up the smell.

Sitting on the rim of the ditch where your virginity, but not your innocence, was laid down for good, you're still a little girl lost in a place that is at times beautiful but always enormous. Look back at the van once again as you stomp out the cigarette. The line of your sight is an invisible tether connecting you to Anthony, an imaginary umbilical cord, which gives what you need to live but also taints you with traces and toxins from whatever he's exposed to.

A punk fanzine recently described you as "the first lady of hard-core." You're the cofounder of a key independent label, a prominent figure in what some journalists and historians will go on to consider the most important independent movement in rock-and-roll history. But you're also sixteen years old, lonesome, and confused. At this moment, it's hard to imagine anyone more dependent than you.

EIGHT

At first, I mistook the telephone for the ringing in my own ears after all last night's noise. I tried to ignore it. The rings refused to stop. I allowed one eye to open a crack, not sure where I was and not yet ready to find out. The phone jangled only a foot from my head. My hand shook as I brought the receiver to my ear.

"Hello?" As soon as the word left my mouth, I wished that I'd dropped the phone back onto the cradle. Or better yet, unplugged the cord.

"Laura? Is that you?"

"Maxine." Real life came back to me in spades. Harsh sunlight poured in through the window. My eyes strained to adjust. I was in my apartment. Still in their cases, all our instruments were piled up on one side of the room. As usual, two bodies were wrapped up and asleep on the floor. But when I looked more closely, I saw that these two weren't the same bodies that I was used to seeing there. Flowing elegantly out the top of the sleeping bag were the shining black curls that I knew belonged to Liz. She was asleep in the pile of down and nylon on my floor, intertwined with Nathan.

"Laura, where are you?"

"Maxine, I'm really sorry. I'm . . . sick." I sat up a little and turned to the other side of me. There was Sean, his lips parted ever so slightly, one hand draped loosely over my waist, in a sleep as deep as he'd been in outside my door a couple short weeks ago.

"Why didn't you call?" Maxine sounded like she might be crying. "I can't have this if you're going to manage."

Nathan stirred a little bit and sat up in his sleeping bag. The dust particles in the air glowed like snow in the sunlight that had no business shining throughout Seattle in late November. Nathan's own eyes struggled to make the adjustment. He smiled at me conspiratorially, with Liz still burrowed in his armpit, as if we'd both gotten away with the same crime.

"Listen, Maxine. I've been thinking over this promotion and it doesn't feel like a good idea."

"What?" She whined like a spoiled child. "This is a great opportunity for both of us."

"I'm not management material. Besides, I've . . ."

Nathan locked his eyes on me. His smile straightened itself out.

"I've got a new band now," I said. "That's got to come first. I'm sorry." I held the phone an inch or so from my face.

"Well, that's just great!" Maxine descended into some less-than-coherent sounds.

"I'm way too sick to come in today," I told her, feeling like a boss all of a sudden. "But I'll see you tomorrow, okay?"

"No!" She was definitely crying now. "If you don't come down here now, and right now, then you can forget about working here ever again. Do you understand me?"

I let out a big breath, which sounded like static as it came back to my ear via the phone. "Okay, Maxine. Put my last check in the mail, then. I'll stop by sometime and drop off my shirts."

"What? No, Laura. Wait a minute—"

"Good-bye, Maxine."

By the time I'd hung up the phone, Nathan's grin had regrown, now bigger and slyer. The two of us lay back against the bodies of lovers that we weren't supposed to have. As I fell to sleep, I took some comfort in the fact that at least I was making my mistakes in a familiar direction.

TWO

NINE

The boys moved out by the end of November. Liz knew of a family from her neighborhood in need of house sitters for the holiday season. We set up our equipment in their plush basement. Every night, after Nathan and Sean finished work, we practiced for hours. It was the most consistent drumming I'd ever done, and my chops improved fast. Having played bass for so many years, it wasn't hard to anticipate Nathan's lines. The style that we developed as a rhythm section was unadorned, but tight and reliable, and let Sean be the virtuoso.

Thieves as Thick booked us as their opening act on New Year's Eve. While I downplayed the significance of that show in front of the boys, it looked to be a huge break.

In the space of a few weeks, my practice room went from a cold storage locker in Pioneer Square to the bottom level of a Ralph Anderson house on Mercer Island. The boys went from sleeping on my floor to queen-size beds. Most nights, I stayed over with Sean. Liz and Nathan got the master, and we were stuck in what must've been a teenage daughter's bedroom. Posters of boy bands and Hollywood heartthrobs lined the walls. A pink canopy covered the bed. Sean moved the pile of pillows and teddy bears to one corner of the floor.

In the mornings, Liz drove us into Seattle proper with her station wagon, like a soccer mom dropping the kids off at school. Sean and Nathan worked at their department store. Liz went to sling coffee at the Daily Grind. I took naps back at my apartment, doodled in my sketchbook, and halfheartedly looked for a new job.

A few days before Christmas, a business-size envelope came from Washington, D.C. Inside was all that remained of communication with my parents: a yearly check for a thousand dollars. The memo line read: *Merry Xmas!* The signature was my father's trembling *B* with a squiggly line, then *L* with a squiggly line. However misguided the intention behind it, the money itself was much needed. My final paycheck was almost spent, and January's rent was due.

Once the check cleared, I bought a bottle of hair dye called Electric Blue. Partly for kicks and—on a subconscious level—partly to ensure I wouldn't get another job, I bleached out several strands of my hair and put in bright blue stripes.

Liz and the boys liked it. Sean ran his fingers through the blue parts. Perhaps it resembled one of the colors he saw in our music. For the first time in years, people did a double take when they saw me on the street. I'd almost forgotten what that was like.

After one good practice, the four of us took a bottle of whiskey from the house's liquor cabinet, some cans of spray paint from the garage, and walked out into the damp foggy midnight. We ended up drinking in the playground of a nearby middle school. Eventually, Nathan and Sean grabbed the paint and went off to vandalize. Liz and I sat on the swings, rocking ourselves back and forth. Above us, chains creaked along the beam.

"Smoke?" I held my pack out toward Liz.

She nodded and took one.

I had a buzz and figured the two of us would be alone for a long span of minutes. "So, Liz"—I lit my cigarette and breathed out—"what's the deal?"

"What do you mean?" She leaned her head toward my outstretched hand, cupped her fingers around the flame.

"Why are you working a shit job in a coffee shop? Shouldn't you be off at college or something?"

"I was in college." She let out a smoky sigh of air. "Technically, I still am. This is supposed to be a leave of absence."

From down the hill, on the street, came the hissing of spray cans and the boyish giggles of Sean and Nathan.

"We had a little family tragedy last spring," she went on. "My older sister died." Liz rubbed the heel of her nonsmoking hand against the side of her eye but didn't lose composure.

"I'm sorry." I wished I'd never brought it up.

"It's okay. She'd been sick for a while."

"Like . . . cancer or something?"

"No." Liz pushed herself so that she swung forward a bit on her swing. "I mean mentally sick. She jumped off a parking garage last April."

I watched my toes drag through the packed dirt under my swing.

"She was in Highline for a while. One afternoon she escaped, probably spent a night on the street, and then jumped the next morning. It's strange. Growing up in the suburbs, you never think stuff like that will happen. You think all you have to worry about is life turning out too boring."

"I know exactly what you mean," I said.

"Anyways, I came back home after that. My parents were a wreck—my mother especially. She blames herself, you know. Thinks they never should've put Allison in that hospital. I couldn't go back to Ohio and leave them—still can't, I guess."

"That's good of you—to be there for them."

"To be honest . . ." She stalled her swinging with her feet and took a long drag from the cigarette. "I couldn't handle the thought of going back. I was at this small private school in Ohio. If you could see it— all these rich kids waiting for their trust funds. My sister was the wild one. She was . . . like you, Laura."

"Like me?"

"You know, confident and creative and stuff. And she loved punk rock. The SCC shirt that I wore at the show—that was hers."

"Your sister listened to our records? They were in your house growing up?"

Liz nodded as she drew on her smoke. "Anything to piss off my parents."

I smiled.

"So, yeah, the coffee shop. I needed extra money, not to mention a reason to get out of the house. But mostly, I went and got a job because I'd never had one before. Your sister dies, and it makes you look at your own life. What experiences have I had in twenty-two years: a lot of school, summer camp, a few college parties, and one fucking awful funeral."

"Does Nathan know about this?"

"He knows my sister died, that I left school indefinitely. I spared him the details. He's got a lot on his plate right now, with the band and all. Plus, my other friends in Seattle, all they think about is Allison. It's nice to get away from that."

The boys returned, their spray cans rattling. Sean took a long pull from the whiskey bottle and handed it to me.

"You guys ready?" Nathan asked.

The four of us walked the middle of the empty street toward our temporary home. Nathan and Liz led the way, arm in arm. I didn't realize it at first, but Sean was quite drunk. With an arm around my shoulder, his weight rested heavy on my spine and his feet tumbled along the ground. I pulled him forward with one hand on his waist, feeling the pelvic bone sticking out through his jeans.

We admired the boys' handiwork as we went. They'd revised all the stop signs on the block so that they now read: STOP HATE, STOP WAR, STOP RAPE, etc. The one they were most proud of was on the street itself, where they had embellished on the big STOP at the intersection. With white paint upon the blacktop, it now read: STOP VANDALISM!

Once home, Sean collapsed on the pink canopy bed and passed out in his jeans and belt. I changed into my surgical pants and lay down beside him. Soon enough, I heard the sounds of Nathan and Liz fucking from the other side of the wall.

I'd never had many female friends and didn't know how those relationships worked. I supposed that now, after our talk, Liz and I would be closer than ever. Besides Nathan and Sean, she was technically the best friend I had in this city. But as I lay awake and listened to Liz moaning and cooing in the next room, with her station wagon out in the driveway, her family that helped each other through a tragedy, and her dewy young skin underneath Nathan's hands, I knew that now another part of me hated her more than ever.

Nathan, Sean, and I celebrated Christmas Eve with frozen pizzas and a bottle of Smirnoff. We ate in front of the TV, watching my VHS tape of *This Is Spinal Tap*. Worn out from wrapping gifts, the boys fell asleep an hour into the film. I knew the whole thing by heart and needed a smoke break. Prying myself from between the slumbering bodies of Nathan and Sean, I went to the back porch.

With the sky covered over in clouds, and all the good children tucked into their beds, the night was dark and quiet. Even the parents in this neighborhood had finished playing Santa, setting presents under the tree and biting off a carrot left out for the reindeer. I smoked and hovered over the coffee can that we'd put out back for butts. Through the picture window, I watched Sean and Nathan sleep. The film had finished and the television screen bathed them both in a bluish glow. I'd ceased to think of them as helpless, but as I looked upon their bodies curled together like puppies on that couch, I knew that they were every bit as fragile as they were talented. Guiding their gift through the world was like carrying an egg through a crowd. I wanted to protect it, but if I held on too tight, there was a chance it might shatter inside my fist. It was a burden, in some ways, but also a privilege. I wondered if I was the best one for this job, if I could be trusted with these two boys, with their hopes and their means of making them real.

Turning away from the window at last, I looked up and around at our temporary squat, this sprawling overgrown house. I took a visual inventory of the suburban toys in the backyard and along the deck: gas grill, out-of-service Jacuzzi, the shed with its riding mowers and power tools, swing set and sandbox. I didn't want all these ridiculous things, but I no longer wanted to be poor either. I turned back to my sleeping boys once more, under the soft geometry of cedar and stone that was the living room, and promised myself that my years of squalor and poverty were about to end. From this moment forward, I decided, I'd no longer wait for free checks and old muffins. From now on, I would get what I wanted.

I decided to seal this pledge somehow and thought of what Boeing Bob had told me about sacrifice. In the pocket of my sniper coat, I found a crumpled one-dollar bill and my lighter. My hands shaking with cold, I lit the bill on fire and held the flame up to my eye level.

"This year," I said out loud, "I will know success."

It burned too close to my fingers, and I dropped the flaming paper into the coffee can, among the spent cigarette butts.

WASHINGTON, D.C.: AUGUST 1979

It's a school night. Sit up in your bed with a notebook and draw a horse-type creature with long spindly legs. The phone rings three times. Don't think much of it.

Billy's been a friend of Anthony's for a long time. He's a year older but socially awkward. It will shock you that he's even able to play with the band. His parents travel a lot. There are rumors that Billy's father is a spy.

In some ways, you feel that Anthony and Billy became such good friends because they so often have that big empty house to hang out in. It sounds funny: your brother will go on to be considered a canonical figure for one of the most noisy and aggressive genres of music in history, but his whole life, Anthony always looked for a little peace and quiet—for a place where he could breathe.

Hear the front door slam and the car start. Lights come on in the house. The car takes off down the street. Both parents' voices sound from outside your bedroom door. It's Anthony who's left. Put your notebook down by the side of the bed and walk up to the door. In the

kitchen, your parents stand in robes and pajamas. Mother dials numbers
off a list by the phone and Father paces around.

"What's going on?" you ask. "Where's Anthony?"

"Go back to bed, sweetie."

Don't think much of it. Your brother never gets into trouble. Go to
sleep and dream of an airplane dropping nuclear suitcases over the playground across from your house. Hear the rest from Anthony later on.

Billy called to say good-bye. He'd slit his wrists and lay down in the
bathtub so as not to make a mess. His parents were in Eastern Europe.
Anthony called 911, then drove over. He climbed into the tub with his
bleeding friend and held him, saying that everything was okay. He was
there.

Instead of an ambulance, two cops come in with their flashlights and
nightsticks drawn. Shining their light in his eyes, they tell Anthony to
get out of the tub. He asks what they're doing here, where the fucking
ambulance is. They order him again out of the bathtub. He says he isn't
leaving Billy until the medics arrive. Then the sentence that's eventually
construed as a threat: "If you don't get that flashlight out of my face, I
swear to God I'll shove it up your ass!"

One cop strikes Anthony across the temple with his nightstick.
They proceed to choke him, ignoring the dying child in the tub. The
cops pull the baton into Anthony's throat until he foams at the
mouth. All the blood vessels in his eyes burst. His corneas are red as
apples afterwards. He has matching black eyes. Anthony is seventeen
years old.

Your parents hire a good lawyer, and you all go to the trial every
day. Impossibly, your brother is convicted of striking an officer. His
flailing arms hit the two big cops a couple of times as he was choking
to death. A minor, Anthony is sentenced to community service.

The rock historians will use this incident as the linchpin to Anthony's career. They'll say that it started his rage against authority, his

distrust of the system. To a certain extent, they will be right. But they will miss the most important aspect: his black eyes.

For a month, your brother goes through life wearing a raccoon mask. People point and stare. Strangers laugh. It hurts at first, but Anthony eventually grows taken by it. For a matter of weeks, his black eyes are a badge of honor. A middle-class white male, your brother has his first taste of what it means to be an outcast. Afterwards, he can't get enough. When the eyes heal, he moves on to spray-painted hair, leather, and chains.

Billy sees a therapist. The doctor finally decides that he is "not a threat to himself or others"—which becomes a kind of inside joke to your whole crew.

TEN

We arrived early for load in. The boys looked nervous as we banged out a tongue-in-cheek version of "My Sharona" to get our levels right. Scanning the bar, I didn't see any familiar faces. I wondered if Thieves as Thick still drew crowds.

After sound check, we waited backstage. Nathan and Sean sat down at a card table in the center. I fell into an old couch. The walls of the room were all covered in stickers—everything from skateboard logos to half-witted bumper slogans. Nathan borrowed my Sharpie and made copies of the set list. From a fifth of Canadian whiskey stolen from our house, Sean took several long pulls.

Every few minutes, I went to the wings and looked at the audience. The bulk of the crowd was the twenty-something hipsters that followed Mark and his band, a few metalheads, and younger punk kids. Finally, I saw who I'd been looking for.

Chip and Doug were the owners and cofounders of Gawk Rawd, the most established and well-distributed of the regional independent labels, the label that Thieves were on. A band they'd developed, called Puddle-jumper, recently signed to a major label for their second album. Rumors of their advance floated around the scene for the last couple months. Now that the higher powers in the music industry saw a need for what they called "agitated guitar music," smaller operations like Gawk Rawd acted as their farm league.

We'd met before. The Cooler Heads had tried, unsuccessfully, to bend their ear. Chip was the spokesman and visionary of the two. He'd started a lo-fi music magazine as a school project in college, and sometimes included sampler cassettes of local bands. Doug was the businessman; he'd staked the label in the first place with cash from an inheritance.

Back in the sticker room, Nathan handed me my Sharpie.

"I'll be back in a second," I said to the boys. "I'm going to the bar."

I ordered a drink. Chip and Doug approached. Chip had grown a bushy beard since the last time I saw him, and couldn't keep his hands off it. Doug wore chunky black spectacles, his hair close cropped, tentative sideburns creeping down along his ears.

"So, Laura"—Chip stroked his beard and grinned through the fuzz—"hear you've got a new band."

"Nothing gets by you guys." I dumped my cigarettes and lighter on the bar beside my Cold War.

"The Cooler Heads are no more?" They both chuckled.

"I don't know what they're doing now." I tried to squeeze the paper-thin lime into my drink. "I quit."

"Mark says this new act has a good sound."

I smiled, thinking of my first jam session with Nathan and Sean. "You're about to find out."

"Yeah." Chip grinned. "Mark called us up a few weeks ago, freaking out about your band, saying we should sign you guys right away and shit." Doug laughed from behind.

At that moment, Liz happened to walk through the door.

"Laura!" She saw me and waved. I motioned for her to come this way.

"Liz," I said. "This is Chip and Doug."

"Hey."

"How do you do?"

"Yeah . . ." I tried to restart the conversation where it had left off. "I'm not sure we want to go that route. I did the indie label thing for a long time, you know." I lit the cigarette and blew smoke out one side of my mouth.

Chip shifted uncomfortably and cracked his neck.

"This band is good. We could go straight to the bigs. Did you hear those guys from Aberdeen might sign to Geffen? What are they called again?"

"Nirvana."

"Right. First Soundgarden, then Puddle-jumper, now them, it's like: Why sign some contract that you're going to have to buy your way out of six months later?"

"The Puddle-jumper situation was not as simple as—" Chip lost his composure.

"Look at me." I cut him off. "How many fucking years did I spend pasting up flyers all day long, getting spit on at night? I'm ready to get paid, you know. Should I be ashamed to say that?" It was a rhetorical question, I suppose, but a part of me did want to know: *Should I?*

Liz looked at me with an awkward half smile.

"Let's go," I said to her. "It's almost time to start." I turned back to Chip and Doug. "You guys enjoy the show."

The stage had a classic look to it—polished wood and ornate trim. It was more intimidating than the Wreck Room. The lighting and sound were far superior. Mark and the rest of his band came down front. Liz worked her way through the crowd.

"Hello, beautiful people of Seattle," Nathan said into the microphone. "Thanks for spending the last night of 1990 with us. We are the Mistakes."

Sean ticked out "Nowhere Fast." It was the perfect opener, with that memorable vamp that you could sing along to even if it was your first time hearing it. We were tight. Sean's whiskey buzz didn't faze him once onstage. A photographer shot from down front. Periodically, a flashbulb went off in my face and I'd have to look away as my pupils constricted.

We played a short set that was high energy all the way through. The closer was a version of that sped-up Irish drinking song that I'd seen them play in Montana. Nathan had written more lyrics and called it "Thin Air in My Arms." At the end, Sean shocked everyone—the crowd, Nathan, and definitely me—by smashing his guitar onstage.

He'd probably learned that stroke from chopping wood back in Montana. The flashbulb went off from the front of the crowd. A cheap guitar to begin with, the neck snapped soundly where it was screwed into the body, and the two pieces hung slack by the strings for a half second before popping apart. Sean picked up both halves and placed them in front of his amplifier. The room was washed over in a wave of feedback. Sean walked offstage.

The drunker elements of the crowd went crazy. Houselights came on. From the foot of the stage, Mark stared at me with an open mouth. I shrugged at him.

"Happy New Year, everybody," Nathan spoke into the microphone. "Thieves as Thick are up next." Before leaving, he picked up the two pieces of Sean's guitar. I followed him off.

Backstage, Sean sat at the little folding table.

Nathan stood over him, shouting, "Dude! What were you thinking? That's our only guitar!"

There was that. Also, it's bad form for an opening band to smash instruments. It's hard to follow. There is such a thing as unspoken rock-and-roll etiquette.

"I don't know." Sean was apologetic, a child who'd knocked a bottle off the table to see what would happen. "It felt right."

The door to the room swung open hard and hit the wall. Mark burst in and confirmed my worries. "What the fuck was that?" He screamed at me first, then turned his boozy rage toward Sean. "I don't know who the fuck you think you're dealing with, but that bullshit will not stand!" He stuck his index finger in Sean's face. "Try and upstage my band! You're done, you hear me? You might as well move back to Montana because you are done playing music in Seattle!"

With one push, Nathan knocked Mark nearly all the way across the room. "Don't ever talk to my friend that way." Besides me, Nathan was the smallest in the room. But he was fearless, his eyes burning a hole in Mark's throat.

I stepped between the two of them. Sean sat still at the table.

"Get out of here," I said to Mark. "You got a show to play."

He tried to look over my shoulder at Nathan.

"We upstaged you way before that guitar ever got smashed," I went on. "You couldn't follow us if you lit yourselves on fire."

Mark made the open-palmed gesture of throwing something away. "Screw you guys." He turned and left the room.

Nathan and Sean both looked to me, as if awaiting orders. There was a second or two in which only the stickers along all the walls did the talking: WHERE THE HECK IS WALL DRUG?

"Break everything down," I said. "Pack our stuff. I'll find Liz and try to get our money."

Out in the crowd, I told Liz to bring the car around. The owner was so keen to have us back that I was able to get our cut of the door without staying to the end. He told me to have whatever we wanted to drink, so I went to the bar and ordered four beers, figuring a round would calm everybody down, even if we took them to go. I picked the bottles up by the necks, two in each hand, and turned toward the back door.

"Laura." It was Doug. He grabbed me by the forearm.

It was the first time I'd heard him speak all night. I looked around for Chip.

"We want you guys." Doug stared at me over the rim of his black glasses, a fold of pale flesh jiggling about his chin. "We want the Mistakes."

I looked down at the hand clutching my forearm. "It's going to cost you," I said. I put the beers back on the bar and took the Sharpie out of my pocket. On Doug's forearm, I wrote my phone number in black ink. "We've got to go now," I said. "Give me a call when you have the best possible offer."

I found Liz and the boys in the alley, hastily loading gear into the station wagon. Having prepared for a quick getaway, they were taken aback when I passed out the beers. I heard the opening chords of Thieves' set and figured we no longer needed to hurry. The cool night air felt nice after the smoky, stuffy bar. The light of the streetlamps shone off puddles on the pavement and made the whole alley glitter like a blackened mirror.

Nathan leaned against the car and took a sip of his beer, one arm around Liz. "I think if we get a new neck for the guitar, I can fix it."

"It's all right," I said. "He needs a new instrument anyway. That thing was a piece of shit. We should buy a new bass as well. I think I got us a record deal."

All three of them stared at me, incredulous.

"We didn't come up with terms or anything, but Gawk Rawd wants us. They definitely want us."

Nathan abruptly let go of Liz and put his arms around his best friend. In an awkward but emotional silence, they hugged together in the darkened alley. Liz and I shrugged. Once they released, we all raised our bottles in the air and made a toast to the Mistakes. I looked at my watch. It was 1991.

WASHINGTON, D.C.: OCTOBER 1979

Your parents sleep soundly in their bed. Since the trial, they've granted Anthony a fair amount of slack. Hear the front door open and footsteps heading to the kitchen. He's home. Sneak out of bed and spy from down the hall.

Anthony opens the refrigerator and drinks from a milk carton. It's a warm fall night; they're calling it an Indian summer. His face is shaded by the light from inside the fridge.

"Where were you?"

Anthony jumps at the sound of your voice. "Laura! Don't sneak up on people like that." His voice is a whispered shout.

"Where were you?"

"I saw a concert tonight." He smiles.

"Was it fun?"

"It was the most fun I've ever had," he says. "It's what I've been looking for."

"Who was the band?"

"They're called the Bad Brains. You should go to bed." He puts the milk away and closes the refrigerator.

Once back in your bedroom, see through the cracks around the door that Anthony's lamp is on. Listen to the pages of a magazine turning.

The very next day, Anthony embarks on his adventures in punk rock. The weather is warm, so he starts by ripping and pinning back together his T-shirts. To a pair of leather boots, he attaches chains and upholstery nails. Your brother's hair is naturally a mess of tight curls. He spray-paints it two different colors but can't make it spike properly. By the end of the week, he brings home a secondhand electric bass.

During all of this, your parents seem to think it best not to over-react. Though they are liberal arts professors, their disapproval is palpable. Perhaps he'll grow out of this phase on his own, they seem to think, if they don't make an issue of it.

Years later, you'll wish you could've been at that Bad Brains show. During the prime of your D.C.-concert-attending years, they were banned or in New York. But more so, when recalling that night, you'll wonder how your life might've been different had your brother attended some other event. He was a free radical, looking for something to which he could bind. Had he gone to a Golden Gloves bout, he may have be-come a champion prizefighter. Had he attended a Hare Krishna meeting, he might've been a top guru. Instead, he saw the Bad Brains and went on to become the high priest and punching bag for the D.C. hardcore scene.

ELEVEN

With phone calls and a couple of meetings, Doug and I hashed out a contract by mid-January. I pretended to be savvy about the whole thing. In actuality, I had no idea what I was doing and nobody to ask for help. After what happened with Mark on New Year's Eve, all my bridges had been burned in the Seattle music scene.

Doug wouldn't budge on the commitment: a single right away and then two full-length albums. At the time, Gawk Rawd operated a subscription service for collectible 45s, a concept that traded heavily on good singles from unheard-of bands. For all this music, the label would advance us three grand. Sean and Nathan thought this was a dream.

We spent all the money we'd made at the New Year's show on a new guitar for Sean. He moved up from an Asian-made Stratocaster to a Mexican one. A beautiful instrument, the color was called sapphire blue; he chose it because it matched my hair.

The first catch was that all our recording sessions started at 3 A.M., when studio time was cheapest. Liz was kind enough to lend us the station wagon. We packed our things, stopped for cigarettes and a two-liter bottle of Mountain Dew, and headed off to record our single.

All the Gawk Rawd stuff was done in a tiny plywood shack of a studio, across from a railroad switching yard. Every side of the place—floor, walls, and ceiling—was covered in a funky layer of shag carpeting. The live room barely had space for the three of us and our equipment. The control booth held the mixing board and two people, tops.

Chip waited for us in an old Autopilot T-shirt and thrift store trousers, his beard a bit bushier than before. He introduced us to the producer. Jojo was an older black guy with a salt-and-pepper beard. He wore dark sunglasses indoors.

Nathan and Sean set up our gear while I talked with Chip.

"I made a cover for the single."

"Oh," he said.

I handed him the black plastic bag with my painting inside. It was basically an illustration for the "Nowhere Fast" lyrics. An over-the-shoulder view of the character from Nathan's song, you could see his one hand on the steering wheel and the other on the bottle, the cab of the car all littered with pills and weapons. I wrote THE MISTAKES in block letters across the top, along the ceiling of the car, and then drew a green road sign through the windshield. It read *Nowhere* like the name of a city, and *Fast* like the number of miles it would take to get there.

"Nice." Chip was unenthused. "Sort of old school, huh."

I felt silly, like a kid showing my dad what I did in art class. "When do we get our money?"

"In the morning." Chip put the painting back inside the bag. "Doug's bringing by a check first thing."

Once Chip left, Jojo got down to business. He tuned and microphoned my drum kit in minutes. Choosing the songs was easy. "Nowhere Fast" had become our trademark. If any of our tunes could get play on the college radio stations, that was the one. For the B-side, we agreed on "Thin Air in My Arms," a nice counterpoint.

We laid down the rhythm tracks in no time. The place was so small and the equipment so scarce that Jojo had to come in and rearrange the live room to do the vocals and leads. My job mostly done for the night, I went outside for a cigarette.

In the railroad yard across the street, a cargo train inched its way across the landscape like a giant metal slug. I thought I saw two hoboes leap into an empty boxcar, but my eyes might've played tricks on me. I put my head against the wall, hoping to listen to the boys, but all I heard was the echo of blood thundering through my ear.

Nathan walked out with the bottle of Mountain Dew in his arms and asked for a smoke.

"That was quick." I handed him the pack.

"It's just a scratch vocal for now; they're doing the lead guitar tracks." He tucked the soda bottle under his arm, then cupped his hands around the lighter.

"How are things with you and Liz?" I hadn't broached this subject before.

"Good." Nathan met my stare and then looked away, nodding his head. "Fine." He took a slurp of Mountain Dew, then handed the bottle to me.

"Be careful. She's from a different world, you know."

"You told me that already."

"A girl like that, her rebellious phase won't last forever."

"I get it." He pulled hard on his cigarette.

"Her future doesn't include following around an aspiring rock star while—"

"I said I get it!" He threw his cigarette to the ground and stomped it out. "The band comes first; nothing's changed with that."

Why did I ask? What was I after? Sometimes, when I look back at things through a certain lens, it's not hard to understand why the public hates me now. "Sorry." I rubbed out my cigarette into the sole of my shoe, then took a drink from the soda bottle.

We squeezed into the control room. The sound of Sean's guitar filled up the tiny space. Everything else was turned down.

Jojo twisted a knob on the sound board. "This kid is good."

He was right. Sean played a lead over the chorus. The three of us stared at him there on the other side of the glass. Sean's big hair puffed out around the headphones. The flannel shirt hung heroically from his narrow frame. His eyes were half-open and darting around the room, seeing right through all the equipment and the gross carpet, seeing something the rest of us couldn't see.

Jojo was pleased. He moved the mic stands around to record the vocals. Sean and I went outside to smoke.

"That sounded great. Jojo was psyched."

"It's easy like this," he said. "No crowd, no band even. There's no distraction."

"Distraction," I asked sheepishly, "from the colors, you mean?"

He sipped smoke from his half-done cigarette. "Right. Just me and the headphones, I can really get into it. Let it take over the whole room."

"What do you see, during 'Nowhere Fast'?"

He looked down. "The song itself, straight up, is red to me. When I play, I sometimes try to match that. Or I'll make it earthier, the color of rust or bricks. Other times I try something different that goes with it, something green, maybe—because green goes with red, like Christmas."

I stood and listened, fascinated. The silence was broken only by the groan of train wheels on the rails and puffs on our cigarettes.

Without warning, Sean leaned over and kissed me on the mouth.

"You don't like doing that in front of other people, do you?" he asked once the kiss was finished.

"No," I said. "I guess not." I summoned an explanation. "Here's the thing, Sean: I don't want people to know about us. Not because I'm ashamed. But girls in bands don't get taken seriously if they're screwing one of the other members. I'd rather we kept it between us."

"That's cool." He took a sip of Mountain Dew. "I don't mind."

"Look." I leaned my back up against the recording shack and stared out at the trains. "I've never been any good at being anybody's girl-friend, okay. It's something I never learned how to do." What might my life look like, I wondered, had my older sibling been a sister, and not Anthony?

"It's okay," he said. "I wouldn't know the difference." We stomped out our smokes and went back into the studio.

"That's good." Jojo spoke to Nathan through the microphone on the sound board. "Now, let's do another one where you open up on the chorus."

Nathan nodded, his hands on the sides of his headphones.

Jojo looked over his shoulder at Sean and me. "He's a natural in the studio."

"What are you doing?" I asked. "Are you double-tracking the vo-cals?"

Jojo pulled his sunglasses down his nose a little bit and looked up at me with bloodshot eyes. "You're goddamn right, I'm double-tracking the vocals."

"No, fuck that." I shook my head. "This isn't a pop song. We're do-ing a warts-and-all recording. This is punk rock. It's supposed to be rough."

Jojo yawned at me. From under the mixing board, he pulled out a stack of stapled-together papers that appeared to be a photocopy of our contract. It was already flipped to a specific paragraph, circled with yellow highlighter.

"Article four A." He turned back to the mixing board and moved several sliders up at once so that a rough mix of our song sounded through his speakers. "The record label shall have final say on all deci-sions related to the production of the aforementioned recordings."

"It sounds good, Laura," Sean whispered in my ear. He was right. The music coming through the speakers sounded very good.

"Listen to your bandmate." Jojo was unfazed by my protests. "And

take a piece of advice from me: Choose your battles in this business."
He scratched at his face. "For crying out loud, John Lennon double-
tracked like crazy."

Doug showed up around 6 A.M. In a tired fog, Sean and Nathan loaded
our equipment into the station wagon.

"So," Doug said, "we finalized the dates and—"

"Not now," I said, looking over to see if either of the boys heard
anything. "I'm too tired to talk shop. I'll call you this afternoon." I was
genuinely exhausted but also trying to surprise Nathan and Sean.

"Fair enough," he said. "I'm pleased by how this recording went.
Should I make the check out to you?"

We bought doughnuts and coffee and waited in the parking lot for the
bank to open.

I cashed Doug's check, then fanned the hundred-dollar bills out in
front of the boys' faces back in the car. They laughed.

"All right," Nathan said. "Now, let's get some sleep."

"Not yet," I said. "We got one more thing to take care of."

They both sighed with exhaustion.

"Don't worry," I said. "This is a good errand. Go south on I-5. We'll
get off right before the airport."

"I'm Laura," I told the attendant at the car lot. "We spoke over the
phone yesterday?"

"Right." The salesman snapped his fingers. "Follow me."

We stumbled our way through a labyrinth of automobiles in various
states of disrepair.

"It's the only one left on the lot." The salesman walked fast. "The miniatures have taken over. Anymore, I don't fuss with the full-sizes too much."

We followed him through the new gray morning, our feet splashing puddles on the patchwork of gravel and dirt that made up the lot.

The dealer turned a corner, and we saw it for ourselves. He wasn't lying—it was old—but an Econoline just the same. This model of Ford vans was the backbone of the eighties hardcore scene. Capable of holding exactly three to five teenagers and their instruments, they were widely available secondhand. I sometimes wonder what would've become of underground music in this country had Ford never produced this model.

"Dude." Nathan stumbled a few steps closer. "Is this an ambulance?"

The van was white with red stripes along the sides, a small siren attached to the top.

"*Was* an ambulance," said the salesman. "Been decommissioned for a while. Some small town in central Washington."

"It's a seventy-four, is that right?" I played it cool, but inside I was psyched. This was the last year that they made the rounded headlights.

The boys looked puzzled.

"Can you give us a minute?" I said to the salesman.

He walked off to a car several yards away.

"Are you going to buy this ambulance, Laura?" Sean asked without guile.

"Me? No. *We're* going to buy it." Did they not see the next logical step in this band's evolution? "Boys," I said. "We're going on the road. We've got a single to promote."

They stood and stared at me. A jet from SeaTac took off right over us with a deafening roar. I looked up and saw the silver underbelly of the fuselage. It looked vulnerable, like I could throw a rock up at it and bring the whole thing tumbling down.

Once the noise passed, Sean smiled and Nathan laughed out loud.

"Our van!" Nathan tried the words out in his mouth.

"A tour!" Sean said.

"It's not a lot," I told them. "Tacoma and Portland, the college towns in Oregon, over to Boise and then up to your neck of the woods, a show in eastern Washington, then back home."

"Four states!" Nathan revised his own mythology, made room for bigger things.

"We're a Gawk Rawd band now," I told them. "That carries a lot of weight in the Northwest." I turned to the salesman, who now leaned against a sedan, his forearms resting on its roof. "You got the keys?"

It started right up. With the transmission still in neutral, I hit the gas. The van revved loud, like a motorcycle. I looked over at the salesman.

"There's a hole in the muffler!" He cupped his hands around his mouth and shouted at me. "It's noisy, but not a real problem otherwise."

Nathan climbed into the passenger seat. From the back, Sean reached between the two front seats and turned on the radio. After some talk and a little static, he found "Sweet Leaf" by Black Sabbath. The three of us smiled and nodded along to the music.

The salesman walked up to the driver's-side window.

"We'll take it!" Nathan screamed over the engine and the radio.

The label sent a box of singles to my apartment. Upon opening it, I screamed out loud. Instead of my design, the cover was a black-and-white photo from our New Year's show, of Sean smashing his guitar against the stage—a sort of homage to the Clash's *London Calling*. In a red strip across the top, it read, THE MISTAKES: NOWHERE FAST / THIN AIR IN MY ARMS. The square Gawk Rawd logo was in the bottom left corner. I called the label's office.

"This is about branding." Chip kept his composure even after my screaming tirade. "Nobody outside of Seattle has heard of your band. Kids all over the country are wearing Gawk Rawd T-shirts to school. This label is the Motown of underground rock. The album covers are part of our image."

"I gave you the design for the record. I worked hard on that."

"And it's a great design. We'll use it for T-shirts and stuff. But this isn't an SCC record. Let it be its own thing."

"We didn't want it to be this thing," I said. "That's the problem."

"Okay . . . here."

I heard the phone being passed around.

"Laura, this is Doug. Bottom line: The contract specifies that we have final cut on all the jacket-design decisions. Express yourself through the music and leave the packaging to us, okay. Good-bye."

He hung up the phone. I remembered my pledge on the deck of our borrowed house, not to be a starving artist anymore. With my pride stuck halfway down my throat, I had another look at the single. It wasn't bad. The photo would stand out among others in the Gawk Rawd catalog. I placed it on the turntable and swallowed my pride the rest of the way.

The boys were out running errands. I switched the record player to 45 rpms. Though it was early, I decided a Cold War would help wash down my pride.

With a drink and a lit cigarette, I set the needle and sat in the easy chair. My hands trembled as the vinyl hissed and crackled. A quick fade-in gave way to Sean's guitar line. The effect was like being woken up suddenly or raising a reclining car seat too fast. It got your attention.

The fade-in, the vamps with all of us, then Nathan's vocals—the first thirty seconds of the track were a relentless buildup.

At first, I didn't believe it was me drumming. On the Autopilot records, the drums always sounded as if they were falling down a flight of stairs. This was crisp and tight. A little slick, yes, but a damn good listen. Nathan's vocals were lush and textured. It was similar, production-wise, to a lot of the other Gawk Rawd stuff. But this was somehow, well, better.

The B-side was a real surprise. Jojo had added all these strange layers of Sean's guitar on different settings. It had a noisy, psychedelic quality, a totally new song.

Nathan and Sean came in a moment later, carrying empty quarts of motor oil and a half-full jug of antifreeze. The record still spun on my turntable.

"It's here," I said. "It's good." I handed Nathan the seven-inch.

"Hey, that's me." Sean looked over Nathan's shoulder. Neither of them remembered my cover design. I'd nearly forgotten about it myself.

"Jesus, Laura." Nathan said, "You look like you're about to cry."

"We should listen to it," I said.

On the floor in front of the speakers, we all three sat silent through the first measure of the song.

Nathan spoke first. "Fuck. Is that really us?"

We sat there for hours, flipping that record over and over on the turntable and listening to those two songs again and again, until darkness fell over Seattle and we were starving for dinner.

The boys turned out to be handy with the van. They topped off the fluids and cleaned it inside and out. So our equipment wouldn't slide around, they covered the floor with a piece of indoor/outdoor carpet. Nathan came up with the brilliant idea of sticking my short sofa right behind the existing seats in the van. It fit perfectly. He used wire to tie it down.

After our Tacoma show, we all drove back to my place and crashed.

It was the first time since the night of our Wreck Room concert that the four of us—including Liz—had slept there.

We needed to leave early for Portland. Liz had work that day. I locked up my apartment, and all of us went down to the street. It was overcast, the sidewalk wet with an earlier rain. In bright-colored spandex, three cyclists passed on their way up the street.

"Hold on a second," Liz said. "I need to get something from my car."

I was anxious to get on the road, and didn't look forward to a sappy good-bye.

"Don't worry," Nathan said as if reading my mind. "This won't take long."

Liz returned with a cardboard box. Inside, there was the beef jerky that the boys so loved, a jar of aspirin, some throat lozenges, two packs of cigarettes, and a bottle of Jack Daniel's. I was speechless. Of all the times I'd toured, nobody had ever done something like this. In SCC, our departures were usually met with a screaming match against somebody's parents. Liz had made us a care package.

"Thanks. This is sweet of you." I did appreciate it. But mostly, I couldn't get over how much punk rock had changed.

Liz put her arms around me. "I'm going to miss you so much, Laura." She said the words into my shoulder. It took a second to return her embrace.

She hugged Sean as well. The two of us climbed into the van, to give Nathan a chance to say good-bye to Liz in private. Sean opened the jerky. I started the engine.

"That was nice of her," Sean said between chomps on the leathery meat.

Through the windshield, I watched as Nathan mussed up Liz's hair and said good-bye. She was on the verge of tears. Perhaps I'd been wrong about them; perhaps she was the one in danger of heartbreak.

Nathan walked away. Liz rubbed the heel of her hand at the edge of her eye the way she had that night on the swings, telling a story of loss. The van door opened and shut. "Let's go," Nathan said.

As we drove south on I-5, the city of Seattle faded and gave way to rural western Washington. The boys watched wide-eyed and pointed with pleasure at everything that passed—cows, water towers, XXX-rated trucker beat-off stops. Nathan rolled down his window and felt the wind. Sean put his guitar across his knee and played along unamplified to the radio.

Let's pause here for a second, shall we. As we headed out on our first tour, in a van that was in my name, which I had purchased with a check made out to me, there were two pieces of paper folded up in my back pocket with all the vital information regarding our shows— times, dates, addresses. It's true that I didn't have a detailed plan of where we'd sleep each night, but in my experience, it was best to find a floor-space offer the night of a show, when the fans were drunk and feeling generous.

While Nathan might've had a vague idea of this tour's overall trajectory, he didn't even know that those pieces of paper existed. As for Sean, forget it. Mind you, I don't hold this against them. But it bears mentioning.

GOLD DIGGER, SLUT, AFTER THE MONEY AND NOT THE MUSIC—all these headlines have been used to describe me. Think about a few of them in light of this crucial moment in our history. Take me out of the picture, and what would happen? Besides the van crashing, of course. Say at the next gas station, a billionaire with an incurable disease stopped for fuel on his way to Seattle. If I were, in fact, the gold-digging slut that all these latter-day fans and rock critics make me out to be, then I surely would've jumped into his limo and given him head on the way north. Where would that leave Nathan and Sean? Without a clue where tonight's show was, for starters, and no idea how to get home or what their next step should be. What I'm trying to say is, there's more to a band than playing music, and—ladies and gentlemen of the press, fans of all ages—it's a bit hypocritical to hate me for undoing something that I myself created.

WASHINGTON, D.C.: JANUARY 1980

In the bathroom the two of you share, come across Anthony leaning over the sink. Still unable to properly spike his kinky locks, he goes after them with a set of electric clippers. With a grimace and a grunt, they soon get stuck in that mess of hair he's thickened with red and green paint. Anthony shuts off the clippers and gives them a pull.

"Let me help." With scissors, you carve out the seized clippers. Your brother sits on the toilet. Colored chunks of stuck-together hair gather on the floor. There's a base pleasure in this, like picking a scab. Once you're down to the short layer of pure hair, you turn on the clippers and finish the job. Without him saying so, know that Anthony wants it shaved to the nub. Sitting on the toilet, your brother can't see himself in the mirror.

Spend a second running your hand over the smooth, bluish bulb of his bare head. The scraps of dead cells on the floor seem like the layers of Anthony that you've clawed through to get to the purest form of him underneath. His head is a cut diamond shining bright now that the excess has been chipped away.

At that moment, your mother walks in and screams. Tears form on her cheeks. "What have you done to yourself?" she yells at Anthony. "Laura?" She sees you with the clippers in your hand. "Did you do this? What will your father say?" She storms out of the room.

Once she's gone, let out a deep breath and run your hand over Anthony's bare scalp a few more times. There's something addictive in that sandpaper texture against your fingers.

"Finished?" Anthony asks.

"I think so." Brush off his shoulders and back up so that he can look in the mirror.

He stands before the sink, turning his head slightly from side to side.

"What do you think?" Look over his shoulder, nervous—as if there were some way you could screw up such a haircut short of drawing blood.

Anthony smiles. Your eyes meet in the mirror.

"I look like myself," he says.

TWELVE

In Boise, Idaho, we had our first bad show. The venue didn't have an all-ages policy. The high school kids loyal to Gawk Rawd weren't even allowed in. The crowd wasn't so much music fans as local drunks who'd been kicked out of other bars.

We couldn't hear ourselves in the monitors. I watched Nathan's hands to follow the changes. A giant crown glowed from behind the drum riser. Taken from a carnival or theme park, it was as big as a sofa and flickered with red and yellow incandescent bulbs. I worried that it might send one of us into a seizure.

Sean drank Jack-and-Cokes before we went on and had three beer bottles balanced atop his amp. Between songs, he took sips. For the first time, the alcohol made his guitar sloppy and off.

We played everything that we knew, including those old SCC covers—though nobody here recognized them. Nathan even took us into "I Wanna Be Sedated" by the Ramones, hoping to elicit a spark from the disinterested crowd.

A big guy with a goatee, seated at a booth to the lower left of the stage, heckled us. He shouted, "Play 'Free Bird'!" The two girls at his table shushed him. The two guys he was with laughed.

"Can't do that, man." Nathan did his best to humor them. "Skynyrd sucks." He turned back to me to try to figure out another song.

"You suck!" said the redneck heckler. "Get off the stage!"

From the corner of my eye, I saw something flutter through the air, like a shiny amber bat. I recognized it as a beer bottle only when it broke against the redneck's face. At my right, Sean leaned forward, his throwing arm still following through.

Everyone at the table jumped to their feet. The two girls huddled around the heckler, checking his face. He pushed them away and shouted, "Motherfucker!" right at Sean.

Nathan turned to me. I pointed to the alley door and said, "Bolt!"

My drum stool fell over as I stood. Nathan unplugged his bass and ushered Sean to follow. The redneck and his buddies were slowed by the crowd.

Outside there was an empty lot between the alley exit and the spot where we'd parked the van. I sprinted ahead, feeling the pocket of my jeans for the key. The tops of my low-cut combat boots bit into my ankles. Over my shoulder, I saw Nathan and Sean run along behind, their instruments bouncing against their hips.

I got into the van and turned the key. With a loud roar from the bad muffler, the engine turned over. The rednecks appeared at the alley door. One pointed in our direction, then ran. I could see the bloody-faced man holding a cloth against one eye.

"C'mon!" I said to Nathan and Sean, though that's exactly what they were doing.

They jumped in through the sliding side door. Before it closed, I pulled into the street. Sean hung out the side of the van and offered the rednecks his middle finger. "Fuck you!" he shouted.

"Get him inside!" I said to Nathan.

Nathan pulled Sean into the van, slid the door shut, climbed forward into the passenger seat, and stuck his head out the window. "They're getting into a pickup," he said. "They're coming after us."

"Fuck!" I looked at Sean in the mirror above the dash. "What were you thinking?"

Sprawled across the sofa, he found the whiskey bottle that we'd left in the van and took a slug from it.

"Take a left," Nathan said. "We need to lose them."

I turned onto a four-lane road and drove fast, trying to make it to some traffic in the distance.

"There they are," Nathan said. "They see us."

I looked into the side mirror and saw the truck that was pursuing. One of those jacked-up jobs, it had a row of lights across the top, probably a gun rack in the cab. I turned into the parking lot of a supermarket and cut through diagonally. Once out on the other side, I drove fast up a residential street.

"You know where you're going?" Nathan asked.

"No idea." I floored it through a neighborhood of modest family homes, hoping no dogs or cats would run out into the ambulance's path. The pickup had yet to appear behind us. I took a quick left, went two blocks, then took another left.

"Uh-oh," Nathan said. "There they are."

I hit the gas again. The pickup gained behind me. We came upon a major street. Shifting the transmission into 2, I sped up and cut the wheel. Nathan put his hands on the dash as the van tilted into the turn. I shifted back to D and hit the gas.

At that last turn, the pickup must've been held up. We gained a little ground, now on a wide avenue without traffic lights, an island of grass and trees between the two lanes, big houses with yards. This must be where the rich people lived. I pushed the gas hard and opened the V8 all the way. Tree trunks whizzed past on either side. The pickup sped up behind us. We looked to be heading away from town.

In the distance, a stoplight appeared, then changed from green to yellow. An old sedan with a pizza delivery sign on top waited at the left-hand side of the intersection. The pickup followed a few car-lengths behind us.

"Hang on," I said to Nathan.

The light turned red as we passed under it.

Nathan leaned out the passenger-side window. "Fuck!" he said.

From behind came the sound of squealing brakes, scraping metal, and shattering glass. I looked into my mirror and saw the pickup T-boned into the pizza delivery car.

"Fuck!" Nathan said again.

We passed a couple of office buildings and one enormous mansion on a hill—an American flag, big as a movie theater screen, flapping above. The road rose upward into the foothills. For the first time in a while, I had a nice view of a clear night sky.

"Look," Nathan said. "It must be a full moon."

We wound upward through a series of tight switchbacks, with drop-offs on either side. I felt sick about causing that accident, but now I saw that it may have prevented us all from a worse fate, had that car chase continued into these hills. In the back of the van, Sean was passed out on the little sofa.

"Where are we?" Nathan asked.

"Not a clue."

After climbing for several more minutes, I saw a dirt lot at the side of the road and pulled into it. Some bulldozers had obviously exca-vated to make room for a house. A concrete slab of a foundation was poured.

I put the van in park and turned the heater on high. From behind us came the sound of Sean's belabored passed-out breathing. Nathan and I stepped out of the van into the cold night air.

The moon was indeed full. Farther up in the mountains, we could see one snow-covered peak, shining bright in the moonlight. Nathan took a piss over by the road. The sound of his urine hitting the frozen earth made me realize how quiet it was. I went and had a seat on the cement foundation. There was a perfect view of this small, sleeping city—a puddle of streetlights and rooftops inside a vast desert of brown.

Nathan walked over to the van and moved some equipment around, then joined me where I sat, the whiskey bottle in his hand. He put two cigarettes in his mouth and lit them both, then handed one to me. "It's beautiful here, huh?" he took a slug from the bottle and passed it over.

The whiskey was warm and soothing in my throat. "Do you think anyone got hurt back there? In the wreck?"

"No." He shook his head. "The truck caught the front end of the delivery car. But the pizza guy wasn't going fast enough to hurt the rednecks. And I saw him get out of his car."

"That's good." I passed the bottle back. The full moon made a shadow on one side of Nathan's face. "What's gotten into him?" I asked.

"Sean? I don't know." Nathan looked down. "This is what we always wanted: play music for a living, not have day jobs."

"He's been drinking a lot. He wasn't like this before."

Nathan flicked his cigarette away and shrugged. "What do we do about the drums and amps?"

"We'll go by in the morning," I said. "Probably won't get paid, but we should get our stuff back."

Satisfied, Nathan stood up and walked to the van. "It's warm now," he called back to me and killed the motor.

Nathan covered Sean's body with a sleeping bag. We both bundled up in our own bags, to a great whooshing of nylon cloth and whistling of zippers.

"Good night, Laura," Nathan said.

"Sleep tight." But even with the whiskey and the late hour, I lay awake for a long while, listening to the pings from the cooling engine and the wheezing snores from my drunken lover.

Hungover and ashamed, Sean kept quiet the next morning. We drove to the club and found a young kid cleaning up. He gave us the benefit of the doubt and let us collect our equipment. While the boys loaded the van, I bought coffee and doughnuts at a place nearby. We gassed up for the long drive to Montana.

The trip north turned out to be beautiful. The sky was clear and blue, with a winter sun that felt luxurious even through the windshield. Up the winding mountain roads, across the rushing rivers, with the snowcapped peaks all around, Nathan did the driving. Sean slept on the sofa in the back. With my sketchbook on my lap, I stared at the scenery and doodled lazily, sometimes writing down the names of towns or roads if I liked them. Early on, the van's radio lost any worthwhile reception. We crossed the pass into Montana with time to spare. I forgot about the troubles of last night and looked forward to Missoula, playing the venue where I'd first seen Nathan and Sean a few months ago.

On a flatter stretch of road, Nathan pulled off into a dirt shoulder next to a walking bridge that crossed the river. He killed the engine.

"What are you doing?" I asked.

"Just a quick stop."

The side door slid open and Sean stood at my window. "Sightseeing."

I followed them across the bridge, over the river, along a well-worn path into the woods.

"Are there bears around here?" I asked.

"Yes," Sean said.

"I'm serious!" They didn't slow down.

Up ahead, a column of white rose through the trees. I thought it was an old building at first, a missile silo or something. As we walked closer, the white looked more like smoke, and I believed we were coming upon a giant, silent fire.

"What is that?" I shouted ahead to the boys.

Sean turned to me and said, "Steam."

At the base of the column was a pool of water, set up with several large stones and fed by steaming cracks in the rocks above. It overflowed on the other side and the water drained down into the river.

"Hot springs?" I asked. They already had their shirts off and their shoes unlaced. I dipped my hand into the pool. It was like bathwater. A naked Sean climbed over the stones and into the water. The taller of the two, his limbs all seemed stretched out an inch too far. The sight of him naked in broad daylight made me think of a carnival mirror. His bushy mop of hair could now cover up his whole face.

Nathan followed, stepping gingerly in bare feet over the rocky ground. His body looked healthier than Sean's, more proportional. He had better posture, coarse black hairs along his chest and legs.

They each found seats in the pool and used their cupped hands to sprinkle the steaming water over their faces.

"Come on in," Sean said. "It's nice."

"Do we have time for this?" The words came out of my mouth in a whining mumble. "What about our show?"

"No problem." Nathan raised his voice a little over the trickling of the water. "It's two hours to town. We're fine."

I stood there for a second, hands in my pockets, and realized that what I was concerned about wasn't the show tonight but the show of my nakedness right now. The memory of Nathan blushing inside my apartment back in November flashed through my mind.

"Fuck it," I said, then untied my shoes.

In jest, Nathan and Sean hooted and hollered as I removed my clothes. Before I knew it, I was indulging them in a sarcastic striptease, rocking my hips back and forth, sling-shoting my bra away, inching my pants off and twirling them over my head.

The boys played along, shouting, "Whooh, baby!" and "Take it off!" Though I was blushing, the joke did relieve the tension.

The water felt amazing after so many hours in the van. Nathan and Sean were kind enough to give me the best spot. My back against a smooth rock, I sat on the sand bottom and closed my eyes. Without deciding to, I found that the three of us were once again holding hands—me in the middle—the way we had backstage at the Wreck Room after our first show.

My eyes opened with a jolt, and I looked from side to side. I must've fallen asleep. Far north and not quite spring, the sun set fast and early. The full moon hadn't yet risen above the mountains at the horizon. The boys released my hands and dressed in the dark.

Because of that stupid striptease, my clothes were scattered all about. Nathan and Sean searched around the rocks with their cigarette lighters. I now felt silly, and found myself covering my breasts with my hands once I got out of the water. Losing patience, I put my pants on over my bare ass. Sean found my bra and brought it over to me while I tied my shoes. I'd given up hope on my underwear and was ready to leave when Nathan said, "Hey, right here."

He walked over, then paused for a second in front of me, looking down at the twist of cotton and elastic in his hand as if considering whether or not he should give it back.

"Thanks." I grabbed the underwear and stuffed them into the back pocket of my jeans.

Right on the cusp of running late, Nathan drove fast and none of us spoke. It was a tense ride on a twisting mountain road. Our van lurched through the corners, and I grabbed at the handles above the door. Nathan checked the clock on the dash.

"It's okay." Sean wasn't worried. "They'll wait for us." He reached up from his seat in the back and turned on the radio.

He found a station playing "Marquee Moon," the old Television classic.

"Not bad for a small town in Montana," I said.

"It's college radio," Nathan explained. "It's good."

"That's where we first heard SCC," Sean said.

The announcer came on and underwrote a couple of local businesses, then read back his playlist, which included a lot of good underground rock. Apparently, we'd just missed the single that Nirvana released a few months back, as well as a Puddle-jumper tune.

"But, of course," went the voice through the speakers, "the big news is tonight's sold-out concert."

"What the fuck?" Nathan said. "Is there a show on campus or something?" He looked to me as if I should know.

"Jesus," I said. "I told Chip to check what was going on before booking these small towns." This was all we needed, second billing in the middle of nowhere.

"Hey," Sean said, "at least it's sold out. Maybe we'll get the overflow."

"That's right, Zoo-Town," the announcer continued. "Tonight only, it's our very own . . . the Mistakes!" The next sounds through the speakers were the fade-in that led to Sean's guitar intro, the three-note crash, and Nathan's voice singing the lyrics to "Nowhere Fast."

"Bullshit!" Nathan said, as if this were an elaborate hoax.

"No way!" Sean leaned his face up from the back.

I turned the volume up. It made perfect sense. The Missoula college station would have been first on the list to receive our single, and

Chip and Doug were wise enough to work the local angle, even if our band had never played one song together in this state.

We shouted "No-Where-Fast!" along with the radio. Nathan honked the horn and flashed the brights as we entered the outskirts of Missoula and prepared for our first-ever sold-out show.

WASHINGTON, D.C.: MARCH 1980

You sit at the kitchen table doing your homework when they come over for the first time. Mother prepares a piece of beef for roasting, covering it in herbs and shining oils. Anthony walks in with two friends in tow.

Billy you recognize. The tall one is vaguely familiar as well. You've seen him in the halls and yards at school. He isn't somebody you ever thought would be in your kitchen. A long curtain of chestnut hair hangs down in one direction before his eyes, the sides cut close. It's the official hairstyle of the small group of skateboarders that have formed at your high school, and he has the T-shirt and shoes to match.

"This is Hank and Billy," Anthony says to you and your mother. "We're going to practice."

Only Hank carries an instrument.

"Will you boys be staying for dinner?" Your mother smiles, happy to see Anthony with friends.

They shrug.

"C'mon," Anthony says. All three go downstairs.

Finish your homework faster than usual. With the light step and quiet creep that grown-ups have begun to notice as extraordinary, open the door to the basement, sit at the top of the stairs, and watch.

Years in the future, you might find this comical. "Practice" is Hank playing his best licks over the three bass notes he's taught to Anthony. Billy flips through your brother's magazines and interjects possible band names. "We should be the Canned Gods! Get it?"

But at the time, what they were doing was the most serious thing in the world—more important than what parents did at their offices all day long, more important still than what the presidents and prime ministers did in their summits and conferences.

Watch Hank again. He flips his flap of hair over to one side, the guitar hanging loose about his waist. He stops Anthony, holds his hands, shows him on the fretboard where his fingers are supposed to go.

"Bah—bah, bah—Bah!" Hank sings the simple bass line for your brother's benefit. At the time, it unnerves you to watch this. You've grown up thinking that there was nobody who had anything to teach Anthony. More unnerving still is to watch your brother struggle, to try so hard to figure out how to do what seems to the other boy the easiest thing in the world.

After all, if Anthony can't do it, then who can?

THIRTEEN

The kids from the meat band fell all over themselves helping us load in.

The leader, the one who'd worn the rib cage last August, handed Nathan a cassette tape. "Give this to the guys at Gawk Rawd, will you."

His bass already strapped on, Nathan looked down at the tape in his hand—probably made on a boom box. "I can't do much with this," he said.

"Just give it to your label," the guy said, as if he knew something about the business that we did not. He patted Nathan on the shoulder and climbed offstage.

Nathan turned to me, holding the cassette by the corner like a dead bird. I shrugged. This was something he'd have to get used to. He took off his bass and went to the bar.

By showtime, the place was packed tight. It was quite a mix. College kids turned out in their finest thrift store wares. The same rowdy crew of punk and heavy metal types from last summer showed up. But there were also high school kids, lots of them.

"Sean," I called out. "Do you know all these people?"

"Almost nobody," he said.

My eyes locked on to one young boy in the crowd. He couldn't have been more than sixteen, wearing a baseball cap and sipping a Coke. His skin had a tan hue that made me wonder if he wasn't part Native American. A big black *X* had been drawn on his hand, as if any bartender would mistake him for drinking age. I watched the way he looked around at this crowd, mostly terrified but also excited. He was unsure of how he'd fit in among all these weirdos crammed together in this tiny room. For some reason, the sight of that kid made me realize that, from now on, nobody would remember me as Laura Loss, Anthony's little sister from SCC. I would henceforth be known as Laura Loss, the drummer from the Mistakes.

Nathan returned from the bar with beers for each of us. He rolled his neck a couple times and passed out the set list.

I studied Sean and how he slurped his beer. Though it was already hundreds of miles away, last night's show was still close to my mind.

"Hello, Missoula!" Nathan shouted into the microphone. "It's great to be home. This is, of course, the first stage I ever played on in my life." The crowd ate it up.

I could tell from the first few notes of "Nowhere Fast" that this was going to be a great show. By the time I hit the drum crashes, I was sure it would be our best to date.

I was right. We killed. Sean was on fire. The crowd went insane. I worried, for a while, that the floor might collapse under the weight of everybody jumping up and down.

Afterwards, I sat on the end of the stage and sold copies of our single while the boys broke down equipment. The guys from the venison band invited us to an after-party at what they called "the North Side House." I was assured that Nathan and Sean knew where. A girl in black with tattoos on her arms bought the last single. I'd seen her in the crowd. She was hard to miss in fishnets and tall boots, showing off several inches of cleavage.

"You were great tonight," she said, giving me a sort of once-over.

"Thanks," I said.

"You're going to the party, right?" A silver stud went through one nostril.

"If the guys want to."

"You have to come," she said with a pout.

At the after-party, the three of us were greeted like . . . well, like rock stars. People cheered as we walked in and ran to fetch us beers from a keg in the garage. The cleavage girl presented Nathan with a single red rose and kissed him on the cheek. "That was beautiful," she said.

The house was one of those Craftsman single-story jobs that abound in the small towns of the Pacific Northwest. The raised lanes of the interstate passed by about a block away. The inside walls were done with fake-wood paneling. Most of the party went on in the garage.

Sean and I took our beers over by the open garage door, which seemed designated as the smoking area. Nathan stayed inside, glad-handing some of his new fans.

"I want to say I'm sorry," Sean said, "about last night, the show and the bottle and all."

"It happens," I said.

"Well, I shouldn't have done it. That guy was an asshole, but it fucked things up for us."

"Sean, I'm not too sensitive when it comes to recklessness. What worries me the most about last night is this: You would never have done it sober. Understand? The same goes for smashing your guitar on New Year's. In hindsight, that may well have been the thing that stitched up our record deal. But it wasn't you."

"I'm sorry." He took a sip of his beer. "There's something about being onstage. It's like I can do whatever I want to, like I'm free or something."

I sighed and took a drag from my cigarette. Though not fully satisfied, I was glad that he had apologized. Also, he was so good. This band couldn't exist without Sean and his gift. Cutting him some slack seemed the least I could do.

"Laura"—he put a cold hand under my sniper coat and touched the skin at the small of my back—"could we get out of here?"

I drained my beer and set it on a shelf along the wall. We slipped out the open garage door, then kissed in the dark backyard.

"C'mon," he whispered. "Let's go to the van."

Hand in hand, we walked around the house and out to the dark street. Sean slid open the side door of the van.

"Whoa!" I shouted the nonsense word, then stood there stunned, trying to figure out what I stared at. The unnatural arrangement of body parts looked like some sort of monster. I saw a woman's fleshy white hip, a pendulous breast jiggling in midair, a silver ring through the nipple. Several arms were pushed into the cushions of the couch. From hours earlier, I recognized Nathan's bare ass, moving in a midtempo thrust. Black jeans twisted around a pair of knees. A woman's face emerged, a disheveled mess of hair hanging down before her eyes.

"Close the fucking door!" the monster's female head shouted at us.

Sean reached across me and slid the door closed. Only then did I realize that what I'd witnessed was Nathan screwing a fan in the small space that our fully loaded van allowed.

"What about Liz?" I stupidly asked.

"We went to high school with that girl," Sean said. "She wouldn't give us the time of day back then."

I made a mental note never to sit on that sofa again.

"Let's get out of here," Sean said.

I followed him down the middle of the darkened street. Semi-trucks whizzed by above on the elevated interstate, as if they were spaceships flying low. I knew that the moon was full but couldn't see it through the ceiling of clouds above us.

"It's cloudy," I said. "I hope it doesn't rain."

"It's not clouds," Sean said. "It's the inversion. In the winter, cold air gets stuck in the valley under a layer of warm air, then the pollution and everything gets trapped inside."

"There's that much pollution in this little town?"

"The mill," Sean said.

"Where you used to work?"

"Yeah. Where my father works."

We walked for a while and came to a one-story brick house. An older pickup truck was in the driveway. Sean lifted the welcome mat, found a key there, and opened up the front door.

"This way," he said.

I followed him down a hall. The house had a sort of chemical smell, like mothballs and ammonia. In the main room, attached to a wall, an animal head with antlers looked to one side. Above the fake fireplace, a stuffed wildcat crept along a branch and growled. Several birds, mounted in action poses, stood on the floor.

Sean led me down a flight of stairs and into a basement. Its cinder block walls were painted yellow. There were more birds down here, and a rack of rifles along one wall. We stood in a big room with a couch and dartboard.

"You grew up here?" I whispered to Sean.

"From high school on," he said. "We moved around more when I was a kid."

I felt guilty for never having asked about his childhood.

"Who's the hunter?" I said.

"The what?"

"All the dead animals."

"Oh, my dad."

"Your mom doesn't mind stuffed heads?"

"My mother's not alive."

"Oh." I didn't remember him speaking of this before. "I'm sorry."

"It's not like that," he said. "I barely knew her. She wasn't a real mom or anything."

"So it's always been you and your dad?"

"And my grandmother." Sean opened a door in the corner. "My room's right here."

It was like entering a whole different house. I couldn't see the ugly yellow walls through the thick layer of posters and pictures taped up all around. It was mostly punk rock, but there was older stuff as well. Sean went to the bathroom, and I studied the walls. The pictures overlapped one another. They showed the layers of his musical evolution, a sort of chronology of the phases and influences he went through. Around the edges, you could still see the Beatles and Rolling Stones. Led Zeppelin and Black Sabbath were featured more prominently. There was a light spattering of Brit pop: the Cure and the Smiths. Then a lot of early punk rock, the Clash and the Ramones, until the hardcore that made up the final layer.

I came across a picture, with Hank in the center, of SCC playing a live gig. He was in his full-throttle guitar stance. On one side, Anthony leapt through the air. An image of me stood on the other side, in a sort of profile, with my bass neck jutting out like a gun I couldn't decide where to aim. I reached out and touched the image with my finger. It was an actual photograph, not from a magazine. I thought of the girl who Nathan was screwing right now—with her tattoos and piercings and sexy black clothes. In this old photo, I was dressed almost the same as I was tonight: jeans, a T-shirt, combat boots. They were boy clothes, really. What might I look like in fishnets? I pulled down the neck of my T-shirt and glanced at my chest, to see if I could show any real cleavage.

Sean walked back in and shut the door. I fixed my shirt.

"Where did you get this?" I pointed to the photo.

"Oh, that." He sat down on the edge of his bed and unlaced his shoes. "It's kind of embarrassing. This older guy named Bruce, a bartender at the place where we just played, actually, saw SCC in San Francisco back in the day. He took a bunch of pictures. I liked that one, and he gave it to me as a gift."

"We look so young," I said.

"It's from a while ago." Sean took off his jeans and threw them on the floor. In only his boxers, he climbed into bed.

"Have you spoken to your dad much since you left here?" I undid my coat.

"No."

I wasn't sure if he meant "no, not much" or "no, not at all."

"Could you turn off the light when you're ready to come to bed?" Sean turned over into a fetal position.

I studied the picture a second longer. It was nice to see myself placed in a kind of unofficial rock-and-roll canon. It was odd to be here now, in one of the basements across America where my records and even my photos were studied. Music was something that was thrust upon me. It certainly wasn't something that I spent years dreaming about. How remarkable it must be for Sean, I thought, to now be living out such a long-held dream.

It sounds funny, but I envied him this dream and its encroaching reality. I envied the fact that now he had me here in the flesh and in his bedroom. Tonight that young kid, the boy in the baseball cap from the audience, might've taken a photo of us to hang on his own wall.

As I undressed, I remembered that my underwear was still in the back pocket of my jeans. It seemed silly to put them back on. This was the first private room that Sean and I had shared in more than a week, and it was surprisingly warm. I took off all my clothes, killed the light, and climbed into the bed behind Sean. I reached around his bony hip and slipped my hand under the waistband of his boxer shorts.

He tensed up. "What are you doing?"

I withdrew my hand, put first my thumb then my forefinger into my mouth, licked the space in between, then stuck it back inside his boxers.

"We'll wake my dad."

But I could feel his dick grow hard within the wet ring of my fingers. I'm ashamed to admit that something excited me about the whole scenario—being inside this high school time capsule of a room. It felt like getting away with a bad thing.

I rolled Sean onto his back and pulled his boxers down to his ankles. He put his palms up as if to say stop, but his erection betrayed him.

"Please," Sean said in a throaty whisper. "Please be quiet."

I mounted and put him inside, held down his arms at the wrists. His eyes closed and his face was caught between pleasure and anxiety. Sean relaxed a little, and then I couldn't help myself. I let out some low moans and he looked worried. I didn't truly think we'd wake anyone, but I loved watching him squirm.

This hadn't gone on for a minute before Sean finally broke my armlock and put his hand over my mouth. The bitter taste of metal strings overtook my lips.

I lay down beside him. He put his head on my chest and I stroked his hair. A heating unit shut itself off, and the house turned even more silent. I suddenly felt sorry for the noise.

With a massive headache, I woke the next morning to the sounds of unfamiliar shouts. I patted the mattress beside me but didn't feel Sean.

The screaming voice came from upstairs. I was able to make out a few of the words: *lust . . . abomination . . . wasted youth.* It must've been a televised sermon, turned up way too loud. My head throbbed. I found all my clothes on the floor and dressed hastily. With my coat and shoes already on—I planned to go outside for a smoke—I left the room and went to find Sean, hoping his family might've made a pot of coffee.

Upstairs, it was not a televised sermon at all. The TV was on, but the sound was turned down. An old woman sat at a dining table in front of the screen, with a game of solitaire before her. In the center of the room, Sean sat in a wooden chair, staring down at the floor. The fire-and-brimstone calls came from a real live human, a large balding man with a Bible in one hand, standing right over Sean.

"Your pride!" the man said. "Your vanity! Your flesh! These things are selfish! If you love your life, you will lose it!" He turned to me as I entered the room. His button-down shirt was tucked into pressed jeans. A boxy pair of spectacles seemed the only part of his face not contorted by rage.

"Morning," I said softly. "I'm Laura."

"Your name," he yelled as if I were in a house next door, "is Jeze-bel!" The black Bible looked like a box of matches inside his enormous hand. He pointed one corner of it at my head like a gun, running it along the blue streaks in my hair. "The painted Jezebel who turned my son away from God!" Everything about this man was grotesque—his long limbs, his absurdly loud voice. It was like speaking to a car-toon character.

"Whoa," I said. "Your son came to me. I didn't turn him away from anything." The old woman at the table seemed unfazed by any of this, laying down her cards then squinting up at the game show on televi-sion. A stuffed wildcat growled silently from its perch above her.

"Don't you raise your voice to me in my house!" Sean's father seemed shocked that I'd responded to him.

I looked over at Sean, who still stared at the ground. "With all due respect, I'm not the one raising my voice. I'm just saying that I didn't steal anybody. Your son and his friend came to me for help." Why is this fact so hard for anybody to believe, even now? "Maybe you should ask yourself why he'd want to leave."

"Don't you dare reprimand me, you little whore!" his voice cracked.

"What did you call me?"

"You heard me. You come into my house and spread your legs all over my boy. I called you a whore because that's what you are!"

Two things went through my mind as this absurd and ugly man stood over me, swinging his Bible and his judgment. I thought of Anthony and how he always defeated my own father with a cooler head. And I thought of Nathan on New Year's Eve, pushing Mark across the room when he offended one of us. Neither of them was here now, so I looked to Sean, whose head still faced the ground.

"Sean," I said. "Did you hear what he said to me?"

Sean's head lifted up and his eyes met mine. His face was red and wet, but he spoke no words.

I turned and walked away, making sure to slam the front door on the way out. The house was set deep inside a cul-de-sac. I headed toward the main road, where a grade school sat on the far side. Moving in what I hoped was the direction of downtown, I fished my smokes and my lighter from my pocket. My hands shook so bad with nerves that I snapped the first cigarette in two trying to light it. I stood still and got it on the second try.

"Laura!" the calls came from behind. "Laura, wait!" Sean ran after me, struggling to get his denim coat on. "I'm sorry!"

I turned back and looked at him, let him catch up. I wasn't ready to forgive him for standing idly by while that awful man called me a whore. But the truth is: I was sorry, too. Sorry about last night and sorry about the years and years that he'd had to spend in that house.

Once we were face-to-face, he paused. I wasn't sure whether I should hug him or slap him.

"That's it," he said. "I'm done. I'm never setting foot in there again."

That was a big step for him. But for me, it wasn't enough.

Just then, a beeping horn sounded from the street and a voice screamed, "Hey, Laura! Sean! Hey!"

We both turned. The van swerved across the road to our side, the wrong side.

"Get in, quick!" Bare-chested, Nathan spoke to us right through the windshield, where glass should've been. Sean and I ran around the van and climbed in the side door. There we saw that Nathan was completely naked, and that every single window in the van had been smashed. Broken glass lay everywhere. I brushed the shards off the passenger seat with my coat sleeve before I sat down.

"What the fuck happened?" I asked.

"That girl from last night"—Nathan drove fast, checking his mirror every few seconds—"turns out she has a boyfriend. We were sleeping in the van and the fucker starts smashing the windows with a tire iron." His teeth chattered with the cold.

I laughed out loud.

"What's so funny?" Nathan put one hand in his lap. "I barely got out of there alive!"

I laughed even harder.

Nathan turned to me. He looked offended at first, then burst into laughter himself. "Fuck!" he said. "Could somebody hand me a sleeping bag?"

Sean found one in the back and wrapped it around his naked friend. I couldn't stop laughing for several minutes. As Nathan drove farther out of town, it grew cold inside the van. Winter air whipped through it like a wind tunnel.

"Are we going to drive all the way home like this?" I shouted over the noise.

"We'll get it fixed in Spokane!" Nathan screamed. "It's not that far."

I looked in the rearview mirror. "Slow down, at least. Nobody's following us."

At a gas station up the valley, I got my coffee, Nathan got dressed, and we swept most of the bigger glass chunks out of the van. With garbage bags and duct tape, the boys sealed up the windows in the back, so that only the windshield remained empty. It was still loud and cold in the van, and we had to stop often, on our way up the pass, through Northern Idaho and into Washington. Eventually, we moved some things around so that Sean and I could sit on the floor behind the couch, with our backs to it, bundled up in our sleeping bags.

In gloves, hat, and sunglasses, Nathan did all the driving; it was his fault. He tied some T-shirts over his face as protection against the wind, as well as the dust and bugs that blew in.

At one point toward the end of the drive, as Sean and I shivered there behind the couch, he reached his hand out of his sleeping bag and touched my arm. "I'm sorry," he said.

I nodded, then pulled the bag up farther around my neck.

WASHINGTON, D.C.: AUGUST 1980

Anthony and Hank work most of the summer at an ice cream store in Georgetown. Two weeks before school starts, they both quit and buy tickets on the Greyhound to California.

While your brother is gone, sneak into his room to play the bass guitar that he's left behind. As younger children, you took piano lessons while Anthony did Little League. Remember the basics as best you can. The instrument is heavy across your knees, the tuning pegs enormous inside your little hands.

The next day, open the piano bench that's been closed for years, and sift through the old sheet music. Find one of your first books, full of simple kids' songs. It has the names of the notes listed above the bars, along with the music.

While your parents sit and study in their separate offices, preparing classes and writing obscure articles, teach yourself to play bass. Soon, you've mastered "Tom Dooley" and "Michael, Row Your Boat Ashore." The sessions last almost three hours, ending only when the summer sunlight through the window becomes orange and low, and the smell of steamed vegetables fills the house as your mother makes dinner. Time stands still there inside Anthony's room—the punk rock posters on the wall, his burgeoning collection of 45s and cassette tapes on the bookshelf. Only once you're finally called down to eat do you notice the pains in your fingertips, the numbness in your legs. Rise from off his bed, put the instrument back against the wall, and hear a sort of unbearable silence for those first few seconds after you stop.

When Anthony and Hank return from California, their stories sound impossible. In the beach towns south of Los Angeles, the hardcore shows were more like gang fights or riots. They took place in empty warehouses and vacant garages. The L.A. bands practice all day, Anthony tells you, spend hours putting up flyers, live in vans, eat dog food.

The two of them managed to hitch a ride to San Francisco with one of the bands. There, Anthony explains, in the fabled Mabuhay Gardens, the punks were still pogo-ing to the music, as if it were London in '77. (Notice the disdain that your brother now shows toward the so-called first wave.)

It was a bloodbath. The Southern California crew punched people in the face unprovoked, stomped around swinging their fists and elbows, and knocked kids over. The venue and the promoters couldn't understand what was going on.

Anthony tells this story with a smirk. As he describes the violence and mayhem to you there in the basement that night, it fills you with an intoxicating mix of fear and awe. Your brother is taken by it because it's extreme, prohibited. Along with Hank, he will be partly responsible for importing this West Coast brand of thuggery to your city and your scene. It won't take long for it to turn on him.

Don't manage to tell him that you've been in his room, playing his instrument. You're not ashamed so much as shy, and afraid of pretending to be something that you're not.

FOURTEEN

In Spokane, a decent crowd of strangers came to hear us. The next morning, we spent several hours—as well as all the money we'd made from the last two shows—on new windows for the van. Our tour was set up to end back at the Raspberry Room, site of the New Year's gig with Thieves as Thick. We were running late. Nathan drove fast across Washington State, while I rode shotgun and Sean slept on the little couch.

"Do you know Sean's father?" I asked.

"Frank Purvis at-your-service? I grew up around him. Did you have the pleasure?"

"Yesterday morning," I said. "He called me a whore."

"Guy's a joke in Missoula. He was a legendary drunk for years. He'd go up to people in the bar and say, 'Frank Purvis, at your service,' and lift his hat. College kids used to beat him up for fun. He'd pass out in the street. Fucker nearly froze to death a couple of times."

"That was Sean's childhood?"

"Not exactly." Nathan squinted at a mileage sign. "Sean was raised by his grandparents. Every so often, Frank would decide to play Dad

and move Sean into his trailer. That might last a month or two before
Frank wrecked a car or got fired from a job. He'd send Sean back to the
grandparents, and somehow make Sean believe it was his fault things
didn't work out. We were freshmen when he got clean, found Jesus and
all. The grandpa had died by then, and the old lady was in bad shape. So
Frank moved into her house. Now he preaches at the church. I guess
he's on the wagon. Guts are so full of ulcers, he'd probably die if he
drank again. His job at the mill is steady, at least. Even as a preacher,
he's still a joke to everybody."

"Except Sean," I said.

"Yeah," Nathan said. "Sean is pretty much the only person on earth
who takes old Frank seriously."

"Does your father work at that mill, too?" I asked.

"My father?" Nathan turned away from the new windshield to look
me in the eye a second. "He's with the same company, but my dad's in
sales."

Two chestnut horses chased each other through a barren field,
steam puffing from their nostrils.

"So." I kept staring out the window. "What about you and Liz?"

"What about us?" Nathan eased up on the gas a little.

"Are you going to tell her?"

"Tell her what?"

"About the girl the other night." In another field, two different
horses reared up toward each other, as though fighting.

"I hadn't planned on it."

We both went silent for a minute and listened to the hum of the
wheels on the road, the revving of the unmuffled engine.

Nathan spoke more urgently. "You're the one who told me to be
careful, not to get too close to her."

"Okay," I said. "It's none of my business." The truth is I didn't want
Nathan to come clean with Liz. "Do you love her, Nathan?" I couldn't
help myself.

"I don't think so." He tightened his grip on the steering wheel.

"You don't think so?"

"Liz is cool and all. We have fun together. But I wouldn't say it's love. Maybe I wouldn't know the difference."

I didn't push him any further.

"Pretty lame answer, huh?" he said.

"Not so much. Don't ask me where love starts and stops." Is it wrong to say that I was relieved to hear this?

From a pay phone at a convenience store on the way up Snoqualmie Pass, I left word at both the venue and the Gawk Rawd offices that we were running late. Dirty snow was piled up in bunches all around the margins of the little store's parking lot. Trucks full of timber and heavy equipment flew by on the steep roads. The boys went inside to buy jerky. Once I hung up the phone, snow crunched and echoed all around. A bird let out a caw. I took a moment to remember that I was on the road again, playing good music and getting paid. Despite all the bullshit, I didn't want to go back to Seattle. I'd rather keep driving around with Nathan and Sean, doing shows and sleeping wherever.

"Get a hold of anybody?" Nathan burst through the door and clanged the little bell.

"No," I said. "I left messages on their machines."

The boys dropped me off out front while they went to the alley to un-load gear. I walked in during the opening act, a band called the Rum-ble Strips—a trio with two gigantic brothers on guitar and bass. Each of them was well over six-three and 250 pounds. Their drummer was a veteran of the scene named Todd. He was Asian and had a slight build that made his bandmates look even bigger. I'd seen them play before. They had a good sound, but their songs were a bit monotonous.

Chip and Doug smiled and shook my hand. Over the music, Chip shouted, "How was the tour?" into my ear.

"Good!" I nodded.

"I want you to meet somebody." He presented me to a thin balding white guy in a wool sweater. "This is Malcolm." Chip kept talking in my ear while I shook Malcolm's hand. "He's here doing a story for one of the British weeklies."

Malcolm leaned into my ear and said, "Pleased to meet you. I'd love it if we could sit down and chat about your band sometime."

"Sure." I liked his accent. "Let's talk later. I have to go set up." I went to find Sean and Nathan in the back.

We unloaded our gear and grabbed a round of beers. In the same sticker-covered room where we'd had the altercation with Mark weeks before, we sat and listened while a band opened for us. Nathan's Sharpie scratched along the back side of some flyers. Without announcement, Sean left the room for another trip to the bar.

The scratches from the marker stopped. "What do you think for a closer tonight?" Nathan asked me. It was the first time he'd ever consulted anybody about the set list. "You think we should wait and save 'Nowhere Fast'?"

I paused. "Let's do whatever we know works. We need to kill tonight, not experiment. There's press out there."

"Got it," Nathan said. I watched him write NOWHERE FAST at the top of the list.

"Hey, strangers," a voice came from behind us. Nathan and I both turned and saw Liz close the door softly behind her back. Nathan put down his Sharpie and stood up.

Liz ran over and hugged him. "I missed you so much."

I lit a cigarette and looked in the other direction. After a couple drags, I was startled by a Liz-embrace of my own.

"I missed you, too, Laura," she mumbled into my shoulder. "Tell me everything about the tour."

"It's not so interesting." I sipped smoke from my cigarette. "Playing to drunks, sleeping on floors, that sort of thing."

Liz nodded. I tried to think of an anecdote that didn't relate to Nathan and that other girl. Good thing we fixed the glass.

"Some rednecks gave us a high-speed car chase in Boise." Nathan jumped in. "You should've seen Laura driving the van. We were up on two wheels and shit." He laughed.

The door swung open and slammed against the wall. "Showtime!" Sean burst in with a fresh beer. I could tell he'd taken shots at the bar. "Hey, Liz," he said, already slurring.

With all the interruptions, I hadn't noticed the Rumble Strips' set end. The two giants walked backstage with their guitars, each a mess of sweat and hair.

"You guys sounded really good," Sean blurted.

As Nathan carried out an amplifier, I walked over to Sean and took the bottle from his hands. I leaned up and whispered in his ear: "Don't get shit-faced tonight, Sean. This is important. No smashing guitars, no throwing bottles. Can you handle that?" It was the first time I'd ever reprimanded him.

Sean scratched the side of his face. "No problem."

I nodded, and set to hauling out the drums.

We had our sound check down to a science now, and took a short break backstage once it was done. Sean gave me the cold shoulder, which was fine by me. The anger seemed to sober him up.

Finally, they killed the houselights and we went out onstage. Sean messed with his pedals, then started off into "Nowhere Fast." He stared at me defiantly as he played it, spot-on.

At the first vamp, Sean jumped across the stage. On the second one, he did a power slide toward the audience and strummed a couple of bars on his knees. Flashbulbs went off left and right.

———

Once the show was over, Chip praised the performance. Doug reminded us of our upcoming all-night recording sessions. Malcolm, the British journalist, found me as we hauled our gear away, and asked about coffee and a chat. I gave him my number.

Nathan and Liz opted to sleep in the van. Sean passed out before we even found a parking spot. Nathan helped me haul him up the stairs.

We plopped Sean onto my bed. He snored instantly, as Nathan removed his shoes and belt. So happy to spend a night in my own apartment, I wasn't fazed by Sean's drinking.

"He's out for the count, now." Nathan stared at the floor, his hands thrust in his pockets and his quilted flannel bunching up around his waist like the first night they'd arrived here.

"I see that."

He looked up at me. "It was a good tour, all in all, wasn't it?"

"It was a good tour," I said. "You've done a great job." Nathan was the real workhorse behind this band, though people were still seeing only Sean's guitar brilliance and, to a lesser extent, my legacy. He was the Anthony of the Mistakes—doing the tireless and thankless work.

"Good night, Laura," Nathan said.

"Sleep tight."

At the studio, Jojo was all business. He planned to plow through a bunch of rhythm tracks tonight. In the other two sessions that were lined up, he'd get the vocals and guitar leads.

What this meant, effectively, was that I wouldn't even need to show up after tonight. While I liked the idea of not pulling another two all-nighters, I hated to be left out. The recording process was the time when I felt most expendable as a member of this band. But after my outburst last time, and the way I'd been proved wrong by the final product, I wasn't about to question Jojo's judgment.

More like a live show, we moved right through the set list, with none of the starting and stopping of the last session. By now, we'd played these songs together so many times, we could do them with our eyes shut. I checked the clock. My meeting with the British journalist was scheduled for the next day, and I hoped to get a nap in beforehand.

Once we both had our coffees, Malcolm pressed down the buttons on his tape recorder.

"Please state your name, and that you know you're being recorded."

I did as I was told. He opened up a flip-top notebook and scanned it for questions. "You've been a part of two different underground music movements. Which do you feel is more important, and why?"

"Excuse me?" I was still waking up and had no idea what he was trying to say. "Which two movements are you talking about?"

"Well." Malcolm smiled awkwardly. "You and your brother were key players in the eighties hardcore scene. Now, you're with one of the up-and-coming bands of the grunge scene."

"The what scene?"

"Grunge. This new Seattle sound. The term's been used to describe the Mistakes several times."

The word didn't sound familiar. "Look, Malcolm, I've been playing more or less the same kind of music since I was fourteen: loud, simple, fast, honest music. The catchphrases come and go."

"Fair enough." Malcolm crossed out a couple of items in his little book. I took a sip of my coffee. "How would you compare the music scene now with that of the early eighties?"

I paused to light a cigarette and gather my thoughts. "It's different now, definitely. Back then, there was no chance of us getting into real magazines or on real radio stations or record labels. So we did it all ourselves."

Malcolm scribbled furiously.

"You have to keep in mind that we were kids. Nobody took us seriously, save ourselves and other bands. The whole thing was fueled off the energy that only teenagers have. We weren't after any payoff, other than not being bored."

I'd never thought about these issues until Malcolm asked. He continued writing, and I enjoyed talking more than answering his questions, so I went on.

"Chip and Doug, they've done a good job with their label. It's not a major, and still the music reaches people. But you listen to them talk, and it's all exposure and marketing and sales. Back in the day, nobody thought like that."

I blew out a puff of smoke. "It was like a shadow music industry, with its own distribution and touring network, built alongside the mainstream industry. The cops would break up the SCC shows. They'd beat us with batons, like we were criminals. Nowadays, in Seattle, the cops probably listen to Gawk Rawd records."

"If I might change the subject," Malcolm said. "There's an old assumption that punk rock is for people without musical skill. This Seattle sound, however, seems to be populated with talented musicians. Sean Purvis, your guitar player, is particularly gifted. How does this distinguish the current scene?"

I shrugged. "Nowadays, these guys see a future playing this kind of music. They can bring crowds, get girls."

"Back to Sean, he has some sort of a condition, isn't that right? He can see music somehow?"

I stomped my cigarette out in the ashtray. "I'd rather not talk about that." It wasn't a matter of protecting Sean. I truly didn't want to have that conversation. Sean's condition shouldn't be the linchpin for the success of the Mistakes.

"I'm sorry," Malcolm said. "The label mentioned it. I didn't know it was a secret."

I kept stomping out the cigarette butt, though it was obviously extinguished. "Next question."

He flipped through the pages in his notebook. "A critic recently stated that punk rock was the only important cultural institution to be entirely created by middle-class white males. I wonder if you agree."

"What about skateboarding?" I said. "Or serial killing?"

Malcolm gave a puzzled stare. That wasn't the kind of answer he was after. "Would you care to speculate on the future of the Mistakes?"

"Our future?" I drained the last of my now-cold coffee. "If we don't end up hating each other and destroying ourselves, then we'll become the biggest band in the world."

At that point, I expected to share a laugh with Malcolm. Instead, he scribbled even more intently in his little pad, trying to capture my sarcastic words.

"Laura, Laura!" Sean shook me awake.

My sleeping habits had turned screwy since the tour and the nocturnal recording sessions.

"Jojo wants us all back in the studio tonight." Sean was giddy. "He wants to do another song."

My vision was still clouded as I opened my eyes. "What other song?"

On the far side of the room, Nathan sat at the kitchen table and tuned my old acoustic guitar. "Jojo wanted a mellow number." He shrugged his shoulders. "So I played him something. He thinks it shows a different side."

Sean shook the bed. "We need to learn it by tonight. It's our last session."

I looked at the alarm clock. With the unpacking, repacking, and driving, we'd have a couple of hours to jam. "I'll make some coffee," I said.

"It's a simple song," Nathan explained as Sean's footsteps hurried down the stairs. "I never brought it up because it wouldn't work in our live show."

In a few quick trips, Sean brought up all our gear. Like Nathan said, it was simple: four chords, no bridge or chorus. Sean set his amp so that it was quiet enough to hear Nathan strumming. I tried to drum softly, but it wasn't working. Finally I switched to bass and wrote a line that both the boys liked.

Nathan sang the refrain several times to get his voice right. It went: *"the devil that you know and the devil that you don't know."* It was nice. We were focused on the music, and he didn't bother singing the rest of the lyrics.

Sean picked up a broken drumstick from off the floor. Sitting on an amplifier with his legs crossed, he used the stick to play a slide-style guitar lick along the neck—something I'd never seen him do before. We sorted out an intro. The acoustic started it out, then the bass and vocals. Sean's lead guitar came in last and built up strong during the refrains. After going through it a few times, we switched the instrumentation so that Nathan played bass and I came up with a quiet drumbeat. By then, it was time to pack up and drive back.

Nathan recorded the acoustic track first, then the bass line. Jojo had a set of drum-brushes. He showed me how to use them and put some extra padding in the kick drum.

Once we had the rhythm track down, I went outside for a smoke. It was a much warmer night than the first time we'd been here to do our single. Making this record almost seemed too easy. I recalled the Christmas pledge to myself on the Mercer Island patio. Maybe I'd only needed to let things be this easy.

I stepped on my cigarette and walked in through the door to the booth. Jojo and Sean were both squeezed in there already. The music in the speakers was turned down low, and Nathan's voice—coming straight in as he sang—was all the way up.

He was on the refrain: *"The devil that you know and the devil that you don't know."* We watched him through the glass, wearing those giant headphones, his eyes closed, his head tilted back as if he sang to the ceiling. After the refrain, he let a couple of bars go, then started up again. The lyrics were the most obscure of all the songs he'd written so far, but somehow they felt more intimate:

> *It was a bad idea taken way too far*
> *on a night too cold to spend alone in a car*
> *He aimed for your head and you didn't flinch*
> *you gave him a mile but he took an inch*

My face turned red. It sounds ridiculous, but I was certain that those cryptic lyrics were written about me, about me and Sean. I turned away from Nathan. Sean was there on the other side of Jojo, bobbing his head to the song. Was this all in my mind?

I tried to think of how that expression actually goes—"The devil I know is better than the devil I don't know." Nathan's song argued the opposite: They're both devils after all, and the devil you don't know might possibly turn out to be better.

I thought it meant that I was with Sean because it happened that way. He was the devil I know. My legs trembled under me as I came to the resulting conclusion: that Nathan was the devil I don't know—the lesser of the two by the logic of the world, but the greater of the two by the logic of the song.

Nathan opened his eyes, looked back through the glass, and seemed shocked to see me standing there. Our stares locked in mutual embarrassment. I turned away, now even more confused.

"That was good," Jojo said. "This time open up on those refrains, okay."

Nathan nodded from his side of the glass and bent to pick up a water bottle at his feet.

"Fucking good tune, huh?" Sean asked.

"I'm going to the van for a nap," I said, thankful the weather was warm enough for such a thing.

I spent the rest of the night on the gross van-couch that I swore I'd never again sit on. There was no sleep, just a lot of nervous twitching. The thoughts grew in my mind faster than I could stub them out. As the night went on, it mattered less and less whether or not those lyrics meant what I thought they did. The question now was, what did I want the song to mean?

WASHINGTON, D.C.: NOVEMBER 1980

After much begging and patience, Anthony takes you to your first hardcore show. It's wintertime. You both wear black leather jackets. You've painted on yours—the silhouette of a cheerleader with pompoms and a little skirt inside crosshairs.

The show is in a community center not far from your neighborhood. A crowd of local kids mill about outside. Some you recognize as friends of Anthony's. Some you've seen around school. At this point, the punk scene in D.C. is still wide open. The homogenized hardcore look has yet to be established. Some of the kids have cherry-red mohawks and bondage trousers. Others have tight jeans and bomber jackets. Eyeliner, dog collars, rude boy hats, a few skinny ties even—anything goes.

Tonight's band is a local act known as the Vegetarian Resistance, which sings about health food—the benefits of vitamin B, the still-secret ills of high-fructose corn syrup.

The two of you watch the first few songs from the back; then Anthony says he wants to go down front for a closer look.

"I'll come with you," you say.

"No. Wait here. It gets rough down there."

Watch your brother disappear into a sea of swinging limbs. Feel awkward in the back of the room without him. Your jacket hangs heavy and makes your shoulders ache.

"Laura?" a voice comes from behind. "Big brother let you come out finally?"

"Hank!" You're excited to see somebody that you know. "Anthony's down front." Hank holds a skateboard at waist level.

"Still doing the health-core thing, these guys." He is unimpressed. "You want to go outside for a second?"

The sidewalk out front is now empty. Hank wears an old army coat and folds up the collar against the cold. He rests his skateboard along the outside wall. With a flip of his curtain of hair, he reaches deep into one pocket and produces a pack of cigarettes.

"Yeah, this band. They're all right." He puts a smoke in his mouth, then holds the hard pack out to you. "It's just too much about the message, you know."

A dozen cotton filter tips stare back at you.

"You want one?" He lifts the cigarettes closer to your face. One has been flipped around backwards, the brown end sticking out like the butthole on a white cat.

"Sure." You pluck one out with thumb and forefinger. "Thanks."

Hank holds his plastic lighter within inches of your face. Fear, for a second, that your hair might catch fire.

"Hey, inhale," he says. "Have you done this before?"

"No," you say with a cough.

Hank demonstrates how to hold the smoke in your lungs, then let it out. According to him, you're a natural. Love the tingling feeling in the back of your throat.

Talking to this cooler, older boy, watching the smoke come out your mouth, and holding fire at the end of your fingers, feel the head rush that you've gone looking for with every single cigarette you've ever lit since.

FIFTEEN

While our record was in postproduction, we had another show to play in Seattle, at a bigger venue called the Sea. Gawk Rawd booked Thieves as Thick to open for us. I told Chip about what happened last time, and he promised us separate dressing rooms—as if that were a solution.

In truth, I felt bad for Mark. It must've been a slice of humble pie for him—to open for us after claiming that we'd never play another gig in Seattle. He'd bent the ear of our label in the first place. On my part, there was no grudge. I couldn't speak for the boys.

Our dressing room was small but charming, full of old wood and long mirrors. On my way to the bar, I noticed that Thieves as Thick hadn't been given a room at all. Their equipment was crammed into the hallway and backstage men's room.

Mark sat at the bar. People filed in through the front door.

"Hey, stranger." I sat on the stool next to his and ordered a vodka and Coke.

"Laura." He smiled at me. "Look at you. The first lady of punk rock all over again."

"The first lady of *hardcore.* I think Patti Smith is the first lady of punk rock." Surely he considered all those titles as ridiculous as I did.

"Whatever," Mark said. "You guys are blowing up."

I took a sip of my drink. "We're the flavor of the month is all."

He smiled and lit a cigarette. "You and those kids from Aberdeen."

"Nirvana?"

"I got to tell you: I didn't see much of a future for those guys."

"Listen, Mark. We're cool, right? No hard feelings about New Year's."

"Hey"—he exhaled and held up his hands—"you were right. We can't follow you. Here we are, a few months later, I'm supporting."

"Now's your chance to smash guitars."

"We're too broke."

I laughed.

"No, I'm happy for you guys, Laura. The band is good. You deserve the success."

"Thanks." That must've been hard for him to say. Surely, he didn't fully believe it. I know I didn't. Thieves as Thick had been playing out in Seattle for five years now, longer than Puddle-jumper. The Mistakes didn't even have a full-length record released.

"Well, showtime." Mark drained the last of his beer.

"Hey," I said as he stood up. "Give me a hug."

We shared a short but tight embrace. "Have a good show," I said.

"You, too." Mark walked off toward the stage.

I turned back to the bar and finished my drink.

"Make up with your old boyfriend?" Sean was suddenly standing beside me.

I didn't know who told him that Mark and I used to have a thing, and didn't much care. "Grow up, Sean."

"If that asshole sticks his finger in my face again, I swear—"

"Forget it, will you?" I put a hand on his shoulder. "Do you know how much Mark did for us? If not for him, we'd still be playing the

Wreck Room for free hot dogs." I picked up my drink and remembered it was empty. "Jesus, you bite the hand that feeds you, but you sure shut up and take it from the people that truly fuck with you."

"Hey, guys! It's here!" Nathan ran up to us from behind. Flanking him were Chip and Liz. At first, I thought our record had arrived early. Instead, what he thrust into my hands was the article Malcolm had written for the British weekly. At the top of the page, in big black ink, it read: SOMEWHERE FAST: FROM THE TRAILER PARK TO THE BIG CITY, THE MISTAKES ARE THE BEST BAND YOU HAVEN'T HEARD OF YET.

"Trailer park?" I asked. "What did you guys tell him?"

Nathan waved me off. "He loved the backwoods Montana thing. We gave him what he wanted to hear."

On the first page was a picture of Sean playing guitar on his knees, hair hanging down before his eyes. The caption read: *Raised by lumberjacks, guitarist Sean Purvis is rumored to have a rare brain disease that allows him to see music.*

"Raised by lumberjacks?" I said. "That doesn't even make sense."

"It's unbelievable." Chip's enthusiasm was even greater than Nathan's. "All day long, the British press has been calling for review copies of the record."

The factual lapses didn't bother anyone except me. In a quick glance, I could see that *grunge* word that Malcolm was so enamored with worked into several of the captions and subtitles.

"Now, I don't want to speak out of turn," Chip went on. "But Doug and I have been talking about sending you guys to Europe. We've crunched the numbers and it makes a lot of sense. This article might seal the deal."

"Europe?" I said. "You're shitting me!" SCC played Montreal once. That was the extent of my international experience.

"I'm serious," Chip said. "It's time to tap new markets."

Just then, Thieves as Thick struck up the first few notes of their set. We couldn't hear one another talk.

Chip leaned into my ear. "I'll speak to Doug and see if we can't iron out the details."

I nodded. Chip walked away and the boys exchanged grins. Liz did her best to put on a brave face, but she knew that, for her relationship, this was not good news. When Nathan turned to her, his smile straightened out. I knew then and there that he would end it.

Sean ordered himself a drink. In the dim light, Nathan squinted and tried to read the article. I went down to the stage and listened to Thieves play their set. Bobbing my head and tapping my foot, I tried to remember that this was the part that mattered, playing quality music for people who cared enough to listen.

This should be enough, I told myself, as Mark and his band worked through the tunes they'd played so many hundreds of times in this town. But all I could think was: *I'm going to Europe.* It's strange; this was the sort of thing I thought I deserved when I made that late-night pledge on the rich family's patio. But standing there, watching the foot soldiers of the Seattle rock scene open up for us—none of it felt fair. It didn't feel like my just deserts. It only felt as if I stood on the winning side of the unfairness for once.

By the time we went onstage, Sean was shit-faced. He played guitar doubled over, staring at his own navel. Every so often, he'd whip his head up and get dizzy with the blood rush. The Gawk Rawd photographer followed his every move, snapping off pictures and blinding us all with the flash. I found myself not caring enough to police up the performance. I was tired of warning Sean about what might go wrong. Let him find out for himself.

Then there was the kick. Maybe I was the only one who saw. Though Sean bounced around like a drunken monkey, his limbs flailing this way and that, there was no doubt in my mind—as his foot connected squarely around Mark's ear—that it was intentional.

Mark fell against some of the other bodies standing down front but not all the way to the floor. He bounced back up with one hand against the side of his head. In a swift lunge, Mark jumped halfway up the stage and managed to grab Sean's foot, sending him down onto his back.

Still playing the bass line, Nathan ran across the stage to put himself between a furious Mark and a dazed Sean. It was hardly necessary. Well before the bouncers knew what was happening, the fans themselves turned on Mark and pulled him down into a sea of elbows and forearms. Sean stood up, looking more sober now, and the three of us kept playing.

Perhaps I should've understood everything then. All those flannel-and-denim-clad zombies turned on Mark—who'd been serving them for so many years now, and who was kind enough to come down front and listen to us play—in order to protect Sean, who started the altercation and was in the wrong but was slightly more in vogue at the moment. All I needed to know about rock fans is summed up in this one thirty-second incident. Why did it take me so long to learn my lesson?

After the show, I had a ringside seat for Liz and Nathan's breakup. The four of us ended up back at my apartment: Sean passed out in my bed, Liz cried in the bathroom, Nathan pleaded and apologized to the locked bathroom door, while I sat on the end of my bed and wished all of them would leave.

"Liz, please understand." Nathan spoke in his gentlest voice. "It's better this way."

"Fuck off!" came Liz's voice from behind the door.

Nathan turned to me and shrugged. Sean's snores sounded from the other side.

"Whatever happens next," I told Nathan, "you guys are getting your own place."

He turned back to the door. "Can we talk this over someplace else, Liz? We're keeping everybody up."

I had to laugh at "everybody," considering Sean was comatose, drooling in his jeans.

"Is Laura out there?" came the voice from the bathroom.

"Yes," Nathan answered. "She's right here."

"Laura, would you come in here, please?"

I rolled my eyes at Nathan. He made a series of hand gestures between himself, the door, and me. I stood up and walked over to my own damn bathroom. "Here I am, Liz."

The knob turned, and the door opened a crack, as if she didn't want Nathan to see her inside. I went in. Liz's normally beautiful face was red and rubbery with the crying. She hugged me and sobbed into my shoulder.

"Laura, I'm so sorry."

I put my arms around her and whispered, "It's okay. Everything's fine." I had no idea what was appropriate.

"He says that if you guys go to Europe, then it's better if we break up. It'll be a long time, he says, and the band will be busy." She pulled away from my shoulder and took some toilet paper to blow her nose and dab at her eyes, checking herself in the mirror.

"He's got a point," I said. "It's hard to do a relationship while you're in a band." I made this up. I knew fuck-all about relationships.

"It makes sense," she said. "And God knows I have my own problems. But something doesn't seem right with him. Ever since you guys got back from the tour, he's not been the same." She turned away from the mirror and looked straight at me. "It's like there's something he's not telling me, you know."

While my mind summoned images of that pierced and pendulous breast dangling in the dark van, my mouth said these words: "He's gotten super committed to the band is all."

Liz swallowed. "You think that's it?"

"Definitely." I dug up the only words of advice that I could think of. "You know what they say about sacrifice: If you let go of something that you want, you'll throw the rhythms of the world out of whack. What you'll end up with is something new, maybe something better."

With the moist toilet paper still in her hand, Liz threw her arms around me again. "Thank you so much, Laura."

Though yet to give us a firm yes on Europe, Chip had us start the passport process. I dragged Sean and Nathan to the post office for photos and filled out their paperwork myself. If I left it to them, they'd screw something up and none of us would get to go.

The boys went through the motions of finding an apartment. Nathan did most of the work. But even for him, it was a halfhearted search. I knew what he was thinking: Why start paying rent right before we take off on another tour? But I'd put my foot down that night, and I refused to back off now. Plus, Europe still wasn't a sure thing, and I would not jinx it.

Each morning, Nathan made calls with the classifieds, then dragged Sean out to look at apartments. They'd return in the afternoon with a list of reasons that none of them worked out, most often: "We can't be loud there." After a few days, this chore became little more than a way to get them out of my hair for a few hours.

It was afternoon—Nathan and Sean jamming together with their instruments unplugged, me on my bed thumbing through a library book on the Louvre, a light drizzle falling against the windowpane— when I got the call from Chip.

"Okay, Laura," he said. "It's a green light."

I lowered my voice to a whisper. "For real?"

"June. You'll start in London. Do you have passports yet?"

"They should be here any day."

"Good. We'll be sending the Rumble Strips to open for you."

"The Rumble Strips?" I said with indignation. I'd be stuck with five stinking boys instead of two.

"That's right. We would be sending Thieves if it weren't for the schoolyard bullshit. If you're going to pick fights with our A-list bands, then you'll have to take what we give you."

"Okay. It's fine." I'd fallen into thinking of this tour as my own precious gift. I didn't want to share.

"I spoke to Jojo. The album's coming along well. We're going to call it *Bad Ideas Taken Way Too Far,* get it?"

"Yeah. That's cool." Actually, I thought it was a stupid title. It paraphrased a line from "Devil You Know." That's a good lyric, but too much of a mouthful for an album title.

Chip said good-bye. I hung up the phone.

"Well?" Nathan asked. "What'd he say?"

"Our record is called *Bad Ideas Taken Way Too Far.*"

Nathan pondered it. "Not bad."

"Could be worse," I agreed.

They both picked up their instruments and resumed playing. I walked to the kitchen and mixed myself a Cold War.

"Oh, guys," I said, still facing the counter, watching the fizz settle atop my drink. "The other thing is . . . we're going to Europe."

I allowed myself a sly smile, my back still to Sean and Nathan. I expected to hear some hooting and high-fiving. Instead, there was silence. Finally, I turned around and saw the two of them sharing a tight embrace, their instruments hanging to their sides—not unlike the one they shared in the alley upon learning of our record deal in the first hours of this year. I took a long sip of my Cold War. Sometimes, I thought about the three of us and wondered if I'd ever be a part of the bond that the two of them shared. At that moment, it didn't matter to me much. I was going to Europe.

———

Every day, I checked the mail for passports. In a dark and desperate corner of my mind, I came up with a list of last resorts if there was a problem with either of the boys' paperwork. If Sean couldn't go, we'd have to find another guitar player. If Nathan couldn't go, things would be more difficult. Maybe I could get Claire from Cooler Heads to play drums. I was prepared to learn all the bass lines and sing the songs myself if I had to. Nothing would stop me from going on this tour, from seeing all those museums and galleries I'd dreamed about for years.

Two days before our release party, I returned from the library with some new Europe books. The mail had come earlier than usual. I put my key into the hole and opened the thin metal door. Inside, two stiff envelopes cut a diagonal across the box. They bore a government seal.

Only two. I closed my eyes and took a deep breath. It would be Sean's that was missing. He always fucked things up when it came to touring. We'd have to bring in another guitarist. It was nothing personal.

With a trembling hand, I removed the first of the envelopes. *Nathan Sullivan* was the name atop the destination address. I reached in for my own passport. A dark cloud invaded my vision. With one arm, I braced myself against the wall to keep from passing out. The name on the second envelope was *Sean Purvis*.

Once upstairs, I slammed the two envelopes into Nathan's chest and went straight for a pile of papers and documents by the telephone. Nathan handed one envelope to Sean, and they opened them.

"Cool." Sean spread the pages of the blue book.

"Where's yours?" Nathan asked me.

"It didn't fucking come." I tore through the stack of documents. Paper flew about the room.

"Why not? We sent all the stuff in on the same day."

"I know we did. It doesn't make sense." Finally, I found the form that

I was looking for, where I'd circled the passport office's 800-number. My next few hours were spent on hold or speaking to a series of clueless bureaucrats, whose final word was, essentially, that they didn't know where my passport was.

Gawk Rawd rented out a local independent record store to throw our release party. It was a strange scene—mostly press and industry types. We signed records for a while, people snapping photos like we were zoo animals.

Wearing a vintage suit and with his beard now in full bloom, Chip gave a speech. He said the normal stuff about how bright our future was. At the end, he paraphrased my only quote in Malcolm's article: If we didn't destroy one another, we'd go on to be the biggest band in the world. That got a round of applause. Nobody understood that I'd been joking.

Finally, they played the record. While I wasn't crazy about the title, the cover looked good. It was a photograph of the three of us onstage: Sean in the foreground, Nathan and I in the back. The picture was out of focus, but they'd double-exposed it with another black-and-white photo, this one of lush vegetation. You could look at it for a while and notice new things—a halo of branches around Sean's head, teardrops made of leaves coming from my eyes.

Once the signing part was over, we milled about in the crowd. A table was set up along one wall with drinks and snacks. I shoved my mouth full of cheese cubes and grabbed a plastic cup of champagne. Chip called the band over to one corner. Sean carried a plate of raw vegetables and ranch dressing.

"You guys feeling good?" he asked. "The record sounds great." He spoke quick and nervous, looking past us into the crowd.

"There's a problem, Chip," I said once I'd worked the cheese down. Sean and Nathan crunched carrot sticks.

"What problem? What's the problem?"

"They got their passports last week. Mine still hasn't come."

"What? Why? You sent everything in, right?"

"Of course. I sent it the same day they did."

"Have you called them? Probably some of that anti-American shit you pulled in the eighties."

"That's not even——"

"Hold on. I have to talk to Doug."

Across the room, Doug also wore a suit, though his wasn't as loud or stylish. He could've been on his way to work in a bank. Chip tapped him on the shoulder and the two spoke vigorously for a span of several minutes. I drained the champagne from my plastic cup. Sean reloaded the tiny plate full of veggies and dressing.

"Okay, I talked to Doug." Chip said this as if we hadn't all watched. "We need to bring in another drummer, just in case." He shrugged. "If Laura's passport arrives between now and then, great. If not, we've got plan B. Maybe Todd from Rumble Strips can learn the songs. That might cut costs."

The plastic cup crushed there in my hand. Loud lip smacks came from Sean and his carrots. Then I heard these words: "No fucking way." It was Nathan. "You go tell Doug, or the Rumble Strips, or whoever, that Laura is our drummer. We don't play without her. Postpone the tour. Cancel the tour. Do what you want. But if Laura's not going, I'm not going, and Sean isn't going. That's that."

I was speechless. Sean stopped crunching.

"Well"——Chip looked at the floor——"that's not a very practical way to solve the problem."

"I'm not a very practical guy," Nathan said.

Over the store's sound system, I heard Nathan sing: *the devil that you don't know.*

Chip put his palms up to face level and shook his downturned head. "Look, why don't we all cool off and hope that Laura's passport arrives within the next couple weeks, okay?"

Nathan nodded at him. Chip walked away. Sean crunched another carrot.

"Thanks, Nathan. Thank you so much," I said. "I need a cigarette."

"I'll come with you," Nathan said.

"No! I need to be alone. At least for a minute. Please?"

He nodded. I went outside and leaned against the glass panel of the storefront. It was all plastered over in posters advertising our album: Sean's image loomed large in the front, Nathan and I stood together in the background. I closed my eyes and took a drag so deep, it made me dizzy. Nathan had done a favor for me that I'd been unwilling to do for him. I needed a second to stew in this. But there was something else as well, something in that second when I was helpless and he stood tall. It was a sensation that I hadn't felt in years—not since that awful night in Philly—like I had somebody I could lean into again, like I didn't have to handle things all by myself.

"Laura? Is that you?"

I opened my eyes and saw a familiar face. "Claire? Oh my god." I stood away from the wall and gave her a hug.

"What are you doing?" she asked.

"I stepped out of the store for a second." I pointed to the strange image of myself there in the window. "That's me. It's my release party."

"I've heard about your new band," she said. "You guys are blowing up."

"We've been lucky." I noticed she was wearing a uniform of some kind: white dress shirt tucked into black pants. "What about the Cooler Heads? I could talk to our label about you guys. They're right inside, actually."

"No. I've got to work. Catering." She used her hand to demonstrate the outfit.

"Are you sure? It might help out."

"Cooler Heads broke up. We never replaced you."

"Really?" I hardly considered myself an asset to that group.

"It was true, what you said. We weren't going anywhere."

"Oh."

"Listen," she said. "I do have to go. But congratulations, seriously."

"Good-bye." I watched Claire walk off. A couple of days before, I'd considered calling her to see if she would play drums if Nathan didn't get his passport. There was that, plus the fact that I'd destroyed her band with what amounted to a temper tantrum. I didn't feel like much as I lit my second cigarette there before my own image in the record store window.

After the party, my passport waited inside the mailbox.

WASHINGTON, D.C.: FEBRUARY 1981

"No, no. That's not it." Hank is frustrated. "The second time through it changes, see." He lets his guitar hang slack about his waist and puts his fingers on the neck of your brother's instrument.

They've been trying this same song for thirty minutes, and Anthony can't get it right.

"What if we changed it so that both parts are the same?" your brother asks.

"That's boring," Hank says. "If we can't figure this out, we won't learn anything."

"Can I try?" Is it your mouth that this question just came from?

The boys all turn to see you sitting there on the stairs. Anthony studies you, confused.

"Do you know how to play?" Hank asks.

Shrug. Stand up. Walk over and take the bass from your brother. The line is only five notes. You mastered more difficult children's songs while Anthony and Hank were away in California. The tips of your fingers have turned tender in the months since you sneaked into your brother's bedroom. Play through the pain.

After a couple bars, Hank strums chords along with you. Suddenly, the music makes even more sense. Billy bangs out a rhythm, and you understand why this is so much fun. The three of you play along for several measures.

Turn to Anthony for approval. Find him looking a little hurt instead. You've stolen his role in his own band.

"Nice!" Hank stops playing. "She's a natural." This is the second time he's described you that way. "How about this?" He strums the chords to "Stepping Stone"—which all of you believe to be a Sex Pistols original. Have no trouble following him on the bass.

Anthony searches the basement shelf and comes back with the broken handle from a set of hedge clippers. Up to his mouth, he holds the piece of wood like a microphone and screams into it. He bounces around on the cement floor, developing stagecraft. Within the two minutes since you picked up the bass, he's already managed to revise his role in the band. Luckily, there's no musical talent required for his new job.

SIXTEEN

I ditched the boys and took the tube to Trafalgar Square. We had several hours before our first London gig, and I didn't intend to waste them. Inside the National Gallery, I walked around as if drunk. My normal museum strategy was to choose a couple pieces and immerse myself. But on this, my first day in Europe, I took it all in at once— the Van Goghs, the Velásquezes, the Rembrandts and Botticellis, the Manets and Cézannes. It was almost too much for my senses. For a moment, I thought I'd developed a condition like Sean's, watching all the colors blur and swirl around me into something beautiful but beyond my control.

Back at the hotel, everyone waited on me. We crammed into a clownish van-type thing the label had rented. Todd, drummer from the Rumble Strips, had gotten an international license and was in charge of driving.

The other five-hundred pounds of the Rumble Strips took up the first row of seats in the back. They were gentlemanly enough to offer me shotgun, while Sean and Nathan squeezed themselves into the last row around all our gear.

The crowd at our first European show was an unruly bunch of drunken hooligans, eager to mosh and break stuff. Rumble Strips went over well. Sean finished his third pint of Guinness and headed back to the bar.

Nathan sweated over the set list like it was a poem he was writing.

"You know about this place?" I asked him.

"What do you mean?" He looked up at me.

"The Sex Pistols played here in the seventies. The Clash, Siouxsie and the Banshees, everybody."

"No shit?" Nathan's Sharpie bled a dot of black ink into the paper.

"The Rolling Stones played here once in the eighties."

Nathan grinned incredulously. He thought I was pulling his leg.

"Seriously! This is like the CBGB of England."

"The Rolling-fucking-Stones out there on that stage we're about to play on?"

"I'm not shitting you." I smiled. "This is Europe, not Montana. Every inch of this city has history to it."

"We better not screw up."

And this is what I did next, as Nathan turned back to his list: I stood, walked the not-even five paces over to him in my softest steps, put my hand on the base of his neck, then leaned down and kissed him on the cheek. He turned up and looked at me. The muscles of his throat contracted in a swallow.

"We'll do great," I said. "We've come this far."

"I love this English beer!" Sean burst through the door with another pint of what was, in fact, Irish beer. He froze as he saw the two of us there, my hand still on Nathan's neck, my face still leaning over next to his. Sean wore the same jealous glare as when he'd seen Mark and me hug back in Seattle. Blood rushed to my face. Why was I ashamed? Wasn't it an innocent good-luck peck on the cheek?

"Move 'Nowhere Fast' down," I said. "Let's start with something noisy." I pretended to be leaning over to see the piece of paper on the table.

"Right." Nathan played along. I recalled a similar conspiratorial moment between the two of us when Liz asked for details of our Northwest tour. In both cases, the deception came quick and natural.

Sean took a long slurp of his beer, his eyeballs going back and forth above the rim of the glass.

It was a gladiator pit out there. The crowd wanted noise and gore. Sean went wild, sliding across the stage, jumping into the audience. His playing was spot-on.

In a pause between songs, I took a hurried gulp from my water bottle. Not having noticed it on the set list, I thought it was a mistake when I heard Nathan play the first few notes of "Devil You Know."

We hadn't practiced this song since the night we recorded it. I assumed we'd never play it live. Nathan went through the bass line, which I'd invented. I hit the drums lightly to compensate for the lack of brushes. Sean took a step forward and reached into the crowd. He came back with a half-full beer bottle. Once he'd drained it, he slid the bottle along the fretboard of his guitar to produce the same sound he'd gotten from that drumstick.

And then, the strangest thing happened. Perhaps the wildest crowd we'd ever played to shut up and paid attention.

With a whisper at first, Nathan sang the lyrics.

It was a bad idea taken way too far
on a night too cold to spend alone in a car.

I looked at my snare drum and tried to ignore the words, convinced that my imagination had gotten the best of me.

I looked up and saw that Nathan was staring straight at me as he sang. He'd turned his mic stand around. A sweating, panting Sean stared at Nathan. Hundreds of eyes in the crowd stared at the three of us.

> *You're not dumb and you're not naïve*
> *but you never learned to tell the difference between . . .*

With his guitar, Sean let out a roar. Nathan matched the rise in volume as he came to the refrain: *"The devil you know and the devil that you don't know."* I picked up the beat a little and threw in some grace notes. Sean chucked the beer bottle back into the crowd and worked the strings with his magic fingers. Nathan sang his one line over and over, the two of them competing for decibels.

I don't know who started it, but all three of us sped up. It wasn't planned, and we didn't signal one another. Little by little, we increased the tempo, playing harder and faster, into a sort of instrumental breakdown not unlike the end of "Free Bird"—something we'd never attempted or talked about.

The crowd slam-danced with renewed vigor. Nathan spread out his stance and dug in harder to the bass line. Sean bounced around the stage, then did a running shoulder check into Nathan—another first. He did it again, and knocked Nathan away from his mic mid-lyric. Looking annoyed, Nathan finally returned the blow, and sent Sean stumbling backwards. Was Sean hearing the same things that I was in these lyrics? Had he seen something that justified jealousy in that backstage moment between Nathan and me?

Still in the middle of a solo, Sean retreated all the way to his end of the stage. Nathan closed his eyes and embellished the words. All the way backed up, Sean put one foot in front of the other like a sprinter on his mark. The crowd cheered. With closed eyes, Nathan was oblivious on his own side of the stage.

Guitar in hand, Sean began his running charge toward Nathan. The audience howled. I almost had to turn away. But when Sean crossed right in front of my drum riser, his foot caught one of the cables taped to the stage. He was running fast, and got a good bit of air. By accident, the Sean Purvis signature belly flop was born.

He fell flat on his face and guitar. It made the most bizarre sound through the amplifiers—every point of every string struck at once, while the whammy bar was pushed beyond its range of motion. It was like a loud electric sneeze.

Nathan's eyes went wide as he heard this and saw Sean lying motionless on the floor. The music stopped. The crowd screamed. Nathan took off his bass and kneeled by his friend. I was about to join them, when Sean crawled up to his knees. From nose down to chin, his face was all blood. Two broken strings hung from the head of his guitar. The volume and tone knobs had shattered and fell off in pieces. One of the single coil pickups was pushed up into the body of the instrument.

Nathan put a hand under his friend's armpit to help him up. But before Sean even stood on his feet, he began playing the chords on his four remaining strings. He wanted to finish the song. Nathan shrugged at me and put his bass back on.

Sean turned to the crowd. They cheered. We finished the verse and did the refrain at normal tempo. By now, the audience knew those words by heart and continued to chant even once we stopped playing. Nathan thanked them and put down his bass. He walked over to Sean and unplugged the guitar cord. I dropped my sticks and joined them. The audience didn't stop.

Under each arm, Nathan and I led Sean offstage. He shook as if cold. Even backstage, we could hear the crowd chanting: *"The devil you know and the devil that you don't know."* Nathan shouted for the Rumble Strips to please pack up our equipment. Sean didn't speak, but misty dots of snotty blood stained our clothes as he breathed out.

At the emergency room, Sean was taken into the back. Nathan and I sat in the waiting room, a kind of temporary asylum full of screaming drunks and weirdos. The main attraction was one skinny guy in a brown leather jacket designed for a woman. He stood atop his plastic chair, shouting: "Won't somebody please help us! We're in pain, for the love of God!" With his big nose and narrow chest, the two long arms extended out at his sides, the man looked like a sick scavenger bird. A girl, who I assumed was with him, sat in the plastic chair at his side and wept into her hands. Neither had any visible wounds. I thought it would make a nice painting, the two of them—one huddled up crying, the other flapping around and shouting.

It wasn't long before we were called into the back. Sean lay in a hospital bed with bandages over his nose and ointment on his upper lip. His teeth were intact. They'd filled him up with pain medication. His eyelids rested in a half-open daze. It was obvious that Nathan felt guilty. I was mixed up, feeling at fault in a way, but also aware that Sean had been heading in this direction for a while now, and that this might be better than a more severe bottoming out.

The doctors sent us home with pain pills and fresh gauze. We took a cab back to the hotel. Sean leaned against the window in a woozy half-awake trance. The beginnings of double black eyes appeared on either side of his nose. Nathan stared out the window at the still-busy London streets.

Finally, Sean broke the silence. "I can totally play tomorrow night, so you guys know. It's not a problem." He said it with the tone of apology, his tongue heavy and dry with the medication.

Sitting in the middle, I reached over and took each of their hands in mine. Both gave me a reassuring squeeze.

Back at the hotel, Nathan helped me put Sean to bed. He fell asleep almost instantly on top of the covers, his bloody shirt bunched up around his chest and exposing his abdomen.

"Jesus," Nathan said, pointing at the yellow bruises around Sean's belly. "Good thing he didn't break any ribs."

I stood by the door. "Good thing."

Nathan pulled the shirt down all the way to his friend's waistband. "Good night, Laura," he said, then left the room.

I killed the light and lay down under the blankets. The sound from the traffic rolled in from the streets. Steady shallow breaths came from my sedated lover. After a few minutes of listening, I knew I wouldn't get any sleep.

I took my cigarettes out to the wrought iron balcony at the end of our floor. From there, the London skyline shone in the clear summer night like all the postcards promised: Big Ben, the bridges, that Ferris wheel from Piccadilly Circus. I was seeing the world, and it turned out to be a lonely place.

After two cigarettes, I walked back down the hall. I passed by Nathan's room and paused in front of the door. I even put my hand on the knob to see how it felt. I wanted to go in there. I wanted to sleep beside him instead of Sean. There was no denying it. I've said before that I don't mind being hated. But will the fans and historians please answer me this one question: What is it that makes somebody a bad person? Is it your desires, these feelings that we can barely control? Or is it your actions, which urges you obey or deny?

That night, I walked back to my own room and swallowed two of Sean's pain pills. Soon, a tingling lightness took over my limbs and I lay down on the bed. It wasn't long before I was in a state not so unlike sleep.

I woke up sometime in the afternoon. Sean snored on his back. His double black eyes had filled in like a raccoon's mask. The nose bandages were brown with dried blood. I put on some clothes and left the room.

Nathan was in the common area downstairs, drinking coffee and working on Sean's guitar. He'd already restrung it and now struggled to get it in tune. "Morning," he said when he saw me.

I nodded, walked over to the coffee table, and took a sip from his mug. "How's it going?" I gestured toward the guitar.

"The intonation's fucked," he said, "and the tone knob doesn't work anymore. But I think it'll be playable by tomorrow night."

"Tomorrow night?" I asked. "What about the show in three hours?"

"I canceled it." Nathan looked up from the guitar and straight at me. "Rumble Strips will do two sets. They were cool about it. I left a message with Gawk Rawd."

"It's our second show of the tour!"

Nathan shrugged. "How's Sean doing?"

"He said he wanted to play. He finished the set last night. My brother played a whole show with a broken arm once." In the other room, a phone rang.

Nathan raised his eyebrows at the mention of my brother. He didn't have to say it, but the meaning was clear: Some things are more important than a gig.

The British girl manning the front desk poked her head in. "Laura? Is there a Laura Loss here? Telephone call."

Chip let out a string of expletives before I could even say hello. "The tour just fucking started! England is a huge market for us!"

"What are you yelling at me for? It wasn't my idea."

"Don't fuck with me on this. This is a major investment!"

"You want me to manage your bands, Chip? Then pay me a salary."

Nathan walked up to the desk when he heard the yelling.

"Listen to me, Laura," Chip growled into the receiver now. "Do not think that I won't cancel the rest of the dates and bring you all back home. . . ."

I trembled at the thought. I couldn't afford to keep traveling Europe on my own. And I knew, for certain, that my band wouldn't survive such a hardship in the state we were in.

Nathan walked over and put one hand on my shoulder. He held out his other hand and gestured for me to give him the phone. Chip still shouted as I passed the receiver.

"Chip, this is Nathan. Three things. One: If you would've built some days off into this tour, then we wouldn't have to cancel anything. Two: This whole city will be talking about yesterday's show for years. We sold enough of your records last night to cancel ten shows. Three: Don't you ever fucking scream at anybody in my band again, ever. Good-bye." Nathan hung up the phone.

Without thinking, without even checking to see if anyone was coming, I threw my arms around him and buried my head in his shoulder. A dull ring still sounded from the old phone, Nathan had slammed it down so hard.

LUCKETTS, VIRGINIA: JUNE 1981

The four of you make the pilgrimage in your newly acquired van. Anthony drives in circles, staring down at crude directions scribbled on the back of an envelope.

"Where are we?" Hank keeps saying. "How do you know this guy again?"

Billy crunches through a bag of corn chips. Stare out the window: cows, barns, fields full of tall grass waving in the wind.

"I think this might be it," your brother says. He pulls the van down a muddy driveway, into the shade of tall trees. You end up in what looks like a decrepit campus or boarding school. Long and low buildings, like cabins, litter the sides of the dirt road. A basketball court lies on the right, weeds creeping up through the blacktop.

Anthony turns off the ignition, looks down at his envelope.

"Is that him?" Spot a man in a tie-dye T-shirt walking toward you and waving his arms. He's got a big belly, an unkempt white beard, and a red bandanna around his forehead—a hippie Santa Claus.

"That's him." Anthony kills the ignition and steps out. You all follow.

Skip's "studio" is just his house. The mixing board is on the porch, with a bundle of wires connecting it to the microphones and reel-to-reel tape recorder in the basement. Much of the equipment is home-made. Everything is held together with clothespins.

The home four-track recorder hasn't been invented yet. For most bands, it is a question of either pressing play-and-record on the boom box or dropping thousands of dollars for professional studio time. Anthony discovered something in between.

There are no second takes, no effects or polish. Go all out for a minute and a half then move on to the next song. A collection of stringed instruments lines the walls of the live room—mandolins, a harp, strange Celtic-looking pieces you don't know the name for. The notes from your amplifier resonate through their wooden bodies.

If you take a break, Skip comes in and tells tales about the sixties. This place had been a boarding school and commune that never worked out. His stories of idealistic communal living are met with eye rolls by everyone except Anthony.

Hank says he's going for a walk and you join him, hoping to share cigarettes. The two of you find a pond down the hill. There's a small dock where you sit and smoke. The whole campus has the smell of moist grass and rotting leaves. Swat mosquitoes and hear frogs.

"What are we going to do with these songs once we record them?" you ask between drags.

"I don't know." Hank shrugs. "Listen to them in ten years and have a good laugh."

SEVENTEEN

It rained hard on our way into Paris. In the back of the van, Sean slept with his head on Nathan's shoulder, no sign of a grudge between them. It was evening by the time we found our hotel, in a tight corner of the Latin Quarter.

We were scheduled to play the very same night. With the van still full of equipment, the six of us went out in search of dinner. The rain came down harder, and we did an awkward, single-file run through the winding streets. Before long, Todd held a door open and waved us in. It was a Middle Eastern restaurant, serving Greek gyros. At the counter, a smiling young man with dark hair and crooked teeth stood beside a rotating column of meat.

The Rumble Strips ordered paper-wrapped pita sandwiches over-flowing with lettuce and lamb, and french fries.

A camera flash went off. Todd snapped a photo of his bandmates with their arms around the smiling sandwich-maker. Through a com-bination of hand signals and broken French, I managed to order falafel. I turned back to Nathan and Sean. They stared big-eyed up at the menu, scared to approach the counter. For a second, in this foreign

land, surrounded by strange food and language, they were those two
timid boys from Montana once again.

They ended up with the same meat-and-potatoes fare as their coun-
trymen. The six of us sat down—Nathan with the Rumble Strips, Sean
and I by ourselves.

"This is good," Sean said, some of the white gyro sauce stuck to his
nose bandages. "It tastes like elk."

"It's lamb," I told him.

The man from the counter turned on the stereo. Some brand of
Middle Eastern music played, a sound I'd associate with belly dancing.
Sean's eyes darted around above the bandages. He put his sandwich
down on the table.

"Something's wrong," Sean said.

"What, with your food?"

"No, this music." He leaned in toward me and lowered his voice. "I
don't *see* anything!"

"No colors?" I whispered.

"No colors. What the fuck?" He took short and shallow breaths, as
if on the verge of hyperventilating.

From the other table, I overheard a joke about french fries and
what they call them here. Their laughter was muffled by mouths full of
food.

"Relax," I said. "Your head's been through a lot in the last forty-
eight hours. Give it some time." I reached out and put my hand on his
shoulder.

He nodded and took another bite.

The venue was a long, low-ceilinged basement with a fog of cigarette
smoke hanging at eye level. From a beautiful French girl tending bar,
I struggled to order a drink through the language barrier. She was tall
and lean with giant eyes, olive skin, and straight hair that hung down

like a frame on either side of her face. On one of her narrow upper
arms, she had a tattoo of an anchor, like a sailor might.

The crowd enjoyed the Rumble Strips. I'd been bad about catching
their sets. Anthony would've been disappointed.

The backstage room was full of mismatched office furniture. Nathan sat at one side of a big executive desk and squeaked out the set list
with the Sharpie. A bottle in one hand and his jar of pills in the other,
Sean sat on a couch that might've been from an airport lounge, beside
a twelve-pack of warm Belgian beer.

Not sure if he'd spoken to Nathan about it, I leaned in and whispered to Sean. "Are you okay? Is it back, I mean?"

"It's back." He nodded. "But it's different now, more yellow and
brown than before."

"Who knows what got rattled around up there." I made a fist and
tapped it on my temple. "Try not to take any more blows to the head."

"I'll try."

"You're not supposed to drink on that medication," I said.

There was a second of silence. Sean stared at the beer bottle.

"Here." Nathan pushed three set lists across the big desk. Suddenly, he was chairman of the board.

I looked over the list on the desk. As the closer, Nathan had put,
"Devil You Know."

Sean did his thing—power slides, stage diving, spot-on guitar licks.
I liked this audience. They were high energy, without that element
of violence that the UK fans had. I thought I heard them singing
along to "Nowhere Fast"—which was doubly odd, given the language
barrier.

We never discussed the arrangement for "Devil You Know," but
the three of us understood and went into a sped-up instrumental part

after the first verse. To the shock of both Nathan and me, Sean again performed a running belly flop—this time on purpose. Hadn't we just agreed that he'd be more careful?

This time, Sean held on to the neck and body of his instrument and tucked his chin into his shoulder. His face didn't take the impact. Instead, the force of the fall landed squarely on his guitar, emitting that same wild sound as two nights ago, and again breaking several strings.

With all the pain pills in his system, Sean recovered quick. He stood up on his own and finished the song with the remaining strings. A fresh gush of blood came from his nose. Watching him in his chemical daze, grinning at the approval from the crowd, I felt a sharp second of hatred, like an insect crawling up my back, for Sean and his talent. He was becoming like Hank, a gifted egomaniac. But he was also worse than Hank. Sean was letting his gift go to waste.

Once backstage, Sean lay down across the same vinyl couch. "Laura," he called out to me. "I want to go back to the hotel."

I was tired myself. "All right," I said. "Let's go."

Nathan cracked a beer from among those remaining in the box. "I'll stick around for a while," he said. "I'm still pretty wired."

Back at the room, Sean threw up in the toilet, took more pills, and passed out on the bed. I slept for a couple of hours, then woke up to the sound of Sean's loud breaths forcing their way through his blood-congested nose.

I sat up in bed and looked him over. His bandages were in desperate need of changing. Crusts of blood lined the bottom of his nostrils. A string of drool went out one side of his mouth. Staring down at him in the dark, I couldn't understand how it had come to pass that we were sharing a bed. I wasn't attracted to him. We hadn't made love in weeks. As far as the label knew, they were booking two rooms because I was a girl and needed space.

Knowing I'd get no more sleep tonight, I picked up my cigarettes and went to find someplace to smoke. Out in the hallway, the whole hotel was sound asleep. I paused in front of the room that I knew to be Nathan's. As in London, I reached out and put my hand on the knob.

Through the thick door, I heard Nathan stirring inside. I turned the knob and held it there for a moment. If he was up, we could talk, maybe share a cigarette. I paused there with the twisted doorknob in my hand, in the hallway of the hotel, our one dark corner of this vast city of lights. It didn't seem wrong as I slowly pushed open that door. It seemed like all I was capable of.

There was a light on inside. I could tell as soon as the door was cracked a little. And there were noises, too. I heard a low grunt, not quite a word. I pushed the door farther.

There was Nathan, all right, though he didn't see me at first. He lay on his back, eyes shut, his torso bare atop the covers. I took another step and then froze when I saw them.

The first face to look up at me was that of the gorgeous French bartender. She and another girl I recognized from the show—this one with a shaved head—were both naked and on their knees, giving Nathan head at the same time. The second girl looked up as well. With their big eyes and wet lips, they could've been two deer drinking from a brook, startled by a hunter.

Nathan saw me. One of the girls whispered in French.

"Laura!" Nathan said. "Do you . . . want something?"

The French girls giggled and turned away from me. I caught a glimpse of the anchor tattoo on the bartender's beautiful forearm, the arc of her small breast peeking around from one side. She was like a statue come to life.

"Could you close the door?" Nathan said calmly.

"I'm sorry." I slammed the door shut. I ran through the hall and then down the two flights of stairs. There was a couch in the lobby. The night auditor slept in a chair. My hands trembled as I lit a cigarette. I got through only a few drags before the tears fell hard down my cheeks and my chest convulsed with weeping. I snuffed out my smoke in an ashtray on the coffee table and used both hands to stop the sobs.

Within seconds, the night auditor awoke and yelled at me in French.

"Leave me the fuck alone!" I shouted at him.

He seemed to get my meaning. I cried myself to sleep on the common-area couch, feeling unwelcome in either of the two rooms my band had booked.

I woke up on that same couch the next morning, to Nathan shaking me and saying my name. "Laura," he said. "What are you doing down here?"

I rubbed my eyes. "I came down for a smoke and must've fallen asleep. Hey, I'm sorry about last night. I woke up and I thought—"

"Don't worry about it," Nathan said. "No big deal."

"Where are those girls?" I sat up and looked around.

"They left," he said. "I need coffee. You want to get some?"

I looked out the window and saw that it was still early, and turning into a clear summer day. "Let me put clothes on." I held up a pinch of cloth from the blue surgical pants.

Nathan and I found a café not far from the hotel and picked out some pastries by pointing at the glass case. We walked along the river and looked at what we guessed were famous sights.

"Good crowd last night," Nathan said.

"Really good," I said. "I'm telling you, a bunch of those people knew the words to the songs. They must've heard the record."

"Maybe they have college radio here."

We passed by an organ grinder with a monkey on a leash—like something from a strange movie. Both of us stared but neither said a word.

"I want to go to the Louvre today," I said. "I've wanted to go since I was a kid."

"The what?" Nathan asked.

"The most famous museum in the world," I said.

Nathan nodded, a little embarrassed by his ignorance.

"It's where the *Mona Lisa* is."

"Cool," he said. "Let's check it out."

It was amazing. Within minutes, we saw the *Venus de Milo,* the equestrian statue of Louis XIV, and *Psyche Revived by Cupid's Kiss.* The two of us walked faster than I would have on my own; I didn't want Nathan to get bored. But it was nice to have somebody else along. We came to the crowd gathered around the *Mona Lisa.*

"It's smaller than I thought," Nathan said. "What's with this glass?"

"It's bulletproof. The picture was stolen in 1911. A janitor hid in the broom closet then walked out with the most famous painting in history under his coat."

Nathan laughed. "Seriously?"

I nodded. "They brought Pablo Picasso in for questioning."

Nathan stared on, attempting to take in all that history. "Did you go to school for this stuff?"

"No," I said. "My parents are both professors. My mom does art history."

By now, the French art students had arrived with their sketchbooks. They stood in corners or sat down on the floor and copied the masterpieces. I stared at one girl with glasses and thick curly hair. She was drawing a lesser-known Renaissance portrait in charcoal. That's the kind of life my mother had always wanted for me. Why had I fought against it so hard for so many years? To Anthony, there was something cowardly about studying the art of the past in those dusty old texts and museums, when you could be out there rewriting the history books of the future. Back then, I agreed with him.

"Check it out!" Nathan said a bit too loudly. "It's the Pogues!"

He pointed at a painting by Géricault. It was true; the Pogues superimposed their own faces over those in the painting for the cover of *Rum, Sodomy & the Lash.*

"It's called *The Raft of the Medusa,*" I explained. "That really happened, the shipwreck. The captain was incompetent. He got his job through political connections, then sank the ship. The survivors clung to that raft. It was the first romantic painting that showed contemporary events, rather than historical or religious subjects. It was revolutionary."

"Wow." He stared on, entranced by this over all the other things that we had seen.

"Nathan," I said, emboldened by the way we both looked straight ahead and not at each other. "I don't want to be with Sean anymore. I want to be with you. And honestly—whether you'll admit it or not— I'm almost sure you feel the same way."

A group of Japanese tourists approached our painting. Their guide explained its history in a language I didn't understand.

"He's my best friend, Laura." Nathan swallowed but didn't turn his head away from the art. "I can't do that."

"You won't have to do anything. I'll end it. We're not happy, me and him. We're not good together."

"No." Nathan turned to me at last and took me by the hand. "Don't break his heart, Laura. He wouldn't be able to handle that. Please."

————————

Back at the hotel, Sean sat up on the couch I'd slept on. "Where were you guys? I've been waiting here for hours."

"Seeing this city," I said. "You can't do anything without us?"

Nathan was more genuine. "We went to the big museum here. And we got food." He placed the two plastic bags on the counter. We'd bought a chicken from one of the rotisserie places along the Marché Bastille. It was impossible not to: the giant glass oven full of golden birds rotating, while a pile of peeled potatoes absorbed the juices and oils at the bottom. The three of us tore into the food without plates or utensils. Within minutes, the coffee table was a mess of chicken bones and greasy wadded-up napkins. It reminded me of the takeout dinners we used to share at my apartment in Seattle.

When Sean did his belly flop that night, he didn't land it correctly and his guitar failed to make that trademark sound. Sean stood up looking more frustrated than in pain. All six strings remained intact. Instead of finishing the song, Sean took off his guitar and slammed it hard against the stage. Nathan winced as the components flew apart. A wave of feedback washed over the crowd and Sean walked off into the wings. Nathan said good-bye, then gathered up the pieces of the guitar.

Backstage, Sean lay down atop the big executive desk. "Laura." He spoke softly from his prone position. "Laura, I don't feel so good. Could you take me back?"

I looked around the room. Nathan chugged from a bottle of water. The Rumble Strips drank beer and laughed.

"Maybe I want to stick around for a while," I said discreetly. "You know, hang out after the show for once. Can't you get yourself home?"

"I'm sorry, Laura. I don't know where I'm going. I don't even know the name of the hotel or anything." He sounded as if he might cry. "Please? I think I might throw up."

The French bartender appeared in the doorway with a cigarette in hand. She looked over at Nathan and he smiled. I wondered: How did they communicate with each other?

"Fuck it," I said to Sean. "Let's go."

WASHINGTON, D.C.: SEPTEMBER 1981

Your brother flips through the yellow pages. Once he finds what he's looking for, he dials the number.

"Yes, I'm calling to ask how much it would cost to have my record pressed."

There's a pause.

"No. I don't have a company. I have a band." He scribbles down some numbers.

Once off the phone, he sifts through a stack of British seven-inches. He finds one in particular and removes the record. With a letter opener, he pries apart the seams of the sleeve. A couple of pops and he lays it out flat in front of you.

You're shocked to see an album cover like this, in only one dimension—a piece of stiff paper, some little tabs and creases with a few flattened balls of glue.

"What I want you to do"—Anthony runs the bottom of his hand across the piece of cardboard again and again, trying to make it smooth—"is draw me something in this same shape. Something for the cover of the album."

"What should I draw?" you ask.

"Whatever you want," Anthony says.

"What's the name of the band?"

"Second Class Citizens."

"What about the record company?"

He pauses for a second. "Autopilot."

Take out your sketchpad and a marker. Trace the shape of the album cover.

Your brother picks up the phone again. "Yes, I called a moment ago. I'd like to go ahead and order a pressing of my record."

And just like that, with the telephone, a letter opener, and a Magic Marker, you and your brother change the world.

EIGHTEEN

The van stank of sweat and farts. My knees dug into the dashboard. In the back, the boys shared a Walkman, one earpiece each, though Sean slept much of the time. Nathan fixed and restrung Sean's guitar as we drove, until it was held together entirely by duct tape. By the time we crossed the border into Spain, Sean's bandages had come off. His nose now bent slightly to the left. The raccoon mask turned a dull green.

Madrid was hot. The Spaniards all wore black clothes and ate rich steaming meals. But I liked the city, more than I thought I would. Not as touristy as Paris or London, it felt like people actually lived and worked here. Rather than a hodgepodge of international influences, Madrid had its own personality.

The first night went well. Sean slept most of the day before and got only moderately drunk. While we played, I was sure I saw some of the kids mouthing words to our songs. And not just the big ones, some of the more obscure tunes from the album. Two boys down front actually had the NOWHERE FAST T-shirts on.

After the show, we all hung out in the back and drank from liter bottles of beer. A couple of teenage girls burst into the dressing room, gushing Spanish. Both carried copies of our full-length and pushed them toward us along with a pen. They wanted us to autograph *Bad Ideas*. Nathan and I looked at each other. Sean was the first to go over and sign.

After the Spanish kids left, I lit a cigarette. "Something's going on," I said to Nathan. "We need to talk to Chip and Doug."

This hotel was the shittiest that we'd stayed in so far. The bathrooms were shared—one on each floor, the drains full of hair, caked-up soap scum all over the sinks.

Nathan brushed his teeth as I came out of the shower. "Morning," he said.

"Hey."

"You going to check out a museum today?" he asked through a mouthful of toothpaste.

"Yeah," I said. "I want to get breakfast first, but I hope to see the Prado."

"Can I come with?" He spit lather into the sink.

We found a small café near the hotel. The waiters wore bow ties. We ate ham sandwiches and slices of cold potato omelet. It was the first time we'd been alone since the Louvre.

Once we entered the museum, I talked about paintings. A crowd gathered around the big Velásquez, *Las Meninas*. We stood on our tip-toes to see it over the heads of others.

"He was the top dog in Spain's golden age," I told Nathan. "This is his masterpiece."

"It's pretty cool."

We went downstairs. I thought that Picasso's *Guernica* was here, but an English-speaking staff member explained that it had been moved to a new building.

"Whoa," Nathan said. "What's this?" He'd found the Black Paintings.

"Goya," I said. "We saw his statue outside. That piece is called *Saturn Devouring His Son*. It's a scene from Greek mythology but also a comment on Spain's civil conflicts. Goya had a kind of mental breakdown and moved into a house outside this city called the Deaf Man's Villa. On the walls, he painted all these, never intending for anybody other than himself to see them."

Nathan stood in front of *Fight with Cudgels*. Before a barren landscape, two men are each poised to strike. We can tell that neither will escape the other's club. Their knees fade into a blur. There will be blows landed, the painting seemed to say. There will be pain on everyone's part. We will cause hurt, and we will suffer, and in the end, we'll be no better for it.

"Fucking hell." Nathan's eyes stayed on the painting. "Do you have to be insane to make something like this?"

I took Nathan by the hand. He glanced down at our intertwined fingers and then back up at my face. His breath came out quick and shallow. And then, ladies and gentlemen of the press, fans of all ages, I leaned in and kissed him on the mouth. It was all me. In this re-creation of a deaf man's house, surrounded by black pictures never meant to be seen, I gave in to my urges.

Now you know. Hurl all your insults this way. Let those of you most seasoned in the suppression of desire cast the first stones.

There was a moment there in which we were both happy. Nathan forgot about the context for a split second and kissed me back. Soon enough, he pulled away and looked at me with awful surprise.

"Let me ask you something, Nathan." I gestured to the paintings all around us—the jealous god eating his offspring, the horned devil holding a Sabbath of witches, the carnival of tortured faces. "What does it mean to be a less-than-perfect friend in a world full of liars and thieves? What does it mean to be unfaithful in a place this fucked up, where happiness is this hard to come by?"

He dropped my hand and ran out of the museum. I followed him outside, shouting his name down the street. He slowed to a walk along the broad avenue lined with marble and iron; I kept running and gained on him half a block down.

"We can't do this!" was the first thing out of Nathan's mouth once he allowed me to catch up with him. "We talked about it already."

"Nathan, I'm not being curious or sneaky for the fuck of it. This is what I want. I've felt this way for a while and it's not going away. You can't ask me to bottle it up. We're all adults. We can figure this out."

"He's my best friend."

"You look me right in the eye and you tell me that you don't feel the same way that I do. Tell me that you'd rather screw groupies than be with me, and I'll leave you alone. But I won't let it be about Sean."

Nathan took a deep breath and then looked me straight in the eye. "I don't return your feelings, Laura. I do not want to be your boy-friend."

I'd forgotten what a brilliant liar he was.

"Fine," I said. Only half my heart was broken; the other half knew that Nathan wasn't sincere.

Back at the hotel, Sean sat in a sort of den on the first floor, with an open bottle of red wine. His teeth and lips were dark with tannins. Behind him, a group of young American tourists watched MTV in Spanish.

"Let me guess," Sean slurred as we walked in. "You guys were at the museum, looking at art." He said the last word sarcastically.

"That's right." I had no patience for his bullshit and was a little disgusted by the sight of him.

"I never knew you were such an art lover, Nathan," Sean said.

I didn't let Nathan respond. "You're judging him for taking in a couple museums? Look at you—been all over Europe and haven't seen shit but the inside of some hotels and a couple of concert halls."

One of the American kids laughed from the couch behind.

Sean turned around to see.

"Grow up, Sean." I walked off to my room. Nathan sighed as I passed him.

Sean lost it during our show that night. He'd finished two bottles of wine before we went onstage, along with God knows how many pills. After his belly flop, the crowd let out a massive cheer. He tried to play the rest of the song, but the pickups shorted out.

In a fit of frustration, Sean took off his guitar and launched it backwards over his head—the way a bride might do with the bouquet. I looked up and saw it coming straight at me. I tried to stand and get out of the way, but my knees were wedged under the snare drum.

To shield myself, I put my hands up around my head. The guitar didn't land on me. It came down on one side of the drum set. The floor tom cracked and the rough edge of a worn-out crash cymbal tumbled toward my head, opening a cut on my temple as I fell backwards.

On the ground, I reached up to my forehead and then saw the blood on my fingers. Nathan was there a second later, digging me out from under the equipment. Sean had walked offstage once the guitar was airborne, never looking to see where it might land.

"I'm sick of this shit," I said as Nathan pulled the drums off me. "I'm fucking sick of it!"

In the dressing room, somebody had set off a fire extinguisher, and the walls and floor were covered with chemical foam. Sean was passed out in a chair. With little discussion, we shoved him in a cab and took off. I stared out the window and felt my anger beat inside my chest like a second heart. Nathan and I dragged Sean up the stairs, the smell of alcohol oozing from his pores.

"I'm over this," I said to Nathan as the two of us looked down upon a comatose, wheezing Sean in the bed. "I want out. I quit."

"Let's clean up that cut on your head."

We went to the common bathroom, and Nathan used a wet paper towel to wipe the dried blood from my brow.

"It's not too deep." Somehow, Nathan produced a Band-Aid. "Looks worse than it is."

"I'm serious about quitting. I'll call Chip in the morning and tell him. I don't even want to go to Italy anymore. This whole thing has been a big fucking mistake."

"Don't say that," Nathan said calmly. He pressed the Band-Aid's adhesive surface into my forehead with his thumbs.

"I'm serious," I said again. The tears flowed and I cursed myself. In the mirror behind Nathan, I saw my chin turn to quivering rubber. "Years and years of boys beating me up onstage while other boys watch and cheer."

Nathan put his arms around me. I soaked his shirtfront in my tears. With my head against Nathan's chest like that, I could feel his heart beat faster than normal. His breathing turned rushed and shallow, almost hyperventilating. I pulled back to see if he was all right. His face had lost all color.

"Are you okay?" I wiped at my eyes with a shirtsleeve.

Nathan leaned in and kissed me harder and longer than in the museum this morning. I kissed back, threw my arms around him, and ran my fingers through his mop of hair. He picked me up off the ground, our lips still locked together. I felt his whole body tremble with nerves.

All the day's wrongs were swiftly reversed. I knew that he'd been lying; he did love me back, even if he was too ashamed to admit it. I didn't care what happened next. It was like waking from a bad dream, leaving the unloved life behind and never wanting to visit it ever again.

Ladies and gentlemen of the press, fans of all ages, let the record show that I was happy then. There are times when it all seems worth it—all the hate mail, all the tabloid stories, all the accusations piled upon me. There are times when all of that seems a small price to pay for a feeling that lasted a few seconds in a filthy bathroom in Madrid. You can bury me in dirty laundry under an upside-down pedestal, but you'll never take away the single moment in my life in which I loved a boy boldly and felt that love returned to me in equal measure.

That's something that a fan could never understand.

Nathan was so nervous, I worried that he might have a panic attack in my arms. There was something about his anxiety—the fact that he owned all his guilt—that made me even happier. This wasn't a late-night moment of weakness. He knew what he was doing. It was practically killing him, but at least he was aware of the consequences.

He put me back on the ground, and our kiss finally came to an end. I leaned up and whispered into his ear: "Breathe."

He took me by the hand and led me down the hall to his room. The door swung shut and the two of us stood staring at each other in front of the bed. Still shaking with nerves, Nathan slowly took my clothes off. Once I was naked, he took a couple steps backwards and looked me up and down as though I were a piece of art.

I stepped toward him and pulled his T-shirt up over his head. Nathan still had his shoes on, and there was an awkward moment where we stopped so that he could undo the laces. His fingers shook so bad that he couldn't untie the knot.

"Here," I said. "Let me do it."

From the instant that I removed his shoes, there was a change in our dynamic. We weren't two unlikely lovers urgently getting it on. I became a kind of nurse all of a sudden, helping Nathan through this act that he'd committed to but could barely handle. I pushed his chest down so that he lay flat on the bed. I pulled off his socks, his pants, his boxers.

Now that we were both naked, I crawled up his body and kissed his lips.

"Relax," I whispered in his ear. "Breathe in through your mouth."

He did as I told him.

"Now hold it for a second. Let it go out through your nose."

He took a few more breaths, each one deeper and longer than the last. It seemed to help with his trembling.

"Keep thinking about your breathing." I kissed his neck and tasted salt. He smelled robust and healthy. I'd gotten used to smelling Sean, whose system was flush with booze, chemicals, and those hormonal scents like animals put out when they're injured to keep scavengers away. I lay my cheek against Nathan's abdomen and felt his lungs rise and fall.

His nervous dick grew like a fetus inside the warm womb of my mouth. Fingers dug through my hair. Deep breaths gave way to short pants.

When I felt Nathan's erection reach its apex, I sat up and mounted him. The sex itself wasn't that important to me. But what I wanted badly was to consummate this night. I wanted for us to be unable to ignore it later. What I wanted was something new.

It was over in an instant. I lay down upon his chest. From below, I felt the tension drain from his limbs, as if I were lying on an air mattress with an open valve. After a glorious span of minutes, the anxiety returned to Nathan's body and he placed a shaking hand around my back. I took comfort in the fact that we were in this together. These mistakes, we made them as one.

I woke up to sunlight peeking in through the window of the room. Suddenly a little paranoid, I dressed and left without waking Nathan.

In my own room, Sean lay asleep. I squinted as the sun came in through our window. Outside, all sorts of people wandered about, busy as ants: Spaniards off to work, students at the cafés, a few tourists with bright backpacks. Watching them, I longed to be the kind of person who was outside during the daylight hours. I didn't want to be nocturnal anymore. How did I get mixed up with this race of vampires, thriving on blood and darkness?

I opened up the window and let the sounds of the street wash in. The air felt nice, even with the heat. At this hour, all the colors were more vivid, the contrasts sharper. It was like the world seen through a newly cleaned windshield after days of looking through a layer of dust. I sat on the sill and let my feet dangle from three stories up.

"Could you close the fucking window?" Sean's whining came from over my shoulder.

I didn't even turn around. "Did you know that you cut my head open last night, Sean?"

"What? I did not."

"You threw your guitar and didn't even see where it landed. It could've hurt me a lot worse." Still sitting in the window, I turned around to face him and pulled the Band-Aid off to one side.

Sean looked at my face and saw the cut for the first time. He threw up on the floor next to the bed—a cupful of half-digested wine as red as blood—then pulled the covers up over his head. That puddle of vomit, the stench of alcoholic bile, that's what sealed it.

"I'm quitting the band," I told him.

"I'm sorry," he moaned from under the sheet. "Don't do that. I'm sorry about your head. I'm an asshole and a fuckup and I can't do anything right." He poked his head out. "I didn't mean to."

I slammed the door as Sean went on. Downstairs, the clerk showed me a piece of paper with several phone messages. All were from Chip—some kind of hassle over the trashed dressing room, no doubt.

As crappy as this hotel was, its staff was the most pleasant and helpful. Through a series of hand gestures, I got the clerk to dial the number that had left the messages.

"Laura! How's it going?" I didn't expect Chip to be so animated.

"Fucking terrible! I just quit the band. I want a ticket home, from Madrid. I'm over this."

"Laura, you don't want to do that."

"Don't tell me what I want! My head's cut open. My room is covered in puke. Sean is a fucking maniac. I'm too old for this."

"Laura, listen to me——"

"No, you listen to me. Get me a plane ticket, or every musician in Seattle will know how you treat your talent!"

The hotel clerk looked at me with wide eyes.

"Your record went gold yesterday. It jumped over a hundred and fifty spots to number thirty-eight on the Billboard charts. Do you understand? It's in the top forty."

"What record?"

"Your record, Laura: *Bad Ideas Taken Way Too Far*. It's insane. Nobody expected this."

"The Mistakes record?" I laughed out loud. "But it's a punk rock album."

Chip let out a deep breath. "If that's so, then it may be the best-selling punk rock album ever. We're swamped here. The orders keep coming in. We already did one emergency pressing; we need to go for another."

"But I quit the Mistakes."

"Laura," Chip spoke slowly. "Your life is about to change. You need to do whatever you can to keep this band together and finish the tour. Doug and I will fly to Italy if we have to, as soon as the next pressing is under way. Do you understand me? I'm begging you here. Keep the Mistakes together at all costs."

I looked out the glass door of the hotel. On the other side of the street, a fruit stand was set up with bright apples and oranges. A dark-skinned man attended it and smiled at passersby. A woman in high heels and designer sunglasses walked past with a well-groomed dog on a leash. With a sly grin, I turned back to the hotel clerk, who stood opposite me at his desk. He returned a timid smile. Suddenly, I knew how to handle this.

"Send us money," I told Chip. "A lot of money. Put us up in a goddamn decent hotel in Italy—three rooms. And buy us some new instruments, for Christ's sake. Our gear is a disgrace."

Chip was taken aback. "Okay, first of all, let me check on the—"

"Good-bye." I took a page from Nathan's book and slammed down the phone.

Nathan and Sean both stood at the bottom of the stairs.

"What was that all about?" Sean asked.

"Our lives are about to change."

WASHINGTON, D.C.: NOVEMBER 1981

Catch your mother in the kitchen before she leaves for work. "Mom, could you Xerox something for me?"

She pauses, coffee mug in hand. "Of course, sweetheart."

Hand her the folder with your album cover. "It's eleven by fourteen. I hope that's okay."

She puts down her coffee cup and opens the folder. "That's a nice composition. It follows the golden ratio. Look how the eye gets drawn in." She traces a spiraling line along the shadow on the wall of your drawing, to the figure crouched in the corner.

"It's just something I drew." Hate it when she applies classical principles to your work. At times, her discipline and her profession seem to you little more than ways to take the fun out of art.

"You're very talented. I want you to know that."

"Helen, are you ready? I can't be late for this." Your father's voice sounds from the staircase. With haste, your mother puts the drawing back into your folder and then under her briefcase—not wanting to betray her closet support for the band.

Father comes to the kitchen, his tie twisted up at his neck. "A little help?"

She steps in close to him, wrapping and pulling on the colored cloth.

He turns to you. "Where's your brother?"

"The bakery." This is the latest in the series of low-paying jobs that Anthony takes on. "He needs money to pay the pressing plant for our record."

Dad rolls his eyes. "If you made music that was a bit more . . . palatable, maybe somebody else would pay for it."

"Whitman paid for *Leaves of Grass* himself." Anthony taught you to use this precedent.

"*Leaves of Grass* is an American classic!" your father snaps.

"Not when it first came out. People said it was trash. Whitman's own brother said it wasn't worth reading."

"Laura"—your mother finishes up the tying—"I wish we could get you to study for some reason other than arguing with us."

"Well." Father steps back. "Do I look like a department head?" He is well on the way to becoming the administrator that he is meant to be.

Your mother nods and gathers her things off the counter.

"What's that?" Father points to the folder with your drawing in it.

"Nothing," Mother says. "Something I need to copy is all."

They head out the door. Wonder if all marriage is like theirs: a subtle balance of secrets and insincerity, motivated mainly by the fear of being alone.

NINETEEN

The Rumble Strips didn't react well to the news of our record sales. They mumbled insincere congratulations and took to calling us "the rock stars." As in, "We can't leave yet, the rock stars aren't ready," or "That's the way the rock stars want it."

We dropped off the van and flew to Rome. Chip came through on the hotel—a cute place in the Trastevere district with air-conditioning. The Rumble Strips' one room was on the third floor. We were on the fourth.

The clerk opened three different doors, two on one side of the hall, one on the other.

"I think there's a mistake," Sean said. "We always share."

"All three rooms have been paid for," the clerk said.

"It's cool." I turned to Nathan and Sean. "I told Chip to get us three rooms. I wanted to boss him around a little." In the room that was alone on one side of the hall, I caught a glimpse of the view through the window—a little piazza with a fountain. Stray cats walked along the windows of an adjacent building. "Can I have this one?" I asked them. "Do you mind?"

Nathan grabbed a key from the clerk and walked into one of the other rooms. Sean dropped his bags in the last room, then came running into mine before I had a chance to shut the door.

"What the fuck?" he said. "What do you want your own room for all of a sudden?"

"You puked on the floor of our last room. There was blood and fire extinguisher foam all over. It's gross. I need some space. Relax. The label's paying for it."

"But I want to share with you!" He sounded like a child. I realized that he'd barely slept alone since leaving home.

"Sean, this isn't a big deal. I'm a girl. I want to take a bath and get my clothes cleaned. I'm sick of being cooped up with five boys all the time."

He looked at the ground.

"Why don't you go out with Nathan tonight? Italy's supposed to have a good rock scene. You might be famous here already." I put my hand on his shoulder.

He cocked his head. My ideas were little revelations to him.

"By the way, what's going on with your . . . condition? Are you seeing the colors again?"

"More or less," he said.

"What's that supposed to mean?"

"I'm still playing okay, right?"

"When you don't get too wasted," I said.

He nodded. We shared a second of silence.

"Get some rest, Laura." He kissed me on the lips for the first time in a while, and left.

I woke up around four in the morning. Outside my window, a couple of streetlights lit up the piazza. An old man pushed a wheeled cart down the stone alley. I smoked a cigarette and did a rough sketch of the way the fountain looked at night, but couldn't get into it. Sleep wasn't coming back to me, so I put my shoes on and left the hotel.

There was something amazing about walking around this city before sunrise. How many centuries had the most important people on the planet ambled these same streets? Without deciding to, I found myself headed toward St. Peter's. The basilica was open, and Catholic pilgrims already came in and out to light candles and pray. Inside, I immediately saw Michelangelo's *Pietà*. The facts that I'd memorized streamed through my head: the masterpiece of the artist's early years, the solution to the composition problem that had baffled his contemporaries— how to make a pyramid harmony from a full-grown man lying across the lap of a woman.

But soon, I forgot the context and saw only the timeless beauty of the piece. I thought of my brother, Anthony, the awful moment of him lying limp and motionless years ago, another young man whose beliefs mattered more than his life, who only in destruction became sacred.

I saw the look on poor Mary's face, the unconditional love. That kind of girl would be good for Sean: someone who cares for him no matter what, who lifts him up each time he falls.

After staring for a while, I didn't have the energy to see anything else. At a café nearby, I had the most delicious espresso I'd ever tasted. It made me recall my old boss Maxine, how she'd come to this country to find the passion that would govern the rest of her life.

Back at the hotel, our floor was a circus.

"Laura Loss!" some idiot shouted as I walked in the door, pointing a handheld video camera at my face. "How does it feel to be in the biggest band in the world?"

I stuck my middle finger into his camera lens and entered Nathan's room. Chip and Doug had arrived, playing the moguls in suits and ties. Doug talked on the hotel phone. A still photographer took a portrait of Nathan over by the window. That idiot with the handheld kept filming. Chip vigorously shook my hand.

"It's still selling." Chip's beard had been clipped in the middle, around his chin, so that now it was a pair of tremendous sideburns. "It's unbelievable. We've got to shoot a video as soon as you guys get home."

"A video?" I asked.

"MTV is pissed off that we don't have anything."

"They're buying us new guitars," Nathan said, as though this was the best news of all.

"Where's Sean?" I asked.

"Talking to Sid next door," Chip said. "He wants to interview all you guys one by one."

"Great," I said.

"Chip." Doug held his hand over the phone receiver. "They need the number."

Chip excused himself and took the phone.

Doug walked over to talk to me. "Laura." He shook my hand. "Congratulations."

"Thanks, Doug. Listen, with the record selling so well, maybe now would be a good time to give us a little money."

"Money?" Doug was taken aback. "Let's see. The royalties schedule totals up at the end of the month. But I could give you an advance, I suppose."

"That would be great, a little running-around cash."

"No problem," Doug said. "Just draw me up an IOU against the July earnings, sign it, and I'll write the check."

"An IOU?" *Was he kidding?* "Where can I cash your check in Italy?"

"Hey, Doug." Chip called him back over to the phone. "They need you here." The two of them again switched places.

"Don't worry about him," Chip said in a hushed tone. "Success has made Doug even more ultra-businesslike. Trust me, somebody on our team needs to be that way." Chip pulled out a big roll of Italian money. "Look at this; I'm a millionaire in lire." He peeled me off a stack of multicolored bills. "We'll call it even for the guitars we're about to buy the boys."

"Thanks, Chip." I sat down on the end of the bed.

Sean walked in from his room, along with the reporter. Sid was an older guy, with a gray Einstein-style mess of frizzy hair retreating up his scalp.

"Hey, Laura." Sean looked well rested for the first time in days. Without warning, he walked over, leaned down, and kissed me on the mouth. He ran his hand through my hair and rested it on my shoulder. A flashbulb went off in my eyes.

I felt the blood rush to my face. I'd been clear with Sean about showing affection in public, especially with the label guys and the press around. My eyes met Nathan's. He was equally shocked.

"Okay." Chip raised his voice to make an announcement. "Guitar shopping time. As most of you know, the venue has been changed for tonight, so we need to get there early for load-in. Nathan, Sean, let's go."

"Sean," I said, "can I talk to you for a second?" I dragged him across the hall, into my room, and shut the door. "What the fuck are you doing? I told you, this thing"—I pointed back and forth between the two of us—"nobody needs to know about it!"

"It's all right, Laura." He wasn't fazed. "I thought about what we said last night. I want to make it right."

A knock sounded on the door, then, "Sean, let's go."

"Can we talk about this later?"

"Fine," I said. "Go on."

We opened the door and Sean joined the caravan. My eyes caught Nathan's again. He looked hurt. I shrugged. As Chip the ringmaster led his circus to the stairs, Sid tapped me on the shoulder.

"Do you think we could talk for a few minutes?"

"No thanks," I said.

"Are you sure? Your label flew me here. I already spoke to Nathan and Sean. I'd love to hear what you have to say."

"Stick with the boys. They'll give you better quotes." I closed the door.

In the dressing room, Sean drank from a bottle of Jack Daniel's. His brand-new guitar strapped across his shoulder, he paced around the room, improvising little runs up and down the fretboard. They bought him a real Strat, made in the U.S.A., gloss-black with a white pick guard.

Nathan sat on a couch with a book on his lap, squeaking out the set list with a Sharpie. His new bass—a cream-colored Fender Precision—leaned against the wall.

The Rumble Strips came back covered in sweat, carrying equipment.

"Fucking tough crowd," Todd said, snare drum and high hat in his hands.

The theater stretched back and upward for what looked like a mile. It was packed with people, many in leather and spikes, spray-painted hair. For a moment, I thought it was a flashback to one of SCC's tours in the eighties, only none of those shows were this well attended.

This was the first place we'd played that had seating, but it was our most nonsedentary crowd. Everyone was down front or in the aisles. Cigarette and marijuana smoke hung in the air. A few rows back, somebody sliced open a chair cushion; foam and upholstery flew about.

There was a riser for the drums, a foot or two off the ground. The boys helped me get my kit set up. Sean brought the bottle of whiskey with him and took a slug after plugging in. I looked at the set list. "Nowhere Fast" was first up.

"Hello, beautiful people of Italy." Nathan spoke through the microphone. Chip and Doug and their entourage sat at the far right of the stage. "From America," Nathan continued, "we are the Mistakes."

Sean started that *tick-tick* line that had served us so well. The crowd dropped its shenanigans and looked up. It was like watching a few thousand people all try to make up their minds at once. By the first vamp, the audience was sold. Moshers took over every open space in the theater. People knew the words. Chip and Doug were pleased.

Sean had one of his high-energy shows. He disappeared into the crowd for a while during the middle of the set. Italian fans climbed up and jumped off the stage.

By the time we got to the closer, I would've called it a perfect show. I turned down to my set list and saw "Devil You Know" at the bottom. When I looked up, Nathan had turned around his microphone stand so that it faced me at the drums. A sudden emptiness overtook my stomach. Sean held the whiskey bottle halfway up to his lips, but paused when he saw what Nathan was doing. The crowd and the label guys didn't even notice.

We started the first slow verse. The crowd was uncharacteristically patient. Nathan sang with his eyes shut. He tortured every word as it came out of his mouth—*"you gave him a mile and he took an inch."*

Sean played his slide-style guitar licks with the neck of the Jack Daniel's bottle.

We hit the sped-up breakdown. It was like a three-way competition
among us to see who could play fastest. The moshing resumed. I stared
down at my snare and let my hair hang before my eyes. When I looked
back up, Sean stood on the corner of my drum riser, looking out at the
crowd. Then, like an Olympic diver, he launched himself up and seemed
to pause in midair, before landing squarely on the stage atop his brand-
new guitar.

He lay motionless, then curled into a fetal position. There was no
chance he'd finish the song. Nathan ran over to his friend. Chip and
Doug dropped their jaws. I was blinded by a flashbulb coming from
their direction.

Back at the hotel, I found Sean his pills. The bottle was nearly full and
the writing was in Italian. I fed him four and it helped immediately. As
he drifted off, he said, "Laura, I'm sorry for all of this shit. I'm sorry
for cutting your face. I'll fix it, I swear."

Finally he faded into a chemical-induced slumber. I left him there
and opened the unlocked door to Nathan's room.

The only light came from the bathroom and lit Nathan up from
the side. He sat on the professionally made bed, elbows resting on his
knees, head hanging forward. He looked up and wasn't surprised to
see me. This is what I'd wanted in Paris when I'd found the two
French girls instead. I shut the door behind me.

"I didn't want to sing it like that, Laura. I just couldn't go through
the motions anymore."

"Don't do this! Don't blame yourself!" I scolded, still standing in
front of the door. "Sean chucks himself off the drum riser, and you
want to beat yourself up about it. Don't you see that he gets himself
hurt onstage whenever he runs out of options? It's his fucking defense

mechanism, and you're the one who falls for it. It makes me crazy!"
Was it possible that I now understood them better than they understood each other?

Nathan dropped his head back down. "You've been right all along,"
he said. "Denying this—whatever is going on between us—that's the
worst thing we could do, to us and to him."

"*This*"—I pointed back and forth between the two of us—"is
called falling in love." Nathan looked embarrassed at the term. "And
we can figure it out. Let me talk to Sean. It's the idea of a girlfriend
that he wants; it isn't me. I'm the last person on earth that's right for
him. Now, with this album out, him on the cover, he can have any girl.
I'm telling you, we can make this work. We can keep the band together."

"You'll talk to him, break it off?" Nathan wanted to make sure he
understood.

"Tomorrow," I said.

"You won't tell him about us, about that night, not yet at least."

"Not if you don't want me to."

"We'll chill out for a while?"

I sat down beside him on the bed. "What do you mean, 'chill out'?"

"I don't want to sneak around behind his back. That wouldn't be
right."

"Nathan." I put my hands up around his face and turned his head
so that our eyes met. "As far as right and wrong goes, the damage is
done."

That night, as Nathan and I made love for the second time, I was
doubly sure that this was what I wanted, where I belonged. I can only
assume that Nathan, too, saw our future couplehood as an ends that
justified these temporarily devious means. The best part was falling
asleep in his arms afterwards. For the first time, we had something
like a plan, a future to look forward to. In a city with centuries of love
and betrayal layered atop one another, there were a handful of dark

hours in which Nathan and I, for the first and only time in our lives, were like man and wife.

As the sun rose out the window, I pried myself from his sleeping arms and went back to my own room, smiling like a teenager in spite of the unsavory task I had ahead of me that day.

WASHINGTON, D.C.: DECEMBER 1981

The records arrive from the pressing plant. Anthony calls a band meeting—not to be confused with a practice.

"Here's some scissors," Anthony says, "and glue." On the table, he places the plastic cubby full of art supplies that the two of you once used to make Mother's Day cards and macaroni drawings. Old sequins and dry noodles lie scattered at the bottom.

"Here are the sleeves." Anthony places a stack of Xeroxed pages—courtesy of your mother's office—alongside the cubby. It's a nice representation of your drawing. SECOND CLASS CITIZENS is written across the top. At the bottom: AUTOPILOT RECORDS in bold blocky letters.

"What we need to do," Anthony says, "is cut these out along the lines here." He demonstrates with the first paper on the stack. "Then put the glue along these tabs. Not too much, or the thing won't open. Once that dries, we stick in a record." He holds up his hands as if to show how simple it is.

Hank's mouth hangs slack and open. "How many of those are there?"

"One thousand."

"You're shitting me."

"I'm not shitting you." Anthony starts on the second sleeve.

"Don't they have a machine that does this?" Hank collapsed his shoulders to show frustration.

"Who is *they*?" Anthony says. "There's no *they* out there that wants to come and record us. Get it? There's us, me and you. And no, we don't have any machines. We got glue, and scissors, and time."

To defuse the argument, pick up another uncut sleeve from off the stack and a pair of scissors. Billy, still silent, follows your lead. With a great sighing and rolling of eyes, Hank joins in. A two-liter bottle of Mountain Dew and a bag of Doritos are passed around the circle. Crumbs and orange cheese powder get caught in the glue along the seams, but nobody minds.

A wide and painful paper cut opens on your thumb, and the next few sleeves have a red circle of blood on the back cover. Ask Anthony if that's okay.

"Fine," he says. "Sealed with blood. It's kind of cool."

TWENTY

I woke up around noon, and went to check on Sean first thing. His equipment and clothes were still strewn about the room, but he was missing. I went next door to Nathan's. Same thing: the room was unlocked, everything there except my bandmate.

I had a paranoid notion that maybe Nathan had taken things into his own hands and decided to talk to Sean himself. On the stairs, I passed Todd from the Rumble Strips. He was eating gelato, his lips and tongue brown with the chocolate.

"Where is everybody?" I asked.

"I guess they're still at the hospital."

"What?"

"Sean banged on Nathan's door early this morning. He was in a lot of pain, once the drugs wore off. They got Chip and Doug up and went off to some emergency room."

"What hospital?" I asked. How long after I'd left Nathan's bedroom this morning had Sean entered it?

"Fuck if I know." He put another spoonful of gelato in his mouth. "It had an Italian name."

Several reporters leapt up at the sight of me, their cameras clicking as I got out of the cab. I pushed through them the way I'd been taught by television and entered the hospital.

Chip leaned against the wall beside a closed door, flipping through a magazine. "Laura!" he called out.

"Why didn't anybody wake me up?"

"I'm sorry," Chip said. "It all happened so fast."

"What's going on?" I looked through the window in the door over Chip's shoulder. Sean lay on the hospital bed, asleep, Nathan in a chair by his side.

"He broke a couple ribs." Chip lowered his voice. "The problem is, his liver is swollen. Normally, with a broken rib, they give pain meds and wait for them to heal. But now, they're concerned about all the pills he's been taking, mixed with the—" Chip made the international sign for drinking, his hand tipping up an imaginary bottle. "So, the doctors are a bit confused, to say the least. I don't need to tell you that it would be best if we could keep this pills-and-booze thing out of the press."

I hated being the last to know about this. "Can't they give him non-narcotic painkillers?"

"That's the thing. The anti-inflammatory stuff is even worse on the liver. They shot him full of morphine just now."

We both turned and looked through the window in the door.

"At least he's got you, though. That must help," Chip said.

"What do you mean by that?" I was dumbstruck.

"You know, a strong girl by his side. That means a lot. Congratulations, by the way. You're good at keeping a secret." Chip smiled.

"What the fuck are you talking about?" I felt the floor move under my feet.

"You and Sean." Chip turned to me. "Didn't you see this yet?" He handed me the magazine he'd been reading, cover bent around to an article in the middle. There was a large photo of Sean with his hand on my shoulder, from the hotel. The caption underneath read: *A Match Made in Grunge Heaven.*

"What the hell? Who told them we were a couple?"

"Sean did. It's full of quotes from his interview with Sid."

"That was yesterday." This couldn't be happening, could it?

Chip shrugged. "Sid flew to London instead of going to the show. He wanted to drop the flag on this one."

"You should've stopped this!" I raised my voice. "You guys should be handling the press."

"Stop it? This is great PR. It's a whole family vibe now. You two are like the Ike and Tina of grunge."

I felt vertigo. I put my hands against the hospital wall for support. A couple lines of text from the magazine caught my eye.

> *"We've been in love for a while," Purvis says. "But we didn't want to go public with it. Now, with the band moving to the next level, there'll be more attention and I don't want to keep any secrets."*

Sean had never once told me that he loved me in person. I leaned over and put my head between my knees.

Chip was confused. He put a hand on my back. "What's the problem? It's cute."

I stood up straight again. "What if I want to break up with him now?"

Chip laughed softly. "I wouldn't do that, if I were you." He looked at my face and saw that I wasn't being hypothetical. "Seriously, Laura— you break that kid's heart, and they'll crucify you in the press. He's the poster-boy for a whole new generation of high school shoegazers. They worship Sean."

Imagine what they'd think of me cuckolding him with his best friend.

Just then, Nathan walked out of the hospital room. The door swung shut behind him. He looked at me briefly and then turned to Chip. "Cancel the rest of the tour."

"Now, don't overreact," Chip said. "We got tonight's show postponed. After that, there's only a few gigs left. He'll be fine if he lays off the booze. Eastern Europe is a stronghold for us."

"I said cancel it!" Nathan shouted. "We're going home."

"I'm sorry to say this, Nathan. But you can't go." Chip did seem genuinely sorry. "You signed a contract. You're bound to finish this tour."

"Is that right?" Nathan stepped closer to Chip and got right into his face. "You want to talk about my fucking contract? That's my best friend on that bed!"

Chip backed away a couple of steps. He held his hands up in the air, waiting for Nathan to calm down.

"Here's a contract for you, motherfucker." In a flash of winding limbs, Nathan landed a solid punch to Chip's jaw. Chip spun around and fell onto his hands.

I cried over by the door and stuffed the magazine underneath my armpit, so I could wipe at the tears with my shirt. Out of the four of us Americans in that hospital, it seemed to me that Chip was the least deserving of a punch.

"That was stupid," Chip said once he was back on his feet. He held his fingers up to his lower lip and saw that it was bleeding. "You belong to my label, all of you do. I own your music! You could've been the biggest band in the world. Now you won't be shit!"

Unfortunately, whenever anybody said something like that to us, it meant only greater and more unwieldy success.

"The Mistakes are over," Chip continued as he retreated under the fluorescent lights of the hospital hallway.

"Get the fuck out of here," Nathan called to him.

I sobbed harder into my hands. I was sad for Chip, sad for myself, sad for both of these boys and what I'd made and unmade out of them.

Nathan put his arm around my shoulder. "We need to find a new label," he said. "Who did Puddle-jumper sign with again?"

Our label problem was a distant second to the most pressing thing on my mind. I held out the magazine that I'd stashed under my armpit. "He talked to that reporter," I said to Nathan in between sobs. "He told him we're in love. That I'm his girlfriend."

Nathan took the magazine from me and wrinkled up his brow. "What? I thought you said it was only the idea of a girlfriend? That's not what it says here!"

I grabbed a hold of Nathan's hand. "I'll still do it. I'll break it off. The press and the fans can stick needles in my voodoo doll. I don't care."

"No!" Nathan said. "Forget it. He loves you. I can't do this. We . . . you and me, can't happen. It's not right." He put his fingers up to his temples and rubbed them. "I want to go home. Last night should've never happened."

That's the moment that broke my heart the most. Not losing the label that had given us our shot, not the public announcement of my relationship to a boy I didn't love, not seeing my band nearly torn apart by chemicals and incest—it was that last part, where Nathan and I ceased to err together and in the same direction, and I was left to make my mistakes while he made his.

THREE

TWENTY-ONE

The boys went off to Missoula. I flew back to Seattle. Royalties poured in, along with apologies from Gawk Rawd. Doug left messages and sent notes with the checks. Their lawyers must've explained that breaking the contract would be the biggest favor they could do us.

With the first couple checks, I made a down payment on a two-bedroom house up on Magnolia Bluff, not far from Discovery Park. A team of movers hauled all the crap from my Belltown apartment, where the Mistakes had started. The new place wasn't convenient for public transportation, so I bought myself a Saab station wagon as well. It was no Mercer Island and still technically part of the city, but going this far from the commercial district—from the homeless shelters, the biker bars, the loud nightclubs—did feel like moving up. My neighbors were upwardly mobile home owners. They had careers, cars, firsthand furniture, even children.

Many of my hours were spent shopping for housewares. I bought nice cooking utensils for the kitchen. The spatulas and ladles had a satisfying weight in my hand—even if I used them only for heating soup or frying eggs. A full set of knives stood like a sentinel inside a wooden block upon my counter.

I took my cigarettes for walks around the loop in Discovery Park, and on clear days had a view of the water. The happy people of Magnolia—now my neighbors, formerly my customers—were out in their Windbreakers, walking their dogs. A family of obese rabbits lived in a bramble of weeds and trees in the center of the main loop. Whenever one wandered too far from their lair, an unleashed dog would chase it back, barking. The rabbit's swollen belly swung and bounced between its two front feet as it hopped back to the safety of the hole. The dog would be stuck sniffing, butt in the air, while its owner called it back.

Bad Ideas continued to climb the charts. Finding a new label wasn't easy. Whoever took on the Mistakes would have to buy out our contract with Gawk Rawd—which wouldn't be cheap, under the circumstances. Furthermore, word had gotten out about Nathan punching our last label executive in the face. We'd gained a reputation, quite deservedly, as a problem band.

After a dozen phone calls, exactly two labels were willing to talk. Kingdom Records, who had signed Puddle-jumper, was very interested and the obvious choice. Eager to secure a bigger piece of the Seattle pie, they seemed to think we'd offer them some kind of grunge legitimacy, even if we didn't earn them a ton of money.

The only other label was SGM, who'd had some financial troubles lately and looked at us as a Hail Mary. They were disorganized over the phone and gave me a bad vibe. Still, I thought it best that we entertain more than one option, for the sake of negotiation.

Nathan called from Missoula, and I told him the details.

"Do you know those guys from Pearl Jam?" he asked.

"I saw some of them in other bands a while back."

"Their bass player is from around here. Who's putting their album out?"

"Epic. I called them. They're not interested in us."

"I see," he said. "Kingdom sounds like the best bet."

"I think so, too. But let's stay open-minded."

"Right on," he said.

"So you'll get the tickets?"

"Yeah, there's a travel agency downtown."

"How's Sean?"

"He's okay, hasn't been partying or anything."

"That's cool."

"I guess I'll see you in L.A."

"I guess so."

"Good-bye, Laura."

"Bye."

I always spoke to Nathan, and our conversations were all business. He tried his best to be cold and distant over the phone. The moment Sean announced our relationship to the public, it began to exist only in the eyes of the public. I hadn't talked to him in days and couldn't remember the last time we had sex. But candid photographs of the two of us—some of which must've been doctored together—appeared on the covers of music magazines, along with articles about our nonexistent love life.

"Where is Sean?"

The voice first sounded in my dream: I stood alone upon an enormous stage, in front of a stadium full of people, all waiting in silence. There was an oversize cock rock drum set, complete with double bass and gong. Marshall amps, stacked several cabinets high, lined either side of the drum riser.

"Where is Sean?"

At the foot of center stage, standing before the sea of heads that stretched on to infinity, was a little girl—much too young to be at a rock concert—asking for Sean. I looked around for anybody at all— Sean, Nathan, Anthony. There was no one to help me please this one little girl and the legion of fans that sat so silent in their seats.

I turned over to my other side, hoping for a better dream. Then came the voice again: "Where is Sean?" more demanding this time. I was too scared to move. Somebody was in my bedroom.

"Where is Sean?"

Like a spring, I shot myself up into a ball by the headboard, bringing my knees and elbows into my body. In the yellowish glow from the streetlamps outside my window, I saw her. She wore a flannel shirt and ripped blue jeans. Her hair was cut with short bangs and a braid on each side. She was tall and chubby, shaped like she hadn't grown into her body yet.

"Where is Sean?"

"Who the fuck are you? What are you doing in my house?" I asked through hurried breaths.

"I'm Andrea." She spoke like a frustrated child. "I'm only the biggest fan the Mistakes have!"

"How did you get in here?"

"Through the window, silly."

My heart knocked against my chest so hard, it hurt. I pulled myself even farther into the headboard, so my feet were underneath me.

"Now, where is Sean?" she said. "He should be here with you."

"He's in Montana." I tried to keep my voice calm. I needed to get out of this room.

"You let him go to Montana by himself? You need to take care of him, Laura!"

"Shut up!" I made a break for it. At first, I considered pushing her down on my way, but she was bigger than me and I couldn't risk a wrestling match. Instead I ran past this strange girl, down the stairs, and into the kitchen.

From the wooden block on the counter, I grabbed the biggest chef knife of the brand-new set. I pointed it toward the bottom of the stairs but didn't see Andrea. My hand shook so bad that I dropped the cordless phone on the counter in my first attempt to remove it from its cradle. It took three tries before I was able to dial 911.

"Yes, somebody is in my house. I think she's crazy. Please come as quick as you can."

"Address, please."

I almost gave them my old Belltown one. Luckily, a piece of junk mail lay on the counter. I read off my street and number. Footsteps descended the stairs.

"Don't you come any closer!" I screamed before she'd even rounded the corner. Standing behind the counter, the knife in my hand, it felt as if I were guarding my refrigerator.

"You don't have to be so dramatic," she said. "We're all friends."

In the light of the living room, I saw that her hair was dyed jet black. She had a silver stud through her nostril. One of the living room windows was still open where she must've come in.

"The cops are on their way," I said. "You stay right fucking there." I did my best to project a false sense of calm.

"Oh my god, Laura. You didn't have to do that. Don't you read my letters?"

"Shut up. Don't talk."

"What are you doing sending Sean off to Montana? You should go with him. Sean is special. He has a gift."

Tears streamed down my face. "Don't say one more word about Sean or me, or I swear to God I will cut your fucking throat!"

"Pshh." She rolled her eyes. "You'll cut me. Well, that's great. You know something, Laura, I love you and all, but you should think about treating your fans a little better."

That's when I lost it. "My fans? Treat my fucking fans a little bit better? Treat you maniacs better? Let me tell you something about fans: I've given my whole life to making them happy!"

The colored lights of police cars danced outside. This emboldened me further. I walked around the counter and waved the knife in Andrea's face. "All you people have ever brought me is misery! You spit on me and my brother. You beat us up, blamed us for everything that was wrong with your own lives. And you didn't even have the decency to kill him! Only you and your fucking fans could come up with something worse than dying!"

I heard the door and intended to open it once I'd said my piece. The blue strands of hair hanging before my eyes were wet with tears and spittle.

"I don't owe you fuckers anything. I don't need to stay in any bad relationship because you assholes want it that way. Do you hear me?" I held the knife right at her eye level. "Say it, you bitch! Say that I can do what I want! Say I can love who I want to love. Say it!"

Andrea remained composed. She turned her face away from the knife a little, as though it had a bad smell.

"Say it!"

The door exploded with a crack. Suddenly, I was face-first on the ground.

"No! You idiots, this is my house. I'm the one that called you guys!"

The cops administered some manner of armlock and cuffed my hands behind my back. I groaned with pain. Andrea picked up the chef knife and put it back in the block on the counter where it belonged, as if this were her house—which was exactly what the policemen believed.

I expected them to choke me with their nightsticks. Instead, the two cops picked me up by my armpits and hauled me out through my own front door. All along, I screamed that they had the wrong woman.

Outside, several of my neighbors had turned on their lights and stood at their doorways in pajamas. Dogs barked from their masters' sides. They must've thought that either I was a prowler or that this was some sort of white trash domestic dispute.

The cops put me in the caged back of the squad car. One officer sat in the driver's seat while the other spoke to Andrea on the stoop.

"Officer"—being in the cage had a kind of calming effect—"I know how this looks. But I swear I'm the one who lives here. I called 911. My name is Laura Loss. There's mail on the counter addressed to me. My driver's license is in my wallet upstairs."

"What were you doing with that knife in her face?" This cop was Latino and had an accent that sounded East Coast. He was stocky, like a former athlete, with close-cropped hair.

"I was protecting myself! What does the victim usually do in a thing like this? Offer her a cup of tea? Ask if she wants to hold the knives?"

We sat there in silence for a few minutes. My neighbors stared on. Some of them pointed. My attempt to live like a normal person wasn't even a week old and already had proved itself a disaster. It wasn't a matter of how I looked or where I lived. I was born into outcast-dom.

Finally the other cop came over and leaned at the car window. He was older, with thick graying hair. There was a distinguished look to him; he could've been a once-famous actor, an aging leading man.

"Get a load of this. She says she doesn't live here. It's her friend Laura's house. She says she came over to visit."

"That's what I've been saying. I'm Laura. It's my house."

The older cop turned to me. "Do you know that girl?" he asked.

"No. I'm a musician. She's a fan. She thinks were friends but we've never met before. She's fucking crazy."

"Run this for me, will you." The older cop handed the younger one a card.

"Bingo!" The younger cop jumped out of the car and drew his gun.

That seemed like overkill as Andrea stood there in the threshold, without any weapons, waiting for this whole thing to be over so that she could give me more advice.

"Ms. Loss," the older cop said, "I am so sorry about this." He unlocked my handcuffs and took me out of the backseat.

I rubbed my wrists and leaned against the cruiser. "Motherfucking cops," I muttered.

"Please accept our apologies. You have to understand how it looked."

"Could you understand how this looks to all of my new neighbors?" I gestured toward the house next door. Looking self-conscious, the couple retreated inside.

"I am sorry," he said again. I could tell he was genuine but that made me no less angry.

"Hands behind your back!" Up in my doorway, the younger cop had Andrea facedown on the ground.

"Is that really necessary?" I asked the older cop.

"Oh, that." He took the handcuffs that I'd just been in and ran them up to his partner. I took several steps away as the young cop led Andrea to the car. The older one walked me back to my front door. At last, the roles were fully reversed. I stood in the doorway while Andrea sat in the backseat cage.

"This girl appears to have escaped from an institution," the cop explained. "If you want to press charges, it probably won't change things much."

"Whatever," I said.

"Again, I'm sorry about the mix-up. By the way," he said, "what's the name of your band?"

"The Mistakes." I looked over his shoulder at Andrea in the car. I felt sympathy for her. It was a thin line that separated the two of us. Tonight was the first time I'd ever called the police to my aid, after years of being hurt and hassled by them. What would Anthony think of this? I was a home owner now—one of the fortunate few they protected.

"The Mistakes?" the cop asked. "The band that sings that 'Devil You Know' song?"

"You've heard of us?"

"My son has your album. Do you think I could get an autograph for him?"

"No," I said, and shut the door. My doorknob was now worthless where the police had broken in, but the dead bolt still worked. With every single light in the house turned on, and all the windows shut tight, I sat up the rest of the night drinking Cold Wars and smoking cigarettes, the chef knife on my lap, thinking about both my fans and my neighbors, wondering if I would ever relate to either of them.

The day before my flight to L.A., I walked through the park. A sunbreak loomed in the sky. The dogs and their walkers all looked up at it.

Then I noticed something. On a bench at the far end of the park, an older man with a beard sat and petted a dog off the leash. I hadn't met any of my neighbors, but this was certainly someone I knew. I walked closer. Then it hit me.

"Bob? Is that you?"

He looked up at me.

"It's me, Laura," I said. "From the Daily Grind."

"Of course, Laura!" He scooted to one side of the bench. "Have a seat."

Bob and I sat down side by side. The dog's owner came by and reattached the leash, careful not to make eye contact with us.

"You must have left the coffee shop," Bob said. "I haven't seen you there."

"Look." I pointed to a roof behind two other roofs on one of the streets below the park. "That's my house—I own the thing."

"Really?" Bob said. "So rock and roll can pay the bills after all."

"The band I'm in, we're huge. We're in the top forty. There are pictures of me on music magazines." Even from my own mouth, I waited to hear the catch.

"That's great!" he said. "Congratulations."

"I guess." I shrugged. "It feels weird more than anything. I never wanted to be famous. But if these kids don't buy our records, they'll buy some shittier music by some other assholes, right?" It made a kind of sense, my justification.

"I know what you mean," Bob said. "In art, and also in life, it's important not to mistake irrelevance for integrity."

Needing to digest that sentence, I nodded and lit up another cigarette. "What are you doing in this neighborhood?"

"I used to live near here, back when I worked for Boeing. I still like to walk in this park sometimes."

I smiled at the thought of it. "We might have been neighbors, if not for all those layoffs."

"I was never laid off, Laura. I quit."

The two of us looked straight ahead, as if he were driving and I was the passenger.

"I always thought you were a casualty of that airline slump back in the seventies."

"That's the rumor that went around. I never did anything to fight it. But the truth is: I never worked on passenger jets. I was part of the Apollo project, and after that fizzled out I worked on Boeing's bid for the new Advanced Tactical Fighter." I stole a glance at his face and detected a somber tone there, like I'd seen in the Virgin Mary's marble eyes back in Rome.

"You did military jets, with weapons and all?"

"For a bit," he said. "Then I left."

"I see."

"I've been thinking about that time a lot lately, what with this Gulf War business. It's as you say, Laura: If I didn't do it, somebody else would, maybe somebody less competent. This was doubly true in that case. We were competing for the contract with several firms, some less responsible than others."

Across the park, a dog chased one of the fat rabbits into the bramble of weeds. I realized that an entire war had begun and ended since I last spoke to Bob.

"But on the other hand," he continued, "I couldn't help thinking that perhaps, if we all refused to do things we weren't comfortable with—pulling triggers, building bombs, designing weapons—then the world might be a bit better off. I mean, what could be easier? Just stop. Stop doing whatever it is you're not okay with."

I was at a loss for words. He needed some sort of consolation, but I was out of my league. Bob was the one who gave me advice, not the other way around. The running dog gained several feet, but the fat rabbit made it into the hole with half a second to spare.

"But as you can see, my not working hasn't prevented any wars."

The dog's head disappeared inside the rabbit hole. Its tail wagged hard.

"Bob, remember what you told me once about sacrifice?" For some reason, I found myself fighting back tears. "Is that like, 'If you let something go, it'll come back to you' sort of thing?"

"No, Laura." Still staring straight ahead, Bob looked as though he might cry as well. "A sacrifice is when you abandon your desire completely. It's not a way to get what you want, but you might get something you didn't expect."

The sunbreak had grown bigger. I looked up and felt the warm light drape over me like a blanket.

"I have to go," I said.

At the house, I was surprised by a young man in white coveralls standing by my stoop, waiting with a clipboard and a toolbox. A van was parked up the street with the logo of a private security company.

"Laura Loss?" The man read off the clipboard.

"Did the cops send you?" I asked.

"No, ma'am. We don't work like that. By the way, it's an honor to meet you. I'm a big fan. That said, we take confidentiality very seriously. Our firm works with a lot of high-profile clients for whom privacy is key. Sorry to hear about your break-in, by the way."

"How did you hear about it?" Speaking of privacy.

"It was in the papers."

I looked at my neighbors' houses. Had one of them talked to the press? Had the cops? "Who the fuck sent you to my house?"

He squinted at his clipboard, using his finger to follow the lines. "Nathan Sullivan. Hey, the lead singer, right?" He looked up, grinning, then seemed to recall the company's privacy policy. "He didn't tell you we were coming?"

My emotions did a 180. In spite of his bulldog front, Nathan was still concerned about me.

"Come on in," I said to the man. "You better get started. I'm leaving town tomorrow morning."

Things would never work out under the circumstances, with all of us in the same band. More and more, I wondered if I wanted to be in this band anymore. As a child, I'd helped make something out of nothing. Now, I had commercial success. What was left?

The royalties from this record wouldn't keep up forever. But I still hadn't been paid for the biggest month of sales so far. With that check, I could pay my house off. If the Mistakes made another record, this time on a major label and with a professional marketing scheme, there was no reason why I couldn't buy another house. I could buy a duplex and rent it out, go back to school perhaps. It might not be the life of a rock star, but I might be happier than most rock stars.

This idea took hold: Stick it out for one more album with the Mistakes, then quit for good. Nathan and Sean could have their pick of better drummers. I tried to stay rational about all this, convince myself that it came down to dollars and cents and our own well-being. But every so often, little thoughts started up like brush fires in my mind, threatening to burn through my whole psyche. Maybe, if I was no longer a part of the Mistakes and out of the public eye, then Nathan and I could be together.

WASHINGTON, D.C.: APRIL 1981

You hang out in the back of the community center, smoking one of Hank's cigarettes. The boys played a couple of bad shows together a while back, but this is your debut.

"Don't worry." Hank reads your mind. "You'll be fine."

Nod and exhale the smoke.

"Trust me. All these kids want is some noise they can slam dance to."

Love the way cigarettes burn in the spring, the smoke going down cold into your lungs and coming back out as a steaming cloud.

"Better go tune." Hank crushes his smoke into the gum-rubber sole of his skate shoe. You grind yours into the brick wall and then slip it into the Dumpster.

Before Hank opens the door to go back inside, Anthony comes out. "There's soda in the dressing room," your brother says.

"Cool." Hank heads in and the heavy door swings shut behind him.

Smile at Anthony, then tilt your head down. Pretend to study the black X drawn on the back of your hand. Anthony has already aligned himself with the fledgling straight-edge movement, but surely he must know that you've been sneaking cigarettes with Hank. Perhaps it's first on the list of things that the two of you don't talk about.

In many ways, straight edge chose Anthony. He never cared for any sort of substances. That monastic quality is what set him apart from the rest of the band. But passing judgment wasn't his style either.

"You feeling okay?" he asks.

"Yeah, good."

"You don't have to do this, Laura, if you don't want to."

"What do you mean?" Isn't this what both of you want? Isn't this what it's all been leading up to?

"Just what I said. It's your choice. Don't perform to make me happy."

"I'm not. I want to." This is true. You want to do it.

"Good. Then remember: If you're not nervous, if you're not scared, then you're probably doing something wrong, or not doing enough."

Nod.

Suddenly, Anthony puts his arms around you and gives you a tight embrace. As a family, you've never been physically affectionate. It feels a bit awkward. Return the hug. Press your head into his shoulder.

"You'll do fine," Anthony says.

TWENTY-TWO

My flight arrived in LAX before the boys. I waited at the terminal where they were meant to disembark.

In their decomposing denim and flannel, they stood out from the rest of the passengers.

"Hey, Laura." Sean smiled.

"Good to see you." Nathan had trouble maintaining eye contact.

Two other boys stood behind Nathan and Sean, in their same disheveled dress code. They looked familiar from the shows and parties in Montana.

"Who are these guys?" I asked.

"This is Brian and Will," Sean said in a self-satisfied tone. "We brought them with us from Missoula."

"You have an entourage now," I said.

Everyone laughed as if it were a joke.

I picked up the key to the room I'd reserved and left the boys to figure out the rest. After dropping off my bags, I smoked a cigarette at the railing above the pool. The sun was strong and felt luxurious against my skin.

By the time I'd finished the smoke, the boys had all piled into one hotel room. They flipped through the channels and joked about finding porn.

"Let's go," I said to Nathan and Sean. "The first appointment."

Their four faces turned to me. I felt like a mom telling them it was time for school.

Nathan stood up and said, "All right guys, let's take care of business."

"They don't need to come." I still hadn't addressed Brian or Will directly.

"I want them to come." Nathan finally made eye contact with me.

"Fine," I said.

Kingdom had somebody waiting for us in the lobby of their building. Our music played in the background. The receptionist told Brian and Will to wait downstairs while we went up to meet with the executive that I'd spoken to over the phone.

His name was Michael Sinclair. He wore a baggy black suit without a tie, the jacket draped over a chair. Full of product, his shining hair lay flat against his forehead. The office windows looked out onto the city, gold records along the walls.

"Now," he said, "let's cut to the chase. You guys need a label, and fast. This is the most important time in the life of your record, and you're walking around in limbo. That's fucked up. We want a video, right away, like tomorrow. The creatives already have a set in the works. An outstanding director, the one who did the Puddle-jumper videos, is waiting for a green light. Then"—he nodded his head and let out a dark laugh—"we've got to get a national tour under way. I cannot believe there's no tour to support this record. Anyways, we recommend Liquid

Management; we work well with them. I will personally handle the buyout from Gawk Rawd."

"Wait a minute." Nathan stopped him. "We just got back from Europe. I don't know if we're ready to go out on the road already. And this video, I mean, don't we get some say what it's going to look like? Shouldn't it be us who chooses the director?"

Michael didn't miss a beat. "Nathan, let me ask you something. Have you tried to find your record in a store lately?"

"No."

"That's good, because you can't find it. Your do-it-yourself label, they can't keep up with demand. Now this is what you have to ask yourselves: Do you want to keep playing for a thousand people, hoping to sell some T-shirts so you can afford dinner, or do you want to go to the next level? With a smaller label, you will have more freedom and control. But I'll tell you what. If you want to stay indie, you better patch things up with Gawk Rawd, because there is no small label out there with the capital to buy out the contract you signed. That I will guarantee you. In a perfect world, things wouldn't be so rushed, we'd have time to hammer out these decisions. But we're under the gun here. This record is hot, and we can't let it slip through our fingers. That's just business."

Michael slid a clipboard across the table. "You sign this piece of paper and you'll be shooting a video tomorrow, touring with Puddlejumper by the end of the month. The figure at the bottom is your advance, but I'll warn you that taxes and fees will take a cut. Still, that's the best I can do, considering what we'll be paying to your old label. Two full-lengths, standard royalties agreement. It's up to you."

"Who's the headliner?" Nathan glanced at the numbers on the contract. "On the tour with Puddle-jumper?"

"Well, guys." Michael smiled and put his arms out at his sides. "I don't look forward to telling Puddle about this. But from what I've heard, there's no way they could follow you."

We all smiled. Sean's eyes lost their gloss and momentarily beamed.

"What if we agree to just one album, for now?" I asked.

Michael looked at me and paused, as if that was the last thing he expected me to ask. "Well, we'd have to cut the advance in half."

I nodded, treating it like a hypothetical question. The contract sat on the table. Both Nathan and Sean looked at me. If it were up to them, they would've signed just to avoid the afternoon meeting.

"It's interesting," I said at last. "We need some time to think about it."

"And you have a meeting with SGM this afternoon," Michael said.

"How'd you know that?" I asked.

"It's my job to know these things. Don't worry. It makes sense. You guys should explore the options. Trust me, I know those guys at SGM." He let out another of his dark laughs. "I'm not worried."

Then an awkward moment of silence.

"So," I said. "We can call you?"

"Of course, here's my card. Let me walk you out."

We went out through the glass doors, where the noise of phones ringing and assistants chatting was suddenly loud. Downstairs, Brian and Will waited with cans of soda in their hands.

"They gave us free pop!" Brian said as we approached.

Michael shook each of our hands. "What do you all want for lunch? It's on us. We'll have somebody take you."

"Hamburgers?" It was the first word Sean spoke to Michael.

"Done."

A limo took the five of us to an outdoor café. It had a fifties theme, with burgers and milk shakes. Once Brian and Will had their mouths full, I brought up the deal.

"So, what do you guys think?"

Nathan shrugged. "He seems serious."

"No shit, he's serious," I said. "It's a lot of money they're talking about spending on us."

"I didn't know we'd have to tour again so soon," Sean said.

"It'll be different this time," I told him. "We'll have a big bus, road-ies, the works."

"Let's see how it goes with SGM," Nathan said.

"Excuse me." Two teenage girls in heavy metal T-shirts material-ized by our table. "Aren't you guys the Mistakes?" one of them asked.

"Guilty." Nathan smiled. I enjoyed seeing his charming side come back out. He'd kept it well hidden from me all day.

"Could we take a photo of you?"

"Brian," he ordered, "take a picture of us with their camera."

We posed for the shot. Sean put his arm around me, the most affec-tion he'd shown since the last time we were photographed together. I went back to my burger while Nathan chatted.

"We can't find your album anywhere," said one of the girls. "My friend has the CD, and we've all been making tapes."

"We heard about that," Nathan said. "We're in town trying to get that sorted out."

"Are you playing a show in L.A.? I don't know anybody who's seen you in concert yet."

"We got back from Europe a couple of weeks ago. We're still set-ting up an American tour."

Brian and Will nudged each other and giggled while Nathan spoke.

"Thanks for the picture. We should let you finish eating. I hope you come to play in California soon."

"We're staying at the Vista Hills hotel!" Will shouted at them. "Stop by later for a drink."

"Yeah?" one of the girls said. She looked to Nathan for confirma-tion.

"Sure," Nathan said timidly. "Stop by if you like."

I took a big bite of my burger and chewed. Nathan sipped on his milk shake as the girls walked away. Once they were out of earshot, he turned to Will. "Please don't go around telling people what hotel we're staying in."

At SGM, we were met by a man with a Southern accent who called himself Jimmy. He chewed vigorously on a piece of gum, shaking hands with all of us, including Brian and Will.

"All right." He grinned. "All y'all in this band or what?"

"Just the three of us." I pointed at Sean and Nathan.

"Well, let's talk, shall we? These guys coming, too?"

All five of us filed upstairs into a conference room with leather rolling chairs.

"Everybody take a seat over on that side there," Jimmy said. "Who wants a drink? You all hungry or what?" He didn't wait for an answer, but pressed a button on a telephone and said, "Yeah, Susan, have somebody run downstairs for nachos and spicy wings. Uh-huh. Cold beer as well. I appreciate it." He chewed away on his gum.

"You didn't have to do that," I said. "We just—"

"It's all right. Shit, I'm not the one pays for it. Now, if you could give me your attention. Our art department has put together a little something." He picked up a remote control from off the shining table and fiddled with the buttons. The lights went off in the room. A screen descended behind his chair.

A projector came on, and a black-and-white image of young Elvis twisted his hips before us. He sang that "one for the money" song. Over the music, we heard a woman's voice say, "Elvis," in a dramatic tone. Suddenly the image changed to the Beatles in their little suits. "The Beatles," the woman's voice said, as if we didn't know who they were. After that we could predict the rest. The Rolling Stones footage was cool, with Brian Jones playing sitar in the back. By then, Nathan and I mocked the narrator out loud: "The Rolling Stones," we said. The voice said "the" Led Zeppelin, which got a good laugh from all of us. The screen went black. "And now," the voice continued, "SGM Records would like to present the new greatest rock band in the world." The opening notes of "Nowhere Fast" sounded. We chuckled at the cheesiness of the whole thing. "Ladies and gentlemen, the Mistakes." Along with our studio track, they'd put a mash-up of still photos and live footage of us playing—some in Seattle, some in Europe. There were some terrific shots of Sean flying through the air. Will and Brian laughed and cheered at the montage of crash landings.

"You should hear the sound it makes," Sean whispered to them.

From now on, I realized, fans will want their money back if they don't see Sean hurt himself onstage.

The video came to a close and Jimmy switched the lights back on. "I got one question for you." He turned to Nathan. "In the 'Nowhere Fast' song, is that dude about to do it with his first cousin?"

Nathan turned red. I barely kept a straight face. Nobody had ever confronted him about his lyrics before.

"Sure," Nathan said.

"I knew it!" Jimmy clapped his hands. He pushed a button on his telephone. "Hey, Chuck, you owe me those Lakers tickets after all!

"So." Jimmy turned back to us as though there were nothing left to talk about. "What's keeping us from doing business today?"

"Well," I said. "What's your plan? What can we expect if we sign with you?"

"That's an excellent question. I'm glad you asked." He looked me in the eye. "My plan, little lady, is to make the Mistakes into the biggest rock band in the world. What do you think of that?"

"Did you just call me 'little lady'?"

The door swung open. "Jimmy, your food's here." Two female assistants in business casual carried in a platter of nachos sagging under the weight of their sauce and cheese, another tray of chicken wings in red grease, and a disposable Styrofoam cooler filled with bottles of Mexican beer.

"Thanks." Jimmy twisted the top off one of the beer bottles and said, "So, we celebrating or what?"

Will went for a nacho at the end of the tray.

"Can we think about it?" I asked.

Jimmy seemed annoyed that I was the one who did the talking. "Anybody can think. You know what a star does? A star acts." The boys snickered. Jimmy picked up a clipboard and a pen and threw them down on the table like a challenge.

"Sorry," I said, "but we're not ready to sign anything right now. We need to talk it over."

"That's fine," he relented. "That's what I like about your band. You all talk things over. You're like a grunge family, as they say."

"Who says that?" I asked.

"You know, the magazines and everybody." Jimmy looked at Nathan and Sean. "Which one of these two is your man, anyway?"

I felt myself blush. "You got a card or something?" I stood up. Nathan and Sean followed suit. Will and Brian made final grabs for the snacks.

"Here you go." Jimmy passed me his business card. "I expect to hear from you-all by tomorrow."

"Can we take some of this stuff?" Will asked sheepishly.

"Take it all." Jimmy brushed the question away with his hand.

We walked downstairs into the lobby, me in the lead, Sean and Nathan at either side, Will and Brian in the rear, balancing those flimsy plastic trays and dragging the cooler of beer.

"Are we all on the same page?" I asked Nathan and Sean as we walked.

"It's a no-brainer," Nathan said.

I walked up to the man attending the building's front desk. "Is there a phone where I can dial out around here?" I fished Michael's card out of my pocket.

He took a phone out from under the desk, dialed a couple of numbers, and handed the receiver to me.

"Michael," I said. "It's Laura from the Mistakes. We're ready. We want the deal we talked about. One full-length for now."

Nathan looked at me suspiciously.

I covered the mouthpiece with my hand. "Signing on for two albums is what got us into this mess in the first place."

That seemed to satisfy him.

"Great," I said into the phone. "Draw it up. We'll sign tomorrow. Send a car to the Vista Hills, and we'll shoot the video."

I hung up the phone. There was a second of breathless silence among the five of us, broken by Will crunching another nacho.

"Brian," I said, "give me one of those beers. We should celebrate. We just signed to a major label, after all."

We clanged bottles and toasted our success in the lobby of the competition's building.

Back at the hotel, we drank the rest of Jimmy's beers around the pool. With my jeans rolled up to my knees and my feet in the water, I sat along the edge and smoked. The whiteness of my legs glowed in the sun. The boys borrowed a pair of scissors from the front desk and made all their jeans into cutoffs. A pile of empty denim tubes lay at one side of the pool. The sky turned a glorious pink as the sun set. The girls in the heavy metal T-shirts finally did arrive, with more beer, and they kept Will, Brian, and Nathan occupied. After that initial toast, I hadn't seen Sean drink any more.

At the deep end, the boys did cannonballs. Sean came over and asked if he could sit beside me. He dipped his feet into the water by mine. I offered him a cigarette, but he waved that off as well.

"You turning straight edge all of a sudden?" I asked.

"No." Sean looked down at the water. His narrow elbows rested on his knees. "Trying to take care of myself is all."

"Good for you." Maybe the liver scare wasn't something he'd taken lightly.

"I got bad genes when it comes to drinking."

"You got bad jeans when it comes to washing, too."

He laughed. Another splash sounded at the deep end, followed by squeals from the girls.

"It was a good choice, what we did today," Sean said.

"You think?"

"Yeah. That guy, Michael, he's all corporate and slick. But he makes no bones about it, you know. He didn't pretend that this wasn't a business or anything. I liked that about him."

"There's no point second-guessing. Between those two, it was a no-brainer, like Nathan said." As if on cue, Nathan did a jackknife into the pool. "I'm more tripping on the fact that we signed to a major at all. I can see my brother's face." I looked into the water, the way it distorted my feet. The lights had been turned on inside the pool and around the patio. The sky darkened.

"You know," Sean said, "if it wasn't for people like you and your brother, there's no way a band like us could ever get signed on a major."

I took another sip of beer. "You think?"

"I'm sure of it. Before hardcore, all the music you could buy was controlled by guys like Jimmy. They didn't have to be nice to people like us."

"I suppose."

"Mainly, I don't want to go back to working at that mill. And I want kids to be able to find our record."

I thought of what Boeing Bob had told me, about mistaking irrelevance and integrity.

"Our fans deserve to hear our music," Sean went on. "Isn't that the whole point?"

"Don't get me started on what I think our fans deserve," I said.

"What do you mean?"

"Just thinking about that thing that happened in Seattle. It got into my head."

"What thing?"

"Nathan didn't tell you about it? This girl, Andrea her name was, she broke into my house while I was sleeping. She's a fan of ours. It was in the papers."

"Jesus," Sean said. "If somebody tried that at our house in Montana, my dad totally would've shot them."

"Yeah, well, she's crazy—like straight-up mentally ill. And when the cops came, they thought I was the intruder and handcuffed me. My neighbors were watching." I felt tears trying to well up in my eyes, but I fought them off and stopped my story there. "It's not a big deal. I felt sorry for her, in the end. I'm going up to my room."

Inside my room, the air conditioner had worked up a nice chill. I lay down under the covers and turned on the TV. A concert film showed Bruce Springsteen performing with the E Street Band. A knock sounded from the door.

"It's me," Sean said. "Can I come in?"

"Sure," I answered without enthusiasm.

"I didn't go back to my dad's house." Sean shut the door behind him. "I said I'd never go back and I meant it. We stayed in Nathan's parents' basement."

Why was he telling me this? He didn't need to stay away from that asshole for my benefit.

"Good for you," I said.

He sat down on the bed.

"Sean," I said. "The girl who broke into my house, she'd come looking for you. She'd read about our love affair in the goddamn magazines and came into my bedroom to find us together. That's how much she adored the rock-and-roll fairy-tale romance."

Sean breathed out. "I'm sorry. I shouldn't have talked to that reporter in Rome. I was fucked up and desperate. I thought it was the right thing to do."

"I don't want to be your girlfriend." Saying those words had caused me so much grief and anguish over the last few months. I'd come to think that voicing them would be like jumping off a cliff. Instead, they changed nothing at all.

"Laura, please. I know I was a train wreck in Europe. But can't you give me another chance? Can you stick this out a little while longer? Get through this tour and see where we are after that."

"I don't want to stick it out."

He closed his eyes and let out a big breath. "I'm so worried about this next tour, Laura. I can't handle a breakup on top of it."

"This thing you're talking about, Sean." I sat up in bed and raised my voice. "It's not even a relationship. It's a fucking joke. At this point, it's a publicity stunt more than anything else."

"It makes me happy," Sean said. He wasn't pleading anymore. He truly didn't care if it was healthy or functional. I don't believe he cared if we were physical or not. He just didn't want to be alone—symbolically or otherwise.

I looked up at the television screen. Bruce sang one of my all-time favorite lyrics: *Is a dream a lie that don't come true, or is it something worse?* But I'd had it wrong. For the first time, I noticed that he was actually singing: *Is a dream a lie if it don't come true, or is it something worse?*

I turned back to Sean. "Fine," I said.

He smiled and lay down on the bed beside me. What had I just agreed to? To pretend to be in a relationship with him for a bit longer? Or to still be a couple, even if that couplehood would seem phony to any sane person?

Still, there was relief in having told him how I felt. It emboldened me onward in my plan: Record one more album and then unmake the Mistakes.

The next day, we were driven to a soundstage and introduced to Nick, a young guy with a shining pompadour who dressed in rockabilly style, his dark jeans rolled up in cuffs.

"So, what I want to do," he said while walking, "is have you guys playing over here." The set was an exact replica of a Middle American supermarket—aisles of food and checkout lanes, deli and bakery counters. I couldn't understand why they didn't just shoot it in a regular grocery store.

"Then we're going to release the bear, and he'll run around at this end."

"Wait a minute," I said. "There's going to be a bear running around?"

"Not a real bear. I wanted a real bear, but it's a big thing, animal rights and whatnot."

"So a fake bear will be running around in our video?"

"It's Laura, right?" Nick stopped walking.

I nodded.

"Have you ever seen a real bear?" he asked.

"No."

"Have you ever seen a guy in a bear suit?"

"No."

"Then how do you know they don't look exactly the same?" Nick resumed walking as though he'd proved a point.

"It's not the realness or fakeness of the bear that concerns me," I said. "It's the irrelevance. This song has its own story, its own imagery. Why not use that?"

"We were doing literal interpretations of lyrics, like, ten years ago." Nick spoke over his shoulder. "I could film a guy in a car driving recklessly for three minutes, but what would be surprising about that?"

He had a point.

"Trust me on this. Lyrics aside, the energy of this song says one thing to me: bear running amok through supermarket. I have a vision."

I looked at Nathan and he shrugged. For their part, the boys enjoyed the surrealism of it all.

Whoever was in charge of set design deserved a promotion. They'd thought of everything. The butcher was an old scary guy, and all his meat was putrid and green. The checkout girls were two leggy beauties with their makeup done like teenage tramps. Nick took one look at Will and Brian and cast them as bag boys.

We did a couple of takes with all of us lip-synching. The biggest cameras circled the band. Men with handhelds went through the set, filming the extras. It was tedious, and the three of us grew sick of hearing our own song over and over.

"Okay," Nick said. "On this take, we can get crazy."

We started the song again, cameras circling. Soon, the fake bear came around one corner and roared at us. I couldn't help laughing, but Sean and Nathan played like they were scared and gave each other a wide-eyed glare. The bear was good. He reared up, knocked boxes of cereal and canned goods off shelves. Another actor played the dorky manager. He wagged his finger at the angry bear. With the manager occupied, the sex kitten checkout girls turned and made out with Brian and Will—flashing plenty of midriff flesh and upper thigh as they did. The bear gave chase to the manager. More items fell off shelves.

Sean was the first to break from the fake playing and swung his guitar into a stack of cans. After that, pandemonium ensued. Nathan axe-handled his bass into the deli case. But there was no actual Plexiglas over it, so the instrument went right into a bowl of potato salad. As he retreated, I went in after that bowl and chucked handfuls of food at everyone around. I scored a direct hit on Sean. He fetched a box of doughnuts and returned fire. The song finished playing over the PA, the food fight still in its prime. The guys with the handhelds continued filming. The music started up again. Will and Brian chased the fake bear with a pile of rancid steaks. Covered in food now, I picked up my snare drum and lobbed it into a shelf of white bread. Somebody found a can of whipped cream. I tried to pick up my bass drum, but it was too heavy. Suddenly the fake bear was there to help. Between the two of us, we managed to launch it into the nearest shelf. The whole works came down with a crash. The manager put his hands up on his head.

Right in front of the main camera, the checkout hotties stripped to their bras and panties. They rubbed egg salad all over their skin and gyrated to the song. By each hand, they took me and led me over to the camera as well. Before I knew it, I was dancing along with them and we were smearing each other with mayonnaise and whipped cream. Soon, a sort of chorus line formed, with me and the checkout girls in front, shaking our hips, while the bag boys, the butcher, Nathan, Sean, and the bear all came along behind. We screamed "Nowhere Fast!" along with the PA as the song faded out. It was the most fun I'd had in months.

The song's last notes sounded. The set went silent.

"Cut. Yes!" Nick was ecstatic. "I love it!"

All of us were panting and laughing. The head came off the bear, and a pink-skinned bald man stood underneath, his face covered in sweat. "You guys rock," he said.

LOS ANGELES: JANUARY 1982

Hank flirts with you all the way across the country. The problem is Anthony. You're always in the same van, on the same stage, or squatting on the same filthy floor as your older brother. Everybody in every scene in every city you've been to on this tour still refers to you as Anthony's little sister. For the first time, you come to resent it.

The show is well attended but wild. Not even halfway through the set, and there's already blood and broken glass everywhere. Earlier, you saw an older girl get carried out by two kids. She looked unconscious. You hoped she was breathing. Anthony seems concerned about things going too far.

"Take care of each other!" he shouts between songs. "Don't prove everybody right about us!" The kids don't understand what he means by any of this.

Hank watches you from the other side of the stage.

Playing in Southern California is a double-edged sword. Anthony says that hardcore was invented here. But as in D.C., there is an underground precisely because the mainstream is so conservative. The cops here are the worst. And the fans are the youngest and rowdiest—pioneering new forms of music-related violence. Playing in L.A., you can never drop your guard.

Anthony must see them come in through the back.

He turns to the rest of you and shouts, "Only Good Cop! Only Good Cop!" which is not the next number on the set list. Nod and start your bass line. Hank and Billy roar in on the second bar. Then you see them, too: LAPD in full riot gear, nightsticks drawn.

"The only good cop!" Your brother belts out the lyrics in his soulful scream. *"Is not the one in the doughnut shop."*

Bodies hit the floor. Cops stomp through the crowd and swing batons as though they're chopping down tall weeds with machetes. Some of the kids fight back. The clever ones grab on to the helmets and cover the visors with their hands. A kid works a helmet off and puts it on himself. The bareheaded pig climbs onstage and cracks Hank on the forehead. He keeps playing. Anthony kicks the cop in the shin. You take off your bass and swing it toward the cop's head like a baseball bat. Both your brother and the cop tumble to the floor.

Hank grabs you around the waist and takes you off the stage. He knocks over a couple amplifiers and leads you down the hallway, then ducks into a janitor's closet with no door.

You reach up and hold your fingers to his bleeding forehead. "It's bad," you say. "Fucking pigs."

Hank leans down then and kisses you on the mouth. His tongue pushes against your still-closed lips. Blood drips onto your cheek. The sounds of nightsticks striking teenage flesh come down the hallway. You wonder, briefly, if your brother is okay, then part your lips and feel Hank's tongue along your teeth.

TWENTY-THREE

I bought framed prints for my new house, including a few Edward Hoppers. In my haste, I forgot to pick up anything to hang them with. Days later, the pictures still stood along the floor, leaning against the otherwise bare walls.

This was not exactly time off. Between Kingdom Records, Liquid Management, and my bandmates, I barely went an hour without a long-distance conversation. Nathan and Sean simply kept their hotel room in L.A., which was good for me. They were the first to be called in for interviews or photo shoots.

Liquid constantly updated the tour itinerary. We would start in San Francisco, go down through California, then do a bunch of cities in the Southwest. The East Coast leg would go from Atlanta up to Boston, then across the Midwest, finishing with a big finale back in Seattle. We would have our own full-size coach. We would play stadiums and arenas.

On the day the buyout was meant to be final, my phone rang at 10 P.M.

"Are you watching?" It was Michael.

"What happened with the buyout?"

"Turn on the television."

I did as I was told. "What channel?"

"MTV, what do you think?"

"Oh my god." There I was, playing drums on the screen. "It looks so much like me."

"It is you, stupid!"

"Yeah, I just mean. I don't know what I mean." It looked amazing. They used some sort of filter on the cameras. All the light was harsh and flat, like old photographs from the sixties. It was kind of disturbing but with a sense of humor. I liked it.

"Looks good, huh? MTV's psyched."

"So, does this mean—"

"Yep." He cut me off. "Gawk Rawd signed the papers this morning. Congratulations. You'll be helping those two hipsters make obscure albums for college students for the next decade."

Good for them, I thought to myself. On-screen, the hips of the girls danced before the camera; then all of us were there shouting along with the song. The final shot showed Sean and the bear regarding each other, both in profile, with the same blank and curious expression. They each cocked their heads. The picture faded to black.

"You have a ticket to San Fran, then?"

"Yeah," I said. "It's sorted out. How are the boys doing?"

"Nathan and Sean? They're fine. All the stories about them, I thought I'd have sprung them from jail a couple of times by now. Frankly, I'm a little disappointed. That Sean is clean and sober."

"More like on the wagon," I said.

"They've been working, doing interviews. There should be a decent media buzz by the time you hit the road."

I wondered how much more media we needed. We had an album in the top forty and our pictures in a bunch of magazines. What did Kingdom have in mind?

In the morning, I took a cigarette out to the front stoop. My neighbors left for the park with their dog. Feeling confident, I offered a wave and a smile. I belonged here. I had money coming in. I was on television. Soon, I'd be the talk of the neighborhood but in a good way.

During the first drag of my cigarette, a gunshot sounded from up the street. I ducked my head down and covered my face with my forearms. The smoke dropped to the steps.

It wasn't a gunshot at all but a car backfiring. I heard a rattling engine, looked up, and saw our old van coming down the street. It stopped right in front of my house. I half expected for Nathan and Sean to hop out. Instead, the driver's door opened and Chip walked around from the side. His beard was in the early stages of filling back in.

"This belongs to you," he said, dangling the keys.

"I forgot all about it." We'd left the van in their care when we went to Europe.

"You've forgotten about a lot of things."

"I'm sorry, Chip. I have no grudge. I appreciate all that you did for us."

"You got a strange way of showing it."

"Come on, Chip. It's for the best. Kids couldn't find our album anywhere."

"We were working on that!" He raised his voice. "We could've done this. Gawk Rawd and the Mistakes could've beaten the majors. It would've been the fulfillment of what you guys started with Autopilot."

"Nathan punched you. You wanted us gone."

He sighed and looked toward the street.

"At least your label is buoyant again."

He smiled. "You got that right."

"I'm happy for you. I'm happy that you stuck it to Kingdom. You guys deserve it."

"Besides," he said, "your next album will probably suck anyways."
We both laughed.

"I'm serious, though," he said more somberly. "We could've made history. The personal differences were one thing. But there won't be another opportunity like that. Now the majors will snatch up acts like you before us little guys have a chance. The Mistakes was our shot."

I picked up the dropped cigarette, took a long drag, and told myself that making music industry history didn't matter to me. That was Anthony's department.

"If it makes any difference, I have a feeling that the Mistakes won't be around much longer." It was amazing how many of my problems seemed to have the exact same solution.

"Too many chefs?" he asked.

A horn honked from up the street.

"That's my ride," Chip said.

A small car pulled up with Doug at the wheel. I waved. He didn't return the gesture.

"Doug hasn't taken this well," Chip said. "He's got loyalty issues."

We shook hands. He dropped the van keys into my palm.

"Good-bye," Chip said.

"Good luck." I parked the van next to my station wagon in my garage, and packed for the tour.

Nathan and Sean, along with Will and Brian, were driven up from L.A. in the coach we'd be using. I flew in and we all met up backstage before the show. The tour manager was a tall skinny guy with a set of nervous tics that included head twitches and a habit of repeating himself under his breath. The boys dubbed him Commander Spaz.

Puddle-jumper got a separate dressing room and their own bus. Rumor was they weren't happy to be our opening act.

Sean tuned up another new guitar. California agreed with him.

His skin wore a healthy glow. Oddly, he stretched his fingers and played some scales. He usually warmed up with little runs of his own creation. I didn't think he knew the normal scales.

Nathan scratched out the set list with a brand-new Sharpie. Will and Brian munched away on sandwiches from the deli tray.

"I think I'll check out these guys' act for a minute," I said. The boys nodded. Around my neck, I hung the string of ID cards and passes that Commander Spaz had issued, and went out to the wings of the stage.

Puddle-jumper played one of their popular numbers. The crowd was into it. I'd seen them perform in Seattle back in the day but was never a fan. They were a brick-and-mortar band: their sound was tight and polished, but there was nothing inspired about their music. Plus, I didn't care for their lead singer. Jeff was an egomaniac, the kind of guy who always wanted to be a star.

Back inside our dressing room, the boys had gotten into the make-shift bar. Only Sean abstained. He paced around with his guitar strapped on, looking nervous.

"How do they sound?" Nathan asked me.

"Tight," I said. "Like stadium rock, you know. The crowd likes them."

Nathan handed me a set list. "Hopefully they'll like us, too."

It could've been anything. We hadn't played together in a long time. The instruments were all new and unfamiliar. The sound system was unlike anything we'd worked with before.

But it was none of those things. I could hear Nathan clearly through those monitors. The rhythm section was all together.

The problem was Sean. He didn't play any of his signature licks. That style he had, of playing in and around the melody, it wasn't there tonight. He mostly strummed barre chords, picked notes out here and there. Onstage, he didn't do anything crazier than bob his head.

I hated to admit it to myself: that his sobriety was the reason we

sounded like shit. For months, I'd wished he'd stop getting wasted, stop hurting himself onstage. Now he'd done it, and we sucked.

The crowd sat there bored. A few people booed. We didn't bother doing an encore. The three of us retreated offstage like losing fighters. Before we got to the dressing room, we came upon Commander Spaz.

Jeff, from Puddle-jumper, read him the riot act. "This"—he held his hand out toward us like we were inanimate objects—"this is your fucking headliner? This is the live show that we can't follow? Are you kidding me?"

Commander Spaz looked at his clipboard and mumbled something about "only the first night of the tour." His shoulder and his left ear pulled themselves together like nervous magnetic attraction.

"I'm calling Michael." Jeff stormed off. "This is bullshit!"

Commander Spaz looked at his watch. "You guys have two hours before the bus leaves. The roadies will pack everything." He walked off, staring down at his own feet. Only the three of us stood there in the wings.

"Well." Nathan broke the silence. "I'm ready for a sandwich."

Sean started to follow him to the dressing room, but I grabbed his arm. "Sean," I said. "It's okay. Everybody has a bad night now and again. This isn't about the booze."

"Laura." He looked down at my hand, gripped on his forearm. "I'm afraid it is about booze." Roadies ran all around us with armloads of gear.

"That's bullshit. I've seen you kill so many times without drinking. You were sober when we started this band."

"I know." He couldn't look me in the eye. "But it's different now."

"You got used to playing buzzed is all. You'll get over it."

"Listen." He took his free hand and used it to hold my other elbow. Finally, he looked right at me. "The color thing, my disease or whatever, it doesn't work when I'm sober."

"What?" I'd almost forgotten about Sean's synesthesia. "No. We used to practice all the time without drinking."

"This is new." The words hissed out. He looked to see if anybody listened. "Remember in Paris, that day in the restaurant when I said it wasn't working? After hitting my head that first night in London, I haven't been the same."

"No," I said. "You slayed it almost every other night of that tour."

"But I was drunk!" Sean struggled to keep his voice down. "The colors come back with alcohol. It's not like before. They have this weird brownish tinge to them. But I can see them, at least."

We stared at each other. I was flat out of ideas.

"Hey, guys." It was Will. "They're about to break down the catering table, so if you want dinner, now's the time."

"We better go," Sean said.

Still unsure how to respond, I said okay and started toward our dressing room.

"Laura, can I ask you something?"

I turned back to him again.

"Do you think it's possible—if that blow to the head in London did this—that another blow to the head might make it go back to the way it was?"

"Tell me you're not fucking serious."

"Never mind," Sean said.

The bus was a top-of-the-line Prévost, the first one I'd ever been aboard. There was a kitchen and TV room in the front, with a dining table and couches; the berths were in back. The boys wasted no time breaking it in. Loose CDs and laundry were scattered about. Bags of jerky filled up the shelves. I felt like I was raiding their clubhouse.

"We saved the best bunk for you." Will was kind enough to carry my suitcase.

"Cool." The berths all had consoles with a reading light and air nozzle, like on passenger jets. "Do you know where Nathan and Sean are?"

"They're still inside," Will said. "They needed to talk."

"I'll go ahead and lie down."

I snapped the curtains shut and lay back inside my dark cocoon. With my hips lifted into a bridge, I fumbled out of my clothes. The nozzle blew cool air against the grimy layer of sweat I'd built up while drumming. The other three boys climbed aboard.

"You guys sounded good tonight," I heard Will say through the curtain.

"We sounded like shit," Nathan corrected him. "But don't worry; that won't happen again. In L.A., you'll see a real Mistakes show."

Finally, the bus pulled out and we started down the road. Inside my womb of black cloth, I felt more restful than I had the week prior in my suburban house. The big wheels beat upon the American highway, the only home I'd ever known.

"Laura," a voice came from outside my berth. "Laura, it's time."

Still half-asleep, I took a second to remember where I was. The curtains came apart with a snap. My eyes squinted against the light. Will stood there with a steaming paper cup in his hand.

"What time is it?" I pulled the sheet up to my neck.

"Five in the afternoon," Will said. "Commander Spaz wants to do sound check." Will lifted the cup a little. "Nathan told me that if I was going to wake you, I better bring coffee."

"Good advice," I said. "I can't believe I slept in so late."

"You didn't miss anything. It's hot as shit. You can see the Hollywood sign, but that takes like two seconds. Puddle-jumper's been giving us the cold shoulder all day."

"They're dicks." I wrapped the sheet around me like a toga, sat up on the bunk, and took the coffee cup from Will. "And their music is lame."

"Can I get you anything else?" he asked. "They got bread and stuff here in the kitchen."

"You don't have to do that."

"It's kind of my job, actually. We're supposed to be earning our keep."

I thought about it. Why not? "Some toast would be great, yeah."

Will walked to the kitchen. Still wrapped in the sheet, I wiggled into my clothes.

"You should probably know"—Will spoke over the ticks from the toaster—"the guys are already hitting the booze."

In the dressing room, Sean, Nathan, and Brian all held cans and passed around a bottle of Jack Daniel's. A mouthful of beer foamed out of Sean's face as he laughed too hard. *There must be another solution,* I thought.

Commander Spaz showed up with a cordless phone. "It's the record company for you." He held it out in my direction.

"Hello?"

"What's all this about you guys having a bad show last night?" It was Michael.

"Who told you that? Puddle-jumper? They should change their name to Sour Grapes."

"I heard the same thing from Liquid," he said. "You didn't even do an encore, they say. People were booing."

"We had some issues last night. It won't happen again."

"See that it doesn't."

"Are you coming to the show tonight?"

"I think I better, yes."

"Then you'll see for yourself." I clicked the button on the phone.

At that point, I so wanted to kill tonight, I was ready to make Sean a pitcher of Long Island ice teas myself.

Commander Spaz walked away with the phone in one hand, his clipboard in the other. I walked around one side of the stage and had a look at the Hollywood sign. It glowed orange with the setting sun. Will was right: it took only two seconds to see it.

Puddle-jumper drew out their closer for a long time. Jeff sported that shorts, combat boots, and long underwear combo that never made sense to me, in terms of fashion or function.

Back in the dressing room, Nathan handed me a set list. "How did they sound?"

"Boring," I said. "Those guys try too hard."

Sean paced around and picked notes from his unamplified guitar. He rolled his head atop his neck a couple of times, then took another pull from the near-empty whiskey bottle on the catering table. "You guys ready or what?" he said.

We took to the stage with a big cheer from the crowd. Nathan went to the microphone. "Thanks," he said. "We're the Mistakes." I saw Michael in the first row.

His back toward the crowd, his flannel shirt hanging unbuttoned on either side of his guitar, Sean stepped on his distortion pedal and half opened up the Cry Baby. When he hit the first line of "Nowhere Fast," I knew it would be a good show.

It was that unmistakable Mistakes guitar sound—the one that tingled in your molars and never sounded the same twice in a row. Nathan sang the lyrics. We hit the first vamp and ten thousand people shouted, "Nowhere fast!" all at once. Kids ran from the back of the amphitheater and formed a mosh pit down front. The industry people in the first row were forced to their feet.

After a couple of high-energy hours, Nathan waved to the crowd and said: "Thank you, good night!"

With all his fancy new effect pedals turned on, Sean strummed his guitar one last time and then placed it in front of his amp. The whole arena squealed with feedback. We followed Nathan offstage. I lit a cigarette and the three of us passed it while the crowd screamed and held up their lighters.

"I feel great," Sean said. "I could play for another hour."

The cigarette circled around until it was nothing but filter.

"All right," Nathan said. "Let's do it."

"Wait," I said. "Which song?"

They looked at me as though I were a fool. " 'Devil You Know,' " they both said at once.

It dawned on me that we'd not played it yet. "All right."

The crowd cheered as we came back out. Sean tapped off all the pedals. Nathan fiddled with a tuning peg. I found the brushes I'd asked for atop my bass drum. After a minute or two, Sean had the tone he wanted. He took a broken drumstick from off the floor by my drum riser and stuck it into the back pocket of his jeans. The kids put away their lighters.

Sean strummed the slow opening chords of "Devil You Know." Nathan lifted the head of his bass and cued me to start. As soon as we were locked in, Sean picked notes out of the basic melody. Softly at first, Nathan sang the lyrics: *"It was a bad idea taken way too far / on a night too cold to spend alone in a car."*

The crowd stayed silent during the verse. I hit a little fill as we came to the first refrain: *"The devil you know and the devil that you don't know."* The audience sang along. Sean tapped his foot on one of the distortion boxes and pulled the broken drumstick from his pocket. Without missing a note, his guitar whined and slid out a lick that mirrored Nathan's lyrics.

We played at this tempo for a couple more bars; then Sean backed up and faced the band. With mouth and eyes held wide open, he nodded his head and cued us into the sped-up instrumental breakdown that nobody in this crowd expected.

I ditched my brushes and grabbed a pair of sticks. The mosh pit returned to life. Sean played a lick at fever pitch. He turned back to me and Nathan and urged us to speed up even more.

I was at the critical mass of my drumming ability—much faster, and I wouldn't be able to keep up. I bent forward, closed my eyes, and focused all my energy into getting more speed out of my arms.

The tempo leveled off. I looked up, hoping for a cue from Nathan or Sean. There was Sean's back, right before my eyes. He stood at the edge of my drum riser.

"No." I said it softly at first, then screamed it the second time. "No, Sean, don't!" But there was no chance that he'd hear me over the amplifiers and the cheers of the crowd. Sean launched himself, guitar first, onto the floor of the stage. Because of the height of the drum riser and the angle of my view, I didn't see the impact so much as hear it. A distorted smack rang out through the whole arena, and echoed over the sudden silence of the band and the crowd.

Nathan looked at me. Both of us cringed. Finally, Sean's head appeared above the lip of my drum riser. His face was bloodless, for which I was thankful. But he held a hand across his chest as though he'd broken one of those ribs that had only recently healed. With eyes and teeth clenched tight, he rose to his feet. It was the usual story with the guitar. Strings hung broken from the head. Knobs were shattered and missing, pushed into the body. A spiderweb of cracks spread across the pick guard.

Hunched over, looking terribly pained, Sean managed to pluck the unbroken strings. I picked up my brushes off the floor and we made it through the second verse. Nathan sang into the microphone, as slow and laborious as a funeral march. Every note from Sean's guitar pierced like a fractured bone. The mosh pit stood still.

After the final refrain, the three of us faded out. My brushes sizzled along the snare drum. Nathan took off his bass. Sean undid the strap on his guitar and let it fall straight to the ground.

Nathan and I ran over to Sean and placed each of his arms over our necks. "It hurts," he said. "I need something for the pain."

As the three of us walked off toward the back of the stage, the crowd exploded into applause. We turned back, like some wounded three-headed monster, and saw the whole amphitheater take to its feet. Commander Spaz met us backstage.

"Get a fucking doctor," I said. Sean's question from last night lingered in my mind: did he really think he could restore his disorder by another blow to the head?

"He's on his way." Commander Spaz turned to his walkie-talkie.

Within seconds, a middle-aged man in a golf shirt came toward us. He told us to back away from Sean. "Put your arm up over your head," the man ordered.

Sean did as he was told.

The doctor pressed along his side. "Does this hurt?"

Will and Brian showed up and watched along with us. "You guys were great," Brian said.

The doctor worked his way down Sean's rib cage until finally, a few ribs from the bottom, he pressed on one and Sean cried out. I winced.

"It's the rib," the doctor said. "Either it's broken or separated from the sternum. In either case, there's nothing much to be done. It'll take about six weeks to heal." He took out his prescription pad. "This should help with the pain. Don't drink on this stuff. And cut out the belly-flopping." The doctor turned and walked away.

Sean sat down on the floor with a great groaning and clenching of teeth. He stared at the piece of paper in his hand and then up at Commander Spaz.

"I'm on it." Commander Spaz took the prescription and read it over.

"I can't get comfortable," Sean groaned.

Just like that. A few beers, a bit of whiskey, and we're back to the same bullshit. "Will," I said. "You guys take him to his bunk."

There in the wings of the stage, save for a few passing roadies, me and Nathan were alone for the first time since Europe.

"We need to talk," I said.

"Buy you a drink?"

In our dressing room, the linen-covered catering table had plenty of food and alcohol left. Nathan made a Cold War for each of us, put two cigarettes in his mouth, and lit them both.

"This is the only answer?" I sat on the table beside the tray of deli meats. "Get Sean wasted?"

Nathan shrugged and handed one of the lit cigarettes to me. "Sean told you about the colors?" He leaned against the table a couple of feet away from me.

"Yeah," I said.

"I thought maybe he could handle it," Nathan said. "You know, moderation. But once he gets started . . ."

"Can he go to a specialist or something?"

Nathan scoffed out a mouthful of smoke. "Ask a doctor to repair his disease? Not likely. Nobody knows what causes it anyway."

"Fuck," I said.

"Tell me about it. This is Sean's dream, too. If you ask him, he'll trade all the broken ribs and busted noses in the world for music. Those are his priorities."

"Yeah, well"—I brought the Cold War up to my lips and held it there—"maybe he doesn't know what's best for himself."

"You want to pull the plug?" Nathan was genuine.

"I don't know," I said. "It's a lesser-of-evils kind of situation."

"I'm going to check on him." Nathan stubbed out his cigarette and stood away from the catering table.

"Nathan, the security system . . . thank you." It was the first time we'd mentioned it.

"You're welcome. You're okay, right? Nothing happened?" His concern betrayed him.

For a moment, my guts twisted with the terror of being alone in that house with Andrea. I kept it to myself. "Nothing I can't handle."

Nathan nodded and left the dressing room. I poured myself another Cold War. The roadies soon came in and cleared out the food and bar. I was now doubly sure that I had to break up the Mistakes. If anything, I now wondered if it wasn't wrong to wait until after we'd completed this tour and a second album. Would Sean make it through all of that intact?

CLEVELAND: JULY 1984

Your brother is like those old-time geniuses, whose ideas come in great bright epiphanies—watching an apple fall or something float in the bathtub. You can see the gears turning inside, the cartoon lightbulb above his head. This one occurs onstage.

The set is halfway through. A bloody face appears in the crowd. Something's going on: a fight in the pit, par for the course. It's the middle of a song and Anthony stops singing. He looks to you and runs his hand across his throat like an imaginary knife. Stop playing and still the strings with the palm of your hand. The rest of the band halts as well.

"What the fuck?" Hank shouts.

"We're not going to play"—Anthony speaks into the microphone—"until you all cut out the fighting."

What? Drop your jaw. This was your brother's big idea? The crowd boils over with boos and hisses. Half the reason kids come to these hardcore shows is so they can fight. What is Anthony thinking?

Hank puts a hand on Anthony's shoulder and leans into his ear: "Have you lost your mind?"

Barely hear him over the hate from the crowd.

"I'm serious." Anthony looks at Hank but speaks into the microphone. "I'm not going to be a part of something that hurts people. I'm not okay with that." He turns to the crowd and keeps talking. "If those two want to break it up, we'll be happy to keep playing."

Standing there onstage without performing is torture. The kids spit and throw cans. Take a couple steps back toward the drum set. It's true, you'd like to see the violence stop, but it seems an effort like defying teenage gravity.

Eventually, the bloody-faced boy leaves. You think it was that same big skinhead who'd beat on him. Anthony counts you all into the next song on the set list, but even then it's met mostly with boos and spit.

Though nobody would've thought it possible, the tour descends from there into a chaos that makes regular hardcore shows look organized and well managed. You never even know if you're going to play songs. Once the rumors get out about Anthony's no-violence policy, kids fight just to spite him.

The worst part is when you have to stand there onstage, holding your instrument but not allowed to play it, while the crowd seethes, meeting your brother in a battle of wills.

TWENTY-FOUR

The Southwest leg was a blur of scorching days and open-air arenas in the cool desert night. I tried not to worry about Sean. He was now an important asset to Kingdom Records and Liquid Management; let them look after him. Who was I to bear that cross? Night after night, as Sean threw himself onto the stage, I did my best to pretend it was happening on a TV screen, many years removed, like that cheesy montage footage what's-his-name had made to try to sign us.

Will and Brian pitted a full-blown prank war against Puddle-jumper. It started one night during the opening set, when they switched the gross bologna from our deli tray for all the good ham and turkey breast on Puddle-jumper's. Puddle-jumper retaliated by trashing our dressing room in Phoenix.

Will and Brian raised the bar. They took the next night's supply of bologna, dipped it in vinegar, and stuck the little circles of meat all over the sides of Puddle-jumper's tour bus. The next day, when the roadies went to remove the slices, there was a big rust stain underneath each one. Apparently, this was a common gag in Montana.

We didn't even notice until the following day, after we'd stopped in Albuquerque. With orange spray paint, FAGGOTS was written along the side of our bus. Sean, Nathan, Will, Brian, and I stood there staring at it, more confused than anything else.

This seemed like the work of some macho hair band from a bygone era, not one of our peers. Wasn't this new wave of alternative rock supposed to be about tolerance and progressive values? Perhaps that, too, was a creation of the journalists.

"Hey!" Sean shouted to one of the roadies in that dry-mouthed, heavy-tongued speech that came with his pain pills. "Have you guys got any spray paint?"

The roadie produced a can marked Caution Yellow. Sean wasted no time amending Puddle-jumper's work. Now, we'd be traveling through Texas with a bus that read FAGGOTS RULE! across its side.

Brian and Will would not be outdone. With a sewing needle and some dental floss, Brian sewed together long strings of bologna slices from our backstage deli trays, until he could drape them over his chest. He stripped down to his underwear. With the help of the other boys, he made himself a sort of bologna suit. They found some clear tape in the road crew's toolbox and were able to encase Brian's arms and legs in the processed meat.

Soon enough, our dressing room was all giggles and the sound of tape ripping off its reel. They did a great job with his head, encasing it in several layers of slices, letting a few hang about his shoulders like hair. Puddle-jumper was halfway through their set once the boys finished the job. The three of them stood back for a second to admire their work.

"So." I poured myself a Cold War from off the bar. "What do you do now?"

"Accompany them," Brian said. "Puddle-fucker could use a good bologna-ist."

Ask a stupid question, I thought.

Nathan took off his necklace of badges and passes and hung it around Brian's neck. "You're authorized, dude."

The boys walked out toward the stage.

"Sean!" I shouted as they left. I hoped he wasn't yet too drunk to have a serious talk.

"What's up?" He stood by the door, the whiskey bottle they'd been passing around still in his hand.

"You okay?" I asked.

"Yeah, good." He put his free hand up near his damaged rib.

"You don't have to keep doing this," I said.

"What do you mean?"

"Getting wasted, throwing yourself all over the stage. We can bag the whole thing. I'm fine with walking away now."

"Fuck that. This is what I've wanted to do my entire life."

"Fine," I said. "Just don't do it for me, is all I'm saying. To my mind, it's not worth it, what you're doing to yourself."

He nodded his head. "Is that all?"

"No," I said. "This thing with us, this phony relationship, I'm over it. It's a joke."

"I'm sorry about that." Sean turned and looked to the ground.

"The whole idea, it's silly. We're not in love. You can see that, can't you?" I shook my head and fumbled through the lighting of a cigarette. "I understand if you don't want to have some big sensational breakup. But I need you to admit, no matter what the magazines say, no matter what anybody else thinks, you and me"—I pointed back and forth between the two of us—"we're over. We have been for a while. You do get that, don't you?"

He uncapped the whiskey bottle in his hands and took a big pull. After a grimace and a breath, he said, "I get it. Thanks for not making a big deal about it."

"No worries," I said.

"Want to check out what Brian does?"

On the wings of the stage, Will and Nathan stood by the security guy on the side. Brian took his first few tentative steps past him onto the main stage. From the back corner, where the band couldn't yet see him, Brian mocked Jeff's poses. Astute members of the audience pointed and laughed. Brian hammed it up—pardon the expression—his little disks of meat flapping all about. Thinking it was part of the act, the light tech shone a spotlight on Brian. That was when Puddle-jumper saw.

A good band would've worked with this. Brian brought the audience to life. But Puddle-jumper got pissed off. In between verses, Jeff motioned for the big security guy who'd let Brian onstage to pull him. The guard was nonplussed—there was no real threat. But after a second, he went ahead and dragged Brian off. A couple of boos came from the audience.

"What is it with you guys from Montana?" I asked once we were all backstage. "You're all obsessed with putting meat into the performance."

Nobody gave me an answer. I fixed another Cold War. The boys passed around the whiskey. Brian kept his bologna suit on. When time came for us to take the stage, nobody discussed it, we just brought him out there with us. It was like: why waste a perfectly good bologna suit, right?

For our entire set, Brian was a grotesque go-go dancer. He jumped around, riled everybody up, dived into the mosh pit at the front. Best of all, he interacted with Sean. The two of them performed running hip checks into each other. At one point, they did the AC/DC thing, with Sean playing guitar atop Brian's shoulders. It was perfect; Sean had another body to bash himself into, rather than the hard surfaces of the stage and our equipment.

At the end of the set, Sean climbed up onto the small ledge of my drum riser to set up for his signature belly flop. Brian was there to break his fall, and the two of them tumbled to the ground like a poorly coordinated pro-wrestling stunt. Both Sean and the audience seemed satisfied.

Backstage, I was surprised that our dressing room hadn't been trashed by Puddle-jumper. Still giddy from the performance, we grabbed some drinks to take along for the ride through central Texas.

There, standing around our tour bus, were the guys from Puddle-jumper. We assembled like two street gangs in an old movie. I was in the front of my band.

"That's it." Their bass player was the first to speak. "It's go time."

I laughed out loud. The boys followed suit. It was impossible to take them seriously. "Get out of here with that macho bullshit. Shake hands or something and let's get some sleep."

"We're way past that," Jeff said. "Now we got to battle."

The five of us erupted in laughter once again.

"Look," I said. "Lighten up. That bologna thing was shits and giggles."

"Dude." Jeff looked at Sean as he spoke. "You better shut your bitch up."

"Shut up, bitch!" Sean said sarcastically. We all had another good laugh.

"You all think this is funny?" Jeff raised his voice. "You think everything is funny, don't you? See if you think this is funny!" He put his hand around my chin and the sides of my mouth, squeezing my jaw. He wasn't choking me, but it hurt—like he was literally wiping the smile off my face.

I heard a bottle break from behind, then Nathan's voice. "Get your hands off her or I swear to God I'll cut your fucking throat." The broken glass was in his hand, held above Jeff's sternum. I was thankful that no press was around for this. Jeff backed off straightaway.

"What the hell is going on here?" Commander Spaz stormed over. Moving with a purpose, his nervous tics subsided a little. "This better not be what it looks like."

"These guys are leaving, to get on their own bus." Nathan threw the broken bottle at a Dumpster.

Jeff led his band away. We all watched as they walked off.

"Michael called on the mobile," Commander Spaz said once Puddle-jumper was out of earshot.

"Oh, Christ." I pulled out my cigarettes, stuck one in my mouth, and searched my pockets for a lighter. "What did we do now?"

"Your album is number one," said Commander Spaz.

We turned and stared at him. My unlit cigarette hung from my lips. "What did you say?"

"You bumped off Bryan Adams's record. The whole industry's going apeshit."

"You mean like number one on the college charts or something?" I said.

"No. Number one. *Billboard*'s number one album." Commander Spaz looked me in the eye for the very first time.

"That's cool," Sean said. "That should shut up those Puddle-humpers about opening for us." He climbed into the bus. Will and Brian followed.

"So what do we do now?" I asked.

"Get some sleep," Commander Spaz said. "Michael says he'll talk to you in the morning. The tour will go on, but we might add some nights in the bigger towns on the East Coast."

The muffled sounds of bottles and cans popping open and clanging together came from inside the bus. Nathan and I stood there in the parking lot, staring at Commander Spaz.

"Congratulations," he said with a smile, then walked off.

"This is fucked up," I said.

Nathan reached out and lit the cigarette that still dangled from my lips.

"What happens now?" I asked him.

"Among other things"—Nathan took out his own smoke and lit up—"we'll have to make a kick-ass second album."

"Don't you think this is weird?" I was surprised by everyone's casual reaction. "We're supposed to be a punk rock band. You're not worried that our record went too mainstream?"

"That's one way of looking at it," Nathan said. "Maybe the mainstream's finally ready to go punk rock."

Somewhere in the middle of Texas, I woke up inside my berth. We cruised along a flat, straight section of interstate. Snores sounded from outside. The boys had gone to bed at last. I knew I wouldn't fall back to sleep. I found a T-shirt there in the berth, pulled it on over my underwear, and climbed out from behind the curtain.

To my surprise, Nathan sat at the dining table, a spiral notebook and a pen in his hand. He scratched hard at the paper, his lips moving whenever his pen stopped.

"Can't sleep?" I said.

He startled at the sound of my voice. The pen dropped to the floor.

"Sorry," I said.

"It's okay." He leaned down to pick up his pen under the table. "I didn't see you there."

I found a Jack Daniel's bottle that was still half full and poured some into one of the Dixie cups from the dispenser by the sink. "Want some?" I asked.

"Sure," Nathan said. His eyes drifted back down to his pad but lingered for a half second on the curve of my hip.

"What are you working on?" I held the paper cup out in front of him.

"Lyrics." He took it from my hand. "All of a sudden, I've got to follow up on a number one album."

I took a sip from the waxy paper cup and looked out the window at
the darkened Texas landscape rolling past. "I lost my virginity here."

A sudden laugh, like a hiccup, escaped Nathan's mouth. "Right
here, huh? No wonder you woke up."

I smiled. "Maybe it was five hundred miles from here. I don't fucking know. The side of some long-ass road in Texas. In a ditch. With
some asshole who always treated me like shit."

"Why are you telling me this?" Nathan held his pen flat against the
paper.

I shrugged. "I've been thinking about my life a lot lately." With two
hands, I sipped from my cup of whiskey. "The music thing, how it's all
come about. In the first place, it was my brother's passion. I went along
for the ride. Then, with this band, you guys literally showed up on my
doorstep. The biggest band in the world, and I would've tripped over it
trying to get home from my job slinging coffee. It's great, you know.
I've been lucky. But still, it's all just . . . happened."

"It didn't just happen," Nathan said. "Without you, we'd still be
two kids jamming in a basement somewhere in Montana, listening to
some born-again drunk asshole call us losers."

"Sure, I've been part of the journey," I said. "But you guys chose
the direction. Same with Anthony."

"Everybody feels that way, to some extent." Nathan scratched at the
waxy surface of the paper cup with his thumbnail. "Like their lives
chose them, rather than the other way around."

"The bands are one thing. I'm okay with that. I'd rather be a foot
soldier than a general anyway. But what I've been thinking about lately
is how I've been this way in all my relationships, too."

"What?" Nathan shook his head, as if I were being silly.

"Yes. That guy, the ditch, this road. That was . . . what was there,
you know."

Nathan poured himself more whiskey, uncomfortable with the conversation's new turn.

"Same with Sean," I said at last. "We were both there and unattached. The only sense it made was convenience."

"What's your point?" Nathan rubbed his temple hard with one hand.

"My point is that I never fought to be with any guy. I never took the hard road, never overcame anything. And I've never been happy in any relationship. I want to change that."

"Laura." Nathan looked up the aisle to be sure nobody else was awake. "We talked about this. It's not happening."

"Sean and I are through. We're not making a big deal about it. What would be the point? Nobody wants another media circus. But it's over. He gets it. Ask him about it, if you like."

"It's not that simple. Even if it was a mistake, you can't erase it."

I had another sip of whiskey to steel myself. "The thing Sean doesn't know is this: After we're done with this tour, and one more album, I'm quitting the band."

The color drained out of Nathan's face. "That's a long way from now. Anything could happen."

"I know. I'm patient. Do you understand what I'm saying? I want to be with you. And I don't mind that it isn't going to be easy."

ST. LOUIS, MISSOURI: JULY 1984

On the way back to the motel room with two cans of Coca-Cola in your hand, realize that you never bothered to check the room number. Dozens of doors line up along one brick wall, all looking the same. In your light and quiet step, put your ear up to each one.

The first is silent. The second has a television playing loud—people cheering, bells, a game show perhaps. On the third try, you're almost knocked over by a maid pushing the cleaning cart out the door.

It's at the next one that you hear Hank's familiar voice from inside. Stack both ice-cold cans in one of your hands, and go to turn the knob.

Then you hear it: "I'll tell you what. He's getting to be one preachy motherfucker up there."

A grunt of understanding from Billy.

"The whole reason kids come to these shows is that they're sick of having rules shoved down their throats all the damn time."

Feel your fingers go numb against the aluminum. Pull your other hand back from the knob and lean your ear in a little closer. There was a difference of opinion about the sleeping arrangements. Anthony is staying at one of the squats. Hank insisted on getting a room. You never thought it was that big a deal.

"It's one thing to rail against the government and the president and all. Everybody's cool with that, or puts up with it at least. But now Anthony wants to act like he's everybody's dad or something. That's fucked up. You watch. Kids will stop coming to our shows behind this bullshit."

Another grunt from Billy.

What do you do now? Your world suddenly becomes less simple. You must choose between your older brother and your lover. Or must you?

Make a noisy show of opening the door, pretend you didn't hear anything, and help pour another round of Cold Wars.

You would like to see the fighting and the violence stop as well. But Hank's right: The kids aren't responding, and you don't believe they will. Take a sip of the drink, smoke one of Hank's cigarettes, wait the last few hours before load-in, and hope that this all blows over.

TWENTY-FIVE

"Did you save me a ticket?" I sneaked up on Nathan as he poured coffee from the big urn in the lobby. A second show had been added in D.C., and the label put us up in a nice hotel for the weekend. It was still early. Everybody else was asleep.

"A ticket?" He stirred in sugar.

"Remember? When you talked me into playing the Wreck Room, I said to save me a ticket when you sell out RFK Stadium." I took a cup of my own and filled it.

Nathan smiled. "It was like pulling teeth to get you to join this band."

"Do you want to come with me today?" I hadn't thought to ask until the question left my lips.

"Where to?"

"I'm going to see my brother."

"Oh my god." She looked so much older, standing there in the doorway. Her face gaunt and wrinkled, she might've been a grandmother.

"Hi, Mom." I wrapped my arms around her. It took her a second to return the embrace. Nathan stood silent a few steps behind us.

"What are you doing here?" She put her hand up to her chest.

"I'm playing music, at the stadium."

"The stadium," she repeated.

"I bought my own house, Mom. This band I'm in, we've gotten big."

Tears crept down her cheeks. She looked confused, as though she didn't quite believe in what I said, or that it truly was me standing in front of her.

"This is Nathan." I held my arm out toward him. "He's in my band."

"Nice to meet you." He stepped forward and offered his hand.

"How do you do?" my mother said.

"Who's at the door?" My father's voice came from down the hall. A moment later, he stood in the threshold behind my mother, one hand holding a crumpled-up wad of paper, latex, and gauze.

"Oh my," he said. "Hello, Laura." He looked tired.

"Hi, Dad. How are you?"

"Good, yes. I was with Anthony."

An awkward moment of silence followed. None of us knew what to say.

Finally, my father broke it: "Did you get my check?"

"Yeah." I wiped at the tears along the sides of my eyes. "Thank you. It helped out a lot. But you don't need to send them anymore. I've got money now."

He nodded, surprised.

"She bought a house," my mother said.

"That's wonderful." My father couldn't take his eyes off me. His hand tightened around the wad of rubbish.

"I want to see Anthony."

"Right," my father said. "I was just cleaning him up. Could you give me one more minute?"

"It's okay," I said. "I don't mind seeing him as is."

Nathan and I followed my father up the stairs to my brother's bedroom. I stopped at the door and wished I'd accepted the offer to wait. Dad had been treating a bad bedsore on my brother's hip. Anthony lay on his side. My first sight of him in years was that big red sore, oozing pus. With Nathan behind me, I watched from the door while my father applied a layer of ointment and then a gauze bandage. It wasn't that this grossed me out, but it seemed disrespectful somehow, like walking in on somebody in the bathroom.

As my father flipped Anthony back over, I turned to Nathan. "If you're not up for this," I said. "It's okay. It means a lot that you came this far."

Nathan nodded. "I want to go in," he said.

"All right." My father wiped at the side of Anthony's mouth with a white cloth. "All set."

Nathan and I entered the room. It was still covered in the pictures and papers that Anthony had adorned it with as a teenager: photos of California and Midwest hardcore bands, my original drawings for the SCC album covers, a tattered flyer from that Bad Brains show that set both our lives into their first real motion. There was a Food Not Bombs logo and an old anarchy flag. These four walls were a document of every punk show that came through D.C. for a couple of years in the eighties. Anthony had saved all the flyers—most of them with crudely altered images of Ronald Reagan committing atrocities: killing puppies, eating babies, shitting missiles out his ass. Only after the tragedy did my parents respect Anthony's right to hang whatever he wanted in his room.

Slowly, like one of those dreams where your feet weigh a ton, Nathan and I approached the bed. Anthony's body was draped in a gown that allowed easy access to all his orifices. Several other bandages poked out around the sides of his back and legs—more pressure ulcers perhaps, all the result of lying in this same position for so many years. His skin was pale and unhealthy, with a sort of bluish tinge. His hair had grown out in those kinky curls that I used to shave away so often. One tube came down from a bag hanging on a metal stand and entered Anthony's arm. Another tube came out from under his gown and filled a bag that hung from a rail along his bed. This is what my brother had become, a filter for bags of fluid.

His face, once the window to his boiling intensity, now wore an expression of tired indifference. It was as though his eyes could barely be bothered to open, like the nose would just as soon fall off. Every part of him looked victim to too much gravity. From his slumped-forward head to the loose flesh on his limbs, it all seemed to want to go down, down, to fade into the ground already, or drain out into a plastic bag underneath the bed.

"Anthony," my father said. "Look who's here to see you."

"Dad, could you give us a minute?" I asked.

"Of course." He tapped on the IV drip a couple of times, then left the room.

"Anthony," I said once the door was closed, "meet Nathan. He's one of your fans."

"Can he . . . hear us?" Nathan was taken aback.

"No," I said. "Not at all."

"Is it like a coma?"

"Technically, it's what they call a 'persistent vegetative state.'"

"Is there any chance he could wake up?" Nathan asked.

I shrugged, still looking down at my brother in bed. "Not really. If somebody is going to wake up, they do so in the first year. After this long, it's next to impossible."

"I'm sorry," Nathan said.

"We have a band, Anthony." I raised my voice. "Me, Nathan here, and another guy. We're playing at RFK tonight." I noticed my voice quivering as the words came out. "We signed to one of the majors. At first, we were on an indie label, but we left." Tears formed in the sides of my eyes and fell down along my cheeks. My face filled up with blood and wrinkled together around the rubbery clump of my chin.

Nathan put his hand on my back and rubbed a circle into it.

"You would probably consider us sellouts or something," I said. "Part of the problem. But it's hard, Anthony. Back then, I didn't have to worry about all these things. I didn't have rent or bills, you know."

Nathan offered me a wad of tissues, and I blew my nose.

"But you know what? We're reaching a lot of people. It's more polished and produced, but the music is good. The kids love us. Is that something I should be ashamed of?" I reached down and took hold of my brother's moist hand. It felt as if the skin might come off there in my grasp like an empty glove, like the unused flesh could break up into a cloud of dust if I squeezed too hard.

"I don't know, Anthony. That's the thing. I have nobody to tell me right from wrong anymore. You were always there to make it clear. Now, look at me." I used my free thumb to point at Nathan. "I love him, and I think he loves me, too."

"Laura, please," Nathan whispered into my ear.

"But we can't be together because of this other guy in the band, because of some fucked-up notion of what's right, because of how it would look to the public, because of how fragile the other guy is."

"Stop. Please, stop it." Nathan's voice grew louder.

"If you were here, Anthony, you would tell me what to do, and that would be that."

I turned away from my brother at last. Looking down at the floor, each of my hands tucked under the opposite armpit, I took a step toward Nathan and leaned forward, all but begging him to give me a hug. He obliged.

There in his arms, with my tears and snot soaking the front of his shirt, I finally said, "Sorry if that got weird." But I wasn't sorry. I was glad he heard it.

Downstairs, my mother made a pot of coffee and set out some cheese and crackers. Nathan and I hadn't eaten all day. The four of us sat in the dining room, enjoying the snack.

"So?" My father wrapped both hands around his coffee mug as if keeping them warm. "Your music is doing well?" he asked.

"Better than we ever dreamed," I said. "Radio, stadiums, MTV. It's crazy."

"That's wonderful," my mother said.

"It's different is what it is." I wiped at the sides of my swollen eyes with the soiled wad of tissues that Nathan had given me upstairs. "I wouldn't say that it's better or worse than the way things used to be."

My mother didn't stop smiling. "So, Nathan, you're in this new band as well?"

I looked around our dining room, the site of so many silly fights. There was still that awkward patch of wallpaper where my father had thrown the Thanksgiving pie.

"Yes, ma'am. I play bass. Another friend of ours—"

"Mom, Dad," I interrupted. "There's something I need to say to you."

Both of them stared down into the darkness of their coffees. My mother's hands gripped tighter around the mug, preparing to weather a confrontation. Nathan sat across the table, in my brother's old chair. He shook his head, as if to say: *don't do this to them, let it go.*

"Thank you, both of you," I said. "For taking care of him. I know we had our differences, all four of us. Anthony and I thought we were building a community. But when push came to shove, it was you guys who stood up. The rest of them—the rest of us, really—can't say that."

My mother let out a sigh, then looked up at me with moist eyes.

She probably thought I was about to insist they pull the plug or something. My father smiled and nodded.

Nathan tapped his watch with one finger. "Laura, the show."

Back at the hotel, everyone had left for the stadium. The front desk called us a taxi.

"Laura, is that you?" A voice came from over my shoulder.

A tall man in a black suit stood in the lobby. He had a distinctive square jaw and full lips. I didn't recognize him at first. Then it came to me.

"Hank."

"I heard you were staying here and didn't have any other way to get in touch with you. I'm sorry if it's a bit stalker. You look great."

"You know me," I said. "Clean living and a pure heart."

"Right." Hank smiled broadly. His chestnut hair was slick with beauty products.

"Nice suit," I said.

"Can you believe it?" Hank picked up the tip of his tie. "I'm in advertising."

"Advertising?" I said.

"Jingles, mostly," he said. "I get to be creative. The money's good."

Nathan stood a few feet away from us, checking the front door for our cab.

"Not you, though, huh?" Hank continued. "You never gave up on the music thing."

I shrugged, hands out at my sides. "Don't know nothing else."

Hank laughed, though it wasn't actually a joke.

"Laura," Nathan said softly, not meaning to interrupt. "Our taxi's here."

"Hey"—Hank spoke to both of us now—"I know you guys are

busy. Let me give you this." He tucked a business card into my hand, the first time he'd touched me in many years.

"Hi, I'm Hank." He shook Nathan's hand. "Love the record."

Nathan nodded.

"Real quick." Hank turned back to me and held his two index fingers upright. "I've spoken to Billy. We agreed that with this new record you have out, there would be no better time for an SCC reunion!" He paused, as though waiting to hear what a great idea that was.

"An SCC reunion?"

"There's nostalgia for hardcore all of a sudden. With this grunge thing, people are revisiting all the old punk rock."

"The band, getting back together, playing music?"

"We got my man right over here." Hank gestured toward Nathan. "I'll bet he knows those old songs by heart." He gave me that same broad grin and raised his eyebrows.

"No, no," I said. "We'll get Anthony to do it."

That caught him off guard. "Excuse me?" Hank managed.

"Yeah, it'll be a bigger draw with the original singer, don't you think? More money all the way around." My body trembled now with years' worth of rage.

"Look, Laura," Hank spoke softly. "I didn't mean to—"

"We could prop him up on a coatrack or something."

"That's not—"

"Or get those thin strings like the magicians use and attach them to his lips. It would look like he's actually singing. In fact, why don't we just wire his whole body up and have him dance around like a god-damn marionette!" I shouted the last word so loud that everyone in the hotel lobby turned and stared.

"Look, it was only an idea."

"Have you ever even been to see him?"

"Laura, I'm sorry about what happened. We were kids."

"Fuck you!"

Nathan put his hand on the small of my back and whispered into my ear. "C'mon, Laura. We've got to go." I allowed him to lead me toward the door.

"Stay the fuck away from me, Hank!" I shouted over my shoulder as we walked out.

Hank stood alone and cast his head downward, once again lifting up the tip of his tie.

"Where the hell have you two been?" Sean was drunk and angry in the dressing room, already wearing his guitar across his chest. Brian and Will sat on a leather couch along one wall.

"It's a long story," Nathan told him.

My face was puffy with so many crying episodes, my eyes all red and bloodshot. Sean mistook this for a look of guilt. Onstage, Puddle-jumper played what sounded like their closer.

"Let's hear it, goddamnit. I've been here for hours, wondering if we were going to play tonight or what."

"Cool it, dude," Nathan said calmly. "Laura's had a hard day."

"I've had a hard day wondering where my band was!"

"Sean!" I turned to him and screamed. "Shut the fuck up. Do you know how many shows have been ruined or canceled on account of you and your bullshit? We're a little bit late. The opening band is still playing, for Christ's sake!"

Sean hung his head and stared at the strings of his guitar. Will and Brian sat silent on their couch, a bag of corn chips between them.

"What's with you?" I said to Brian. "Where's your bologna suit?"

"I wasn't sure you were going to show up." He spoke in a whisper, scared I might turn and chew him out next. "Commander Spaz is pissed. He was talking about refunding the audience their money and stuff."

"Jesus!" I threw my hands up in the air. "Isn't this supposed to be rock and roll? When did punctuality become such a big deal?"

"Okay, I spoke with Michael." Commander Spaz walked in, staring at the ground. "According to the contract—"

"It's okay," I said. "We're here."

Commander looked up from his feet. "About time."

"We heard."

Puddle-jumper quit playing. Even all the way in the back, we could hear the sounds of a restless crowd. Nathan checked the tuning on his bass.

"Fuck it," I said. "Let's play this show, shall we?"

We took to the stage and the audience cheered. I looked forward to performing—an escape from everything that had happened today. Nathan never had a chance to make a set list, but we'd been playing the songs in mostly the same order for so long now, it didn't matter much.

Sean did nothing but scowl at Nathan and me after the argument in the dressing room. For the first time in a while, the three of us and our problems didn't feel so important.

Nathan chatted to the crowd while I adjusted my kit. The lights from above were blinding, after hours without seeing the sun. Sean tapped his pedals and rolled his neck as if ready to start. I took a deep breath and stretched my arms, preparing to hit hard on the "Nowhere Fast" bits.

But Sean shocked both Nathan and me by starting off with that slow and haunting chord sequence from "Devil You Know." I looked at Nathan. Nathan looked at Sean. Sean stared straight down at his fingers on the fretboard. Without a set list, he technically wasn't in the wrong. When Nathan approached the microphone and sang the first line—*"It was a bad idea taken way too far / on a night too cold to spend alone in a car"*—the audience erupted.

We put the song through its paces. It felt different from playing it as the closer, when we were all exhausted. Toward the end of the final verse, I looked up at the boys to see how we were going to end this. Surely, we wouldn't go into that extended jammy breakdown we did during an encore.

Without warning, Sean sped up his line. The crowd responded with a wave of cheers and hoots. Apparently, we were going to do that sped-up instrumental part, whether we liked it or not.

Within seconds, I was sweating, head down, hair flying everywhere, drumming as hard as my arms would allow. I thought of my brother's near-shapeless body spread across that bed like thick jelly. I thought of my parents, keeping him alive. I thought about the community that Anthony and I had worked so hard to create, how they'd abandoned him and abandoned one another until they thought there might be a dollar in exploiting it as "nostalgia." I thought about these boys in my band. One could go through with the theatrics of hurting himself only because he's never been truly and irredeemably hurt. The other can get caught up in caretaking only because he's never really had to try to heal a loved one.

I channeled all that frustration into the eighth and sixteenth notes on the high hat and snare. I didn't even notice what was going on with the guitar.

Sean still managed to play, in a sense. He turned on all his effects pedals. The digital delay bounced every single note back over and over again, so that it sounded like more music than it actually was. With his guitar still strapped on, Sean climbed up a rigging on the side of the stage, pausing every few steps to hammer down on the fretboard and send another wave of notes echoing through the speakers. His eyes were wild and drifting, as if seeing nothing solid, only the colors of the music.

Into the microphone, Nathan sang a sort of improvised version of the song's refrain. He hadn't noticed what Sean was up to.

"Nathan!" I screamed, though it was impossible for him to hear me over the instruments, the monitors, the crowd. Sean had already climbed up six feet or so. The audience pointed at him and cheered. Finally,

Nathan turned and looked to stage left. He missed a beat or two on his bass line as he saw what his best friend was up to.

Sean freed one hand and made to send another shower of distortion through the PA system and into the air. With that one hand on the guitar, he lost balance and the other hand slipped from off the rigging. He fell backwards onto the stage.

Sean's body made a dull thud as it hit. The brunt of the landing was borne by his upper back and head. The guitar clanged down and then fed back with a piercing whine.

Nathan, Brian, Will, and I all waited in the dressing room for word on Sean's condition. It was silent but for us sucking on cigarettes and shifting around on the leather couches. Someone had been sent out to the stage to apologize to the crowd.

"Nathan," I finally spoke up. "I can't do this anymore."

Nathan nodded back at me. "It'll soon be over. We'll be safe and sound inside a recording studio before long."

"I don't think we'll make it."

"Laura," he said. "Don't take this the wrong way. But after what happened with your brother, did you ever think about giving up on music altogether? I'm not trying to judge. It just seems like a bad blow, you know. It might've soured me for good."

I plucked at the side of my eyebrow. Nobody had asked me that before. "I tried to stop," I said. "I swore to myself that I'd never pick up another instrument again, never set foot onstage. But it's like I told Hank today: I don't know how to do anything else. That, and I missed it. It's like an addiction, I guess. You know it hurts you and your family and friends, but still you can't live without it."

Commander Spaz walked in. "Good news," he said. "Sean sustained a bad concussion, but he's all right now. They want to keep him overnight for some tests and scans. You all can stop by and see him.

I've left messages with Michael, but I don't yet know what the policy is on the show tomorrow night."

"Forget the show," I said. "That's my policy."

"Excuse me?" said Commander Spaz.

"I'm done. No more tour."

"I'm afraid that you signed a contract."

"You're afraid, are you? I'm afraid, too. I'm afraid to watch another talented young man self-destruct onstage. I'm afraid of having that on my conscience all over again. What I'm not afraid of, however, is Michael and his fucking contract."

Commander Spaz gave a satisfied nod, then turned and left the room.

"Do you want to go to the hospital?" Nathan asked me.

"No," I said. "I can't keep indulging him. He gets all weird and jealous about the two of us spending the day together—which isn't any of his business anyway. And when being pissed off doesn't get him the attention that he wants, he goes and hurts himself all over again. I'm not playing this game anymore."

"Will I see you back at the hotel?" Nathan asked.

"No," I said. "I'm going home."

PHILADELPHIA: AUGUST 1984

Maybe word of Anthony's new policy didn't reach Philly yet. Maybe the idea is finally working. For the first few songs of the set, the kids don't fight. The slam-dancing goes on as expected, but your brother chooses his battles. It feels good to play a normal show again. You're reminded of why you enjoy it. Watching a roomful of people sing along to a song you're playing—is there anything more moving?

Then you see him at the back of the hall—the skinhead you've never even learned a nickname for. Your eyes meet Hank's. He tilts his head in a kind of semi-shrug. Anthony dives off the stage and disappears into the crowd.

You've come to think of that skinhead the way that other kids might think of the devil—pure evil, lurking in the background, someone whose very mention could bring trouble to you and your loved ones.

Focus on your bass line. Try and play him away, keep him at the back. Walk to the edge of the stage and play to your fans. Reward them their good behavior. This grueling tour is almost over. Look forward to going home more than ever—a soft bed, square meals. Fuck music.

Fuck art. Fuck history. You want to sit in front of the television and fall asleep to reruns for the first time in so many months—though you'd never admit to any such thing in front of your brother. He's taught you to think of those desires as a weakness. Along with your fondness for cigarettes and alcohol, it's something to feel guilty about.

Realize, as you watch your brother float atop the hands of kids considered unreachable by parents and teachers, that this is a fundamental difference between the two of you. Anthony looks for ways to make life harder, not easier. He reaps short-term pain, as though it might lead to long-term pleasure somewhere down the line. Punk rock is a form of piety for him. Later, you will wonder if your impurity of heart isn't the reason that things went so wrong.

TWENTY-SIX

I came home to my house in Magnolia, my fancy knives and ladles, the art propped along the walls still waiting to be hung. For twenty-four hours, I sat inside and did nothing. I lived off a few canned goods that were left in my pantry and listened to the hums and clicks of the refrigerator turning itself on and off.

The phone rang, but I didn't answer it. Michael's voice on the machine sounded suspiciously pleasant. He said that the boys had gone back to Montana for a while, but things were in the works for recording a second album. There was no yelling or blame or talk of breach-of-contract.

"I hope things are all right, Laura." My ears pricked up when the voice turned personal. "I'm not sure how to say this, but we take it seriously—or I do, at least—the health of the band, physical and mental. You guys are human beings, not just a commodity. Give me a call when you get a chance."

The next day, I drove my station wagon downtown. The parking space I found happened to be across the street from the Daily Grind. I walked in the other direction, straight to the SAM, to look at the collection I'd seen so many times before.

I found myself in the European section and got hung up on Cranach the Elder's *Judgment of Paris*. I couldn't recall how the Greek myth went—only that the mortal Paris was supposed to judge a beauty contest between three goddesses. There was a golden apple involved somehow, and the whole thing ended in a long and terrible war.

A couple of things struck me this time around. Paris looks to be sleeping there in the grass, too tired or indifferent to be much of a judge. And the three goddesses—standing naked and blushing—looked exactly the same. Maybe that was the painter's point: It was an arbitrary contest over nothing, a judgment among equals, that caused all the bloodshed and discord.

Back at my car, I went to open the door, but then looked across the street. A mix of attraction and repulsion came over me as I saw the Daily Grind. But I did want coffee.

The place was busy. Suits came in for their afternoon fix. Kids fresh out of school killed time. Much to my surprise, Liz stood behind the counter.

"Laura!" She was shocked to see me. "What are you doing here? I figured you all moved to L.A. or something."

"No, just Magnolia."

We stared at each other from our opposite sides of the counter. She looked exactly the same.

"You're famous now," she said.

"Could I have some coffee?"

"Of course." She filled the portafilter with grinds.

"How are you?" I raised my voice over the clangs and whirs.

"I'm good, same old thing." She had learned her way around the espresso machine. "How's Nathan?"

I considered telling her everything. That I was in love with Nathan, and that he was—in spite of himself—in love with me. And that this was one of the ways in which the band was tearing itself apart.

"He's handling things as well as anybody is, I suppose." Which was also the truth.

Liz nodded. "This is what he always wanted."

That fact had become meaningless to me. Wanting fame was a desire as universal as it was foolish.

"This is on me." Liz placed my drink on the counter.

"Liz, maybe it's none of my business, but you should be glad that things ended when they did. It would've gotten worse if you and Nathan had stayed together."

She looked down at her hands. I couldn't help but feel a sudden fellowship with her. We'd both been undone by the same confused boy.

"And as far as the band goes, you were along for the best part of the ride. Playing to kids for nothing here in Seattle—that was the golden age of the Mistakes." I didn't realize how true it was until I'd said it.

But Liz took my words as condescension. Like all reckless lovers, she didn't want to be told what was best for her. Her eyes grew puffy and moist. The glossy shine of her black hair faded a little. "Well," she said. "I better get back to work."

"It's good to see you," I said.

"Laura?" A voice came from behind. "Would you mind signing this?" A stranger held out a copy of a magazine. A flashbulb went off and blinded me. I understood why the line in the store hadn't grown impatient. They were watching. Now they wanted autographs.

"When are you playing in Seattle?"

My pupils readjusted. The magazine was thrust closer: a posed shot of the band, Sean standing in front with his hair in his eyes. The headline read: WHY THE WORLD NEEDS THE MISTAKES.

"Leave me alone," I muttered, and ran out of the store.

I jaywalked across the street toward my car. A bum was set up on the corner with a cardboard sign. NOW ACCEPTING TWENTY-DOLLAR BILLS! I thought it was Boeing Bob—the beard and body type were the same—out raising funds for his cappuccino. But it took only a second to see that it was a much younger man. I opened up my car and climbed inside. My coffee in the drink holder, I turned over the motor.

At the Daily Grind, a couple kids pointed toward my car, too shy to approach. I looked back at the beggar on the corner and thought of what Bob had told me about sacrifice: If you give up what you want, then you can trick the world into changing, force something new and unexpected to happen.

I turned off the engine, grabbed my coffee, and stepped out of the car. Across the street, the fans and coffee customers had lost interest. The bum glared at me suspiciously, as if I might beg something from him.

"Here," I said, holding out the car key. "That green Saab there. It's all yours. The title's in the glove box."

In his face, I saw that he was nothing like Bob. Twitchy and nervous, he hadn't taken up this lifestyle by choice. There was a good chance he suffered from mental illness or a substance-abuse problem. Somebody else must've given him that clever sign.

"Go ahead." I jingled the key in front of his face. "Drive it, sell it, whatever. I don't want it anymore."

He took the key from my hand, stood up, and walked away from me in the direction of the car. I was surprised by how smoothly he backed up and then pulled out.

The car disappeared down the street. Walking toward the bus stop—my low-cut Docs now well broken in—it seemed a thin line between that man and me.

"Oregon?" I asked. "Why the middle of nowhere?"

"Nathan made the call. He wants to record with Sheldon Quest. You heard of him?" Michael was pleasant over the phone.

"Sure. I like his stuff. But it's real lo-fi. Are you guys okay with that?"

A loud breath echoed through the earpiece. "In my personal opinion, the Mistakes have earned it. However, there are elements here at Kingdom that are concerned, to say the least. Nathan fought hard."

"I'm surprised you all still put up with us."

"The truth is, Laura, we're kind of off the map here. Your first record defies the logic of the market. Why should we try to tell you what to do? At this point, it's better to duck and get out of the way."

And let the product keep selling, I thought to myself. "So, Quest has his studio in Bend?"

"Just outside of town. Apparently, he lined up a house for you guys."

"Are there any airports there?"

"Not big ones. But it's only a day's drive from Seattle. You can drive, can't you?"

"Of course." I neglected to mention what had become of my car.

It was a gray day in Seattle. The drum set I'd ordered for this recording needed to be picked up downtown. In my garage, our old ambulance van waited for me like a sly dare. It started up on the first try. The noise of the bad muffler echoed throughout my concrete basement, and as I pulled into the street, many of my neighbors came to their doors—worried perhaps that a gang of bikers was coming to take over the block. It was a good feeling. As the yuppies stared and covered their ears, I couldn't help but smile. An old van, a pack of cigarettes, and a long drive—these things made me remember the best parts of my life.

And a wonderful drive it was. Down I-5 and through the fog to Portland, then inland to the back roads and the sunshine. Good radio stations came in most of the way. I tapped my hand against the steering wheel as the mountains and rivers blew past.

The directions Michael had dictated sent me through town and out to a neighborhood of fields and farms. It was a small back road where I finally found a little house with a light on. What looked to be a brand-new Chevy Blazer was parked in the driveway. The screen door swung open, and out stepped Nathan and Sean.

"No way!" Sean said. "Our van!"

"Where was this thing?" Nathan was equally surprised.

"In my garage," I said. "Is that yours?" I pointed to the Blazer.

"Nathan bought it," Sean said.

I looked past them at the little ranch-style house. "So this is the place?" It was good to see the boys. Sean looked healthy and whole. We were like old friends from years ago.

"C'mon in," Nathan said. "You want a drink? I bought vodka and Coke."

They helped me move the drums into the house.

On the walls were corny oil paintings of Western scenes, all done up in lush pastel colors: cowboys riding and roping, smoking around a campfire, always in front of a glorious sunset, as if that was the only time of day that existed in the West. The furniture was semi-ratty, like it had all been bought new but then allowed to age and wear a bit too long.

"What is this place?" I asked.

"Some farmer's tenant house." Nathan dropped ice cubes into a glass. "Not a lot of rentals around here." He handed me a drink, then pointed at Sean.

Sean held up a palm and shook his head no. This made me as happy as anything had in days.

"Where's the studio?" I asked.

"A couple miles down the road, inside a converted barn. It's pretty basic, but ten times better than that closet we used for the last record."

All of us laughed out loud at the thought of that tiny, funky room at the side of the railroad yard. That had seemed like an amazing opportunity for us, not so long ago.

"What's Sheldon like?"

"He's not as crazy as everybody says—a little intense is all."

"Do we have songs to record?"

Nathan shrugged. Sean nodded.

"We've finished some," Nathan said. "A few more need lyrics. We'll do rhythm tracks in the morning."

"Laura," Sean said. "Let me show you your bedroom."

He took the duffel bag with my clothes and things and walked down the hall. "It's the master," he said. "Has its own bathroom."

No bullshit about staying with him or sharing a room. Finally, Sean understood that we can't be a couple. Now, I only had to convince millions of fans around the world.

"Thanks, Sean," I said as he put my bag down at the foot of the bed. "I appreciate it," as if only thanking him for carrying my luggage.

We both walked back into the living room. Sean didn't drink—only chewed on pieces of peppery jerky—but didn't seem to mind that Nathan and I did. The three of us sat together talking and laughing until late.

Though we could smoke in here, I put on my coat and took a cigarette outside. The moon was nearly full. It lit up the tall brown grasses like some kind of sea. In the distance, where the sky met the land, I counted four separate snowcapped peaks, moonlight reflecting off their glaciers. Maybe I'd been wrong. Maybe it was possible for the three of us to work together for more than one more album.

PHILADELPHIA: AUGUST 1984

Feel something grab your pant leg. Next thing you know, you fall to your ass there onstage. The side of your head slams into a monitor, and the sound through the speaker deafens one ear.

When you look up, the nightmare skinhead looms over you, standing at the foot of the stage. His fist is cocked back, ready to strike. But he thinks better of it and puts both meaty hands around your ankle. All you hear is a ringing sound from that one ear, but you see that the band is still playing—Hank strums chords and faces the other way, your brother lost in the crowd somewhere.

Put your arms up around your head and prepare for a beating. Somehow land on your feet once your attacker pulls you off the stage. Your bass has disappeared. With a muscled arm on either side, he pins you against that half wall at the stage-front. You expect punches but instead there's only pressure.

Just above your asshole, feel what you first think is a knife about to stab but then recognize as an erection pressing through denim. The skinhead's wet tongue flickers against the inside of your ear like a snake's. Scream as loud as you can, but hear nothing save that ringing whine from one side of your head. Tears flow. You're in hell.

The blow landed by your brother is the first sound that breaks through the ringing in your ear. He slams the microphone into your attacker's shining bald head so hard that it comes apart upon impact. The sound echoes through the PA system like an atom bomb. The skinhead steps away and releases you. See a transistor and a piece of wire from the broken microphone stuck to the bloody side of his head—as though he's a cyborg whose human layer was just pierced by your brother. His hands go up over the robotic wound, and he stumbles off toward the exit.

Anthony's back is to you. His bare shoulders rise with each panting breath as he watches the skinhead disappear.

Your sense of sound returns in time for the first shout.

"Fucking hypocrite!" one fan yells.

TWENTY-SEVEN

Sheldon was hardly the imposing presence his reputation suggested. No taller than me, he had thin limbs and narrow shoulders. He kept his reddish hair in a kind of mullet and wore all black clothes.

"Set up your drums over there and let's get the microphones checked," were his first words to me.

"Nice to meet you," I muttered under my breath.

A rogue figure in underground music, Sheldon Quest had recorded some of the great post-punk cult classics. But his temper and eccentricity were legendary. Despite all my indie cred, I was intimidated by him. One trademark of his recording style was a raw and powerful drum sound. I wasn't sure if I had the chops.

Once we were set up, Sheldon spoke to the three of us through a microphone from inside his booth. "Okay," he said. "I'd like to do the track we talked about yesterday."

Nathan nodded. Sean tapped on a few of his pedals.

"Hold up!" I shouted. "I haven't learned any of the new songs."

A deafening burp echoed through the speakers. Sheldon almost wrapped his lips around the microphone as he finished belching, then hit a digital delay switch, which made the burp bounce off the studio walls for the next several seconds. Nathan and Sean giggled at the prank.

"Well," Sheldon said, his voice still echoing through the mic, "I hope you learn fast." He left the control booth through a back door.

"Okay." Nathan turned to me. "It goes like this."

It was a good tune. The verse was slow and dark—not unlike "Devil You Know"—but then a loud and hard chorus. I had no trouble coming up with a drumbeat.

I hadn't even heard the lyrics yet, but I could tell that this was as good as any tune the Mistakes had ever made. If the rest of Nathan's material was like this, our new album would kill.

Sheldon came back to the studio with a carton of chocolate milk and a plastic package of waxy doughnuts. "Are we ready?" he asked.

"We're ready," Nathan said.

At my insistence, the bass line was put down first. Nathan nailed it in one take. The drum track took longer, but Sheldon seemed happy with what he got.

Sean hesitated once it came time for him to enter the live room. "I'm just doing the rhythm track for now, yeah?" He asked the question to Sheldon, but looked to Nathan for some kind of confirmation.

"Right," Sheldon's voice came over the speakers. "We'll get this, get the vocals, then do the leads later."

Nathan and I went into the booth and sat down. In the live room, Sean played guitar with headphones on. He kept screwing up. He played the wrong chord, fell out of time, paused for too long. It was painful to watch, like waiting on a stutterer to finish a sentence. Sheldon sat there stunned.

On the seventh or eighth unsuccessful take, Sheldon looked to Nathan and me. "Is there something going on here that I'm not aware of?"

I rubbed my temples with my forefingers, wondering where to start.

"Could you give us half an hour?" Nathan said. "We'll sort it out."

Sheldon nodded and turned back to the mixing board.

I sat in the back of Nathan's Blazer as the three of us took a silent drive. In the front passenger seat, Sean stared forward. Nathan pulled into a small shopping center, parked, and walked into the liquor store. Sean and I stayed in the car.

"I'm proud of you, Sean." I thought he deserved that much. "For cleaning up and for being cool about us . . . us being over and all."

He gazed straight ahead as the fall day came steadily toward its end and the air grew cold. The back passenger door opened up beside me. Nathan placed a large bottle wrapped in a shopping bag on the floor behind the driver's seat. The black-and-white Jack Daniel's label showed through the thin plastic.

Back at the studio, the sun was low and orange in the sky. The three of us stayed inside the car even after Nathan had turned it off. The new engine pinged a couple of times as it cooled.

"Could you hand it up here?" Sean said.

I took the bottle by the neck and passed it to the front. Sean puffed out his cheeks in a strong exhale.

"Sean," Nathan said. "You don't have to do this if you don't want to. Seriously. Fuck the record. We don't need to make music anymore. Say the word, and we'll go home." I'd never loved Nathan any more than I did at that moment.

But Sean shook his head. "I can handle this," he said. "It's like a light switch, you know, once I start seeing the shit. If I drink the right amount, I'll be cool."

Sean broke the seal. Lifting it up with both hands, he took a gulp. I watched the bubbles swim up through the amber liquid to the inverted square of the bottle's bottom. I cringed the way I used to when he'd leap off the drum riser. It was like watching a samurai shove a knife into his belly—all a part of some code as strict as it was arbitrary.

We got out of the truck and shared a cigarette while Sean took more swigs from his whiskey—the medicine meant to restore his disease.

"Okay," he said. "I'm ready."

I took out another cigarette and passed the pack to Nathan. "We'll see you inside."

A gust of wind blew in the first wave of chilly night air. Sean walked off toward the converted barn. The tails of his flannel shirt puffed in the breeze. The oversized whiskey bottle hung at the end of his arm like a claw he'd neglected to trim. A few strands of blue hair whipped in front of my face. Nathan cupped his hand around the lighter and held the flame out for me. I leaned into it and lit up, my eyes still on Sean as he entered the studio door.

"It might work." Nathan shivered with the sudden chill.

"Thanks for giving him the choice," I said. "That was good of you."

"It's always been his choice," Nathan said. "You were right about that part."

"If we get through this album," I said, "there's no way he'd survive the road again."

"I thought you were quitting after this record anyway." Nathan looked at me. The sun was setting behind his head, and I had to squint a little to look him in the eye.

"That's right." I never thought he'd taken me seriously on this count. "But I'm replaceable."

"No." Nathan lifted his chin and made a trumpet of his lips, blowing the smoke upward. "There's no Mistakes without you."

Inside the studio, Sean was slaying it. His mop of hair stuck out around the sides of his headphones, the Stratocaster—a newer blue one—hung too low at his waist. The jug of bourbon rested on a stool nearby like another instrument.

"Whatever the fuck you guys did"—Sheldon stared down at his mixing board—"it worked."

Nathan and I exchanged a look that wasn't exactly a smile, more like a mutual acknowledgment that this hadn't blown up in our faces yet, but still could.

"The way it's going," Sheldon went on, "we'll need to record the vocals tomorrow."

"That's cool," Nathan said.

Back at our house, Nathan put on a pot of coffee and opened up his notebook. It dawned on me that he hadn't yet finished the lyrics he needed to record in the morning.

Sean forgot all about handling his problem. "C'mon, guys." His speech was slurred. "Let's go check out this town. I haven't partied in a long time."

"I'm going to bed." I didn't want to see Sean like this, didn't want to start hating him again. Inside my bedroom, I drifted off to the sounds of Nathan's pen scratching against his spiral notebook, and the occasional grunt or sigh as Sean took another swig of whiskey.

I had a dream of performance, this time inside a sweaty basement venue. Below the stage was a sea of pale limbs and black cloth swaying back and forth in waves, screaming out my name. My old bass was in my hands, but I couldn't figure out how to play it. It was as if the strings were thin beams of light. My fingers went right through them. The crowd screamed: *Laura! Laura!* But I was powerless to satisfy them. Once again, none of my talented boys were there to help me out. *Laura! Laura!* My fingernails bled as I bashed them into the fret-board, just under the less-than-real strings. I tossed and turned into wakefulness.

"Laura! Laura!"

The calls were real. This wasn't coming from my dream. I let out a quick and sharp scream, thinking of Andrea, wondering how she could have found me here, and why Nathan didn't stop her. Then my eyes adjusted to the light, and I saw the figure calling my name.

"Laura, wake up." It was Sean. He was naked and on his knees upon the bed, hunching over me.

I curled myself into a ball against the headboard. Sean attempted a clumsy lean-in and ended up falling against me. He tried to kiss my lips, but I turned away. The smell of bourbon oozed from his pores.

"What the fuck?" I put my hand on the bony center of his chest and pushed him away. He tumbled to his side on the edge of the bed.

"I thought you might want to . . . fool around." The idea seemed to strike even him as silly by the time he'd finished the sentence. With my eyes adjusting, I could make out a boner between his legs, now hanging at half-mast.

"Get away from me."

He stared back, surprised.

"You get drunk and think you can rub your dick all over me whenever you feel like it? Get out of my room, now!"

He hung his head. In a shameful drunken stumble, he pried himself off the bed and out of the room. I got up behind him and locked the bedroom door. The pile of clothes he'd shed lay on the carpet like a puddle of vomit. My heart still beat fast from the scare as I lay under the covers. The digital clock by the bed showed 3 A.M. I heard another lift-and-drop from that big jug of whiskey.

PHILADELPHIA: AUGUST 1984

Anthony still looks away, making sure that your attacker has gone for good.

"*We* can't fight, but *he* can beat *us* up? Fuck that!"

You don't understand what these kids are talking about until a group of four or five of them bum-rush your brother from behind.

"Practice what you preach, motherfucker!"

More kids join in. The music stops, and beating your brother becomes tonight's main event. One word repeats through your head like a single-note bass line: *no, no, no.*

Run around the sides of the circle looking for any point of entry, a way to go in and get your brother out. Feel your hands tingle and shake. A taste like metal fills your mouth. No, no, no, no.

Push your way through them. They are a raw mass of angry teenage energy—the very resource that's provided fuel for your brother's music, for this whole scene—exploding right on him. Push back against the swinging arms, the kicking legs, the violently twisting hips and pelvises. You don't have the strength to break them apart. The fists and steel-toed combat boots swarm like a cloud of negatively charged electrons around the positive nucleus that is Anthony.

"Stop it! Stop it! He's my brother!"

Somebody turns the houselights on. Kids scatter like cockroaches to every side of the floor. They may act bold and brash toward authority figures from a distance, but their fear reveals itself in the face of any real threat. Blood pools up beneath your brother's head and neck, but that's not what scares you the most. He lies motionless, with a vacant sort of peace in his eyes. It's the first time you've ever seen anything resembling rest painted on Anthony's face. So many years spent in fear of nuclear weapons, and now your world is destroyed by knuckles and kneecaps.

Everyone has gone. It's only you and your brother, on a floor covered in sweat, blood, bubble gum, and cigarette butts. Kneel down next to Anthony and pull his upper body into your lap. Your family has never been physically affectionate, but now you stroke his stubbly head and softly kiss his brow.

When the paramedics show up, they have to pry Anthony's limp body from your lap in order to set him on the backboard.

TWENTY-EIGHT

I lay awake until the sunlight came in through the curtains. The smell of coffee brewing crept into my bedroom. I got up to see Nathan.

"Morning." I rubbed my upper arms with my hands, chilly in surgical pants and T-shirt.

Nathan was startled. "Oh, hey. I didn't know you were up. Coffee?"

"Please."

He poured us each a cup. "What's with him?" Across the room, near the bathroom door, Sean lay facedown on the floor, naked and passed out.

"Same old story," I said. "I used to think that drugs and booze were like throwing yourself a one-person birthday party, you know? In the end, you don't get any presents that you didn't have to begin with."

Nathan snorted out a laugh through a mouthful of coffee.

"But with Sean, it's a Jekyll and Hyde thing. He's a whole different guy when he's drinking."

Nathan swallowed.

"You get those lyrics written?"

"I think I'm done, yeah." He looked at his watch. "We need to get down there. What should we do about . . ." He motioned toward Sean with his chin.

"Leave him," I said. "He doesn't have anything to record this morning." Neither did I, actually. But I wanted to get out of the house.

Nathan set up inside the live room. Sheldon turned the knobs. I went outside into the warming daylight and smoked.

Seeing Sean behave that way last night had shaken me up. He couldn't handle this; moderation was not an option. His choice now was between his music and his health.

But in another sense, this simplified things. The band could not work. Recording was barely possible, and the only way I'd let Sean onstage again was inside a straitjacket. If nothing else, I could quit the Mistakes once this album was done and not look over my shoulder.

I walked back into the booth. Sheldon had Nathan's vocal track cranking loud through the speakers, the music a bit softer underneath. On the other side of the glass, Nathan belted out the words with closed eyes, his face clenched up tight as a fist.

"Fucking amazing," Sheldon said over his shoulder—the kind of compliment that flew in the face of his reputation.

Though I came in partway through a line, it didn't take long to pick up the thread of Nathan's lyrics. The second I understood what he was singing about, I began to suffer.

True to his style, Nathan again had manipulated a common truism. I assumed the song was named "Best Two out of Three" based on the chorus.

> The best two out of three
> how's it gonna be?
> First you add him
> Then you subtract me

Never good at math
but even I can see
this division is long
and the remainder is me

I had a hard time listening as he sang on, but the lyrics all seemed to follow that basic mathematical theme:

You carried the one that wasn't me
Now I wait and wait to get a fraction of peace

Big tears welled up inside my eyes. I told myself it was only a song, that I'd read too much into Nathan's lyrics before. But in my heart of hearts, I knew that his quiet stoicism, along with his confused loyalty to his best friend, made it so he could communicate only through lyrics. Most likely, he meant for it to be lighthearted—chalking it all up to a problem with the numbers. But the anger and resentment seeped through.

Sooner or later, you'll have to choose
who's greater than one
who's less than you.
Best two out of three, who's it gonna be?
Why live a dream if you can't even sleep?

It was killing me, but it was a wonderful song. His vocal track was spot-on. I stood behind Sheldon as the tape rolled. It hurt to hear Nathan tell me what was essentially true: that I'd gotten us into this mess, that I had to make up my mind. But at the same time, there was a measure of relief in hearing him let it out.

He finished, opened his eyes, and was surprised to see me standing in the booth. I gave him a moist-eyed nod from behind the glass.

"That kicked ass!" Sheldon said into his mic. "Let's do another one, for texture."

Nathan's gaze lingered on mine as he replaced the headphones over his ears. Sheldon turned the music up on the playback. I listened to the song from the beginning. Once Nathan screamed out the choruses, I had to get out of there. Through the back door and out into a bath of warm autumn daylight, I burst into wailing, moaning, screaming sobs. The sun was in my eyes and the gravel crunched under my feet. I walked over to Nathan's Blazer and put my head into my hands upon the hood, banging my fist against the metal.

I wore myself out after a few minutes of high-impact weeping. With my head buried in my elbow like that, I was transported through time. Back to the years I'd spent with my head down against a school desk after other kids made fun of me. To my head buried in a pillow after watching something on the news about nuclear bombs or the ozone layer. With my hair in my face and tears wetting the flesh of my forearm, I was inside a time warp of shame. Hours may have passed before I felt Nathan's hand upon my back.

"I'm sorry," was the first thing he said.

"Nathan." I turned around, wiped at the side of my eyes with the heel of my hand, and squinted against the sunlight. "Don't ever apologize for your music."

He nodded, looked to the side. "There's a problem with one of the guitar tracks. Sheldon needs Sean to come in."

I snorted up the snot that was forming in my nose. "Let's go get him."

Sean lay asleep on the couch. He'd managed to get himself dressed, hopefully had taken in a little water. I gathered up his guitar and put it in the case while Nathan shook him awake.

"Rise and shine!"

Sean snapped awake, red-eyed and jittery.

"You need to come with us," Nathan said.

Sean sat up slowly on the couch, in his jeans and T-shirt, then suddenly stood and ran for the bathroom. Nathan grimaced as Sean vomited into the toilet. I tasted bile in my own throat.

"Sheldon needs you to redo one of the leads." Nathan stared at the ground and spoke over the sounds of the flushing toilet and running water.

Sean stood in the doorway to the bathroom, swishing around a mouthful of tap water and toothpaste. He held up one finger, then spit the minty foam into the sink.

"I have to play again?" he asked.

Nathan and I nodded. I held out the guitar case in his direction. On the arm of the couch, he found a flannel shirt and put it on. He took his guitar from me, then grabbed the half empty jug of Jack Daniel's from an end table and carried it by the neck in his other hand.

"Let's go," he said.

At the studio, Sheldon had pizzas waiting. The four of us lingered over a silent meal. Nathan and I went outside for a cigarette break. The sun set behind the snowcapped peaks in the distance.

"I don't think I can stay here for this." What did I mean by that exactly? To watch Sean get wasted again for the sake of the song? For Sean to hear the vocal track that Nathan had laid down earlier today? To simply listen to that song again myself?

"Fuck it," Nathan said. "We don't have to stay. There's nothing for us to do anyways."

We asked Sheldon to call the house when they got done.

"That's fine," he said without paying us any attention. He touched a button on the board, then spoke into his microphone. "No. That's not it. It's too low."

Sean nodded from behind the glass.

"Give a call to the house then, and we'll come pick him up," Nathan repeated.

"Got it." Sheldon pressed against one side of his headphones.

We drove off in Nathan's truck on the darkened gravel road.

"This song is turning out good," I said, both our faces looking forward.

"Sheldon seems to like it."

"The lyrics are amazing."

"Just something I came up with last night."

I looked down at my hands, trying to find a way to truly talk about the song, to truly talk about his words, and his heart, and what this was all about.

"Fuck!" Nathan screamed.

My chest bounced against the seat belt and my hands slapped the dash. Nathan's body became a right angle of rigid arms and legs against the brake pedal and steering wheel. I looked through the windshield and saw the reason that he'd stopped.

The doe turned and looked straight at me, her big ears out at her sides and her dark eyes full of fear. Behind her followed a speckled fawn, struggling to walk upon spindly legs.

I watched them wander off into the woods on the other side of the road, their bodies lit up by the headlights of the truck. At the time, I found them beautiful and was glad that Nathan's reflexes had been so quick. In the years and years between that night and now, I will look back upon that doe and wish we would've hit her. They might've been one last escape clause sent to me, to us, by nature or the cosmos, a god of some kind.

"Fucking came out of nowhere!" Nathan panted in the driver's seat, the transmission now in Park.

"Good save," I said. My heart beat hard in my chest, but for some reason, I wasn't nearly as rattled as him.

"A doe that size will stop a car dead in its tracks," he said. "Send you right through the windshield." He put the transmission in Drive and rolled down the road.

Back at our house, I went to the refrigerator and immediately set about making myself a Cold War. "Drink?" I offered Nathan.

He looked at his watch. "A drink?"

"You better have one," I said. "Calm you down a little." Something about this situation—the way that he was wound up about our almost-crash—tilted the balance of nerves between us. I felt more at ease. I handed him a Cold War and lit up cigarettes for each of us.

"We need to talk," I said.

Nathan took a long swallow and then looked me in the eye.

"I am quitting after this album," I said. "My mind's made up. If you want to keep making music with Sean until it kills him, that's up to you. I won't do it anymore."

"All right, then." Nathan nodded. "One more album. Then it's done. I can live with that." He slugged down another sip of his drink. There was a minute or two of silence. We finished our cigarettes at exactly the same time and snuffed them out in the ashtray.

"You know about my brother; everybody does." The composure I'd been holding over him abandoned me. I took another cigarette from the pack and worried it between my fingers, but couldn't manage to get it lit. "But what nobody understands is this: He was everything to me. I depended on him for food and shelter most nights. He taught me about hard work, right and wrong. He was my one true family, and I loved him so much. For the past eight years, I've pretended to be this tough-ass punk rock chick—to need nobody. The truth is, I've been lonely and scared for most of that time." My hands shook so bad, I brought them together around my unlit cigarette. "Those two nights with you—in Madrid and then in Rome—were different. For the first time since 1984, I felt like I didn't have to deal with this world all by myself. Please don't ask me to give that up."

Nathan put his hand over mine and removed that poor cigarette from my nervous clutches. He laid it on the coffee table next to our drinks and put his hands on either side of my face. He kissed me deeply, then pulled his mouth away far enough to say: "I don't want you to be alone."

We kissed again, urgently now. My shirt came off over my head. I pushed the plaid flannel down Nathan's arms. A wad of denim formed around my ankles like a restraint. Our bodies clashed together on that couch—up and down, one above the other—like two horses fighting. I could barely stop kissing him long enough to take his T-shirt off. So much had been pent up inside each of us for so long. Once we let it out, it was an almost violent drama of physical affection, with a soundtrack of smacking lips and undone zippers.

I managed to work Nathan's jeans down around his ankles as well. Before I could pull them off completely, he fell on top of me again. It was then, from over Nathan's shoulder, that I saw him. On the other side of the screen door, his guitar case in one hand, whiskey bottle in the other, Sean stood staring in.

Slowly, I took my hands from out of Nathan's hair.

"Stop," I whispered. "Look."

The screen door swung open as Nathan turned around. We lay still against the couch, paralyzed, shame slowing us down like two feet of snow.

"Come in," I said stupidly. Sean was already inside.

"Sheldon decided to save you guys the trip, said it was on his way home. He dropped me at the end of the driveway." Sean put his guitar on the floor but kept the whiskey bottle in his other hand.

What happened next, I must admit, has been faithfully rendered by all the articles and rumors that have mythologized it. Sean took those few steps over to the couch, where Nathan and I sat half naked and wide eyed. He turned to Nathan, leaned over, and kissed him on the lips. Then he turned to me—his cleft-palate scar showing in the low-angle light—and said, "Good-bye."

It wasn't until he'd walked back out the door that Nathan spoke. "Sean, wait up! Let's talk about this."

The loud motor turned over and yellowish light came in through the doorway and windows.

"Sean! Hold on!" Nathan fumbled with his jeans and redid his belt.

The van bounced down the dirt-and-gravel drive. I put my hand on Nathan's shoulder.

"Maybe," I said, "we should let him go." We had to tell Sean somehow. There was never going to be a good time. I didn't feel great about being caught like this, but I did finally have the biggest, heaviest, most unbearable monkey of my life off my back.

"He's wasted," Nathan said. "He could kill somebody in that thing." He laced up his shoes.

I was still mostly naked as he put on his flannel and grabbed his keys off the end table. "Can I come with you?"

"Wait here, in case he comes back or calls."

I nodded and wrapped my arms around my chest, suddenly embarrassed by my nakedness, like Adam and Eve after the fall. Nathan drove off in pursuit. I put on my clothes. It wasn't anything new to see Sean behave recklessly. I figured he might find a bar downtown and pass out inside. At worst, I worried that he'd hit a deer.

I sat inside on that same couch, chain-smoking and imagining a still life of the contents on the coffee table: an ashtray, a couple of sweaty glasses with that colored half inch of water that once was ice, a couple of guitar picks, a coffee cup from this morning, the notebook that Nathan had used to write those lyrics. Did that have anything to do with Sean catching us? Did he listen to the song in the studio and suspect something?

I was about to pick up Nathan's notebook and have a look at what else he'd written, when headlights came up the drive. Fully clothed, I hopped off the couch and ran outside. The screen door shut behind me. A brood of moths swarmed the outdoor light. It wasn't Nathan's truck but Sheldon's station wagon. Somehow, this told me it was bad news. Sheldon stepped out and opened his passenger side door for me. We didn't say a word. I had no idea what had transpired, but in my head, I kept thinking that something horrible had happened to Nathan. The idea of losing him now, after all this, was too much to bear. It was the fear that held captive my imagination.

And so there was a certain relief that splashed down upon me when I first saw Nathan's blond mop shining in the headlights and then the rest of him standing in the middle of the road and staring forward as if in a trance. I ran out of the car toward him.

"Oh my god!" I said. "I thought that something awful had happened."

Nathan turned to me with a contorted face, as if offended by my words. He didn't speak, only raised his hand, index finger extended, toward the hunk of metal on the other side of the road.

How is it that I didn't even see the van on my first glance? It's not something I can explain. Perhaps I was careless. Perhaps I should be hated for this. But I believe I was so overthrown by my feelings for Nathan—and by the fact that a possible future for us had finally come into focus—I literally didn't have eyes for anything else.

But there it was, whether I wanted to see it or not: our beloved van, with its ass in the air at a most unnatural angle, the front of it pinching around a big pine tree like an oven mitt made of steel.

I took a few steps closer. My feet crunched glass. I looked down and saw the remains of the whiskey bottle—clear angles and curves ground into the gravel. More steps toward the van. A scrap of denim through the crumpled opening that once was a door. A piece of plaid flannel pierced by the steering column. A shock of unwashed hair matted with blood hung where the windshield was meant to be. I'd been wrong. More was at stake in this game than money and emotions. It was life and death. I could hear my brother's mid-eighties mechanized breathing. The thing I'd feared most—another boy's body, another unbearable aftermath—was happening in spite of all the selfish plans I'd made to prevent it.

The nerds who write rock history can argue endlessly about whether or not this was an accident. But for me, standing in the moonlight on a road paved with gravel and glass and blood, I understood what Sean meant when he'd told me good-bye.

"Nathan!" I turned to him. "Nathan, you need to know that this isn't your fault." I went toward him and held out my hand. He didn't budge. I reached for his wrist.

He pulled his hand away and looked at me as though I was something to be feared.

"Don't blame yourself." I spoke desperately now. "Don't blame me. This was out of our hands."

"Look." He backpedaled. "Leave me alone, okay?" His head turned to the side so that he didn't have to look at me. "Please, leave me alone."

Sirens careened down the dirt road, and soon the scene was flooded in red and blue light. An ambulance appeared along with the police, but there was no point even pretending that the broken body in that metal coffin was anywhere near salvation.

Nathan climbed into his Blazer and drove off, without saying good-bye or looking over his shoulder. Most likely, he drove all the way to Montana that very night. Sheldon asked me what I wanted to do and I said, "Go home."

Once we were both inside his station wagon, he popped open the glove box and took out a plastic Baggie full of yellow pills.

"Take this," he said, and placed a small disk on my tongue.

I swallowed it without water and reclined the passenger seat.

WASHINGTON, D.C.: APRIL 1981

In the minutes beforehand, wonder if this is truly what you want. It's the same community center where you saw your first punk rock show, but everything looks different from this side of the stage. The sea of swinging teenage limbs churns. Feel like the figurehead on a ship that's about to sail through it. Your hands are foreign objects—two swollen, helium-filled things attached to your wrists.

"Stretch out your fingers," Hank whispers into your ear. "Don't worry."

Nod and do as he says. Your heart is a flightless bird inside your chest, flapping around but going nowhere. Recheck the set list.

Anthony speaks to the crowd, a slight whine of feedback through the microphone: ". . . and so the world ends not with a bang or with a whimper, but with the sound of two politicians patting each other on the back, and congratulating themselves on the outstanding job that they're doing."

Then the count, sooner than you expect: "two, three, four!"

Hit the first few notes with a forward-hanging head. Hair covers

your face and protects you from the audience like the proverbial os-
trich with its eyes in the sand.

After a bar or two, your brother screams over the music. You look
up and see the crowd go crazy. From the other side of the stage, Hank
gives you an encouraging smirk. Anthony was right; you'll be fine.

In fact, as you see the kids reaching up for a chance to touch
Anthony's hands, to scream into the microphone, realize that you'll
be better than fine. Within the first few seconds of performing live
onstage, feel certain that it's the cure for a disease you've had your
whole life but never diagnosed. Look down and see your hands upon
the coiled wires of the bass. Touch the notes and listen as the music
does exactly what you say.

The instrument suddenly becomes a magical thing. You're convinced that by holding it in your arms—by merely touching it with
your fingertips—you, too, can be saved.

TWENTY-NINE

I woke up in Sheldon's car, driving through downtown Seattle, still fuzzy from the effects of his pill.

"Where's your place?" he asked.

With a dry and scratchy throat, I gave him basic directions. My head was a warm marshmallow.

"I've seen a lot of shit like this," Sheldon opened up. "It seems to me that there's this critical window for young men. Twenty to twenty-eight or something, it's not an exact science. All the musicians and artists and punks I've been around, if they make it through that gauntlet, they're usually golden for the rest of their lives. The ones that we lose, we always lose them in that time frame, you know. Sean was one of those. He had that look like he was fated or something. A tragic flaw kind of vibe."

I'd never thought of it that way.

"The important thing"—Sheldon turned onto my street, apparently unaffected by the all-night drive—"is that you don't beat yourself up over this."

As it turns out, I was the last person I had to worry about beating me up over this.

"Thanks for the ride," I said at my driveway.

"One more thing." Sheldon took a cassette tape from the front pocket of his shirt. "You better take this."

"What is it?" I twisted the tape in my hand, as if I didn't know what a cassette was.

"It's the track you guys made, a rough mix. I'm not supposed to do this. Technically, that belongs to the record company. But I think you should take it, in case things get weird."

I was confused by the gesture and what he meant by "things getting weird," but thanked him again and said good-bye.

The door to my home swung shut behind me, and the effects of Sheldon's pill wore off in an instant. Staring at the brand-new furniture, the expensive prints propped against the walls, I felt the same way I did in that hospital room in Philadelphia years ago. I walked to the kitchen trembling and took out the big chef knife that I'd used to fend off Andrea. I ran my thumb along the cutting edge, felt the weight and heft of it in my hand. I lifted it up to shoulder level and karate-chopped it through the air a couple times.

Then, without deciding to, I swung it into the wall, where the kitchen met the living room. It went easily through the Sheetrock. I chopped away some more, until I'd made a hole the size of a snare drum. Insulation poked out in tufts of pink fur. I grabbed the second largest knife from the set—the one I used for cutting cheese and slicing up frozen pizzas—and stabbed at the walls with both hands. I stood on a chair to reach the higher spots, then moved all the furniture and art away from the walls and into a pile in the center of the floor.

For hours and hours, with only my knives, I stripped the living room of all its drywall, until it was a thick pile of dust and rubble along every side. I took a broom and brushed the scraps into the center, right into the furniture pile, so I could get an even better look at the skeleton of my house. My skin itched from the fiberglass, and my eyes stung with plaster dust. Fingernails bled where I'd pulled stubborn pieces of wall from around the nails and off the two-by-fours.

The downstairs now done, I smoked a cigarette and rested my knives on the counter. The sun had already set. This felt like my first full day's work in a year. I paused for a second once the cigarette was spent, then threw the butt right into the pile of junk in the center of the floor and went upstairs.

All night, in a trembling trance of guilt and heartbreak, I deconstructed the rest of my house, this possession I'd once been so proud of, the only thing that made me feel like a grown-up. A couple of times, I laughed out loud, thinking of the stupid bullshit I worried about only a few short weeks ago: when I should quit the band, whether or not our record would be too poppy or not poppy enough, if I was a sellout by some rock fan's ridiculous standards.

By the time I had the entire house gutted, the sun had come back up through thick clouds. I sat on the floor, thinking the whole thing quite beautiful—the studs like a spindly skeleton, pink insulation playing the tender flesh. If you crossed your eyes just so, it could be mistaken for a living thing—the belly of a whale. I'd not taken food or coffee in days. With my eyes stinging, my body aching, my clothes white with dust, my mind almost too tired to feel pain, and nothing left to destroy, I finally opened the front door.

A bright light blinded me. I squinted hard, and then saw them camped out there on my front stoop. In rumpled raincoats and running shoes, they jumped to attention as I tried to step out.

"Laura Loss, why did you do it?"

"Was this an act of revenge against music fans?"

"Laura, is it true that you slept your way into this band in the first place?"

Journalists. Or so they call themselves. I slammed the door shut and paced around the pile of paper and dust that was my living room.

Luckily I had a few cigarettes left. I checked the freezer and found some coffee. As the brown liquid dripped down into the pot, I curled up next to the counter and lit a smoke. Suddenly, there was nothing beautiful about the exposed boards. They now looked to me like what they were: the bars of a cage that I had built around myself.

I waited until night. From my upstairs window, I saw that the reporters were gone.

The still-bright moon lit up a layer of clouds that hung above the city. The sidewalks were wet and shone under the streetlamps. Walking downhill, there was a moment in which I feared I was hallucinating. A witch, dressed in black and with a pointed hat, came toward me, two small figures in tow. One was a skeleton; the other, a superhero. They carried bags. It was Halloween.

I kept walking, and passed more ghouls and goblins along the way, until I came to an all-night convenience store. I paid for a hot dog and ate it while I shopped, preparing for what could be a long siege: eggs, bread, canned goods. On a stand by the checkout sat the *Seattle Times*. There was a picture of our wrecked van on the front page, beside another picture of some teenagers in tears—holding candles, wearing the T-shirts that I'd designed. The headline read: SEATTLE MOURNS TRAGIC LOSS OF LOCAL MUSICIAN. There must've been a candlelit vigil the night before. Nobody bothered to tell me. I didn't buy the paper.

From the opposite side of the street, I approached my house, wanting to get a clear view in case any more reporters were around.

Three figures boldly milled about on my stoop. I hid behind a tree. There came sounds like hooting and laughter, then the rattle and hiss of aerosol cans. They weren't journalists. They were kids, Halloween pranksters perhaps. One wrote the word SLUT across my front door. From the tone of their voices and the geometry of their postures, they appeared to be two boys and one girl. All three wore denim and flannel. The other boy struggled to write BITCH underneath the lamp. The girl worked on something more elaborate along the front wall, below my window. After a frustrating minute or two of pausing to reshake the sputtering can, she finally managed to spell out: YOU KILLED HIM. It wasn't a Halloween prank. They were Mistakes fans.

I sat down there in the moist earth, among the trees, and recognized for the first time that this was the way the world would see it, no matter what the truth was. The teenagers giggled as they finished up. A light came on at my neighbors' house, and they ran away in a flurry of flapping plaid cloth and worn-out sneaker soles slapping wet pavement.

Perhaps a week had passed when my doorbell rang. Almost exactly one year since the day I came home to discover those two boys outside my Belltown apartment, I found myself staring at Nathan on the stoop of my Magnolia house—the inside stripped to the studs, the outside covered in spray-painted expletives. Looking into his haggard face, I realized that all this time I'd been holding out some vague hope that he would come and find me, make everything right.

Words failed, so I reached out my arms to hug him.

He put a palm up around my sternum and stopped me. "Here's how this will work. I've got some papers that you're going to sign. Then I'll turn around, drive away, and the two of us will never speak again."

For a moment, I wished to wake up in a darkened bedroom, waited for an end to this nightmare that wasn't coming.

"It's a fair agreement." Nathan took the papers out of the envelope. "You'll receive all the royalties due you."

I stared into his eyes as he looked down at those papers. He was nervous the way he'd been during our first night together in Madrid—committing an act that he considered both wrong and inevitable.

"Why are you doing this, Nathan?"

"Initial here. Sign at the bottom."

I looked down at the highlighted passage of legal jargon. It translated into me giving control of the Mistakes' music to Nathan Sullivan and "the estate of Sean Purvis"—which I could only guess referred to that miserable excuse for a father. Nathan had made a deal with the devil and retained lawyers to seal it.

"They'll put out a kind of compilation album: live tracks, covers, some stuff that didn't make it onto the first record, and that last song we did in Oregon."

"I love you, Nathan." That finally got him to look me in the eye. His face was gray as newspaper; bluish bags hung below his eyes.

"He was my best friend, Laura. He was a brother to me."

"You don't truly think this was our fault, do you?"

"I'm not like you, Laura." He turned his head to the side.

"What the fuck is that supposed to mean?" In my mind, he was the only person on earth who was like me.

"I couldn't have kept on playing music after what happened to Anthony. You sure as shit won't see me onstage anytime soon. Remember what you told me—about knowing that a thing has brought only pain and trouble to the people you care about? That's how I feel about you and me. It hurt people. It killed my best friend. I won't do it anymore." Nathan wanted something different from the world, and I was the thing he'd sacrifice.

"Fuck that!" My voice rose to match his. "Sean is dead. We're the ones that have to keep on living."

"Why are you making this hard? Sign these so I can go."

"If you'll be with me, Nathan. If you'll stay here tonight and we give this thing a proper try, then you can have everything: the music, the fucking film rights, whatever. But if you leave me now, I'll give you the fight of your life." I meant every word.

"Are you insane?" Nathan wrinkled his brow. "The press already blames you for this shit. The fans are out for blood. This is a fucking gift I brought you. You're the one who stands to lose everything if we get into a battle."

"If you walk away now, then I've already lost everything."

"Fuck!" Nathan threw the papers onto the threshold and stepped back from the door. "From now on, you *did* kill him—that's my side of the story." He pointed to the graffiti on the front wall of my house, then backed off toward his car.

"I won't give up my band without a fight!" I shouted as he opened his car door.

"Remember this, Laura: I tried to make it easy. You're the one that made it hard. Good-fucking-bye!" He slammed the door and pulled away.

Let the record show that this is how my star burnt out: not with a whimper or a bang, not with a drug problem or a late-night wreck, but with a stack of legal documents and flurry of pointed fingers.

From that same wooden block, I took out the kitchen shears and brought them upstairs to the master bathroom. I shook my head in front of the mirror, until my hair draped down before my face. Starting with the long blue strand hanging in my eyes, I chopped away. Straight and fine, it was much easier to cut than Anthony's dense curls all those years ago. It took me back, giving a crude haircut in a small bathroom. The sink and the floor filled up with my own dead cells. There was a new-enough razor in the bathtub, which drew only a few beads of blood. The shape of my bald head looked remarkably like my brother's. It freaked me out. I waved to that face in the mirror as though it was somebody I hadn't seen for a long time.

It was at the airport that I first saw the magazines. "Band Wrecker" was the title that they invented for me. *She Seduced Us Both!* by a picture of Nathan. There were so many photos of my scowling face, looking annoyed while the boys smiled, flipping the middle finger to a camera—it wasn't hard to see myself as the villain.

I managed to get a plane ticket within the next couple hours, a window seat.

"Excuse me." A preppy-looking girl took the seat next to me on the plane. "This sounds odd, but are you famous, by any chance?"

"No." I reached up to touch the bare skin of my scalp, as if to double-check my disguise. "I'm nobody."

It was true, in a sense, because all fame is relative—to other celebrities and to all the other moments of one's life. But in another sense, it was something that I only wished were true.

The engines grew loud as the big Boeing jet prepared to leave its home. I was happy to be by the window as we rose up into the stratosphere. Good-bye, I said to Seattle as the city shrank below me. Good-bye to your coffee and good-bye to your beer. Good-bye to your flannel and your torn jeans, to your clouds and rain and your smoky basements and your independent credibility and your greasy-haired teenagers with their cigarettes and their hate. Good-bye, Seattle. I leave you to your sound and to your fate.

Again, I traded one Washington for another. From the moment I came home, bald and wrecked, I knew what I had to do. It was time for me to take care of Anthony, to shoulder that burden in place of my parents. I bought a one-bedroom condo with the next month's royalty check. For the first time ever, my brother moved out of his childhood bedroom and into the downstairs of my place. Call this penance, if you like. It's really not about that anymore. I don't expect to make things right.

The dining room is a mess of documents, manila folders, and one overworked telephone. For years and years now, it's been my full-time job to maintain a legal battle against Nathan. "Best Two out of

Three" has never been released. This, of course, fuels the fire of hatred among the fans—all of whom take Nathan's side. In addition to being a "band-wrecking" slut, I'm also a greedy, money-grubbing bitch who's keeping the music from its audience because there might be a dollar in it for me. By some accounts, I'm a shitty drummer.

With the lawyers and all, I lose money every day that this thing goes on. So why do it? The fight is the only way I have left to communicate with Nathan. I did love him, in the truest sense, perhaps I still do. I can't call or write him; we haven't seen each other since that day on the doorstep. So the legal action is the last way to have any sort of back-and-forth, to be a part of his life at all.

And I understand that, in the public eye, he has to hate and blame me. I always enjoyed watching him perform, his skill with satisfying the masses. This isn't much different. Also, there's a piety to it, a sort of morbid obligation, for his best friend. In that sense, it's similar to what I do now. Wiping away Anthony's spittle, changing his catheter bag, treating his bedsores—these things are a little easier than coping with loss, and a whole lot easier than moving on.

I don't leave the house much these days. There's a patio outside where I can smoke, an awkward teenager named Scott who delivers groceries— and thinks my name is Laura Hopper. Caring for Anthony isn't all chores. I like to sit with him. We watch TV together, and sometimes I play songs on the acoustic guitar. Every couple of days, I play the cassette of "Best Two out of Three" that Sheldon gave me. Eyes closed, holding my brother's hand, I listen to the music that the three of us made—Sean's supernatural leads, Nathan's lyrics pushing at the bounds of truth and secrets, me doing my best to hold the beat together.

I miss Sean as well, more than I thought I would. His death made me and everybody else involved filthy rich, which isn't easy to swallow. But in spite of how hard I've tried—and how much harder everyone else has tried——I can't blame myself for it. He was the most gifted and self-destructive individual I've ever known. To hold myself responsible seems egotistical somehow, an overestimation of my powers.

But in the public eye, there's no overestimating one performer's powers. We watched the news today. They're still deep into the coverage of the school shooting in Colorado. I knew, even before they brought it up, that rock and roll would catch the blame for this. Parents, teachers, elected officials——they all get a free ride. Perhaps I should call the press and take responsibility. What have I got to lose, after all?

Many things have changed since the hardcore days. But one thing has stayed the same: this country is incapable of taking teenagers and young adults seriously. The fault, dear anchormen and analysts, lies not in their rock stars, but in themselves.

The television grows tiresome. I turn it off and pop in the cassette. As the first notes of the Mistakes' last song sounds through the speakers, a knock comes at the door.

"Hey, Miss Hopper." It's Scott, the grocery boy. "I know it's early, but it turns out I'll be away this weekend." He hands me a paper bag and receipt.

"That's fine. Come on in. Let me get my wallet."

He steps inside and pulls down the zipper on his coat. I look over and see that he's wearing a Mistakes T-shirt under his winter layer, with the NOWHERE FAST logo that I'd drawn up years ago. If he did know who I was, he'd be obliged to hate me.

"What's this music?" he asks.

I hand him a wad of bills. "It's some band that I knew out West. They were good for a while, but they broke up."

"It's pretty cool. What are they called? Do you think I'd be able to find a copy?"

"No." I stop the tape deck with a click. Anthony's mechanized breath sounds from the other room. "It's never been released. It's just a demo, really. The musicians never learned how to cope with the industry, you know."

"Whatever." Scott shrugs and says good-bye.

Once he's gone, I pick up the acoustic guitar. All the tragedies associated with both my bands, and I still can't quite quit playing. My parents crammed Shakespeare down my throat when I was a kid, along with the other major works of the canon. We went to the Kennedy Center often for plays or symphonies. On my own, I've seen the great paintings and sculptures of the Western masters. But none of it, I'm almost ashamed to say, has ever moved me as much as a good rock-and-roll song.

So it's hard for me to fully return the hate that I get from the fans, especially kids like Scott. I want them to lose themselves in the music, as I've done. I want them to feel three chords resonate deep in their bones, with some words screamed out over the top that—for a minute or two—make them feel a little less lonely. But more than anything, what I want those kids to do is what Anthony and I and Sean and Nathan did. At some point, I want them to turn off the stereo, leave their bedrooms, take hold of their hearts with both hands, go out into the world, and make their own mistakes.

ACKNOWLEDGMENTS

This book owes a gigantic debt to the work of Michael Azerrad. His histories of American music, *Come as You Are* and *Our Band Could Be Your Life,* were a major factor in both the inspiration and the research for my novel. Anyone interested in further reading about Seattle's early nineties sound, the eighties hardcore punk scene, or other forms of underground music in late twentieth-century America must start with Azerrad. Jem Cohen's *Instrument,* as well as Steven Blush and Paul Rachman's *American Hardcore* were also crucial resources. Thanks to Erich Schweiker, an invaluable authority on Seattle geography, architecture, and demographics. My heartfelt thanks go out to Poor Man's Whiskey: the band that taught me more than I ever wanted to know about touring the Pacific Northwest in a van full of unwashed musicians.

This novel would not exist without the insight, hard work, and perseverance of Jennifer de la Fuente—the amazing agent who stuck with me through several manuscripts, market crashes, and tough calls. Thanks to Hilary Rubin Teeman for making this book into a reality, and for making it a much better book.

Thanks to the wonderful community of writers, teachers, and

friends at Boise State University's Creative Writing Program. A special measure of gratitude is owed to J. Ruben Appelman for being this novel's first true reader. His feedback was invaluable, and his enthusiasm meant everything. Thanks to Paul Diamond, my original writing teacher. This or any other book of mine would be unthinkable without his relentless encouragement and unconquerable faith.